THE FOREVER BEAT

John Cline

THE FOREVER BEAT

DUTTON NEW YORK

DUTTON
Published by the Penguin Group
Penguin Books USA Inc., 375 Hudson Street,
New York, New York 10014, U.S.A.
Penguin Books Ltd, 27 Wrights Lane,
London W8 5TZ, England
Penguin Books Australia Ltd, Ringwood,
Victoria, Australia
Penguin Books Canada Ltd, 2801 John Street,
Markham, Ontario, Canada L3R 1B4
Penguin Books (N.Z.) Ltd, 182–190 Wairau Road,
Auckland 10, New Zealand

Penguin Books Ltd, Registered Offices:
Harmondsworth, Middlesex, England

First published by Dutton, an imprint of Penguin Books USA Inc.
Published simultaneously in Canada by Fitzhenry & Whiteside, Limited.

First printing, June 1990.
1   3   5   7   9   10   8   6   4   2

Copyright © 1990 by John Cline
All rights reserved.

Library of Congress Cataloging-in-Publication Data

Cline, John. 1955–
The forever beat / John Cline.—1st ed.
p. cm.
ISBN 0-525-24855-2
I. Title.
PS3553.L547F67   1990
813'.54—dc20   89-23828
                                             CIP

Printed in the United States of America
Set in Century Expanded
Designed by Earl Tidwell

Publisher's Note: This novel is a work of fiction. Names, characters, places,
and incidents either are the product of the author's imagination
or are used fictitiously, and any resemblance to actual persons, living or
dead, events, or locales is entirely coincidental.

Without limiting the rights under copyright reserved above,
no part of this publication may be reproduced, stored in or
introduced into a retrieval system, or transmitted, in any form,
or by any means (electronic, mechanical, photocopying, recording, or
otherwise), without the prior written permission of both the
copyright owner and the above publisher of the book.

For My Father,
Robert Charles Cline
1923–1989

For My Father
Robert Church Clinch
1929–1988

Part One

NEW YORK

1

I had piled them all on the coffee table, six screenplays of varying quality, six shining covers glossily refracting the television's lonely sitcom. The transformation of artificial light into a swirling hallucination seemed healthy and ironic, as if TV had finally succumbed to my vision of it.

I had another glass of wine.

It was ten to seven. In another ten minutes I could blow that joint I was staring at, drift away in a state beyond phone calls. But not till seven. Some one of the many producers with copies of my soon-to-be-hailed screenplays might put finger to the touch-tone and kill a little time before dinner by commissioning a rewrite, or saying thanks but no thanks, or making himself feel sexy by saying maybe. Then he'd have something to talk about at Raoul's or Positano or the Century Café. He could always say no tomorrow, at no expense.

Seven o'clock ticked into place. I held the joint in my hands, twisted it lovingly, inhaled the palpable aroma. I struck the match, but even while I was doing so I could hear the soft knocking on my door.

* * *

Billy was the kind of boy only adults appreciate. We'd met six months ago in the lobby of my building as they were moving in. His attractive mother was newly pregnant and unable to carry much, so I helped. If she hadn't been with child I'd have sought her company; instead, it was Billy who became my friend. It wasn't until later that I realized with profound regret that I was his only friend.

We'd thrown my football around Washington Square a few times. Between passes I learned that at the ripe young age of twelve he'd already lived in seven states and nine cities—an IBM baby.

From a distance all one could see of Billy was his long nose and big eyes and lanky figure. He was Buster Keaton in miniature. He couldn't throw a football, but his intelligence was haunting. He seemed to have a sixth sense about people; he could put his finger on exactly what was bothering them. A month ago he had ruined a dinner party of mine when he dropped in for one of his little visits. Within minutes and from out of the blue he rudely blurted out the precise nature of the marital problem that had plagued my best friends, Marty and Rosiland.

"Religion," he mused. "It's at the core of your mutual distrust." Marty was a Jew, Ros a Catholic. And, according to Ros, Billy was a little snot.

"Hey—shut up—he's just a kid."

"Don't tell me to shut up."

I led Billy out the door and down the hall, and all the while heard the escalating pitch of voices spewing from my forlorn apartment. We stood before his mother's door for an awkward moment.

"I'm sorry," he whispered, as if he'd unleashed a force that had created a monster.

"It's OK," I said, and meant it. "Just don't ever be proud to know what bothers others. It's a matter of honor to keep it to yourself, unless asked."

"OK."

"Billy?" My voice trembled a little. I'd never been a father.

"Yeah?"

"What bothers you?"

He smiled, so sadly, I thought, for a youngster.

"It's a matter of honor," he said, then stepped into his apartment and shut the door behind him. I was angry. In my hurt I conjured that I'd avoid the kid from now on. I leaned against my door and paused, listening to Rosiland and Marty quibble over who should sleep where for the evening. Then at the other end of the hall I heard Billy's door crack open. He stood there in the hallway and said nothing. I moved to him quickly. I wiped the tears off his cheeks, then hugged him, unsure just why I felt so deeply for the boy. He whispered in my ear.

"He's still alive."

I stared at him without speaking.

"My father's still alive. He just . . . ran away."

His mother appeared at the door quietly. One of her pale hands rested softly on the crest of her pregnant womb; the other alighted on Billy's head. She ran her fingers through his hair and spoke to him in gentle tones that somehow reminded me of my own mother.

"You shouldn't make things up, Billy. Mr. Byman is your friend. Don't lie to suit your purpose."

Billy's wide eyes stared at me pathetically. He took my hand, and for the first time I realized how small he was, why it was so hard for him to throw a football. His thin fingers placed something in my palm. He attempted to smile and I tried back. Neither of us made it.

When the door closed I saw that he had slipped me a rabbit's foot. Its hairs were worn smooth, so smooth that he must have been rubbing it all his twelve years.

And now he was at my door again, tonight of all nights, when my own luck seemed to running dry. I knew his knock, and thought of not answering. How could I play surrogate father to a troubled boy when my own troubles weighed so heavily? A stack of bills sat on the kitchen table, each telling me politely that it'd been three months since the last check and, sorry, but the lawyers must be contacted by the end of April. Pay up.

It's difficult to scare up romance in New York without money. I'd stopped trying. I'd stopped trying on a lot of counts. Things get that way, sometimes. Sometimes things stay that way. Billy didn't let that happen—his voice cut through my self-pity like a knife, two words I'll never forget.

"Please, Luke."

He was crying when he took my hand and pulled me down the hall. I followed silently. At his door I stopped short with sudden panic. On the other side Billy's mother screamed and howled like a lonely, wild animal trapped inside a cage. Billy was trembling. He stared up at me, a little boy now, not the adult he'd been pretending to be.

"Go! Get someone else, Billy. A woman!" I heard the terror in my own voice. Billy fled. I opened the door. His mother lay writhing and moaning on the sofa I'd helped carry into their apartment. All sorts of things sped through my brain except what to do, here and now. She was dripping sweat and said with a gasp, "It's close!"

I comforted her as well as I could, then I went to the bathroom to wash my hands and phone an ambulance. I had to walk through the bedroom, and it wasn't until I was on my way out that I saw the money. It lay near an open briefcase, stacks upon stacks of hundred-dollar bills. A suitcase, packed with her clothes, sat near it. A note lay on the bed, on top of an envelope stuffed carelessly with a handful of hundreds. The note read:

> *Mr. Byman, please take*
> *special care of Billy*
> *for just a few months.*
> *I'll be back, I promise.*
> *Thank you—Julia.*

I took a second to rifle through her things and found her airline ticket, a one-way to Los Angeles.

A terrible scream broke the momentary silence. Simultaneously, the apartment door opened. I bolted out of the bedroom and was relieved to see Billy leading an elderly woman through the doorway. Discreetly, I stepped back into the bedroom and threw an afghan over the money. I held the envelope in my hands for a moment, considering. It wasn't the money precisely, it was Billy, whether I could handle him or not. I made a quick decision. He would be mine for a few months, regardless.

I felt sleazy slipping the envelope into my breast pocket. Somehow, though, I sensed that I'd be needing what it contained.

* * *

The old woman was marvelous. Her name was Rita. She'd been a nurse, I learned, for she talked incessantly, as much for our benefit as for hers. A nurse, then in research, then a mother and housewife, and then a nurse again.

"Full cycle," she chimed as the baby's head came into view.

Blood and water poured across the sofa, and Billy went into the bathroom to vomit. I could hear the long pause after the toilet flushed and knew he'd just seen the money and the ticket and the suitcase.

I held the baby in my arms, bloodying my shirt, as Rita cut the umbilical cord. A tiny girl cried up at me. Her frightened little heart beat against my chest. I almost cried, thinking of my own, long-gone mother. My heart must have once beat against her chest. I couldn't help feeling that Life's first few minutes are a sad miracle. The glory goes quickly, and we spend the rest of our years trying to find a piece of it again.

Rita took the child from me and washed her in a pan of warm water I'd managed to organize. The baby's arms flapped up and down like a new butterfly's.

Julia's eyes were closed. The tips of her fingers were touching a scar on the side of her chest, as if it still hurt. It was a round, protruding scar, an old bullet wound.

Billy appeared in the bedroom door frame.

"I guess we were going on a trip." But he didn't believe his own words.

His mother stared at him with a curious, wistful gaze. She turned it on me and I knew, then, that I'd never be the same. Her thick hair had fallen from its bun and drifted down across her shoulders. Its brown and auburn hues made her lovely face stand out in pale relief. Through the daze of the moment her green eyes lanced me with an affecting melancholy. I didn't hold her hand, I seized it. She smiled a smile for the ages.

"Billy . . ." she whispered, but his name floated raggedly across the room. It was hard for her to talk.

"Billy," I repeated, my eyes still locked with Julia's.

Then hell broke loose.

The door was kicked open with a crash. There were several figures in shadow, but the first thing that I saw was the barrel of a gun. What I heard was a deep baritone voice underscoring Rita's terrifying scream.

I stood up and received the butt end of a revolver across my face. The fall to the floor seemed to take a long time. I landed on my right cheek and heard teeth break. I was on the verge of darkness but managed to push myself up on one elbow in time to see Billy appear in the bedroom doorway holding an old .45. My father had had one, navy issue, and for a moment the thought ran through my brain that the gun Billy held was his.

"Go away!" he said with a boyish finality.

"No, Billy!" My words were lost under slices of gunfire. Billy's blood spattered back against the bedroom door. His body crumpled on the carpet. I saw a giant, wide and powerful, with long red hair, step over Billy's frail legs and scoop up the hundred-dollar bills.

I could hear Rita whimpering like a lost child. Another gunshot and there was silence. Her body slumped over me.

Down the hall I heard the elevator open. Julia cried out, "No, not my baby!"

I didn't hear or see much after that. There was a silenced shot and then a deep, rich, powerful pain spread from the center of my body through to each limb. I hadn't felt the bullet enter. Later that night, police would pick it out of the floor.

It was weeks before I regained consciousness.

2

Rosiland and Marty helped with my medical expenses. I had no insurance and was broke and there was no more loving family to fall back on. I was on my own, save for a few wonderful friends. Anyway, that's all anyone ever needs.

They were all there—Ros, Marty, Jim, even Amanda had shown up. They held my arms and patted my back and made loving noises as I shuffled with my new cane out of the hospital and into Jim's old Pontiac.

"Home, James," Amanda said as she squeezed my arm in the back seat. There was sadness and pity and possibility in her pretty brown eyes, as if the bullet that had passed through my gut had taken with it the part of me that had fallen out of love with her. I smiled, rather nervously.

"No," I said.

"Luke, I'm going to sleep on the couch and take care of you for a few days, that's all."

"Don't get all worried, Jack," Ros said. She called me Jack when she was talking man to man.

"All right, I'm not all worried. I just need to do something first, right away, before anything."

There was a disappointed silence.

"Well?" Marty was annoyed. They were all annoyed. Maybe they'd baked a cake or something and it was waiting at Amanda's, but a cake was not what I needed now.

"Fourth Street between First and Second, Jim."

"What the hell is there?"

"The ninth precinct. I called Detective Cussone and he's expecting me."

Amanda was gentler than the rest of them. "They've gotten your statement already, Luke. What gives?"

I was my usual blunt self. "Listen, I know this pisses you all off, but imagine my position. I need to know if there's anything to point to why this all happened, and if I'm still in danger. And I need to know now. It's been burning inside of me—literally—for weeks. Please?"

"Of course," Jim said with feeling. "As a matter of fact, I don't blame you."

"Can't say as I do, either," Marty admitted. But the women were silent.

"Then . . ." I smiled at Amanda, "then I'll hightail it to your apartment and allow myself to be waited on hand and foot."

She produced a wan smile and squeezed me again, harder this time. A shooting pain soared from my abdomen up and into the back of my neck, but I didn't tell her.

We sped down Second Avenue in silence.

3

He wore a tacky tie and blue knit pants, out of which a polyester short-sleeve was half untucked. A sandwich filled his cheeks, but his expression wasn't foolish. There was a keen awareness sparkling in his eyes, one that I appreciated. He seemed to be honored by my trip to the station. He was the only one.

"Detective Sergeant Stanley Cussone," he said formally, dripping olive oil from his hero. My friends all shook his hand and sat down behind me as if they were being arraigned.

"Now . . ." But he was still chewing. He took a swig of something in a plastic cup and was intelligible again. "Now, tell me again why you're here. Why you'd ever want to see me again."

"You're not so bad," I said.

"Talk to my son about that, or my second wife."

"Why *are* you here?" Ros's voice from behind sounded like my conscience. Truth is, I had no idea what I was doing in a detective's office. The thought occurred to me that it might be a halfway house between hospital and home. I turned and saw four blank human beings peering at me from behind those inner walls that folks construct for themselves in situations like these. Cussone's voice was gentle.

"You're here for a reason."

I said with some trepidation: "Where's Billy?"

"Cold storage." It was a cruel answer.

"And Rita?"

"Had a grander funeral than you or I'll ever have. Forest Lawn."

I leaned forward. "And Julia Denig?" I could feel Amanda's eyes on me.

"Gone. You're the only one that can actually place her there. Besides you, all we got is a sofa soaked with blood and water and part of an umbilical cord."

"And no trace of the baby?"

"No trace of the baby. The neighbors heard it crying as it was carried to the elevator."

"Why would they have stolen a baby?" I asked.

Cussone stared blankly, as if allowing for an answer to float through him like a cipher. None came.

"I simply don't know. It's one of the big questions in this case. See, though we don't know the reason why Julia Denig had so much money lying around, we can hypothesize that she'd stolen it or embezzled it, because she'd planned a trip to Los Angeles at the peak of her pregnancy, and that's desperate. She must have known she'd been spotted—that danger was imminent. Anyway, the baby came before she could take off. Then the money was robbed and the burglary turned ugly. They often do, you know. But why she disappeared—well, it's another big question."

"How do you know she wasn't abducted?"

"One of the neighbors got up enough courage to open his door a few minutes after the shooting. He saw her stagger, literally, onto the elevator, carrying her suitcase. She left her son's body behind—and you. Prob'ly thought you were dead, too."

"Yeah." But knowing this sent a cool shiver down my spine. Maybe she hadn't cared.

"And by the way," Cussone continued, "Denig's probably not her real name."

"You checked with IBM?"

"We did. There's a couple of Denigs under their employ. One is an old man, retired now, an old parts designer in Arizona. Lives alone." He paused for emphasis. "In a wheelchair. The other Denigs are a family out of Boston—husband, wife, three kids, family dog. Both Denigs have been given a clean sweep and we've turned up no connection. The IBM management's been more than cooperative in allowing us access to their personnel records, and there's no history of a Denig or any other similar name who's been transferred a number of times as you say they had been."

I echoed what Billy had told me: "Nine cities in seven states," then had the queer sensation that he'd just spoken through me, a hot breath from somewhere beyond. With that sensation came a certainty that he had not been lying about his travels.

"Any clues as to her real name?" I asked.

"Nope, not a one. The apartment's clean. Down payments and rent to the landlord and utilities were all paid through a checking account in her name, so if Denig was an alias then she was using a phony ID. There's no reference anywhere to credit cards, or any other financial history."

"And all the money's gone?"

"Of course. But we've checked on the bills you stuffed in your pocket." He paused and took a bite of his sandwich. I sensed infuriation behind me—they were getting interested.

"Go on," Jim said, almost involuntarily. Cussone chewed his words.

"They weren't traceable, actually, but they're not phony. Just laundered. We still have a guy running the serials over the wire, tracing robberies back three, four years, but no one's responded yet. It doesn't look good."

I touched my chest. "Their bullets?"

"Interesting you should ask. Two varieties. The gun that killed Rita Vitario was a twenty-two. Scratches on the casing verify your observation—both weapons were silenced. The gunman who shot you killed Billy."

There was a natural pause while we all registered the magnitude of Billy's death and thought about the kind of man who could pull the trigger.

"He used a Russian weapon. A Kalashnikov pistol." Cussone leaned forward.

"His voice wasn't Russian," I said, "though he had some sort of vague accent."

"It doesn't really matter. Those guns don't circulate on the street. They usually get sold in big crates to foreign governments." He paused. "That means the international crowd." Cussone let his eyes drift toward a solitary window. Through it he pondered obscure lands beyond his city, provinces he'd never see. His voice was suddenly hopeful, like a breath of spring.

"Can you remember anything more about him—anything?"

"His head scraped against the top of the door frame."

"As you've said. He even left a red hair or two there."

"You checked?"

"We checked. As much to assess your memory as for blood type."

"Well?"

"Tall guy. Type O. Nothing in our files, nor in the FBI's. We checked photo and fingerprint and vehicle records. Nothing. No arrests or wanteds, no shinola anywhere. Not in fifty states."

"Jesus," Marty whispered. Maybe he was finally turning Catholic.

"He wore a black suit . . . it was a strange suit."

"How?"

"I think it was shiny, like plastic."

"Or that spandex stuff?"

"Maybe. And boots."

"Army boots?"

"No . . . no, more like plastic again. Now that I remember it, there was a buckle. They might have been galoshes."

"It wasn't raining that day," Cussone said, but he made a note of it in a little spiral pad.

"Can a shipment of bullets or guns be traced?"

"Sometimes. In this case, no. Keep remembering."

"Guns . . ." I muttered to myself. A thought struck me. "What about the forty-five . . . Billy's gun?"

His big basset hound eyes squinted. "Are you absolutely sure that the boy had a gun?"

"A forty-five. I'm absolutely sure."

He leaned back and his old chair moaned under him. It moaned for both of us, because I knew as he did that without that gun all hope of tracing Julia Denig or her missing husband may have vanished. We stared at one another for a long moment.

"Gone," he finally said.

"Like Billy's father."

"Yup." He emptied his paper cup. "But she took the gun. I'd bet my shield on it."

I had to agree with him, but didn't say a word. Somewhere in the deep shadows of my mind a thought fluttered as if it had wings. A sour image. Julia was lurking with a suitcase full of cash in one hand and a .45 in the other.

But there was an even deeper nagging, something akin to the pull of the moon. I had held the child in its first seconds after birth. Now I wanted her back. Even more than I wanted her mother.

I bade good-bye to Detective Stanley Cussone and said that I would call him tomorrow.

"It's your dime," he said cheerfully.

Back at Amanda's, a chocolate cake waited patiently on the kitchen table.

4

Hurting as I was, after being bedridden for twenty-seven days, I was anything but sleepy. It was I who ended up on the sofa. I must have fallen off to sleep somewhere in the middle of a classic old film noir, *Detour*, because I dreamed in black and white, dreamed that I was making love with Julia as we listened to the national anthem. It was lonely music from far off, like sounds of a postnuclear broadcast.

When I woke up Amanda had already taken action. She was sucking me, and I just lay there like an invalid with a smile on my face, thinking: I like this . . . would that all love were this easy. She smiled through the darkness and straddled me. That sudden rush of passion that sweeps over a man as he enters a woman now swept over me, and I realized how much I'd needed her, wanted her, loved her. We came together. Then we fell asleep in one another's arms, the television a glowing eye in the night.

I woke up screaming. I hurled Amanda off me, thinking she was Rita.

Amanda, who'd always thought me a bastion of strength, cried up at me from the floor. It took me a full minute to shake the feeling of Rita's dead body slumping over me. She kept landing on my back, again and again and again.

I finally stood up, but not for long. A red dot had poked its way through the bandage wrapped around my chest. It was growing. Pain seemed to have exploded from within. It grew until I collapsed.

This time I woke up watching a white ceiling speed by overhead. I lifted my head up as far as I was able and saw that I was heading for the doors of an operating room. Making love with Amanda had ruptured my wound and I was bleeding internally.

Would that all love were this easy.

5

Again I was leaving the hospital, but this time there were no friends to greet me or provide the wheels. I hailed a cab on Second Avenue and hoped New York Hospital with all its interns would float out of my life for good. I watched it through the cab's rear window; plumes of black smoke rose from smokestacks on its roof, as if the doctors were burning their dead inside.

I'd been anxious to get home, but when I actually saw the place again I wasn't glad to be there. My old stale life rose up to greet me with a musty breath. Dust had thickened on every bookshelf. Chinese takeout still sat on the counter growing blue fungus. My stereo had been on for weeks. The apartment seemed like a museum built to preserve an attitude of stultifying inertia.

Luckily, Amanda had asked my next-door neighbor to collect my mail. I knocked on her bright blue door.

Gina smiled and was glad I was back, and with her tiny frame she hugged me gently. I was glad to see her. Everyone else I'd seen had treated me with a certain attitude of reproach. Not

Gina. This was a woman who took everything in stride. With great tolerance she'd managed to weather a violent husband, whom she'd finally up and left only after he'd caused the death of their child. She was no stranger to tragedy, wasn't frightened of it anymore.

She boiled a cup of herbal tea and seemed to know instinctively that I was interested in talking about anything but myself. She gave me a rundown on the local news, scandals in local government and down on Wall Street that I'd missed, and in great detail spelled out the joy and beauty and profound sadness of the Van Gogh exhibit at the Met. Our one-sided conversation was interrupted by a phone call. She shooed me away with a mischievous grin that could only mean that this was one of her boyfriends. So much for the girl next door, I thought.

I carried my mail back to my apartment and spread it out over the wooden table in the living room. Dust rose up like a cloud. In it, I saw the letter. It stood out among the bills and junk mail. It was pink and square and there was the faintest odor emanating from it—perfume, or the scent of dried flowers.

The letter was written in red ink on blue stationery. It didn't take long for my palms to sweat and smudge it. It read:

> Mr. Byman.
> I am taking a great risk writing you. Please don't take this to the police. It can only endanger my life and I assure you I am in danger—my whereabouts must remain unknown. To know that you are in the hospital and are not dead gives me great joy. We will, more than likely, not see one another again, but I had to write, to tell you that I am safe for now, recuperating. It's somehow important to me that you know I'm innocent of any wrongdoing. Very important. I seem to have gotten caught between two dark clouds converging, caught in the middle. And that's all I can say— plus this: that little Genna is still out there. She may not yet be a casualty. I will, I assure you, spend the rest of my life looking for her, if I have to, if I'm able.

> *Good-bye, Luke. Thank you for your kindness toward my dear son—I miss him so. Please—*

But the final sentence was tear smudged. I could barely read the last word: *funeral.* I presumed she meant Billy's.

I searched the envelope and held it up to the light. It was empty and faintly postmarked from Los Angeles.

6

I sat there for over an hour, holding the letter in both hands while listening to my telephone messages. Out of twenty-seven calls only one had been professional. Half of them had been hang-ups.

I didn't know what to do about the letter, but I called Cussone anyway. He picked up on the first ring.

"Cussone."

"It's Luke Byman."

"How's the gut?"

"Tender. Any news?"

"Plenty. None on your case, though. Have you read the papers lately?"

"A little."

"Read anything about a multiple homicide in your neighborhood?"

"A family, wasn't it?"

"Three kids and a mother and her lover. Just down from you, on Bond Street."

"That's terrible, but why tell me?"

"It's my case."

I sighed. There was a point to this, and it didn't take a genius to figure it out.

"So you're dropping my case, is that what you're trying to tell me?"

He hedged. "We're . . . not dropping it. I just wanted to give you an idea of what my current priorities are. I've got six other cases, some just as nasty, and this family murder is serious stuff, all over the press. Please, understand. This is a terrible time. We've gotten nowhere on your case thus far—after a hell of a lot of work. We're relaxing our efforts a bit."

"Euphemistic, isn't it?"

"Listen, don't piss me—"

"I'm not trying to piss you off. Hell, I understand. Just . . . Just give me one more favor, then I'll leave you alone. I want to see Julia's place, the apartment. I want to see where I was shot."

"We've scoured—"

"Not with me you haven't, and I think that's an oversight—don't you?"

"Well, if you would stay the hell out of the hospital long enough . . ." Cussone said he'd meet me himself, after his day was over—anywhere from six to ten o'clock.

He rang my buzzer at eight-thirty. I decided that I wouldn't show him the letter, not just yet, anyway, maybe never.

He was in a gruff mood. His clothes were as unkempt as his personality. We exchanged a few nonpleasantries, then I led him to the apartment. He unlocked the police security bolt with a long piece of metal that looked like a modern skeleton key, and led me through the narrow hallway into the living room. I stood in the shadows a moment, poised but frozen. I could see bloodstains on the sofa and on the rug next to it—my own—and over by the bedroom door, where Billy had fallen. Then everything turned to shadow, a swirl of swimming lights and flashing darks. I felt Cussone's hand take told of my elbow.

"Easy, now," his faraway voice whispered. It took a moment before his stern, blank, expressionless face came into focus.

"Guess I'm not very good at this," I said.

"Wanna leave?"

"Not on your life."

"Good. Let's begin." He told me to sit where I'd been sitting that night, on the couch. Its soft cushions were still stained. A rush came over me again as I realized how the baby girl had been born into a room of death. Her primal seconds had been spent in my arms; after that, her first minutes were spent witnessing the death of her brother. The impact of such a beginning to her life hit me with a wallop. The moon felt as if it shifted. A pull surged within me and gave me the impression that I could follow the child's trail instinctively, by lunar tracking. It was a queer feeling of identification. Perhaps my own childhood was welling up in me.

Cussone stood in the shadows of the corridor.

"OK," he said, "how many were there behind the big man?"

"Two—and I think there was one who waited at the doorway."

"What did they look like?"

"They were in shadow—"

"Their clothes?"

I tried to remember but nothing came. Julia's hallway was today as it had been then, a dark tunnel where men became shadows. A faint fluorescent glow from the outer corridor had silhouetted the killers in a garish light just as Cussone was silhouetted now.

He moved into the light.

"Tell me anything that comes into your head. Just look around and keep talking, maybe something will pop out." He didn't sound too hopeful.

I rose and circled the room, my eyes drifting along its perimeter. I touched on details as a camera would, a morbid home movie. The bookshelves were sparse, each book in them of a surprising quality. Huge tomes on war and history and economics were piled high on one shelf. On another, *Moby Dick* sat alone. I picked it up and opened to the middle. Its pages were as soft as tissue, worn from use. Passages everywhere were underlined. There was an inscription on the flyleaf:

To my beloved Ahab,
Julia

Cussone's voice made me jump.

"We flipped through every page of every book, if that's what you're wondering." I heard a little squeak of metal, turned, and saw him unscrewing the cap of a silver flask. He swigged what might have been vodka down his throat, then smiled. The smile vanished.

"Off duty," he growled.

"I don't give a damn."

"Good. Keep remembering."

He was like a broken record. I wasn't there to remember, exactly. I had come to see if I could find anything in the apartment that might give me a hint as to Julia's whereabouts in Los Angeles.

I kept looking. In one corner sat a baseball mitt, a ball, and a bat, and the football I'd bought for Billy's birthday. Also a banner. Cussone was eyeing me, so I tried to be nonchalant. I lifted the banner with a disinterested swagger. It didn't work.

"You're not bad, kid. You've already hit two of the salient points in the whole place. The book and now the banner."

"What is this, a quiz?"

"It's what you wanted, isn't it?" He maintained his impassive gaze, but his eyes were smiling.

I had to admit he was partly right. Julia's letter had once again roiled up in me the need to penetrate a shining and comfortable surface, where explanations were referred to fate. The violence that had happened in this room was part of a larger scheme of violence that was still going on. I'd never been a saint, but I felt like stopping this particular scheme, or doing anything I could to stop it, to keep Cussone on the investigation.

I spread the banner out in my hands. It was a triangular piece of felt that had faded with the years, but its white letters hadn't. They screamed brightly: CLOVER HIGH. At the end of the wide part of the banner was the circular insignia of Clover High School in Black River, Michigan. I spoke to Cussone in a low whisper.

"You've checked—"

"No such person as Billy Denig in Clover High, or even a

Denig in the whole city of Black River. There is an IBM, though, a big one."

I tossed the banner back into the corner. "What're the other salient points?"

"What?" He was playing with me.

"You said I've touched on two of the salient points."

"Yeah, I suppose I'll be nice." He got up and went to the bookshelf. "This I wouldn't have expected you to find. This takes good, old-fashioned, thorough police work."

He reached for a hardcover on a bottom shelf. It was a junky novel by an unknown author titled *Love's Labor*. Its inside flyleaf revealed it to be a library loaner. The card was missing, but imprinted on the back cover were the words: POUGHKEEPSIE PUBLIC LIBRARY: POUGHKEEPSIE, NEW YORK. The book had been published in 1977 by E. P. Dutton, New York City.

"At least," Cussone whispered, "we know your little friend might not have been lying. There's an IBM in Poughkeepsie, too. But there are seventy-five employees and their families who've been transferred from Black River to Poughkeepsie. We simply don't have the time to trace each one."

"Show me what else you've got."

"First," he said, "you look."

He led me into the bedroom. Billy's blood had dried on the carpet and on the bedroom door. The closets and dresser drawers seemed tousled and torn apart, as if Julia had packed in a hurry. I rifled everywhere but turned up nothing that had any significance. Cussone watched as I willingly tried to play his little game. Finally, I threw my hands up.

"Keep going." He took another swig from his flask.

I ducked into the bathroom once again. Nothing in the medicine cabinet had any doctor's labels or local stickers. I closed the door and stood motionless. My breathing echoed off the white tiles. Hanging from the hook on the back of the door was a gray tweed sports jacket. There was nothing in its pockets, but the inner label cried out at me with the importance of an archaeological discovery: BEVERLY HILLS DESIGN.

Cussone spoke from the bedroom. "Try it on."

I slipped the jacket on and opened the door. I felt both spooked and foolish, modeling for a cop only inches from where Billy had died.

"Fits you, almost." He smiled. "Would never get around my gut."

"So?"

"Well, it's probably Miss Denig's husband's, the same guy she gave the book to—'Ahab.' At least now we know how big he is. He's just about your size."

7

Cussone led me into the building's bleak corridor and locked Julia's door. I asked him why he hadn't mentioned any of these particular bits of evidence.

"Evidence toward what?" he rightly asked back.

"Clues?" was my halfhearted reply.

"One." His voice was gruff again. "I don't go sharing my cases with every bozo who gets shot, you know. Two. We didn't check the books until last week. Three. Besides running a check in each of these three towns—L.A., Black River, and Poughkeepsie—which we've already done, I have no idea what to do with the information we've accumulated." He raised his hands, then let them drop at his sides. "I'm sorry, nothing holds together. I've notified the Division in Los Angeles, but I can't put out an APB without justifiable cause. She very well may be there, but unless LAPD finds her . . ." He slashed the air between us in half with a karate chop. "Forget about her, will you? Forget about the whole thing. Get on with your life."

He jabbed the elevator button. The door opened immediately.

He stepped inside and before the doors closed I caught a glimpse of the tiny silver flask gleaming in his hands.

I got on with my life. What a life. There were more bills, now, more every day. My landlord served me a two-week notice. I decided to take out a loan to pay my rent and bills, but the bank representative just laughed outright.

"You've got to be kidding!" he said. I wanted to belt him.

I sat at my phone for days and dredged up numbers from dog-eared address books. Producers and production companies and advertising agencies that I'd worked for in the past now fielded my calls with aloof pleasantries.

"Aren't you writing scripts now?" they all seemed to ask. The question never failed to seem like a dig. I'd left their businesses to become a haughty film writer and hadn't made it and now they had the upper hand because they knew I was crawling back. Oh Lords of the Sacred Buck, I'll do anything you want—just pay me.

It was Amanda who finally lent me a couple of thousand, her savings. My humiliation seemed complete when she handed me the check; it took me days to deposit it. Days of walking, gaining back my strength. I even managed to face the typewriter and begin another screenplay.

Weeks later a doctor unwrapped the bandage and felt my wounds with the tips of her fingers. The scar on my chest had healed nicely; the one in my back, where the bullet had made a quick entry, still hurt badly at times, was slower to heal. It made me feel as if there were someone behind me constantly jabbing with the point of a knife.

"Be careful," she said with a mischievous grin. "Don't try and make the earth move, not just yet."

With some of Amanda's grocery money I bought a nice bottle of champagne and a dozen tulips. Roses were too romantic, too expensive. When she arrived home from work we made love on her kitchen floor and my head ended up underneath the kitchen table, cut off from what was happening between us by the checkered tablecloth. It was dark and musty under there. I saw Julia's face in the darkness, as if it were projected on the bottom of the table.

8

Finally the call came, at six A.M.
"Luke—can you be here in ten minutes?"
Shit, I thought, just call me boy.
Ten minutes later I was there.
The commercial was selling processed pink granules packaged in a cellophane-type wrapper, one per serving. All you had to do was add water and it became a healthy fruit drink, or so they said. Water, and imagination.
I worked the phone and called crew, stages, camera facilities, and caterers. There were some special effects involved. It took a lot of research to find that special gymnast who could dive through a gushing sea of fruit juice.
I ended up at a grungy soundstage on Fifty-fourth and Tenth, overseeing the construction of a funnel that could properly pour a ton of pink water into a plastic swimming pool. The first week of preproduction ended after five sixteen-hour days. The producer had talked my rate down, so I was making only one seventy-five a day. It used to be two-fifty. I guess she smelled my desperation.
Anyway, I was grateful to be working.

Finally, the shoot day loomed before us. Late that night, after a grueling day of final prep, I took the Lexington Avenue IRT down to Astor Place and walked past the crowds that were filtering out of the local off-off-Broadway theaters. The shows were over; now it was time for the audience to go onstage in several of the chic restaurants that had cropped up in my neighborhood.

NoHo was changing like every other part of the city, gentrifying. It wasn't bad, exactly, it was just that true feelings seemed to echo off the walls of these new establishments like lonely vapors. I was white, thin, brown-haired, blue-eyed, and raised a Catholic. Still, New York made me feel like a member of an ethnic minority constantly trudging through the confines of a restricted country club. Money buys all, I thought, and without it joints like the one I always passed on my way down lower Broadway were off limits. It was a double-decker job, decorated with enormous palms and sprinkled with elegant blue lighting. Every person at every table looked at me as I walked by, then looked at the person who was walking behind me, then at the one after that. A muscular fellow wearing a dark suit and white shirt and loosened red tie smiled at me. "Money buys all," he seemed to be silently reiterating. But his eyes were sad and frightened. "If you had it you'd be in here, too—wouldn't you?"

Lonely vapors.

I bought some milk and a sandwich at a deli and turned the corner onto Lafayette Street. I had found some solace in the balmy night. There was nothing but a song on my lips: "I know what I know" was the chorus.

Before I stuck my key in the lock I turned and faced the night. I felt as if someone was watching me. It was an uncomfortable feeling. Inside, I pulled some more bills out of my mailbox and took the elevator to the second floor.

I stood before my door and fumbled with my keys. There was a noise inside. Then my door swung open. His face was horrible, bloody and wild. He howled as he lunged for me, tearing at my hair and face with his left hand, punching me with his right.

"Damn you!" he shouted.

My bag of groceries crashed at our feet as I tried to fend him off—but he collapsed on me with all his weight. Together we sprawled in the doorway. He'd stopped moving. I screamed again, remembering Rita. It took all my strength to slide out from under his body. I got to my knees. It was then that I saw the knife handle sticking out of his back.

With the force of a baseball bat a gun butt slammed me across the side of the face. I fell into a shadowy world, my cheek against the tiled floor. It was cool and pleasant compared to the hot liquid filling my mouth. I tried to open one eye but couldn't. Instead, I opened my lips and let the blood spill out. The last thing I remember is hearing the sound of a woman in high heels stepping over me and running down the corridor, into the elevator.

9

The hospital felt like my second home. Shit, I thought, the least they could do was paint the place, add some color, maybe a little furniture. Somehow the blank white walls made the inside of my head feel like it had been whitewashed and sterilized.

As if God had rigged a special irony, I turned my hollow head and faced the not unpleasant sight of an attractive black nurse. She was about to pat my forehead with a damp cloth.

"Welcome back." She smiled with such natural beauty that I was almost glad to be there. "You've been having a bad dream."

She was right. Sweat dripped from my arms and hands. She saw me notice, and rubbed the cool cloth all the way from my shoulders to the tips of my fingers. Nothing had ever felt quite so welcome.

"Thanks," I whispered.

"You've had a rough time."

I nodded. "What's your name?"

Her big brown eyes twinkled with a mixture of mischief and suspicion.

"Lola. Now go back to sleep, Mr. Byman. Another day and you'll be out of here. You just need rest. Lots of rest."

"Luke," I said, trying to appear halfway suave in my polka-dotted hospital pajamas.

She smiled again. A feast for the eyes.

"Luke," she repeated.

A warm hand touched my wrist. I grinned, thinking it was Lola. But when I opened my eyes Detective Stanley Cussone's mug was peering directly down at me.

"Time to go," he said quietly. "I'll take you home myself."

Lola stood behind him holding my trousers. She jerked a thumb at Cussone.

"Outa here," she said to him. "Wait in the hall."

I sat up and let my legs dangle over the edge of the bed. She sat next to me as I slipped my pants on; it was an unusual thing for a nurse to do. I was groggy, but not stupid. I took Lola's hand and leaned against her fine shoulder.

"Thank you," I whispered into her ear, then kissed it.

She withdrew, inching away. Her dark brown eyes rolled sideways to me. We sat there for a quiet moment.

"You look terrible," she said finally.

"I may need treatment."

She smiled, openly, a fresh burst of white teeth.

"You better call me for a consultation."

I may have been in pain but I was grinning. It was a crisp June day, a deep blue Manhattan sky. Once again, New York Hospital grew smaller in the rearview mirror. Lola had made me feel like I was surging with a refill of fresh new blood. Cussone broke my surging silence.

"Nice nurse." He turned to me and for a brief moment flashed a yellow smile. Then, as if feeling he'd given too much of himself away, his gruffness returned.

"Says there wasn't any bleeding inside. Says you're lucky."

"Lucky," I mumbled.

"Yeah, that's you."

He turned right on Third Street and passed what seemed to be a thousand bums all panhandling on the same block.

"Salvation Army," he said.
"Yeah," I answered. "Maybe I'll end up there."

It was true. I'd missed the commercial's shoot-day and, in fact, hadn't called the production company until the following Friday, the day I regained consciousness. The receptionist there took my call and trembled slightly for a few seconds before talking.

"I'm glad you're alive," she said. "But you might as well not be. Hold on."

There was an interminable wait. Then the executive producer came on the phone. He took a deep breath before speaking.

"Shit!" I knew I was in for it. "You're all right." Nothing but death would have done for an excuse.

"Yes, I'm all right. I was in the hospital—"

"And you didn't call?"

"I was—"

"Shit, Luke, you fucked up!"

I let a moment float in silence. "I'm sorry," I said, then tried to give him a brief rundown of what happened, but he cut me short.

"Listen, it sounds terrible. I'm sorry I yelled, but I'm angry at you. I have to be honest. A hell of a lot went wrong the other day on the set and we all blamed your absence. We were wrong, of course . . ." But he wasn't so sure about that. I told him I'd make it up to him by coming in for a couple of days and working for free.

"No—no. I'm glad you're all right, Luke. Really. But . . . listen—take care of yourself."

He hung up.

Cussone parked his car on the corner of Great Jones and Lafayette. We walked to my apartment, a block north, past a few of those bums. I limped.

"How's your other case?" I asked him. "The family shooting."

"Terrible. There's evidence that it was a mob hit on a black drug dealer's family. A mother and five kids. The black community is pissed off, crying for Giuliani's boy to do something." Rudolph Giuliani had been Manhattan's extremely high-profile DA. He'd made great stabs at cleaning up the mob and fraud on Wall Street and fraud in government. Since he'd left office, his onetime second-in-command, Ronald Dyson, had been taking a lot of heat. The press, and just about everyone else, still called him "Giuliani's boy." Cussone was an obvious supporter. Passion found its way into his speech. "They bust people right and left but they insist that Dyson's blind to anyone who kills a black. It's a bum rap and a bad scene." He collected himself. "A lotta pressure," he added.

Walking into my apartment did not produce a comforting feeling. There were chalk marks in the doorway that outlined where the dead man's body had fallen. Bloodstains had been left on the floor of my place, but not in the outer hallway. They'd been washed clean by my super.

Inside, nothing was as it had been. The apartment had been torn apart. Books, records, lamps, and kitchenware lay strewn on the floor. In my bedroom, clothes and shoes and personal files had been rifled through. Tubes of toothpaste had been emptied on my bathroom floor, along with my shaving kit and lotions and my soaps and shampoos. In the kitchen, food had been dumped out: rice, flour, liquor, cornflakes.

Also, my mail and bills had been sifted through. Julia's letter was missing.

I sat down on the edge of my sofa with my head in my hands.

"What is happening?" I asked pathetically.

"I wish I knew," Cussone answered. But he was staring at me with those patient dog eyes again, poised on another set of questions. I pulled myself together.

"Go ahead, ask." I moaned.

He leaned even farther forward. "Did you ever know or hear of a man named Bridge. Henry Bridge?"

"No."

"Are you sure?"

"I'm sure. Is he the one—"

"I'll ask the questions, for now. Think hard—does the name Ridley mean anything to you? Peter Ridley?"

"No!" I was frustrated. He was being mysterious.

"Be patient, now—one more question."

"All right."

"Does this mean anything to you?" He opened his palm and in it I saw Billy's rabbit's foot.

"Yes—yes! Billy—it was Billy's!"

"Did he give it to you?"

My voice fell to a whisper: "Yes."

"Well."

"Well what? Tell me something, damn it." I was still whispering.

"The man who tried to kill you, the one who died in your doorway . . ." He paused and looked to the door, as if my memory needed refreshing.

"Go on."

"His name was Henry Bridge. I knew him."

"Who was he?"

"A private cop. Co-ran a small detective agency on Forty-sixth—Bridge and Ridley. Never heard of them?"

"No. Why'd he attack me?"

"Maybe he thought you were somebody else."

"He was in my apartment, for Chrissake!"

"Calm down, will you?"

"All right, all right."

"I knew Henry, long time ago. Hadn't seen him for years when suddenly he popped into my office a year ago or so. He was looking for a guy, needed my help to track him. License rundowns, stuff like that. He'd been to L.A. and they'd helped him there, but what he was asking was against policy. I refused. He told me to go to hell, and left."

"Who was he tracking?"

"A man who had disappeared off the face of the earth. He said it was the man who had killed Peter Ridley, his partner. I knew Peter. . . . And, damn! I wanted to help him."

Cussone clasped his hands and lowered his head. A bald spot was widening on his crown.

"Did he tell you the name of the man he was tracking?"

"No." Cussone's voice was glum. "I'm afraid he might have taken that knowledge with him to his grave."

"How could Bridge think I was the guy?"

"He'd never really seen the suspect. He just had this terrible picture, a grainy newspaper photo, out of focus. Ridley had given it to him. Bridge showed it to me and asked if I'd ever seen him."

"It looked like me?"

"I don't remember."

But remembrance crossed Cussone's brow. His features seemed to sag with sadness.

"How did Bridge know this man had killed his partner?"

"His partner—Ridley—had been following this guy the night he was killed."

"Killed how?"

"Gunshot. A forty-five to the side of the head."

"Why was Ridley following him?"

Cussone's voice rasped: "I don't know. Bridge wouldn't say. Only said it was big, important. But Bridge was always saying that." He seemed to be making excuses for himself.

"Bridge followed this guy here from L.A.?"

Cussone nodded. Just then another nasty image flitted through my head. An image of Julia slamming her .45 into my cheekbone. I touched the painful place with my fingers. It was still swollen.

"Who could the woman have been?"

"I don't know," he answered almost imperceptibly.

"She killed Bridge?"

"It looks that way. But for all you know it could have been a guy you heard, wearing high heels."

I dismissed that thought with a wave of my hand.

"Did she come in before or after Bridge?"

Cussone perked up. He leveled his eyes at me. "It's a good question. Frankly, there isn't much to point against the possibility that it might have been she who ransacked the place. There's no fingerprints except for yours in here, and your friend Amanda's. They seemed old. So she may have hidden away as he came in, then jumped out and killed him." He sighed. "But I tend to doubt it."

"Why?"

"Two reasons. One: Bridge was a trained detective and this place has been professionally scoured. Very thorough."

He wiped his brow and fidgeted for a moment. I knew he was thinking about that little silver flask in his pocket but was hesitant to unleash it, not just yet.

"The other reason . . ." Once again he held out Billy's old rabbit's foot. ". . . is this. We found it clenched in Bridge's fist. Took a lot of force to pry it out of his fingers. It may have been what she was looking for. Who knows?"

He handed me the token. I thought of Billy and how his miserable luck seemed to be rubbing off on me. I thought of his pathetic eyes as he'd handed me the good-luck charm. I stared at the rabbit's foot in my hand as if it were a relic from another age.

"Open it," Cussone said.

"Open it?"

"Yes, open it."

The tarnished silver tip pulled off easily. Inside was a slip of paper like the ones found in fortune cookies. On it, a few words had been scribbled—hastily—probably the night Billy had given it to me. He had written: *"She's not my mother."*

10

It took me a long time to absorb Billy's words and to understand Cussone's train of thought.

"You think Julia killed Bridge."

"Yes."

"She couldn't have."

"Why?"

"She wrote me a letter that came when I was in the hospital. From Los Angeles. The letter's gone, now. Somebody took it."

Cussone sat for a while, his blank gaze working overtime. I knew my protestation seemed feeble.

"What'd the letter say?" Cussone asked.

"Nothing much, really. 'Thank you, glad you're alive,' that type of thing. She was in danger—"

"She said that?"

"Very definitely so."

"What else?"

"That two dark clouds had been moving together and that she was caught in the middle."

"Poetic."

"And one other thing. She said the baby was still alive. She knew it was alive and said that she would keep looking for it, if it took the rest of her life."

We sat for a while, like two followers of an Eastern religion who needed a fix of meditation. Cussone let his chin find a home on his chest. I sprawled out on the sofa, hurting all over. I tried to let myself be convinced that Julia had slugged me and that she'd killed a man—in my apartment, of all places. But it didn't sit right.

"Wait a minute!" My voice sounded like a news flash. "She couldn't have known what Billy had written in that rabbit's foot. And—anyway—it wasn't worth killing over. Neither was the letter, or anything else I had."

"How do you know?" He was playing cop.

"Oh, come on—"

"You're right, you're right." Cussone held up his hand. "I've been thinking the same thing. It sort of saddened me."

"Why?"

"Because that means that Julia—or whoever—followed Bridge here for the purpose of killing him. Who knows why? We may never know. Maybe he'd stumbled onto something. Or maybe he'd just become too big of a nuisance."

"Why kill him in my apartment?"

"Again, who knows? Convenience, maybe." Then Cussone smiled and snapped his fingers. "Because . . . Julia still had the key to this building. She could easily have let herself in after Bridge had picked the lock, made her way up to her old floor, followed him into your apartment, and . . ." He sat back, saddened again. ". . . and crept up behind him . . ."

We listened to some more silence, more of the distant sirens and faraway laughter and screaming that mingled with the rush of traffic down Broadway, that river of sound always droning from over the alley rooftops.

"You know what that means," I said. It took a while for Cussone to answer. When he did, the weight of the case seemed to have grown and to have deposited itself squarely on his shoulders.

"Yes."

"It means," I continued joylessly, "that Julia—or whoever— is working with the man that Ridley and Bridge had been trying to follow."

I locked eyes with Detective Stanley Cussone.

"Julia's husband," he said softly.

"Yes."

Cussone's eyes tilted toward my dirty windows; he seemed to see Julia's spirit fly out of my heart and disappear into the alley.

"I'm going to have to call L.A." he said, hoisting himself out of the chair.

"Yeah," was my only reply.

"Yeah," he mirrored.

I walked him to the door.

"Don't stay here, Luke." It was the first time he'd called me by name. "It's not safe." He produced a card that had been folded and had picked a few teeth after a few lunches. "Here. Ever need a place, call me. It's a nice sofa."

"Thanks."

"If I'm not there, my wife'll know about you."

"Your second wife," I said.

He smiled wanly. "You catch on."

11

I hefted the phone receiver; it felt as if it weighed a hundred pounds. Dialing Amanda's number did not console me. The digits seemed to unlock an inner vault where the ghosts of tear-filled evenings lurked. Even before she answered I was restless to get away from her, release myself before the anger and recriminations welled up again. Once had been enough between us; we were skating on fragile ice.

She knew. I'd not been prepared for what she had to tell me.

"Luke, we have to talk."

The tone of her voice told the story. "Talk," I said weakly. When it rains it pours, I thought.

"When it rains it pours," she said aloud, as if she'd plagiarized my mind.

"*Uh-oh.*"

"Yeah." There was a pause.

"You might as well go ahead and say it now."

She took a deep breath.

"Well, for the last few weeks you've been on my mind a lot, Luke, you know that. You also know that I've been grappling with thoughts of—of us getting back together. Or, more to the point, dealing with your lack of interest in the face of it all. I thought . . ." She sighed such a familiar sigh. "You seemed so helpless, you know. So in need."

"You've been wonderful to me."

"I know." She paused again.

"Now you don't feel like being so wonderful."

"No. Because all I get back is lukewarm sex where you're looking up at the ceiling."

That hurt. What she said next hurt even worse.

"And, Luke"—her tone was condescending—"you never should have borrowed money from me. I've thought about that a lot."

I thought about all the dinners and rent checks I'd paid for, and my stereo and typewriter and books and records on the shelves in her apartment. I was angry. I get that way when I'm humiliated.

"I'll pay it back." She heard me sinking.

"I'm sorry, Luke—it's just me. I don't mean to be cruel. My shrink would say I'm just finding excuses. What I really mean to say is that I shouldn't get back into the same old relationship. That'd be retreating."

Those, too, had probably been her shrink's words.

"I feel the same way." I tried to sound like I meant it. This seemed to cheer Amanda, take some of the heavy burden off those fragile shoulders. There was a silence. Neither of us knew how to continue. "I'll come by and pick up my things," I said with a feeble finality.

"I feel so guilty, after all that's happened to you."

"Shut up and be a man," I said, and hung up.

12

I gathered a few things and threw them in a suitcase and gave a farewell nod to my bills and books, screenplays and toothpaste, that were spread out in piles on the floors of my apartment. Before I closed the door behind me I had a vision that the place was actually floating in space, like a time capsule of my discombobulated past.

I knocked on Gina's door. There was a faint hello that sounded as if it came from a deep, dark dungeon that lurked behind some secret wall. She was probably in her bathroom.

"Be right out," I heard.

When she opened the door it looked as if Gina had just been applying a deep, seductive eyeliner that she'd chosen not to wear for me. There were faint smudges around her eyes where she'd wiped it off.

"Hello," she said breathlessly.

"Hello."

The awkward moment disappeared, and once again I found Gina in my arms. There was a difference this time, though. The hug was not so maternal. "It must have been horrible," she moaned as she pulled me into her apartment. "Want tea?" She turned with a coquettish smile that completely disarmed me. Today was one of those days that a female could pulverize my heart.

"Yes, but not the herbal stuff. Real tea."

"Great. I have this Irish blend."

She bounced into the kitchen. I sat on her couch and watched through the kitchen's doorless entrance as she put water on to boil. It was a brief few moments, but it gave me a chance to study her from behind, her fine form, a body that usually remained hidden under sweaters and baggy pants. Today she wore blue jeans that wrapped tightly around a fragile waist and fine ass. A loose T-shirt allowed her breasts to sway happily. Her bright blue eyes twinkled as she spooned an aromatic tea blend into our cups. Her blondish hair was close-cropped in a sort of pixie-ish style that lent her a youthful charm. She might have been a full head shorter than I was, and five years older, but she was quite a package.

"You know," she chimed, "you almost caught me at an awkward moment."

"How so?"

"I was trying out makeup—which I never wear and have no idea how to put on."

"Why?" I asked, but she misunderstood my question.

"Because I was never into girls' stuff," she said. Then a harsh memory briefly transformed her expression. She squinted maliciously at her kitchen wall. "My mother and sister always played with makeup. Not me."

Her sour expression disappeared, a smile returned. She stepped out of the kitchen balancing two hot mugs and handed one to me. I tried my question again.

"Why were you trying on makeup?"

"Because—I will confess this to you, Luke, because, well, somehow I feel close to you . . ." She looked me right in the eyes. "I seem to be single again." Her wan smile spoke volumes.

I fidgeted.

"My . . . boyfriend," she continued, "just left me. Again. Dropped me like a hot potato."

She sat down next to me and sipped her tea.

"Funny . . ." I knew deep down I shouldn't be saying this. "My girl gave me the can, too. Just now."

"She did that? The day you got out of the hospital?"
"Yup."

I had said the magic words and produced the magic smile and now wished I hadn't been so clever a magician. She leaned her body against me, lightly as a feather. Any harder and she would have been throwing herself at me. Yet there was something queer about her passion. And something bothered me about what she'd just said. I just couldn't figure out what it was.

She let her forehead lean against my shoulder a while, but I did nothing. After a few moments she pulled her head away from me slowly, methodically, and rested it on the back of the couch. Her eyes remained open, feigning dreaminess, avoiding contact.

I remembered why I had come in the first place, and tried to break the silence. "Gina, will you collect my mail for a few weeks more?" There was no answer. "You still have the key, right?"

She nodded, almost imperceptibly. Otherwise she remained motionless, in tragic repose.

I let myself out.

13

I dialed Lola's number from a pay phone on the corner of Eighth and Broadway. A receptionist said he would page her and if she answered I was having good luck today. He didn't know how wrong he was. Or maybe he did—I waited the full three minutes but decided not to burn another nickel. Times were tough.

I walked aimlessly a while, carrying my suitcase into Midtown, feeling like a bag man. All those men and women wearing business suits and carrying briefcases were on their way home to Mamaroneck or Larchmont or perhaps one of the lofts that lined my old avenue—where I used to live, I thought—I certainly couldn't afford it anymore. Perhaps all these folks I watched scurrying were just floating a lie like I had been for the last nine years. Living in a tiny little personal hell with no light that cost hundreds a month with all of it on credit because we were going to make it in New York City, in the big time.

I delved into my wallet and pulled the last twenty of real green money. The rest was plastic, nearly unusable considering all my present debts. I stopped at a deli and bought a roast beef sandwich on a soft roll with butter and a chocolate milk. I sat eating it on a sidewalk wall that looked out over Radio City and the rest of the glistening tunnel of steel they call the Avenue of the Americas.

Big time.

Finally I jumped the West Side IRT. It rumbled up to Broadway and Seventy-seventh, and I spewed out with hundreds of others into the waning light. I walked through the river of humanity that is Broadway, over to Seventy-sixth and Riverside, and rang Amanda's buzzer. There was no answer, so I used my key to enter. I figured that I'd pick up my necessities and find myself a place to stay tonight, or forever, either one.

Once inside, I tried Lola again. The first receptionist transferred me to the same man I'd talked to earlier. This time, he said, she was gone for the day. Then I dialed Marty and Ros and got their machine. I left a meager message, then phoned Jim.

"Look, Luke," he said, sounding like a college student, "if you can't scare up any other place, of course you're welcome. But there's this girl coming over tonight . . ."

I kept trying. I got a few machines and a few apologetic no's. I felt as if the violence that had welled up in my life had made me seem cursed. I was beginning to feel desperate, when the phone rang. It was Ros.

"Get over here, Jack."

Ten days later I was still waking up on their couch. Hospitality was wearing thin, mainly because with me there they couldn't hash out their troubled marriage. After a while they began to look at me each day as if I was the trouble with their marriage. That's when I knew it was all over.

Repeated attempts to call Lola left me frustrated. She was never there. Reluctantly, I ended up at Jim's place, sleeping on the floor as he boffed his girlfriend for what seemed like the whole damn night. He lived in a studio with a loft bed. It squeaked above me, and squeaked and squeaked.

The next evening, wearily, and even more reluctantly, I dialed Cussone's number. I was surprised when he answered.

"Cussone."

"Byman."

He breathed a ninety-proof sigh. "Thought you'd call. How long?" He was not a man of many words tonight.

"A couple of days."

He cupped the phone and I heard him mumble loudly to his wife. Then he came back on, a little annoyed. He spoke in a louder tone.

"She says she'd love to have you. Charmed."

"I bet."

"Well, do you need a place?"

"Yes."

Jim lent me twenty for a cab and a couple of meals, and without adieu I found myself standing before Cussone's tenement on Fifty-forth and Ninth. Hell's Kitchen; a block from the last soundstage I'd worked. The neighborhood was a reminder that there might still be a life for me in commercials. I'd spent the last two weeks moping and now it was time to, as Cussone had once put it, get on with my life. Tomorrow I'd make some calls.

I rang his buzzer; it growled back at me. I climbed three flights up to a surprisingly homey little two-bedroom. It was clean and well furnished, with a worn-in quality that implied love and use but not shabbiness. If there had been any resentment at my showing up, his wife, Anne, didn't show it. She was younger than her husband by quite a few years. I placed her at twenty-eight or twenty-nine. But her homeliness suited Stanley's. She stood at the door with a ready-made mug of tea waiting for me. Tea, I thought, everyone wants to give me tea.

Before resigning ourselves to the privacy of sleep, Cussone sat with me a while. He didn't say much when I asked him about the case, how it was going, if there was progress. I got the impression that things had come to a standstill.

"You'll be happy to know," he did finally say, "that I've asked the boys to do a thorough sweep of Bridge and Ridley—every case in their files. We hesitated to before because there weren't the men to spare. It's a large piece of grunt work."

"How much would you pay me to do it?" I asked.

"Listen, we can't—"

"Just as a drone, a research assistant, whatever you wanna call me, Stanley. I need a job."

His jaw slackened and with an exaggerated puff on the cheeks he blew out a brief gust of alcoholic air. For the first time I'd called him by his name and, subtly, that was working on him. I managed to achieve my poor, broke, about-to-starve expression—which wasn't difficult—and he succumbed.

"Oh, shit, all right. Eight A.M. we're outa here. One day, maybe two."

"Stanley, thank you—"

"It's Detective Cussone, damn it all." He stood up. There was a glint in his eyes but he wouldn't yield a smile. "Good night." He ducked into his bedroom and shut the door behind him. A few minutes later, when we were both in our underwear, he cracked the door open to give me my good-night blessing.

"Minimum wage," he conferred.

The offices of Bridge and Ridley were on the third floor of a decent building on the corner of Forty-sixth and Broadway. Decent, meaning it had an elevator. The lobby was a checkerboard of missing tiles decorated with red graffiti and permeated by the smell of urine. The neighborhood was not what it had been thirty years ago. It was then that two young rookies, discharged from the force for having sex with prostitutes, started this towering outfit.

The elevator threatened not to make it to the third floor. Finally the doors opened and Cussone and I strode the length of a hallway that had been painted as recently as twenty years ago. "Bridge and Ridley—Private Investigations" was stenciled on the frosted glass that rattled in the upper door. Cussone unlocked another police bolt, but stood before the open door without entering. I noticed he was breathing heavily.

"Anything the matter?"

"I hate this place, that's all." He turned to me. "I had to come here, once. My case is in one of these files." He gestured to the room, a dour-looking but functional office, with three desks and walls lined with cheap file cabinets stacked two high.

I said something that probably hadn't needed saying. "Is that why it took you a month to get to this?"

No answer.

I stared at the file cabinets. "Your first wife?"

He nodded.

* * *

The afternoon droned on after sandwiches and soda. At three P.M., Cussone rose to leave. Before he did, I aired something that had been on my mind for weeks.

"I know you're being kind here, letting me help. But I've got to ask a question you may not like."

"Shoot."

"That money, Julia's money."

"It's state's evidence."

I quoted him. "Evidence toward what?"

He smiled.

"Don't get me wrong," I said. "I don't want it for myself, though I could use it. I wanted to bury Billy. Give him better than potter's field." Finally, a permanent home.

This one surprised Cussone. It was language he could understand, a sign that I, too, had my codes and partners, just as all cops had theirs.

"I'll think about it."

But it was a yes, I was sure. I waved to him as the elevator door closed.

The sun dropped beneath the smokestacks of New Jersey. They were fuming a putrid orange out across the river, which was visible from the office's Forty-sixth Street window. Below, Times Square was beginning to boil like a neon stew.

Night came and I still hadn't discovered anything unusual, though I'd searched two of the four file cabinets. The only working lamp in the place was a tiny desk lamp that I had to stick the files directly under in order to read them. My eyes were sore. At one point I found that they'd closed—who knows for how long.

When I opened them, someone else was in the room with me. He'd just switched the lamp off. A gun's tiny barrel winked at me from corner shadows, catching glints of the neon "Coke" sign across Times Square.

"I won't hurt you," he whispered, "if you do what I say."

From there, behind the files, his voice seemed like it came from all around me, or was my own voice talking back to me in a dream.

"Go to the middle row of files, over there."

I moved to where his gun pointed. It jutted in and out of the shadows and pointed toward the left bank of cabinets, near where I'd been looking.

"Under T—May 1987."

"Which file?"

"Just open the drawer."

I did as he said, leafing through the folders till I came to the Ts.

"I've been watching," he suddenly said behind me. "You need to be infinitely more clever than you are to continue, and I don't suggest it, Mr. Byman. Please—withdraw." An unexpected force found its way into his voice. A misery that was palpable. "My life . . . my life's been ruined by them. And my wife's . . . My God, they killed our little boy. And now, now perhaps, the very core of Julia is missing. Her daughter."

"Denig . . ." I whispered.

"Your life will end up as mine has if you continue to pursue this. I came here for the key, yes, but also to tell you that."

The horns and sirens and shouting from the streets below surged up like din from Hades. For a queer few seconds I had the sensation that Denig and I were standing on a ledge above it all and that he was going to push me over.

"Key?" was all I asked.

He sighed. "The last folder."

I reached in and found a safety-deposit key taped to the back of the last folder. The cover of the folder was marked only with a triangle and was Scotch-taped shut. I ripped the key off and held it for a moment in my palm. It was weighty—the box it would unlock was old.

His gun hit me perfectly—a precise dab below the ear. My poor damn head, I thought, as I heard my nose crunch against the floor.

14

I imagined that I'd arrived in purgatory, waking up with the worst headache of my life as I was being lifted off the cold floor into the sweaty, coddling arms of an aging black transvestite.

"Comforting to see you," I said mushily.

"Oh, hush up, dear, you hurt bad."

His blue mascara was running. His ruby lips were cracked. A blond wig had slipped to one side. He lifted me into his arms and literally carried me down three flights of stairs and into a taxicab.

"My name is Danny," he said in the back seat. I found out later that he worked in an "office" down the hall. His clients knew him as "Danielle."

The taxi driver hadn't seen the blood. He turned and raised his fluffy eyebrows and intoned: "Where you lovebirds off to?"

"Roosevelt," said Danny. "Emergency."

"New York Hospital," I corrected.

Then the driver noticed the fine sheen of dried blood that had hardened across my right cheek. It had painted a reddish mustache across my upper lip.

"Just my luck," he mumbled as he headed east on Forty-eighth.

I fell asleep in the emergency room. When I woke, I felt as if I were trapped in some second-rate Fellini movie. There I was, lying in another hospital bed, half drugged with painkillers, and surrounded on all flanks by Lola, Cussone, Danny, and Amanda.

"This is your family?" Lola quipped.

"We all ended up here at once," Amanda said shyly. A slight glance in Lola's direction betrayed her suspicions. She'd brought flowers that now seemed to be wilting in her hands. "I felt so bad when I found out. So guilty, Luke."

"Don't." I wasn't in the mood for guilt. "How did you find out?"

"I called her," Cussone answered.

"Ah."

"I have questions," he said with a smile.

"You always do."

"You up for them?"

I really didn't know how badly I'd been banged on the head. All eyes drifted toward Lola for an evaluation.

"Don't worry. He'll be outa here tonight," she said. "Minor concussion." Then she leaned back against the wall and smiled her wonderful smile. She lifted one leg and tapped the side of my bed with her foot. "What is it with you, anyway?" Her gesture and voice implied a familiarity that went a bit beyond the normal nurse-to-patient repartee. A signal well perceived by both Amanda and Cussone. Even Danny noticed the seductive quality of Lola's stance. He looked as if he were taking mental notes.

"I've been asking myself that lately."

"I've been asking *my*self that question for the last seven years," Amanda offered. Then she stood up and placed the wilting flowers on a windowsill.

" 'Bye, Luke."

I watched her walk out the door.

" 'Bye."

A second later she was standing in the open door again.

"Stop this, Luke. Please. Stay the hell out of"—she spread her hands toward the others—"out of all this."

There was a silence in the room after she'd gone. As usual, Cussone broke it. "Guess I blew it by calling her?"

"An honest mistake. Ask your questions."

Lola said directly to me, "I'll be back."

Danny stood up. "Not me. I'm goin' ta sleep, honey. It's been a looong night . . . day. Whichever."

"Thanks, Danny. I'll stop by when I get back." He smiled a mischievous smile from the doorway. "Don't get any ideas," I said with mock severity.

Just then another nurse appeared at the door. She stood there with an inquisitive expression and spoke to Lola with a feigned politeness:

"Nurse?"

"Coming," Lola said. She left quickly, pulling the other nurse's arm. The small scene left Cussone and me wondering for a moment.

"What a parade!" he finally chimed.

"Yeah. Feels like they've been dancing on my head."

"Someone else was dancing on your head. Do you know who?"

"Yes." I smiled with an unaccountable feeling of pride.

"You going to share it with me?"

"Him," I said with force.

Cussone said with spite: "God sapped you?"

"Denig."

He seemed trounced by my revelation, and saddened. The bags under his basset-eyes sagged. Years of walking a ragged sidewalk beat shone from behind them.

"Did he—did he take anything?"

"A folder, and a key."

His head bowed even farther. He scratched his neck nervously. "To what, do you know?"

"Looked like the key to a safety-deposit box. It was brass, had a good heft to it. Like one of those old ones."

"I know the ones you mean. They're still fairly common. Old banks, even postal offices . . ." His voice trailed off.

"What's the matter?"

"I—I've failed you all, really." I'd never heard the Cussone that was talking to me now. "For weeks I delayed searching that damned office. My own personal—lousy personal reasons! I should be taken off this case." For the first time I realized how seriously

Stanley Cussone regarded his work. He was tearing into that regard like an animal with teeth.

"That goddamned night ruined a marriage; now it's ruined a case." He paused, it seemed, indefinitely.

"Take it easy on yourself. I don't know exactly what you're talking about, but I don't think Denig came just for the key."

"Whaddya mean? What'd he say?"

"He probably could have gotten the key anytime. But he wanted to see me."

"What? Why?" Cussone was alive again. He locked two of his fingers together.

"To warn me not to continue."

"What!? What'd he think, you were a cop? Jesus!"

"He thought I was too interested."

"Maybe you are!"

"Maybe I am."

We stared at one another like rivals.

"What else did he say, for Chrissake?"

I recited my account of the conversation, word for word. It helped me, also, to refocus.

He wiped his brow. "Desperate guy."

"And sad."

"You're lucky he didn't do worse than tap you on the head."

"Yeah, well, I don't believe that. I don't believe he'd have killed me. He could have, you know, easily." Something struck me. "And there's one other thing."

"What?"

"I don't believe he killed Ridley."

"Aw—" Cussone stopped himself. "Who'd he mean," he asked, "when he said 'they'—that 'they'd' ruined his life?"

"That's what we have to find out."

"Me. It's what *I* have to find out. You should give your head a vacation."

As if on cue, Lola strode through the door.

"Not a bad idea," she said to Cussone, then turned her gaze on me. We shared a troubled look that did little to refresh my spirit. When I turned back to Cussone he was already up and on his way out. He didn't say good-bye.

Lola sat at the very end of my bed, out of arm's reach.

"You never called," she said.

"I've called once a day for the last three weeks."

For a moment she stared at me in disbelief. Then a realization came over her and she stood up angrily.

"I can't believe he's done this."

She exited the room with a flourish. I was in a daze, unsure of what the hell she was talking about. I closed my eyes. Hours later I opened them again. Lola was sitting in a chair at the end of my bed. She'd woken me by wiggling my toes.

"I . . . they're going to ask you to leave, Luke. The hospital needs the bed. And you'll be all right."

"Yeah."

But when I finally stood up, the world wobbled. Lola had to hold me. I wrapped my arm around her. Underneath her smooth white uniform a golden black body was heated electrically. Feeling it pumped me with the will to walk again.

"I wanna see you," I said groggily.

"I . . ." She hesitated. Her eyes avoided mine for a moment while her face went through a series of subtle contortions. "Yes, I know." It was not a very encouraging phrase. But I remained undaunted.

"How's tomorrow night? Dinner."

She sighed again, with some sadness: "All right."

"Don't get too excited."

She didn't smile. I tried to figure out her mood on the way to the elevator.

"What was all that about the phone calls?"

"I'll tell you tomorrow night."

Later that day, Anne Cussone boiled me another cup of tea. She offered dinner, but was too shy to wake me when it was finally ready. I slept a fitful sleep, with fitful dreams, the kind where men and women struggle against the unexplainable, dreams played out as theater, nothing but blackness surrounding the stage.

Fourteen hours later, when I finally woke, Mrs. Anne Cussone cooked a special breakfast for me: three eggs and strips of ham with pan fries and coffee. She sat down at the small kitchen table and watched in silence as I devoured her food. I smiled gratefully with every bite. Then, when I'd finished my last gulp of coffee, she spoke with careful hesitance:

"Luke. Stanley and I . . . we think that you should find another place to stay." She went to buy groceries and left me to pack my things in peace.

15

Lola sat down across the table from me in a restaurant many times more expensive than I could afford. A smooth sheen of sweat graced my palms: I hoped that at least one of my credit cards wouldn't bounce. Anyway, I was used to the feeling.

"So." She smiled. "You've been shot and jumped on and beat over the head."

"What about it?" I said humorlessly.

"Oh, come on. Don't get all hard-lipped."

"All right."

She twinkled her big baby-browns. "You don't want to tell me anything about anything—how it started? Or why?"

"Not really."

"What a nudge."

"That's me. The original nudge."

This made her smile. I relaxed a little.

"Listen," I said, "I promise to tell you about it someday. Just—not tonight. It's not a sexy subject."

"Ah! Do we presume . . . ?"

Now I was grinning. "I love to presume."

She leaned back and eyed me with a surprisingly serious gaze. It gave way to another twinkling half smile. She ran her fingers through a wonderful mop of half-straightened black hair and let them trickle down across the thin white turtleneck that clung beautifully to her breasts.

I felt something fiddling between my legs. It was her foot, shoeless. Her toes groped. I let them find what they were looking for.

Her eyes had stayed riveted on me, and half serious.

"What is it about you?" she said again, her voice drifting.

I poured her a glass of wine.

By the time we'd polished off the bottle I'd already spilled all there was to know about Julia Denig and her husband and Billy's murder—and only once did I hold back tears. I guess I'd needed to talk, to tell my troubles to someone other than a cop. Nevertheless, the tingle between my legs was no longer there.

"Thank you," Lola whispered. "At least now I understand you better. It's good for friends to understand one another."

"While we're on the subject of understanding," I drawled, for with my concussion and with the wine I was feeling loose-lipped, "tell me about those goddamned phone calls."

She grimaced. "Ronald, the receptionist."

"Is that supposed to be an explanation?"

"Two months ago I turned him down . . ."

"So he stopped forwarding your calls?"

"From men, anyway." She sighed with soulful sadness. "I had him fired."

I slept on her sofa. Another sofa. After all our conversations I was anything but sexy. And after my concussion all I seemed to want to do was sleep, anyway. My eyes closed immediately. Her lips touched mine as she swept a blanket over me.

Early the next morning I cooked Lola breakfast before letting her trudge off as the Woman in White. She gobbled up the scrambled eggs voraciously.

"First time a man's cooked for me in years." She laughed. "I could get used to it."

Our eyes met and in the warm silence she realized what she'd said and how it might have come off.

"How 'bout I cook for you tomorrow?" I asked.

"Tomorrow sounds good," she said with some relief.

One day at a time, we both were thinking.

That day I talked to every one of the producers who had ever read any one of my scripts. Or rather, talked to their receptionists. Most copies were heading back in the mail. But one producer had liked my last script, a horror thriller.

"Call back tomorrow, Mr. Byman," the secretary urged. "I know Mr. Weiss'll want to talk to you." She added: "Where've you been, anyway?"

Rather than call my machine, I decided that I'd better drop in to my apartment and pick up some more clothes. That way I could pick up any mail that had been collecting at Gina's.

When I got there, a dark sky hung low over Lafayette. I had a terrible feeling of dread outside my building, as if more violence was sure to happen here and I was sure to be a part of it. I rode warily up the elevator and tiptoed down the hall. My apartment—police lock still in place (Cussone had given me the key)—was exactly as I'd left it. I listened to my messages as I quickly piled some shirts and socks and underwear and another pair of trousers into a paper bag. I threw some sneakers in, too.

I reached into my dark tunnel of a closet, where stacks of old screenplays and stories collected dust, and pulled out my guitar, an anonymous brand I'd bought years ago. A bum-around instrument, beat-up but unbeatable.

Before leaving I knocked on Gina's door. There wasn't any answer and I cursed myself for not calling first. I'd have to make another trip to collect my mail.

But when I brought my bags into the hall and locked my police bolt, Gina's door cracked open.

"Luke?" she said groggily.

I left my bags in the hall and slid into her foyer. Then I saw why she'd only cracked the door slightly. She wasn't wearing much. A long T-shirt, panties, that was it. I could see the fine curves of her body under the thin cotton.

"I was . . . I was sleeping." She'd been doing a lot more than sleeping, I thought. Her face was red and blotchy. Sweat rimmed her forehead and her cheeks. Her delicate hands were clammy and hot when she handed me my mail.

"Thanks, Gina. Sorry to bother you."

"No bother. How—how've you been, Luke?"

But I didn't have a chance to answer. Another voice whined childishly from the bedroom.

"Moooommmmy . . ." A girl's voice. Its timbre was low and sultry, but there was no mistaking it for a woman's. When she appeared at the bedroom door, I gasped. She was a dark beauty, no more than sixteen, Spanish or South American. Her long black hair drifted down over her pale breasts, which were large and barely covered by a slip that was so short it revealed a tremendous black bush between the girl's skinny legs. The child leaned against the door frame, dazed and flush. And something more.

"Go back!"

Gina's bark soothed a little. She spoke in Spanish to the girl. She used the word *niña*. Reluctantly, the child disappeared again. When Gina turned to me she was mortified, unable to look me in the eyes.

"So now you know." She sounded as if she were going to be burned at the stake.

"I suppose I do." I tried to smile, and I touched her shoulder reassuringly, but both came off condescendingly. "She's awfully young, Gina."

"Seventeen," she said emphatically, as if this made it all right. I kept my trap shut about the age, but something else bothered me.

"And she's high."

She looked at me and blinked. She said quietly, "Of course she is. She's from the clinic."

"The one you run?"

"I manage it. But it's not our methadone she's on. She's back, Luke . . ." She turned toward the bedroom. "Back on the stuff." Then Gina stared up into my eyes. "I try and help, I really do. Her being with me is a positive step. Really it is." Her eyes tilted down. "For both of us."

"You're not supposed to be . . ." I found myself speechless.

"My job is to treat children who are born addicted. I went to school for it." She pointed weakly toward a diploma that hung in a black frame on the near wall. She'd graduated with honors from the Psychiatric Center for Child Therapy. It was a faded diploma. Gina stared at it as if it were a clue to her pain.

I suddenly felt for the woman. Her job was a full-time losing battle, and she had partly succumbed to the forces she was fighting. Anyone could see that it had begun to eat away at her. There was no more pride left inside. Just sexual confusion.

She glanced back at the bedroom, as if a magnetic pull was coming from inside of it. She clung to the door frame.

"Sondra has been addicted since birth, Luke."

All at once I felt like a shit, asking all these questions as if I'd had the right to judge.

"I'm sorry," I mumbled.

"It's OK. I chose the job. Sometimes . . . sometimes it gets the best of me. You see, I provide her with limited doses. I can tell you, Luke, because I trust you to understand. I don't want her buying it on the street—and she surely would—so . . ."

"So you get her high."

"Yes. I give her small amounts." She sighed. Her hand cupped her breast, as if contained Sondra's heroin. "You see, Luke, when you were here a few weeks ago, that was when . . . when Sondra had disappeared, you know. I told myself then that I'd had it with her. No more teacher, mother, doctor . . ." Her eyes twinkled guiltily. ". . . and other things. I needed a man, you know. But . . ." Gina stared at me with wide eyes. The smile she wore seemed nearly religious. I thought then that I'd never seen her so beautiful. "She came back to me, Luke."

We stood there like two shadows in the tiny hallway. She leaned against me. I felt her warm tears soaking my shirt.

"God, Luke." She clutched my arm. "I love her so."

16

Compassion notwithstanding, I decided that it would be best to change my mailing address so that Gina didn't have to deal with it, or me, and so I'd not have to feel the way I felt now as I rode down on the elevator—as if the world were turning in concentric circles down toward hell.

I knew that I shouldn't tip the precarious balance that existed between Lola and me, so I wouldn't ask her to receive my mail. And I didn't want to have to deal with Ros and Marty. It was obvious that their patience for favors was, at best, threadbare. That left Jim or Amanda. I decided, after a short walk, that Amanda would understand my need for a proper mailing address. Besides, we'd lived together not so long before, and I still had her key. I could let myself in at prescribed times, and she'd never have to see me. Or vice versa.

I called her office and apologized for my behavior at the hospital. She accepted, and, with some coaxing, agreed to receive my mail.

"One of these days you're going to have to cut the umbilical, Luke." It seemed to make her feel good to say this and to hear me agree. I hung up feeling a little like the child she'd always wanted me to be.

Then I took my bags and guitar and my boyish spirit and walked them over to East Fourth Street and up into Cussone's office. He was sitting with that blank expression aimed toward his one blank office window. He looked as if he were receiving signals from it. When he turned to me, he seemed dazed.

"What's the matter?" I asked.

He registered my presence without surprise, as if nothing could surprise him anymore. He slid a manila folder across the top of his desk. I sat across from him and opened it.

I didn't even make it to the bathroom. Somewhere near its door I vomited profusely, all of my breakfast. I was on my knees and trembling when his hands touched my shoulders.

"One of the boys has gone to get a mop. Clean your mess and come back to me." He walked back toward his desk.

I heard myself calling out to him. "Bastard."

Half an hour later I'd cleaned my mess and was able to confront Cussone and what he'd shown me.

"I'm sorry," he said peremptorily. "I forgot that you have no experience." He was being cruel, and it took me a while to understand his motives. He was pushing me away. Trying to make me realize that what Denig had said was true: I was not up to the task of investigating my own shooting. It was a crueler world, and a more violent one, than I could handle—or stomach. It had only been a picture that he'd shown me, a flash of what a police camera had captured with overexposed clarity: a pile of limbs cut from a butchered Latin family. They'd been stacked in their own kitchen. I couldn't shake the image, nor could I shake thoughts of the Plasticine Madonna that hovered over them on their kitchen wall.

"No, I'm the one who's sorry." I'd been doing some thinking while sluffing the mop. "I've been bothering you—"

"No, not bothering."

"Yes, plaguing you. Selfish. I feel selfish."

"There's no good feeling after seeing something like that. I thought you should see it, though. Because it's going to officially take the heat off your case. I wanted you to know why."

"Yeah," I whispered. "Now I know."

"And we believe these murders are connected to the black

family killed weeks ago." He threw his hands up in the air. "Drugs." He let them slap on the table. "Always drugs."

We stared at one another for a moment. "By the way," he added, "sorry Anne and I had to boot you out. But this . . ." He opened the file and glanced at the picture. "This one demands privacy." He looked me in the eye, but said no more. He didn't have to. A good cop is not so different from the rest of us. He'd need to go home and get drunk, or cry, or both. Maybe he'd take Anne to bed tonight and start a family of his own.

"And my case?"

"We found nothing in the remainder of Bridge and Ridley's files. I honestly don't know what else to do. The whole thing draws a huge zero. A blank. Any suggestions?"

He was being kind. I had none, and told him so. My mind was mush now, anyway.

"How many were there?" I asked.

"What?"

"Kids." I pointed to the photo.

"Three. And their parents. The father—small-time drug runner." He scratched his neck. "But there's no rhyme or reason to this—to the connection between the two family murders. I mean, ballistics proved that some of the same bullets were involved in both. And the MO is gruesomely the same. Both families shot, then chopped. But the dealers—they ran in different crowds. With entirely different sources. Apples and oranges." His eyes drifted back toward the window, blank relief.

"I didn't know . . ." I said weakly.

I sat there a moment, staring with Cussone out his webbed window. Then I wrote Lola's home number down on his notepad, thinking that someone should know where to reach me. It might as well be Detective Stanley Cussone.

That night at Lola's I didn't sleep, not a wink.

Lola lived in a brownstone off Central Park West on Eighty-second, a nicely tended block whose trees were blooming. Their leaves rattled through the night. Heavy winds leaned one branch against the window of Lola's living room, and from my position on the couch its black, mysterious fingers seemed to be groping for me. Every now and then a distant scream drifted in and out of hearing, as if other trees on other blocks had succeeded in clutching their prey.

The next morning I phoned the producer who'd been interested in my script. With haggard voice I got through the conversation without betraying my general apathy. His name was Richard Weiss, and he wanted to meet with me at ten o'clock on the following Tuesday.

When I hung up I used the tiny spark of energy this small hope provided to call my friends and let them know where I'd be staying; all but Amanda. I couldn't face telling her that I was staying with another woman. However, I did write the post office and had them reroute my mail to her address. Then I tried jotting down some notes for my next screenplay, and that's when I finally fell asleep.

Lola woke me at six o'clock. She was talkative; in a sort of singsong "LaDiDa" she described her day. She cooked a wonderful dinner of chicken and wild rice and string beans, and generously poured red wine until I was smiling again. After dinner she led me to her bed and massaged my aching back and legs and arms and fingers. She whispered in my ear to have hope. I said I would.

She got up, leaving me glued to the mattress. My eyes remained half open, staring at a wall of childhood photographs near her window. They were arranged in an organized pattern, a dozen weathered shots of a miniature Lola in various stages of her youth: riding a swayback horse, on a beach, in her First Communion dress. Some of the photos in the cluster had been removed recently. Little square spots of bright white remained where they'd been hanging, perhaps where her last boyfriend's pictures had been mounted. I was reminded of how I'd taken down a photo of Amanda from my own bedroom wall a year or so ago. It'd been difficult. Now here I was, teetering precariously on the rim of sleep, lying on another woman's bed, and still dreaming of her. Remembering those nights when she would slowly unbuckle my belt, undo the button on my pants with her teeth, slide my zipper down.

Only I wasn't dreaming. Lola was pulling down my pants. She rolled me over onto my back, then straddled me. That same sultry smile graced her lips. I marveled at the body that hovered over me, and I smiled with her. She lowered her lips to mine, brushing her soft breasts against my chest, and our smiles met. My palms caressed her deep golden skin, satin to the touch. I let them drift down along the curves of her ass and stroke between her legs. She began to gyrate, ever so softly, her wet hair sliding against me like the whisper of a possibility. Her tongue entwined with mine, then, slowly, she lowered herself onto me, a deep heat. We both shuddered. There was a life for me inside her, a passion that I touched, darker than the middle of the earth. Her brown eyes stared wide with wonder—and confusion.

We woke grasped tightly in one another's arms. Fresh morning light breathed in. Never letting go, we risked making love without protection, and came together.

"We've made a mistake," she said after it was over. Trembling, she softly pushed herself away. "History repeats itself," she whispered to the ceiling.

I wanted to ask her how but she'd already gotten up and closed the bathroom door. She didn't say a word to me before she left.

That day I was alive, like I hadn't been for months, not since that bullet had passed through me and taken with it any remembrance of romance. Along with a few arteries. Now romance felt somewhat restored. My bruises were fading. There was a thrilling bounce to my step.

A June rain fell with a quiet hush, as if trying not to disturb anyone who might be sleeping. Rainwater touched the tiny flowers outside Lola's window, slapped them awake. Their eyes opened and they fed upon the rain like voracious babes. I could hear them grow.

Lola had left me a shoddy umbrella. With it I danced to a Korean vegetable store, then around the corner to a Food Emporium. Satchels in hand, I literally sang my way home. I did the Gene Kelly sidewalk step. A young actress type who passed me by shouted that I should go into another line of business.

I was now prepared to cook a grand dinner. I covered a steak with lemon juice and oil and fresh-cut garlic and set it aside to marinate. I sliced carrots and zucchini. I snuck a glass of sherry with my lunchtime soup: black bean with fresh Parmesan.

The phone rang. Lola whispered on the other end.

"Last night may have been the best night of my life."

"This morning wasn't half bad, either."

"Joker."

"Mm-hmmm."

"Mmmmm. Gotta go."

" 'Bye."

She hung up and I slurped another few gulps of soup. With a grandiloquent swig I finished my sherry. The phone rang again. I lifted the receiver.

"I'm terrified," she whispered.

"You're not pregnant."

"I'm nervous, Luke. We have a lot—so much else to talk about." She sighed. "It would complicate things—more than you know—if I was pregnant. What if I was?"

It was a question I'd run through my brain all morning and still couldn't answer.

"We'll have it," I heard myself say. I didn't know if what I felt was real or the sherry or if I was calling her bluff. Or all three.

"We'll talk," she said. "Later."

I hung up wondering if I was suddenly to become a father. I almost hoped so. Her whispering voice and the sherry and warmth in my loins and the flowering trees and the passion in my sudden feeling of release from the previous few months seemed now to conspire as the ingredients of a religious experience. At this very moment I'd have married Lola on the spot. When the phone rang again I leaped for it.

"Baby," I breathed into the phone.

"Luke!"

A cold shudder quashed the joy. I'd never heard Amanda's voice squeezed so painfully.

"Amanda?"

"Luke!" she cried again.

"What is it, Amanda? What?" She'd inspired terror.

"The package . . ." She started to cry.

"Amanda—what package?"

"A box—steel box!"

"What's in it, Amanda?" My voice was rising. It had to be Denig's safety-deposit box. "What's in it?"

"My God, Luke—my God. Take it away. Hurry! I'm home—hurry! Come take it away!" She was screaming. "Take it away!"

I was out the door without the umbrella and running—six blocks south on Amsterdam, then over past Columbus and Broadway to West End. I fell between West End and Riverside, muddying myself in a puddle. It was then that I realized that I'd forgotten her key. I threw open the building's outer door and rang Amanda's buzzer—but there wasn't any answer.

I was panicky. Her voice, that voice!

No one came. The rain had emptied streets and sidewalks. I grabbed one of the white rocks that surrounded a sapling growing near the curb and slammed it into the glass door. After three tries the thick glass shattered. I cut myself opening it, and blood trickled down my arm as I leaped up the stairwell. I reached the third floor. Above me, the fourth-floor stairwell door closed. I began to shake. Without thinking I burst into the hallway of the third floor and made my way around a corner to Amanda's door. The lock was shattered—forced! I kicked the door open, screaming her name. I didn't care about the consequences.

"Amanda!"

She lay sprawled on her own kitchen floor. Blood was flowing from her mouth and from her heart. Her limp body lay in the puddle of blood, as if she were the origin of some otherworldly river that would forever run its red course through the rest of my life. I knelt in it and stared at her. Disbelief still had me in its clutch, and shock. I allowed myself to smile at the sweet manner with which she'd fallen: one arm circling her head, as if for comfort's sake; the other clutching her ovaries. In that hand she held a picture. A picture of a baby. I couldn't tell for sure. It appeared as if the baby was dead.

A siren whined out the west windows. Its presence seemed to generate the slamming of the stairwell door on the third floor. I heard feet descending the staircase. They were muted steps, muted by thick rubber soles. I hoped that the police would recognize the killer on his way out.

For the first time, I noticed the box. It was made of thick brass that was green around the edges. It sat on her table, where my cake had once waited. The box had fallen sideways and spilled its contents out onto the table and the floor.

More pictures. All Polaroids. My eyes began to take them in, scattered around Amanda like surreal confetti. All were of babies, babies both dead and alive. Some of the dead ones had been stacked in piles. The photographs were made more horrible by their simple setting in a pastoral pine forest. Babies leaned against saplings or on beds of pine needles, saucer-eyed, lifeless. I plunged my hand through what remained in the box, and when I came to the bottom I found a half-torn sheet of white paper. Its bottom edge was stuck in the box's corner groove. There was blood on it. I knew that whoever had killed Amanda had tried to extricate the sheet of paper and had torn it in the process. My ringing had scared him off. Then the sirens had stopped him from coming back and finishing the job. Finishing me. I held the torn page in my shaking hand and tried to read.

It contained part of a list that must have corresponded to the numbers on each of the pictures. Staring at those pictures had made me dizzy. The room swirled. I fell to my knees.

I'd not yet loved anyone as I'd loved Amanda. I tried to stop myself from saying her name aloud, but couldn't. The way it rolled on my tongue seemed to signify everything.

"Amanda."

Somewhere deep inside I knew that I was making a mistake, but I didn't care. I lifted her dead and bloody body into my arms and cried as I have never cried before, or will ever cry again.

17

Time gradually made itself noticeable. I wasn't sure how much had passed, but I sensed that someone was watching me from the apartment's entrance. Cussone leaned there, a silhouette, head down.

Some uniforms stood behind him. One of their walkie-talkies buzzed for a split second, like a signal from the planet Earth. They were all waiting, waiting for me to put her down. Cussone must have known, known that you have to put the dead down of your own volition. Let go of them yourself. Otherwise, if they're pulled out of your hands, their eternal weight might cling to you forever.

I laid Amanda back in her own river. Fresh blood still pumped from the hole in her heart. I remembered a quiet little puddle of springwater high in the Adirondack Mountains, a place she and I had visited only two years ago. We'd made love there, and passed the day. Tiny falls had trickled down from us to become a river, one of the oldest rivers, one that flowed past Manhattan. It had been the Hudson's source.

It was strange to realize that I'd been dreaming of the river. I opened my eyes in time to see a police photographer squeeze a shot off. It flashed directly over me, and for a moment I thought I'd died and was the subject of the photograph. Or maybe I was trapped in an Emily Dickinson poem. When I fully awoke I realized that I was lying on her sofa, just steps from where her body had been. Amanda's chalk line had already been drawn.

Cussone sat down on the arm of the couch. He was grimly compassionate, like an undertaker.

"Can you talk?"

I said nothing. I didn't know if I could. Cussone went away. I watched as he motioned for a uniform to get me to an ambulance.

Another hospital.

I sat up and eyed him from across the room. He walked slowly to me, as if I might bite him. But he was just giving me some time. I felt as if I was listening to my own voice from just above the ceiling:

"Not another hospital! Not another—"

"OK, all right."

"Just put me to work."

"I can't, you know—"

"I'm involved now, Cussone, like it or not." I glanced at myself, a downward look. My jeans and oxford shirt were smeared with her blood. I held my hands out to him. Cussone grimaced at their color and sighed. He didn't want to argue.

"Maybe some light work."

"I'm certainly no good at anything else."

"You do all right. Did you see them?"

"Him. No."

"Him?" He had his notebook in his hands.

"Sounded like there was only one. Rubber soles."

"What?"

"Soft steps. On the stairwell."

"Oh."

"Galoshes."

A long pause. "The big man?"

"I didn't see him."

"Then you don't know it's a him."

"No."

"What else?"

I stared at the bloody pile stacked on the table. "The pictures."

Cussone rubbed his palm across his forehead and sighed. "Yeah, more pictures."

"Yeah."

"Do they mean anything to you?"

"No. But there's a list—"

"We found it."

"It's what he was here for."

"We figured. It means we've scored."

The comment felt like an arrow. Amanda's chalk line seemed to cry to me.

"Sorry," Cussone added.

I regained some composure. "What does it mean?"

"Addresses, is all. Corresponding to the numbers on the photos." But he was steering his opinion away from me, as subtle as a bus driver. We stared at one another.

"No," I said. "I want your take on it."

Cussone shot me his hard look, but his pad and pencil were trembling in his hands.

"Smuggling," he said.

"Babies."

"Yes."

18

The rain still fell.

Cussone monologued softly: "I've had some experience with these operations, not much. Drugs, yes. Arms, in small-time quantities. And certainly money can be smuggled, laundered, set out to dry somewhere, then finally brought home again. But—but car parts, that's what we're hottest on these days. They steal the car here in New York and within seconds it's in a chop-shop being disassembled. Its parts are boxed and sent in freight containers to South America. There they're sold for huge profits—a spark plug sells for twenty dollars in Brazil—and those profits are used to buy drugs and then the drugs are shipped back here and the circle is complete. They skim a little profit every now and then to expand the number of chop-shops, and the thing keeps growing. Every now and then we get in between a ring and bust it, every now and then—not often."

He turned to look behind him, saw that his officers weren't paying attention, then reached into his pocket for the silver flask. His gulp was bigger than usual. He handed it to me. I let the vodka run down my throat unfettered by a swallow. Cussone had to grab the flask away from me.

He continued: "I've seen babies smuggled before, phony adoption agencies; big money in it. People pay—yuppies, you know, and older couples—the kind who've outrun their biological clocks but still need to parent a child." He seemed to be speaking with some experience. His gaze drifted past me, as if the wall were transparent and he was staring through it, to a living room from a previous era in his life.

"Like you?"

I'd startled him. His thoughts sprang back to the present. "I'll tell you about it sometime."

"OK."

"Anyway, as I said, I've seen this kind of stuff before, but never this big an operation. Never this . . ." He peeled a bloody picture from the pile and held it in his hands. ". . . this brutal."

"How did they die?"

"In transport, probably."

"From where?"

"Well, the photos are in black and white and it's hard to tell, but the kids look Mexican or South American. They're very young, a lot of them. Just a few weeks old. Stolen from the mothers or—" He stopped abruptly.

"Or maybe seeded for this purpose," I conjured.

"It's a horrible thought, but it's possible."

"What's the motive?"

"Money, what else? As much as twenty grand a baby."

"And these adoption agencies take orders?"

"Oh yeah. There are huge waiting lists in the legitimate agencies. Couples could wait years for a child. They—they might be too old to take a child by that time, so they get desperate, seek out the not-so-legit brokers. Or maybe there's a contact at the legitimate agencies—a spy who collects the addresses of the couples in need, then sells them to these bastards. . . ." Cussone gestured to Amanda's chalk line. He was thinking aloud now, trying ideas on for size. I helped.

"Then it's possible that a lot of the adoption agencies have been infiltrated."

"Possible."

"And you were saying that the money made could be being used for something else? To support another purpose?"

"Maybe. There are ingredients here that point to a larger operation, perhaps international. The Kalashnikov—pistols like that, they aren't your everyday Saturday Night Special. And the Los Angeles connection—Julia Denig, her husband, Ridley and Bridge—all seemed to have followed some piece of this case there."

"Then what are you saying? That you don't believe Julia and her husband are guilty of anything?"

"I didn't say that. They very well could have been mixed up in this and gotten in over their heads."

"Or stolen some of the money."

"Everything points to that conclusion."

"There's another angle," I said wearily. "They could have adopted and in the process discovered who it was they were adopting from. Maybe they went to the police, the authorities, and tried to blow the whole thing open, and in doing so found themselves at the end of a gun. Maybe they've been on the run for the last twelve years."

"I can check with the police in Black River—"

"And Poughkeepsie."

"Yeah, there too . . ." His voice drifted, then rose again into a question. "Why twelve?"

"What?" I was fading again.

"You said twelve years."

"That's how old Billy was."

Cussone was silent for a while. "You're saying that Billy might have been adopted."

"Yes."

"And that Denig's been hunting these killers for all these years? That's hard to swallow."

I had to agree with him.

"Why would he expend so much effort?"

I didn't have an answer—and I didn't have the stomach to continue. Glimmers of sunlight sparkled through the cascading rain and turned the dull puddles of blood on the carpet into crimson lakes. Amanda's genes were still alive and swimming in them. I stood up—had to get out of there. Cussone let me stumble on my own to the doorway. I tried to step out into the hallway but something in that apartment held me like a magnet. I'd told Cussone that I wanted to be involved in the case but now I knew that I was wrong to try, wrong to shoulder the responsibility, afraid to. Scared to death—of death, or worse—scared of becoming another Denig. No more for me; I'd done enough.

Again I tried to extricate myself from Amanda's doorway, fighting the invisible force that held me. I lost. Falling to my knees, there in the door frame, I heard Cussone's words low and clear, as if the room behind me were talking.

"You know as well as I do that you can't leave yet. You've got to try and find her—in the pictures."

With his eyes locked on mine Cussone raised the stack of blood-soaked black and whites and held them to me like an offering.

"Julia's baby," he said.

He led me by my elbow into Amanda's bedroom. We sat on her bed with the pictures between us. A little blood smudged onto the pink-and-white bedspread, the one her grandmother had crocheted for her when she was just a girl. The one we used to sweep over us after making love.

The pictures all began to look alike. After an exhaustive hour I'd peeled through more than two hundred of them. Some were old and yellowed, others more recent. All had been photographed with an old-style black-and-white Polaroid camera, the kind whose body springs open like an accordion. I'd used the same kind of camera scouting locations for commercials, centuries ago.

Little Genna was not among the Polaroids. My vision had been numbed by the overwhelming number of dead children captured by a butcher's lens.

When I finally left the room Cussone clung to my side, preventing my taking a spill. I stopped him at the bedroom's entrance. On the wall near the doorway was a picture of Amanda as a baby, dressed in the frills of innocence and smiling at the camera. I touched the photo with the tips of my fingers, trying to extract some special feeling from it, but I couldn't. I found it impossible to differentiate her face from all the other pictures I'd just sorted through.

Cussone led me past a uniform stationed in the hall and walked me into the elevator. "You need some air," was all he said.

The ride down seemed interminable. Cussone still clung to my arm, my very own Virgil. He led me through the dark, pine-paneled lobby that was littered with cops and bystanders out into the rain. We walked together toward the river.

"Listen, they know what to do up there. Fingerprinting will take hours. A thorough search. Let me drop you somewhere. I could call the nurse . . ."

"Lola—no . . ." Then I reconsidered. "Yes."

He dropped a quarter into a pay phone on the corner of Riverside. He dialed the hospital, asked for Lola, then waited on the line for the full three minutes, till his quarter had run out. Maybe that same switchboard operator had been rehired and was up to his old tricks. It didn't matter. As I waited, the hum of traffic along the West Side Highway mesmerized me. It sped in both directions parallel to the Hudson River. To the south, the sea opened its mouth with a consoling finality. To the north, more than a hundred miles away, was the town where I'd been born and raised, and where my family had died. I longed for them now. Longed to be a child again. I found myself experiencing some strange sympathetic feelings of déjà vu with that day I'd been told my parents were dead. I'd been only nine. Now, again, I felt myself sinking, stepping over yet another threshold. Loneliness, complete and pure, was on the other side.

Cussone grabbed both of my shoulders and shook me out of my stupor.

"Don't do that!" I growled at him.

He led me down through Riverside Park and then up again, a gentle walk that brought us back to the phone booth.

"Anybody else I can call?"

I said with some reluctance: "Just take me to Lola's. I should make a phone call from there."

"Amanda's parents?"

The thought made me tremble.

The car felt like a rocking chair. I didn't sleep, but was relaxed by the ride. Cussone understood, and drove in a circuitous route toward Eighty-second Street.

"I've been thinking," he began, "that you should sit down with one of our sketch artists in Midtown and try to reconstruct a likeness of Denig—and, for that matter, of the Big Man."

"A little late for that, isn't it?"

"Yes, I'm sorry. But that one's just for us to keep searching our records with. Denig—well, I want to put out an APB on him. He may not have killed Amanda. But then again, he may have. Either way, my hand is forced. He has answers to a hell of a lot of questions."

"If . . ." My voice didn't connect with my thoughts, but Cussone did.

"Yeah, if. If he's still alive."

We rode with that thought awhile. His windshield wipers squeaked back and forth along the curved glass that framed the city's blurring reds and greens and grays. I didn't try to make a picture of them; color was enough.

Cussone asked the inevitable. "Why would he have sent the box to you?"

An answer mulled about in my brain but I didn't care to articulate it.

"He was in trouble," Cussone offered. "A deep threat suddenly loomed and he needed to get the evidence to someone else. But why you?"

We crossed Broadway. In the splashing rain dark figures ran for cover, like spirits, or rats. The avenue shone like the surface of a river under garish neon, light that emanated from a hundred pulsing storefronts. Across the surface, at the end of the tunnel that was Seventy-sixth Street, Central Park's dark boughs beckoned with an eternal gloom.

"Because," I finally answered, "he was passing on the torch."

"Hmmm." He stopped at a red light. "You gonna carry it, Byman?"

"I dunno." The light turned green. So did my expression.

Cussone swung his Chevy up Amsterdam. Far ahead, the steeple of Saint John the Divine rose briefly into view, like a shard of hope. Then it disappeared.

"Where we going?" I asked.

He nudged his car close to the curb just above 101st Street.

"Here," was all he said for a moment. Then he broke into a rambling explanation. "No matter what you decide to do with your life, you're in deep shit now, kid. Trouble. Frankly, I'm worried for you—babe in the woods, all that. You can steer away from the trouble by leaving town. Or you can confront it and help us. Your decision. I don't have to tell you that if you stay you're in danger. You can identify a murderer. I'd prefer that you leave; I'll understand if you stay. You don't have to decide now, but I wouldn't dally. I mean, if you stay then you have to be prepared. I'll insist that you go inside. Today, tomorrow, whenever. It's against policy but I have to insist. And I'll handle the paperwork."

I got out of the car and walked through the rain toward the bolted storefront. The display behind its thick glass window gleamed in the dull light.

"My treat," Cussone said without enthusiasm. He handed me a hundred-dollar bill and walked back to his car. He knew it was up to me to make my own decision. I stood there a long time, perched at the store's entrance, the C-note flapping in the wind. My wet clothes sagged over my limbs like the burden of a faintly possible future.

I went in. A little bell rang over the door. I noticed Cussone nodding to the proprietor through the window. The old fellow wore a printer's smock and waved to the detective with a stiff gesture that resembled a salute. Then he turned a sour smile on me. My dejection seemed to hit him like a wave: He stepped back a pace and rocked on the balls of his feet. He spread his arms as he was rocking, and gestured to the glass cases that lined the walls behind the counter.

Ten minutes later I went back out into the pouring rain. I held a handgun in both palms. A .45, like my father's.

Cussone had to run back in and buy the bullets.

19

Amanda's mother had fainted. Her father now wept. I wept into the telephone. Stanley Cussone remained composed.

He spoke to Amanda's father and consoled him with some of the bare facts, facts that weren't reasons, not even remotely so, but seemed to dull the pain, for now. The man who had almost been my father-in-law hung up while quietly cursing the city that had taken his daughter.

When Lola finally came home she wept, too: for me, for the woman I'd once loved, and, in some way, she seemed to be crying for herself. Amanda's death had opened gates in her as yet unlocked in my presence. Gates to another world below her smiling surface, where sorrow lingered, and self-hate.

We stayed in one another's arms for hours. The rain ebbed, and an eerie twilight gripped Eighty-second Street. When the phone rang it punctured a hole in the fragile cocoon we'd spun around ourselves. I picked up the receiver.

"Cussone here. You OK?"

"Yeah." My voice had nearly disappeared. "What is it?"

"Something strange."

* * *

I was down at the precinct half an hour later. "Keep moving," I'd said to myself in the cab. Keep moving. Lola must have felt the same way—she was emphatic about coming with me. When I faced Cussone she sat next to me and leaned her head on my shoulder. Both of her hands clutched my upper arm.

"Look." Stanley shoved a piece of paper toward me.

"No more pictures," I said.

"No, no more pictures." He pushed the paper closer. "Read."

It was a photocopy of the list from the safety-deposit box. Three addresses had been circled in red. The first was in Los Angeles: 2122 Century City, 15th floor, Suite 7, zip code 90024. Several lines down was the second circled address: 44 Elm Street, Black River, Michigan 85126. The third address was near the bottom of the page: 300 Mildred Avenue, Poughkeepsie, New York 12919. Three addresses that matched the evidence found in Julia's apartment. There were no names on any of the addresses.

"We have to contact the local police." My voice rang with a dull excitement that was not so innocent anymore. "I can help you—tomorrow."

"It's been done," Cussone said with monotoned restraint. He made me ask.

"So?"

He replied with sobriety. "There's many levels to this. I don't pretend to have a clue, really, past the smuggling of the children."

Lola's big eyes bore down on me. "Smuggling children," she whispered; a statement, not a question.

Cussone continued. "And I have to tell you right now—and it's going to frustrate you—this case is out of my hands."

"What?"

"Smuggling is a federal offense. FBI—those dickheads—have assumed control as of an hour ago."

"No . . ."

"Yes. And they weren't very polite about it. I'm not off the case, exactly. They still need me. But I'm only here to assist them. And you—they'll want to grill you, for sure."

We both inhaled, then exhaled, tired but in sync with one another, like the proud, relentless bellows of an old factory that had just been bought by an anonymous investment group. This was a personal case now—now that Amanda had died. No one, not the FBI, not anyone, could dissuade me from following its course. My voice took on a power and maturity that had rarely made itself heard. Lola let go of my arm.

"What about the other towns?"

"This is where I get confused." In full view of the officers on night shift, Cussone took a snort—but the flask was empty. He held it upside down for a moment, contemplating. "Men on duty in L.A. can't say much for that particular address except that it belongs to"—he searched his notepad—"Trion. An entertainment group of some kind."

"The file in Bridge's office . . ." I whispered. "The triangle."

"Yep, I've already thought of that. We'll be able to find more about the place tomorrow."

"What about in Black River?"

"We hit something. The first of two curious coincidences. That address now belongs to a nice family by the name of . . . Ansen. New house. But the old house that used to be there burned down seven years ago. Arson. A man and woman were killed. Couple by the name of . . . O'Reilly." He paused. "Burned to death, along with the house. Officer there says it's common knowledge, though still not proved, that it was the daughter who burned the house down. Killed her own parents."

"My God," Lola blurted.

Cussone turned to her, then turned back to me. He just sat there with a dumb look on his face.

"How old was the daughter?" I asked.

"Twenties. Pale skin. Brown hair. Quite beautiful in a plain sort of way. That was the cop's description."

This sank in for a moment. Now I was the one with a dumb look.

"Name was Julia O'Reilly," Cussone added.

My heart flip-flopped. All this was too much for one day.

"The same Julia?" Lola asked.

But I didn't answer.

"I think that banner in her apartment—Clover High—may have been hers as a kid. And we may know more about her parents' death in a couple of days, when the senior officer returns to duty after his vacation. Until then . . ."

I stammered: "Poughkeepsie."

"Yes. Another coincidence, and they're beginning to pile up in my life, all around me." He considered this. "All around."

"The O'Reilly family?"

"No. Their name was Farrer, and they owned the house on Mildred Avenue eleven, twelve years ago. Husband once worked at IBM. They had a child, a few years old. A girl." He paused. "They were killed. Terrible death, apparently. We'll know more tomorrow, the whole report. But the cop on duty in their downtown station remembers only too well. Old geezer by the name of Stephano. And what he had to say makes the whole thing . . . more complicated. Says the child disappeared on the night of the murders."

"He's sure it was a girl?"

"Yes. And he said something else—that the next-door neighbors disappeared, too. For good. Left their house standing as it was." He looked at his notes. "Three-oh-two Mildred Avenue."

"What year was this?"

"Seventy-six. Bicentennial. Statute of limitations has run out on those next-door neighbors, by the way. But for seven years they were wanted for murdering the Farrers. And for kidnapping the girl. Big scandal in Poughkeepsie, to this day."

"What were their names?"

Cussone's heavy lids blinked. "Denington."

"Jesus—Denig."

"Yeah."

I had to pause, to think, but I couldn't think; events collided. Julia's face stared at me from her sofa. Denig's from the corner shadows where he'd held a gun on me. I just couldn't picture them together, killing together. And if they had kidnapped a girl, where was she? Who was she?

"It's hard to believe . . ." I said.

"I know."

"That they're wanted in two states for killing . . ."

"Four people. Two couples. One of them her parents."

"Jesus," Lola said.

I had a thought. "What'd Denig do? For a living, I mean."

"I asked the same question."

"Great minds think alike."

"Yeah."

"Well?"

"He worked at IBM, computer analyst. Until . . ." Cussone's lips curled upward but he was simultaneously trying to prevent himself from smiling. The result was a grimace. ". . . until he became the co-founder of Poughkeepsie's first adoption agency."

After the worst day of my life, it was hard to justify a feeling of exhilaration. For the briefest of moments, I felt close to understanding the case's origins. Then grief and pain and guilt crept in and clouded my overview. Amanda was gone; that sad thought was thick, and powerful, and squeezed the wind out of me.

Lola's eyes were closed. She was shaking. But I couldn't think of her, not right now. I missed Amanda. Anger and bitterness took hold of me, and I locked eyes with Cussone. He didn't say a word, but seemed to understand the alternating currents running through me. Half of me wanted to bury myself, hide from the world and everyone in it. The other half wanted to do something—anything—to avenge Amanda's death. And heal my guilt.

Stanley slid the photocopied list closer to me. I took it carefully, my nerves brittle, and folded the paper twice. Then I slipped it into my breast pocket.

20

The interrogation was scheduled for two P.M., in an office adjacent to a federal courthouse down on Chambers Street. Cussone sat at the far corner of a long table carved from blond oak. Its glossy surface reflected a haphazard pattern of fluorescent tubes dangling from the twenty-foot-high ceilings. Among these patterns, two dark reflections that wore sunglasses were wavering like ghosts. I saw them before seeing the men themselves.

Cussone introduced them as agents Chase and Goody. I laughed.

It wasn't the thing to have done.

"Sit down," Chase said. "And shut up."

I sat. I listened. Chase briefly summarized the case, especially as it related to the smuggling of small children and the possibility of white slavery. Chase was cold but thorough, an ex-marine type whose crew cut and dark suit and Ray-bans extinguished all hope of finding an identifiable personality. Goody sat patiently, across from Cussone. He took his shades off briefly, exposing two green glints of humanity, then replaced them.

When Chase had finished he leaned against the windowsill and folded his arms, at ease. Goody continued, as if their act had been rehearsed.

"We'd like to know what your involvement is in all this. We're very interested. From the beginning."

I began. It wasn't easy, thinking back to Billy, to the beginning. I told them about his death, and Rita's, and of the bullet that had passed through me. I told them of Julia's letter, and of my belief in her innocence. Then in the very next sentence I told them of Billy's rabbit's foot and the note inside of it—"She's not my mother." Billy's words had, then, nearly shattered Julia's credibility for Cussone and me. A lot of other things had done far worse since.

I proceeded with a description of the night that Harry Bridge attacked me, then died, in the doorway of my own apartment. I told them about the mystery woman who had smacked me in the side of the face with a revolver—the woman who'd apparently killed Bridge.

"Is there anything that suggests that it could have been Julia Denig?" Goody queried, pronouncing each word perfectly.

"Nothing. If I thought there was, my feelings would have changed about her."

"Are you in love with her?" Goody's eyes bore down on me from behind his shades.

"I'll be straight with you," I answered. "She's the kind of woman I could fall in love with, but—"

"You hardly know her."

"That's right."

Goody rolled a pencil between his fingers. "Go on."

It took a moment to wipe Julia from the brain. I took a deep breath and continued. I told them how I'd been searching the files at Ridley and Bridge when Denig had appeared, and what he'd said to me.

"What was your impression of him?" Goody asked.

"That he was an innocent man, frankly."

"What is it, you love this whole family?" Chase asked.

"Well—" I tried to dignify him with an answer. "He struck me as a good man who had been on the run too long. He was getting desperate, strung out on a limb. But he didn't strike me as a murderer. He could have easily killed me."

Goody spoke calmly, flatly. "He's still a suspect, though. Do you agree he should be?"

"I suppose so. I sure would like to question him."

"We do the questioning," Chase said, as if I'd threatened his domain.

"Finish." Goody gestured for me to go on.

"OK." I spoke briefly of Lola, how she put me up and how I'd changed my mailing address. But I wasn't prepared for the tears that welled up when I began talking about Amanda. Nor were they.

"Any other facts you can add?" Goody asked, when I was finished.

"You can check Detective Cussone's report; maybe I missed something or other. I don't think I did."

"We'll cross-check the reports. It's our job," Goody replied. "But you seem to have covered everything, if memory serves. I've been up all night reading this stuff. Gruesome. And"—he removed his dark glasses once again—"we're sorry about the girl." He looked down at his notes. "Amanda."

"Thanks."

"In fact, you've been through enough. You can go now, if you don't mind following this up at another time."

"No. What will you do?" I still had more to say, to ask.

"That hasn't become clear." Chase's voice was formal. "Thank you for your time."

I sat there, unmoving.

"Do you have more to add?" Goody leaned forward.

"Yes. Opinions, though."

Chase moved toward me. "That won't be—"

"You need to hear them."

There was a silence. All eyes were on me. Stanley smiled.

"Let him tell you what he thinks, for Chrissake. We owe him that."

"We don't owe him anything," Chase growled.

"But we'll listen," Goody said, feigning a smile.

I took a plunge into the puzzle. "It appears—knowing what we know right now—that it all began in Poughkeepsie. Two families, living next to one another. The Farrers and the Deningtons. The Farrers had a child. A girl. I don't pretend to understand how or why it happened, but the Farrers were killed. The neighbors—the Deningtons—disappear, and so does the girl. Perhaps, though, they all ran away from the same violence that killed the Farrers. I have no idea what happened to the girl. But Denington and his wife, Julia, ended up in Black River, I'm sure of it. Under a new name—obviously on the run. Maybe they had witnessed the murder."

"Maybe they are the murderers!" Chase broke in.

"Of course, maybe they are. But I believe they're not. I think they're on the run. I don't know from who. I don't know why. And I don't know if Billy was their child, or how he came into the picture if he wasn't. But Denington ran an adoption agency. Maybe he stumbled onto the smuggling ring—perhaps his own office had been infiltrated. Can't you see? There's the possibility that they've been running from the same thugs who killed their neighbors and Julia's parents—maybe the same men who tried to kill me."

"What about the money?" Chase asked.

"I don't know about the money!" I stood suddenly, toppling my chair. "I only know that I saw a huge man with red hair kill a child without a second thought! Kill a child! Don't you see! He's your man—not Denig!"

I'd surprised myself with my own passion—and my inability to articulate what I knew was there, there like one of those ancient images carved by Indians into the earth, images drawn by men on the ground but only recognizable from aloft.

"Thank you for your time," Goody said with a voice as dry as sawdust. He didn't even look up.

Our meeting was definitely over.

21

A week passed, a week of healing. I must have showered three times a day, each day, but still the odor of Amanda's blood would not disappear. I reeked of death. Or maybe it was the guilt that stank. A guilt that clung to me like a slimy film of stagnant oil. It wouldn't wash away. And all the ifs—they wouldn't stop tormenting me. If I hadn't used her place as my own mail depot. If I hadn't been such a selfish jerk. If I'd never left her—or let her down so bad that she'd had to push me away. If I'd never even known her—maybe that would have been the best. She'd be alive, now. Smiling somewhere.

There was no news from Cussone. The Feds had taken control of our case, and part of him was grateful. Part of me, also. I'd come to feel that I needed no more of that nightmare. How and why it all happened began to mean less and less to me. My apathy had begun when I'd tried to learn to load and cock and shoot the .45 at Cussone's instruction. I'd been dulled into a bleak sadness by the touch of flesh to steel. And the shooting gallery down in the cellar of his station had brought on a migraine so bad that he'd had to drive me home to Lola's, briefly parking off Herald Square while I opened the door and tossed the lunch he'd bought me onto Thirty-fourth Street.

"This was a bad idea," he'd said. But he made me keep the gun.

"They don't want me anymore," I protested, trying to give him back the .45. "I'm nobody."

He wouldn't listen.

"I'm nobody." I repeated it like a mantra.

Another week at Lola's and I was finally able to make some appointments with friends. Ros and Marty and Jim took me out to dinner at Knickerbocker's and we listened to some soft jazz. I thought it best to go alone, without Lola. The evening's unspoken dedication was to Amanda; they'd have considered Lola an intruder.

That week I finally managed to get in to see Richard Weiss. It turned out that his interest in my horror screenplay was genuine—but before producing that particular movie he wondered if I might agree to turn one of his own ideas into a screenplay. The money he proposed to pay me was low by industry standards—two thousand—but I agreed on the spot.

Money!

The proposed schedule was for the writing of the outline to begin on Monday, July ninth. On that day I'd be paid half: one thousand. The other half was due upon completion. We'd sign a contract before beginning.

A day ticked by.

That evening Anne Cussone called Lola, inviting both of us to a Fourth of July barbecue on their rooftop patio. Lola accepted, with some reservation.

"A cop's house? On the Fourth of July?" she quipped. She had a point. It was a strange concept, being friends with a cop. Incidents in the last three months had drawn us together, as they had Lola and me. Perhaps now I was running the risk of getting too close to Stanley; perhaps friendship was unwise. But he understood, like no one else, the gravity of the convoluted events that had been happening around me, to me. And Lola, also, understood; indeed, she'd seen them cut me open in the operating room. Seen a doctor hold a couple of my arteries in his hands. We were all partners, now, forever, like those diverse fellows who had once shared a trench in Southeast Asia; men from every walk of life who still needed one another's company from time to time, because they were the only ones who understood.

Stanley understood.

The barbecue was a bigger party than we'd expected. Lots of cops were there, from Cussone's division and from Vice, the cops no one ever saw. Some of Anne's friends were there, too: a housewife and her quiet husband, a couple whose child dragged both of them in tow; and Anne's younger brother, Robert. He and I talked for an hour. He played bass in a band that was doing the music for a Broadway show. It was his first gig in New York, and a good start. He was ten years younger than me, with an unfettered smile. I envied him.

There were hot dogs and hamburgers and a river of vodka and beer. Toward the end of the evening a group of vice cops set off fireworks that sailed over the tops of the buildings across the courtyard. They lent a curiously stark glow to the treetops below, like a scene from a dream, or a war. As I was standing there, on the edge of the flashing darkness, Stanley approached me and for the first time that evening spoke of the case.

"They're off, Tuesday, off on the hunt."

"Jesus, took 'em long enough. Where they going?"

"Poughkeepsie. And I think you had a hand in their decision."

"How?"

"Chase didn't take you seriously, but Goody did, and he holds sway."

"He agreed with what I told him?"

"Well, pretty sketchy theory, even I'd have to say. But it gave them something to consider, which they did. They agreed with one thing you said—Poughkeepsie was the beginning."

I felt the sensation of someone watching me. When I turned, Lola was standing silently behind us. She flushed, as if we'd caught her eavesdropping.

"Please, you guys," she said strangely, "don't talk about that stuff now."

I said OK—Stanley even kissed her cheek.

"Back to the twilight's last gleaming," he mumbled, and staggered as he stepped away. Lola and I faced one another under the fireworks. Their bright white light made Lola's black skin seem ashen.

22

"Listen, I'm really sorry," Weiss said. "I hope you don't ditch out, but I don't blame you if you do."

His voice oozed sincerity. I held the receiver as if it were a ticking bomb.

"What's the problem?" I asked with that same old shudder. Regret could so easily turn to melancholy in a conversation like this. Hold your chin up, I told myself silently. I smiled. "Can't be that bad."

"Cash flow," were his only words for a moment. The problem was they couldn't pay me anything up front.

Fool that I was, the next day I began a script outline of the two-page story he'd given me. It was a hackneyed story, one that seemed to have spewed from a computer programmed with the plots of every third-rate action picture on those dusty back rows of video rental stores. But it seemed like a job, one that could take my mind off Amanda and the case that still loomed around me like an emotional shroud.

Jim allowed me to use his word processor. Each day, beginning on the tenth of July, I'd arrive at his house after a three-egg breakfast, use a copy of his key to let myself in, and write for six hours straight. Exhausted, I'd buy groceries on the way back to Lola's and then, after a nap, cook for her. For a week this went on happily. I'd practiced chicken, pork chops, steak, spaghetti carbonara, then chicken again, before Stanley Cussone called me. Lola's kitchen was too small to fit a chair, but when I heard the tone of his voice I instinctively knew that I should sit. I slid down the wall and onto the linoleum.

"They're missing," his thick voice told me. "Gone."

I knew who he meant but I couldn't believe it.

"Chase and Goody?"

"Gone," he repeated. I could tell by the timbre of his voice that he was sitting with that blank look on his face, staring out his opaque office window. An empty silver flask was probably rolling between his fingers.

"I'm in my office," he said, as if he'd heard my thoughts. "Can you come down?"

I said that I would. I told him to stop drinking. He hung up on me.

"This whole thing is in my hands." His voice echoed back and forth off the walls of the precinct's outer foyer. A tired cop, near the end of his day's duty, watched us from the front desk with two dulled, globular eyes. Cussone led me through the doors and down the steps onto Fourth Street. "The whole damn thing."

"Good," I said.

"Not good."

We walked in silence past rows of blue-and-whites that lined one side of the street. A family speaking in Spanish sitting on their stoop hushed their conversation until we'd taken several strides past them. There was a local theater on the block, an off-off-Broadway venue run by New York University. A group of pale students stood outside in the heat, glumly waiting to be baked alive inside. Posters advertised a production of Sam Shepard's *Buried Child*. That made me think of Genna, an alarming stream of images.

Cussone broke the stream: "Not good." He was repeating himself tonight. "A Fed's coming by day after t'morrow, Agent Haley—bigwig, pissed off. Says for now let it wait. One more day.

Says maybe they went under." His voice rose with frustration. "If they didn't, I dunno what to say to him, Chrissake."

"He won't blame you for their disappearance."

"Feds blame everyone but themselves for everything."

"Oh."

He quieted. It seemed to make him feel better to have gotten that off his chest.

"Will you go?" he asked.

"Go where?"

"Poughkeepsie. Tomorrow."

"Shit," I said, stopping on the corner of Fourth Street and First Avenue. The writing job was just on speculation, and I could easily take a day off, but I had another one of those rushes that ran through my veins with a vengeance, a rush that trumpeted the unknown. A bleak unknown that made my breath quicken and palms sweat. Thoughts of the .45 danced in my brain.

"Shit, shit, shit." I kicked the corner deli.

"Thanks," Stanley said in response. He waved his silver flask like a sword. "I need somebody else who's as stupid as I am."

23

Stanley wove his Chevy Impala through a section of the Major Deegan that glides between the ramps and girders of a dozen highways. There, breaking through the tangled junctures and roaring echoes, we crossed the city limits and sped into suburbia.

Route 87 soon evolved into the New York State Thruway. It led us past Ardsley and Worthington, onto the Sawmill River Parkway, and finally to the treacherous Taconic. Cars barreled along the highway at sixty, tires treading the outer edges of their narrow lanes. For an hour and a half I clutched Stanley's dashboard.

Finally, a ramp led us to Route 55, a two-lane stretch of shopping malls and stoplights, fast-food joints and movie octoplexes. It was the kind of crass red carpet that most towns had built for themselves in the last twenty years. It pulsed like a consumer's nightmare—or wet dream.

It led us to the dirty edge of Poughkeepsie, a half city whose Victorian splendor had faded long ago. A few brave souls were trying to rebuild that splendor; renovations stood out like oases amidst the surrounding dead weight of welfare neighborhoods. But the air seemed infected by an indescribable torpor, a strange pall, as if the town and everyone in it were victims of a toxic leak from the dark vats of their own history.

302 Mildred Avenue was a huge old dilapidated manse sitting on a corner, as if perched on a cusp, between two neighborhoods. Its southern side was dappled with a precious sun that seemed to emanate from Mildred Avenue. Its northern face rose like an outpost against a cascading hill of slums. Across a small thoroughfare, a neon Miller sign glowed in the shadows of a bar's torn canopy. A few black men sat dull-eyed on the sidewalk outside, watching as Cussone and I cased the old mansion.

It had been quite a house. A shabby porch still slumped around the front door. Its steps squeaked. Two fine old banisters rotted. Elegant shutters hung loosely from all the windows; over them, capulets rose like tiny churches. Cussone and I walked the length of the porch. We stood on its edge and peered over a row of bushes to the Farrers' old place. It had been built around the same time as the Deningtons'—the turn of the century—but was smaller and in better repair.

"The old cop said this used to be a damn good neighborhood." Cussone looked at his watch. It was quarter to eleven. "He should be here by now."

As if on cue, a patrol car swung around the corner from the avenue and parked. An old man dressed in a blue uniform, yet not wearing a gun, exited from the passenger door. The driver, a boy who swaggered like a rookie, shut the car off and indulged us by sauntering to the porch. He cocked his head back and looked down the length of his nose.

"Mornin'," he said.

The old cop walked up the steps and extended his hand to both of us. He introduced himself as "Sergeant Stephano, semi-retired" as if that were a rank.

"Pulled the same duty for the Feds couple days ago," he said. "What gives? Where are they?"

"That's what we're here to find out," Cussone replied cordially. But there was concern in his eyes, and the old man picked up on it. His own eyes shrank among their wrinkles.

"Feds just don't disappear."

"We know." Stanley's voice carried weight now. "We'd better go inside, take a look. You can fill me in on the details later."

"Right." Stephano turned to his partner. "Williams, draw your pistol."

"Don't tell me—"

"Shut up, ya little brat. Do as I say."

There was some affection in Stephano's abuse. Perhaps he and the rookie were related.

"Nephew." The old man gestured. "Part of him is good Italian, but his uppity father gave him some snotty WASP blood. Forgive him."

Stanley and I shared a smile, then together knocked on the front door.

"They'll be no answer," said Stephano. "No one lives here anymore."

He unlocked the door with a master key of some sort, and we went inside. Cussone, too, drew his gun.

The place smelled of rot, of water-soaked carpeting and furniture. Indeed, the plaster ceiling of the dining room had already fallen, leaving a network of copper pipes unmasked. The living room was empty but for a shabby couch and an old TV. The kitchen was bare, except that a Formica table stood at its center, flanked by two empty vinyl-covered chairs facing one another. I shuddered. The Deningtons had lived here, eaten at this table. Newlyweds, not rich, not poor, but comfortable. And childless.

Perhaps Julia had thought herself unable to have children, and her husband had started his adoption agency from an idea borne of necessity. Perhaps I was dreaming. After all, I couldn't be sure that they had adopted Billy.

Stanley and I searched the three bedrooms upstairs and the attic, but found nothing. The rooms were stripped. Stephano and Williams searched the cellar, with similar results. We all congregated in the living room and sat on its wide windowsills.

From where I sat, I could see the faint, aged outlines of a path that connected the back doors of the two houses. I was fairly sure, now, that the Farrers' little girl had witnessed her own parents' deaths in the house next door—the presence of death still seemed to preside—and had run for shelter into the arms of her next-door neighbors.

"We're sitting in the wrong house," I said.

Stephano's voice boomed across the empty living room: "Well, ya got a point. We'll go over, like all the others—"

"Chase and Goody?" Cussone asked.

"Yup. And those others."

I shared a quick glance with Stanley.

"What others?" His voice rose.

"Oh . . . two years 'go—year and a half. You know, a lota folks always wonderin' 'bout the Farrer murders, how and why, all that. Some amateur detectives bothered us over the years. But these guys were pros. From New York."

"Their names!" Cussone barked, impatient with the old man's rambling.

"Oh, hell, there must be a log. I don't remember."

"Was it Bridge and Ridley, Ridley and Bridge?"

"That's the ones. That's them. Bad dressers. That's why I like the uniform, see, 'cause—"

I cut in on him. "Did they see both houses?"

"Well, yes."

"What happened the night of the murders, best as you remember?" I was annoying Stanley, but he kept quiet.

Stephano replied warily: "I brought the report, you know, 'cause I don't remember so well."

"Try your best," I said. Cussone cast a dubious glance my way. His mouth puckered disparagingly, but there was a hint of tolerance in his eyes.

"You're the boss," Stephano said with a smile aimed at Stanley. "I was on duty, sure. Younger then, too. I remember there was this frantic call that come to the front desk downtown—that's the district we're in now, of course—but the lady just gave her address, crying, then hung up. We were on our routine patrol nearby, so we took the call. First my partner—dead now, poor Frank—checked this house. But there was no one here. Dinner was still fryin' on the stove. Chops. We went next door, knocked— just to follow up, ya know. Routine. That's when we found the bodies."

Young Williams leaned forward, listening to his uncle, his guard momentarily down. Fear crossed his countenance like a shadow. He seemed to age with the story.

"Routine," Stephano said again. For him, it was a sad, honorable word. Perhaps something akin to his life.

"Tell me what you found." I hated to ask.

He sat there holding his knees. Silent.

"Tell us, Uncle Pete." Williams seemed transfigured, now, into a human being. Temporarily.

"Man. Woman. Cut in pieces. Arms, legs, off. Heads." He stood. "What more do ya wanna know!?"

"Only—" Cussone was gentle. "Only the pictures. In the report. For ID, that's all." But something took hold of Stanley's eyes and drove their gaze into the ground. He seemed shaken.

"Stanley?" I whispered.

He shook his jowls, trying to slap himself out of it. "Nothing," he answered. But there was something. He breathed: "Let's just get the hell over there."

"One more thing," I said.

Stanley was already on his feet. "What?"

I asked Stephano: "Who owns this place, and why isn't it rented or sold?"

"Some company or other owns it. An' they haven't got an offer meets their askin' price, so I understand."

"For eleven years?"

"Neighborhood's gone to seed."

"Can you get us the company's name?"

"Town records," he said triumphantly. "Anyone has access." He rose to his feet.

"Let's get over there," Cussone growled.

We walked the child's path to the Farrers', number 300. Cussone and I wandered the perimeter of the house before entering. Besides the front and back doors, another possible exit or entrance was a sliding glass window in the kitchen, which seemed recently built, and an older window from an attic that opened out onto an oak tree's heavy bough.

A young woman appeared on the back steps, hands wringing. She wore a pale blue summer dress covered by an apron, and would have been pretty were it not for the matching shade of blue makeup that streaked over her eyes. It had been hastily applied, like smudges on a football player. Its color clashed with the tassels of brown hair that hung around her cheeks.

"Sergeant Stephano," she whispered hoarsely.

"Ma'am." The sergeant took his hat off. "These are the folks I called you 'bout."

"Yes. I just don't know why they have to keep coming back and back." Her voice had the tremor of hysteria. "I just don't understand."

"This may be the last of the visits," Cussone said kindly. "May we come in?"

She composed herself. "Yes, come in." She opened the back door for us, swaying slightly. When I walked in, past her, our eyes met for a moment. She breathed a gin-soaked "Hello" into my face. It washed hot around my ears.

"Hello."

She said to all of us: "I'm Helen Gladden—funny name, isn't it?" Her voice was humorless. "If you need me I'll be upstairs. The sergeant knows the whole score, anyhow. He's been here enough times." She whisked herself away with an awkward flourish, still wrapped in her kitchen apron. The light caught right and I could see why. She wasn't wearing much under that pale blue summer dress.

I moved instinctively through a wide arch that connected to the living room, if you could call it that. Its furniture was perfectly arranged and seemed to have been bought only yesterday. There wasn't any trash in the baskets, nor any lint; no books. A television sat like a lifeless eye watching us from a far corner. It was on one of those swiveling pivots, built into a cheap Formica cabinet. Its huge presence contributed to the feeling of hotel room sterility.

"Been here three years," Stephano said with some amazement. "House stood empty for a good long time, though." There were blotches of sweat, darkening under his arms. He wiped his forehead. "I don't need to tell why."

"Where were the bodies?" Cussone asked.

"Mainly in here, all over. All the fingers we found on a plate in the kitchen."

That stopped us for a moment.

To let some air in, I opened a huge window that looked out toward the Deningtons' old place. A bird had built its nest over one of the cathedral capulets. It perched there and faced me, screeching like a Banshee.

"Upstairs," Cussone said. We all followed him.

The attic was as organized as the rest of the house. I looked out its upper window and onto the branch of the tree that sloped down toward the ground. Little red flowers were still struggling out of its brown buds.

"This is getting us nowhere," Cussone said. "Call the lady upstairs." It was hot in the attic. We waited in silence as Stephano brought Mrs. Gladden up the dimly lit staircase.

"Yes?" she asked hoarsely, a bit more far gone than before.

"The two federal agents who were here last week," Cussone began, "did they ask you any questions while not in the presence of Sergeant Stephano?"

"Not that I remember. They came up here, too."

"Ah. Did they have any ideas about what they were seeing?"

"They didn't share them with me. Frankly, I try not to think very much about what happened here all those years ago."

Cussone scratched his neck and faced Stephano. "Anything you can add—hell, anything? What were they looking for?"

"They were more closemouthed than you are," the sergeant said carefully.

We all stood in sweating silence. The air up there was stultifying.

"OK," Cussone finally drawled, "downstairs."

"In a minute," I called to Stanley as he was halfway down. Stephano and Williams followed close behind him. But I wanted to stare out the attic window a moment longer. From it I could see directly down, across the overgrown yard, into Julia's old living room.

Helen Gladden stayed in the attic with me. She moved closer, through the shadows, and stood by the window. She stared at me quietly.

"Did you . . ." Suddenly I was nervous in her presence. "Did you find anything in here when you moved in—anything at all?"

"Some stuff." Her voice whispered to me. "We threw most of it out."

"What didn't you throw out?"

She trembled for a moment. There was something else on her mind.

"Why don't you come back? I can show it to you then."

"Come back?" Now I was whispering too.

"Tomorrow." She loosened her apron and it fell to the floor, letting light stream through her pale dress. A thin body curved beautifully underneath. But sweat made her streaks of blue makeup bleed like dark tears. "My husband works days." She added bitterly: "He sleeps nights."

She ran her pale hands over her breasts, then let them slide down to her thighs. Her thumbs made little circles there.

"I need it."

"I'm not it."

Her thumbs stopped working. Her eyes glazed. She tried to lean back against the window, but instead she staggered.

"C'mon," I said to her gently, and took her arm. "Show me what you found."

I let her fall against me for a moment. Her heart pounded a frantic rhythm into my chest. Soon mine was pounding, too. But I had no desire to make music. Carefully, I pushed her away.

Like a zombie she led me down the dark staircase to her bedroom. I stepped just inside the door, but no farther. In it were the only signs of life in the house, if you could call it life. Clothes were strewn on the floor and hung out of drawers. Plates of half-eaten food littered the room, and empty gin bottles. One that was half full lay on a canopied bed that was cluttered with magazines and makeup. It sat propped up on a blanket like an idol.

She went to a far wall and took down a picture. Slowly, as if in a trance, she walked back across the room and handed it to me.

"Ed'll miss this but I don't care. He always thought this had some kind of country charm."

It was an old sepia-toned photograph in a country oak frame. In a dappled light two young boys stood in their knickers on a rickety dock, dangling a huge river bass between them. A sign on the building behind them read: FARRER'S DOCK. LIVE BAIT. Someone had penciled the date at the bottom of the photo: 1949.

"May I keep this?" I asked her.

"Sure. He doesn't come in here much anyway. Anymore."

"Where is your husband, Mrs. Gladden?"

"Out fucking Wendy Lynn Harrison, if you really wanna

know." Her voice was thick with alcohol. "Some nights he doesn't even come home." She looked as if she was about to cry, and slammed the door. "Just go away!" she yelled from behind it.

I stood at the top of the stairs a moment, Cussone watching from below. To my right, across from Helen's door, was a small guest room. It had been used for months but not cleaned. Dirty clothes lingered on the floor, men's clothes. A shotgun stood in the corner.

Mr. Gladden's separate bedroom.

A loud clanging of glass against glass came from Helen's room. And the faint sound of liquid being poured.

24

Cussone put his hand on the ignition key but didn't turn it.

"I have a bad feeling. An ache."

"You sick?" I was half joking, but he replied seriously.

"I'm worried."

He started his car. As planned, Williams and Stephano led us in their black and white to the Town Hall. They honked as they drove off, their hands waving out of their windows. They looked like little wings whose flapping was responsible for the car's acceleration.

The Town Hall was a misplaced cube of academia, a squat brick building that was smothered by ivy and surrounded on three sides by fast-food joints.

Inside, after some bureaucratic confusion, we were finally directed to a section presided over by the fattest woman I had ever seen. The nameplate on her desk read MRS. FULPONE. She swayed down a row of files to find us a record of ownership for the old Denington place. When she disappeared, we sat down.

We sat for half an hour. When Mrs. Fulpone finally reappeared, she was sweating. She sat at her desk before speaking, and wiped her chin and forehead with a cloth.

"Took a while," she wheezed.

"Find it?" Stanley held out his hand.

"Two dollars."

He produced two crumpled bills and she gave him the file. Her fingers had made sweat marks on the manila folder.

Sitting there, over the open folder, it was hard for us to understand the meaning of what we saw. We stared at it, then at one another, then at it again.

Ownership of the house seemed to belong to the man who had died next door, over eleven years ago, Mr. A. J. Farrer. We showed Mrs. Fulpone the document.

"I don't know nothin'." She smiled, toothlessly. "Try upstairs."

We tried upstairs, but no one knew the Farrers, or how a dead man could own a house. Cussone dialed Stephano's precinct number and got him. He gave the sergeant the queer identification, but, even over the receiver, I could hear Stephano laugh at our confusion.

"No, no, no," he boomed, "A. J. Farrer's the old man. Lives down by the docks still. Even though he sold the marina. Go down there and ask around; everyone knows him. You'll see why." Stephano paused a moment. I moved closer to the phone in Stanley's hand. I heard the old man breathe out, as if whispering. "You sure the house is in his name?"

"I'm sure," Stanley answered.

"Well, don't make sense. You'll see that, too. Call me afterwards. OK?"

"OK."

We had to ask how to get to the marina several times before actually finding someone who knew. An aging black woman practically drew us a map before asking: "That old place still standin'?"

"Guess so," I answered, feeling a lump in my stomach. We drove for a while before Cussone spoke.

"I don't like this," he muttered. "Your gun loaded?"

"Yeah," I said with some hesitation.

"I don't want you using it unless I'm down."

We drove the rest of the way in silence.

* * *

The marina was as it had been in the picture, a rickety operation at best. Its use seemed to be relegated now to the storage of a few odd craft; there was a mast-hoisting rig and a launching ramp. When we drove up a family of five was happily backing a small Hereshoff on its trailer down the ramp. The sailboat almost floated away without them.

The sign above the slumping wooden building set back from the shore read SONDRA'S SAILBOAT MARINA, where it once had read FARRER'S DOCK. No more LIVE BAIT.

The building had two sections. The first remotely resembled an office. It was a spacious room with cement block floors and a desk that had one leg missing. A phone sat at an angle, along with the woman on it. She babbled in Spanish, her voice rising and lowering on an invisible tide of emotion. When she hung up, she faced us with a dubious look.

"You don't look like sailors."

"Sondra?" I asked.

"Ha—no. Sondra's the owner's daughter. He named the place for her. Whaddya want?"

Stanley said: "We're looking for old Mr. Farrer."

"Wafor?" She smiled queerly, at some inside joke.

"Questions." Stanley did what all cops do best. He flashed his badge.

The woman went silent. "Oh," she finally said.

"Harmless questions," I added.

She gave us a nasty once-over. "Guess I'd better."

"You'd better." Stanley was annoyed.

She pointed a scabby finger away from the docks, up toward the small hill that rose over the river.

"He lives up there. The trailer. Now git."

We made our way by foot up a series of rotted stairways and gravel roads that interconnected without design. I carried the picture along.

A small dilapidated trailer stood at the top of the hill. It was surrounded by old tires and other rusty car parts. A rowboat sat upended on a pair of sawhorses. An old man was lying on top of it; his head popped up when we arrived. The rest of his body didn't move.

"Don't come any further," he said. "I told you folks, I haven't made any decent wages so I don't owe no taxes."

"We're not taxmen." Stanley held up his badge. "We're just here to ask a few questions."

"Questions," he groaned wearily. "Always questions."

We moved closer, and only then saw that his right arm was missing. White stubble covered his face. His body was thin and taut, like a sailor's, but his eyes were blurred with alcohol and age.

"Cigarette?" he asked.

We both signaled a negative response.

"What good are ya?"

"Not much," I said. "Maybe you can be—"

"I'll handle this," Stanley interrupted. He sauntered around the old man and stood behind him. "How long you been here, Mr. Farrer?"

After an unsure moment Farrer replied: "Goin' on ten years, suppose it is. Why?"

"We're interested in the house you own."

"Ha! I don't own no house."

"Yes, you do. It's the house next door to where your son was killed."

He got off the rowboat and sat down on an old bucket. He covered his face with his one hand. His voice echoed inside of his palm.

"Not again."

"Has someone else been here recently?" I asked. "Asking questions?"

"Them two other young fellas from the IRS. Why do you all keep comin' back?" He added weakly: "Statute's run out."

"When were they here?"

"Oh, days ago. I dunno how many."

"Did they ask about the house?"

"Everyone seems to think I'm some sort of real estate baron!" His voice was charged with an excitement that withered as fast as it grew. "I'm just who I am."

"What is that?" Stanley probed.

The man looked him dead in the eye. "Nothin'."

"Did you once own the house?"

"No."

"Do you think your son bought it for you?"

A memory flashed behind his cold eyes.

"That's a laugh. He came beggin' for money to me, the day before . . ."

"Before he was killed?"

He didn't answer the question, only bowed his head farther toward the ground he'd soon be buried in.

"What happened?" I asked. "The night of your son's murder?"

"I get the call, Molly and me. We lived down on Grove then." His eyes bugged. "I was once regular." He let his eyes close. "Wish yous had a cigarette."

"Go on, Mr. Farrer."

"So anyways, like I told the other fellas, like I told everybody in the whole world, I identified their—" His voice broke. "Their bodies." His whole body shivered. He added, with a voice that teetered on the rim of total despair. "My son was once a good man."

I knelt by the old man and put a hand on his thin shoulders. He was trembling.

"Who killed him, Mr. Farrer?"

He spoke as if in a trance, with better diction than he'd used before. And a queer smile.

"In a way he killed himself. He was a computer programmer for IBM, you know, smart as a whip, but he liked the wild life. He himself was wild. Got that from his mother. Molly's dead, now, 'course. Car accident. Anyway, Sonny started hanging with those—those . . ."

"Who?"

He stared at me, visibly shaking. His voice reverted again.

"I can't talk about nothin', mister—maybe just the jibs and spinnakers that stretch by here, like dreams afloat, yessir . . ." He stood, one shirtsleeve dangling. "But not them." His eyes glanced at the emptiness at his right side. "I learn lessons good."

I was horrified. "They cut off your—?"

Cussone interrupted. "Can you tell us their nationality?"

The old man threw us a stone-cold glare. "Them other dudes wasn't taxmen, was they?"

After some hesitation, Cussone answered: "No."

"They're missin', right?"

"Right."

Farrer just shook his head, swaying it back and forth like an unhinged rudder.

I stepped forward with the picture and handed it to him.

"Was—was one of these boys your son, Mr. Farrer?"

He took the picture in his weathered hand. It began to tremble, then shake. His body convulsed. Stanley and I stood by in shock as the old man fell to his knees, moaning. He slammed the picture over and over onto a rusty bucket, shattering its glass and frame. He took the sepia photograph and knelt on it, ripping it into little pieces with his only hand. Then he got up and threw the pieces over the hill toward the river. They fluttered and descended in the wind, catching the light the way geese do, flying their faraway rounds.

25

Cussone and I backed off, leaving the man on his knees and bent over the same bucket. It seemed to be his altar.

"You have a way with people," Stanley said as we marched downhill.

"Thanks."

When we arrived at the car, the family of five was just a white speck on the river. The haze had burned off, leaving the sky a deep blue. Sondra's proprietor snickered from the shed:

"Have a nice conversation?"

"Splendid," Stanley replied.

He leaned his arms on the roof of the Chevy and yawned.

"I guess we should give the place a once-over, just to say we did."

"That's what I like about you, Stanley, such a good attitude."

We went back to the "office." I greeted the woman with an overly cheerful smile. "What's your name?"

"Don't bullshit me, pink cheeks. Whaddya want now?"

"Just to check the place out," Cussone said with authority. "The second section to this building."

"An' if I don't let yous?"

"We'll get a warrant. And give you a lot of hassles about regulations. Do you conform to all the regulations?"

She said with a quicksilver smile: "Of course not. C'mon." She led us around to the end of the building and unlocked a garage-type sliding door. Inside, a huge white speedboat sat polished and gleaming on a brand-new trailer. Cobwebs had overtaken all the corners, but the place still looked well used. There was a wall where tools hung like artwork, a small shed with a generator and a boat pump, ladders, an old conveyor belt, buckets, fishing gear; even a gas pump outside, and electrical outlets.

But there was nothing that registered as important.

"Seen enough?" she asked.

We looked at one another, nodded, and left in silence. We thanked the woman perfunctorily and walked through the heat to our car. Its interior was all sizzling vinyl.

"Let's get going," I said. "Let there be wind!"

"Wind," Stanley repeated as he put the Chevy into gear. But as we climbed the gravel driveway I saw something in my side mirror that made my insides turn to jelly.

"Stop the car, Stanley."

"Stop—what?"

He stopped. I got out and stood on the hill and looked down at Sondra's Sailboat Marina.

"I can't tell," I said to Stanley.

"Tell what?"

I led him down the hill, to the back wall of the slouching building. Large hooks that had been hammered into its wooden slats had rusted over. From them hung a variety of fishing gear: rods, baskets, nets, waders. Boots were stacked in a row underneath. A faded rental sign was pinned to the wall. Its prices were dated and cheap.

"What?" Stanley demanded.

I pointed to the row of rubber boots that lined the bottom of the wall. Some had an odd, new, shiny spandex quality. They looked as if they could conform to the foot, or to a shoe.

"They're the same. Same as the ones the big man was wearing."

Once again we found ourselves in the front office, but Sondra's keeper had disappeared. We called for her; Cussone tried a whistle. The shrill sound lingered on the breeze for a moment, then the breeze carried it off to sea. In the stillness that followed, Stanley drew his gun.

"I suddenly have a very bad feeling," he said.

He wasn't kidding. The stillness seemed to carry with it a theatrical quality. I felt as if I were acting out a part in an old western. The townsfolk had fled, leaving Cussone and me alone to fight the killers, their rifles poised on ledges above.

Our car seemed a thousand yards away; it was only fifty. I turned to Stanley with what felt like the stupidest expression I'd worn in a long while.

"Let's get the hell—"

He was already running. I followed, then passed him. Our tires kicked up a cloud of red dust that seemed to follow us into Poughkeepsie.

"Glad we got out of that alive."

Stanley gave me one of his dubious smirks, but kept silent. I joined him in the contemplation, watching out my window as a corroded slum evolved into a finely trimmed neighborhood in about as many stages as it took for Cro-Magnon man to turn into yuppies. Then the business district took over.

I shared a thought with Stanley: "Both apes and men get hungry."

He looked at me as if I were crazy, but pulled in at the next coffee shop. It was one of those places that look like silver-shiny versions of a train's caboose. Our waitress had a matching head of silver-shiny hair. She took our order with a seasoned dubiety, as if she mistrusted our motives for eating. Cussone ordered a BLT and I had a hot open turkey sandwich.

I ate it in seconds flat. Afterward, I sipped coffee as Cussone called Stephano. When he returned he didn't sit down. His nerves seemed open-ended.

"C'mon, let's go."

"What'd Stephano say?" I asked.

We were steaming on the vinyl seats again before he answered me.

"Said we should go back to the Hall of Records and find out who owns Sondra's place. But he bets it's in Farrer's name."

"What? Why?"

Cussone didn't answer. He started the car and put it into gear. He almost hit another car backing out of the parking lot.

"You're in an awful hurry," I said.

"Yeah." He sighed. "Your friend, Mrs. Gladden. She just called Stephano."

"Is she all right?" I remembered her husband's shotgun.

"She's all right. Says she was looking out her window a half hour ago. That damn attic window. Says there was a delivery made to the Denington place."

He spun around onto Hudson Avenue, cutting off the onflow of traffic. Everyone honked. We headed for a patch of green at the end of the avenue, a small park. It seemed to recede farther and farther from us as we approached it, like an apparition. Cussone screeched onto another, smaller avenue. The tires screamed to a halt in front of the old bar, where a row of black men still sat quietly under its flayed canopy.

Cussone asked of them quickly: "Anyone see the delivery across the street, anyone know who delivered?" He got a silent chorus in return. A lot of dull, wagging heads.

We ran across the street. Stephano's car was parked outside, empty. We didn't even get to the porch before Williams came running out, carrying his uncle in his arms. He was crying. Sweat ran down his forehead and cheeks. He tried to speak to us, but couldn't. Stephano's eyes were closed. His jaw was as slack as a dead animal's. Cussone felt his pulse.

Williams eked out the words: "Heart attack."

Cussone replied: "He's alive—hurry."

Williams ran with his uncle down the bluestone walk. Cussone called after him: "Which hospital?"

Williams wailed back: "County."

"Draw your gun," Cussone commanded.

I drew.

He kicked the front door open, and I almost fell over. The smell hit me like a punch. My eyes began to tear.

We faced a small hallway. In front of us, the staircase. To our left, the hall to the kitchen. To our right, the living room. Cussone waved with his gun: Go left.

The floorboards creaked under me. I was nearly crying with fear. The gun in my hands felt like it weighed a hundred pounds. I couldn't have fired it steadily. I prayed I wouldn't have to. I stopped praying, forever, when I reached the kitchen.

An ordinary white kitchen plate with pink-flowered trim sat on the Formica table. On it was a pile of men's fingers.

I bent over the kitchen sink and threw up, once. I pulled myself together very quickly. There was no sound from the living room, and I thought, momentarily, of running. But I couldn't.

I aimed my gun at the archway and went in after Stanley.

He was alive. Call it that.

He stood in frozen silence with his eyes riveted on the horror spread around the empty room. Bloodless limbs were strewn on the floor. Arms, legs, torsos. The heads of Chase and Goody stared at us from the mantelpiece, still wearing their sunglasses.

I, too, froze in place, as if touched by Medusa's eyes.

"Stanley—" My voice broke. But he didn't answer. He'd gone way past answering. His arms were trembling as I led him out into Julia's old backyard. I laid him on the ground, in the sun, and took his jacket off. He complied; it was a bad sign.

Helen Gladden stumbled out onto her back porch.

"Whatcha doing? What is it?"

I stood and yelled at her. "Call an ambulance, damn it! Emergency!" In one blink, she seemed to sober. She went inside without a word.

I knelt over Stanley and slapped him. "Goddammit, Stanley! Sit up!"

He sat up. Tears fell from his eyes like thick drops of pine sap. His shoulders slackened. He rubbed his eyes with his thumb and forefinger.

"Wow," he whispered. "It all happened at once. I couldn't handle it."

"Yeah, I know," I responded, nearly hugging him. He talked in a tremulous half whisper.

"Everything—all together."

"Yeah, I know," I said again.

"Stop saying that. It's aggravating me. Don't ya see? All day I knew. I knew! Don't you see?"

I grabbed both of his arms and shook. He seemed on the verge of hysteria. "See what?"

"It's the same. Same as the murder eleven years ago."

"I can see that—I saw." I saw.

"And—and all of them! My families."

Now I could see what had rushed together in his mind and collided like a freeway accident. The black and Hispanic families that had been killed in New York City had been dismembered, too. The MO for four disparate crimes, identical.

I stood and walked to the nearest tree. Somehow touching it grounded me. I rubbed my hand against the bark and had a queer thought, given the moment, about an old Greek philosopher named Parmenides. In college, I'd disagreed with his theory that a tree was like life itself, solid and immutable. I thought then that Heraclitus had been right, that life was like a river, ever changing, never stable.

Stanley whispered from behind me: "It's all one case."

Sirens howled like a pack of lonely wolves. Cussone pulled himself to his feet and slipped his jacket on. He wiped his eyes, put his gun back in its holster, then walked around front to greet the police.

I hugged the tree.

26

After the dozen police units came an ambulance corps, two fire trucks, six federal vehicles, a half-dozen unmarked cars driven by police detectives, a tow truck, two insurance men, the press, the neighborhood, and all the curious passersby. Each seemed like a stratum in vehicle geology. At their core was the Denington house, pulsing with police and federal agents.

Stanley had asked me to disappear, at least for the moment. Things were difficult as it was for him, without having to explain my presence to the Feds. I agreed and chose to retreat to Helen Gladden's living room.

She sat quietly on a sofa, hands folded in her lap. She was wearing that same summer dress, but she'd put panties on, and a bra. A pot of brewed coffee sat before her on a low table along with cups and saucers, sugar and milk. I stayed at the window watching as she tried to pour a cup, but her hands shook with such force that the coffee spilled in a puddle on the table. Sober tears slid down her cheeks into the puddle. When I sat down next to her, I saw her face reflected in it.

"Let me pour," I said gently.

She cried quietly, leaned her head on my shoulder—then withdrew it, remembering our scene in the attic. She stared at me with wide wet eyes that dripped indigo.

"Sorry."

"Don't be."

There was a box of Kleenex on a far table, housed in a little plastic replica of a log cabin. I walked to it and grabbed a wad, then walked back to her.

"This is not a day to mince words," I said. "I'm going to do you a big favor. Don't shy away."

I pressed the tissue above her left eye and gently wiped away its streak of blue makeup. I performed the same operation on her other eye, and used one final tissue for her lids.

"You're too pretty to wear so much makeup."

When she opened her eyes again she stared at me like the dog no one had ever cared to pet.

"Thank you," she whispered, holding her gaze on me.

Suddenly I wanted to take her in my arms. My limbs still ached with fear—I needed the comfort of a woman. But Helen was teetering on that vulnerable precipice of losing self-respect. I didn't want to upset the balance—not for my own selfish fix of comfort. I could do without it. Anyway, I still remembered what a woman-friend had told me once, a long time ago. That it's the "good guys" who can do more damage than the lousy ones.

I got up slowly, stroking Helen's hair just once, and walked to the window again. Outside, behind the Denington house, a huge man in a dark suit was shoving his finger against Cussone's chest and chewing him out. It looked like a pantomime of anger.

I faced Helen. "Can you answer a few questions?"

"Of course."

"Did you see the delivery truck?"

"Not exactly. I saw the back of it. It was white, a cube-shaped van, you know? Two men got out carrying a trunk—like the kind I packed for college. A black trunk. There were bodies in it, weren't there?"

"Yes."

She hugged herself and shivered.

"Could you recognize the men?"

"I really wasn't paying attention—I was—I wasn't sober." She lowered her eyes. "I'm going to stop my drinking. Really."

"I believe you will, Helen." For some reason I thought of Cussone's question to the old man. "Could you tell the nationalities of the two delivery men?"

"Dark skin."

"Black?"

"No . . ." She squinted her eyes and peered back into her memory. "They were . . . more like Puerto Rican, or—something like that."

"What did you see them do?"

"Open the door and walk in—just like that! They must have had a key."

"That's when you called the police?"

Her body fell at an angle against the back of the couch. "No." She leaned farther forward, humiliated. "I took a shower first."

I walked to her and touched her back. It burned.

"You still did the right thing, Helen, after you'd thought about it—sober. I used to drink. I know how it can be."

"You did?"

I'd had a bout with the bottle—a minor fight, which I'd won. But that short battle left scars of humiliation that never seemed too far from breaking open and bleeding again.

"I did, yes. And you're like me, I can tell. You're one of the ones who're going to get over it."

She stood up, head level with my shoulders, eyes staring up into mine.

"I don't even remember your name."

As fate would have it, the door opened and Cussone rushed in. The large man who'd been yelling followed close behind. A federal agent with sunglassed eyes waited at the door.

"We need this house," were the fat man's first words.

Stanley just wagged his jowls, rolled his eyes.

"Any news?" I asked Cussone discreetly.

"No news."

"Who the hell is he?" The fat man lit a cigarette and stared at me as if I might be a suspect. He looked hungry for one.

I looked at Helen. "Luke Byman."

"Private operator," Stanley added quickly. "He's been involved—"

"Well get him out of here." The big man blew a puff of smoke, a cloud that made all of us cough. In it he turned to Helen and gestured with two sausage arms. "We need your house, ma'am. I'm Agent Haley—FBI."

I left through the front door, bumping into a team of young agents carrying mobile telephones up the steps. A polyester photographer scurried around the corner of the house like a little rodent and froze just long enough to snap a picture of me.

"Who are you?" he asked.

"Nobody."

He frowned. "Oh." His quiet feet padded around the corner again.

Then Cussone was standing next to me, his arms folded. He looked as if he was restraining them from swinging at Haley.

"Sorry," he said finally. "But I'm going to have to be here all day. You could take a train back to New York if you want. Or wait. Might take forever."

"Can I use your car?"

He cast a sideways glance that mingled worry with envy.

"I suppose." He let the unspoken question dangle.

"Hall of Records—again," I answered.

"Ah." He handed me the keys. "Be careful. And let me know where you go from there."

I drove away through a flock of crane-necked passersby. They gawked as paramedics transported the plastic-wrapped remains of Chase and Goody to an awaiting ambulance. Some of them were loudly counting the number of pieces.

". . . six . . . seven . . ."

Miss Fulpone had a delightful way with words.

"You again?" she wheezed.

"Me again."

"What is it this time?"

I asked to know the owner of Sondra's Sailboat Marina. She didn't move until I produced a ten-dollar bill. She gave me eight dollars in change, then hoisted herself out of a sagging chair and disappeared down the aisle.

I waited another half hour. When she came back it was three-thirty.

"You come up with 'em, don'tcha?" She collapsed back into her chair. "Had a hell of a time findin' this, too."

The folder was yellowed around the edges. When I opened it a familiar name screamed up at me. A. J. Farrer still owned his old marina. He appeared to have sold it to himself ten years ago, a year after his son's murder. Instead of being privately owned, though, it now was held by his corporation—Farrer Enterprises.

I sat pondering for a moment, until Mrs. Fulpone broke my thoughts with her gentle manner:

"Place closes at four—sharp."

I smiled at her hazily and glanced again at the information in the folder. Much of it was just a record of the real estate transaction: the first offer had been accepted; it had been paid in full, in cash; and there were signatures. One of them was of the real estate broker. His name was Peterman. The firm was Peterman and Decker Real Estate, 1022 Hudson Drive. A twinge of fear and triumph passed through me like a spirit when I read the name. It was the same firm who'd listed the Denington house.

I asked Mrs. Fulpone if it was possible to reference all purchases by A. J. Farrer in the last ten years.

"Possible . . ." She equivocated. "Not today, though."

I handed her my eight dollars.

"Still not possible," she said, fanning herself with the bills.

I rummaged in my wallet for another ten spot. My last. The rest were singles.

"Here." I grimaced as the bill left my hand.

Twenty minutes later she emerged from a back room with two three-by-five file cards. On them were a string of numbers: 3, 12, 77, 109, 136, 197, 210, 331, and more.

"Take these upstairs. They know you're coming. They'll reference these numbers. I'm going home."

Upstairs an old man with spectacles hovered over an enormous computer. It groaned like a lawn mower as he ran the numbers into it. Ten minutes later the machine finally began to print the list.

"Old model," the gentleman said with a smile. "Nineteen sixty-six." He tore off the page when it was finished, and waited with a sly grin before handing it to me. I produced two dollars. He stared at them in disbelief.

"Leave me two for myself, will you?"

I showed him my wallet. With a sour chortle he crumpled the two bills in his skinny fist and dropped the page in my hands.

"Good-bye," he said.

Outside the sun slanted down and hit me. Even so, I had a dark feeling, as if my shadow were alive. I sensed that I was being followed. Two dozen car grills smiled at me from the parking lot, but none of the vehicles was occupied. I walked hurriedly to Stanley's Chevy and climbed in. Somewhere a car door clicked shut— but there was no one getting in or out of any vehicle in sight. I started my engine. Another started with mine—but I couldn't tell whose, or where the sound was coming from. I nearly ran over Mrs. Fulpone trying to race out of there. She cursed me as she trudged to her car, raising her middle finger to the heavens. My eighteen dollars hadn't bought away her bitter weight. And from the direction in which her finger pointed, neither had her prayers.

Some blocks away I pulled over, under the shade of an elm that had been gouged with initials, and took a minute to calm myself. I unfolded the list.

There were thirty-five businesses owned by Farrer Enterprises in Poughkeepsie, and six domestic residences in A. J. Farrer's name. The list was varied: He owned everything from trucking companies and cement mills to video stores and shopping malls. He owned only one marina: Sondra's. And two clubs. Six contracting corporations. Peterman and Decker's real estate brokerage. A law firm. And, most frightening of all, Farrer Enterprises owned the Child Resource Center. An adoption agency.

I pulled the car onto Hudson Avenue, stopped at a phone booth, and dialed Helen Gladden's number. Stanley was in conference. I left Peterman and Decker's address with a federal agent who spoke in yachtsman.

"Right, old boy," he drawled. He made me feel like hitting the phone booth.

The offices of Peterman and Decker Real Estate were small and unpretentious. The storefront window was alive with a cheerful diorama of a white house, a picket fence, and a family of four waving at me with mechanical arms. Inside, half a dozen desks were spaced equally. Behind the farthest desk was another office marked PRIVATE.

"May I help you?" a young saleswoman asked. A name tag labeled her as "Linda."

"I'm here to see Mr. Peterman."

"He's not here."

"How about Decker?"

"Your name?"

I told her.

"Do you have an appointment?"

"No."

"Then I'm afraid—"

I pointed to a Xerox machine in the corner. "May I copy this sheet and ask you to hand it to him?"

Linda was easily flustered. Her pale cheeks turned red. "I guess so." She did as I asked, and within seconds Decker was standing before me. He was a big, gruff man in his fifties. A tuft of gray hair kept falling down over his right eye. He kept pushing it back again.

"Who are you?" His voice was thick, like an old prizefighter's.

Again I recited my name.

"I mean who do you represent?"

"I'd rather not say."

"Then you're not a cop."

"No."

"That means you're a loner."

The tiny features of Genna Denington flickered through my mind and filled me with purpose.

"No, I'm not alone," I said with some conviction. "I have a client." Julia, Genna. "And you've got some explaining to do."

I must have sounded awfully confident. Fear pulsed behind his black eyes. "Come with me," he mumbled shakily. When we'd entered his office Decker closed and locked the door.

"Who are you?" he demanded.

I let my jacket fall open. Decker's eyes riveted on my .45. I tried to maintain my confident tone.

"The man who could put you in jail."

He laughed out loud. "A junior gumshoe!"

My face reddened. I felt like running back to my typewriter. Instead, I tried again:

"I need some explanations, Decker. That's all."

He unfolded the list and spread it out on his desk.

"So you think you found some connections, eh? Think you've got me by the balls? Whaddya think—we're stupid? All this is kosher, junior G. Legal."

"The newspapers would love to hear the story, though: Town drunk owns half of Poughkeepsie's businesses. All of them mob-related, I presume."

"You presume way over your head, kid."

"Just tell me who the old man is fronting for. Who's put everything in his name?"

"A philanthropist who wishes to buy property anonymously."

"And his nationality?"

"American, of course."

I was getting nowhere except deep in trouble. I tried a different tack.

"There's a team of Feds back at the old Denington place who'd just love to know who carved up two of their own." A queer expression reorganized his face. "Whoever did," I continued, "is looking for trouble. There's an army of them. They'd just love my little bit of research here. If I walk out of your office unsatisfied, I go to them—and give them you."

"Listen . . ." he said thoughtfully, "we're businessmen, right? If you press us any further there's going to be—" He sat so suddenly that the room shook. "I'd hate to say what could happen."

"Nothing has to happen."

He misinterpreted my meaning. "Good," he said. "Sit down." He untaped a key from the bottom of his desk blotter and opened a large bottom drawer. In it he found a metal box; he unlocked it. There was money inside. I couldn't tell how much. There were pictures, too. Decker riffled through the bills and came up with a wad of them in his fist.

"How's five hundred?"

"I don't want your money. I want the name."

He shrugged. "Trust me, it's a name you don't wanna know." He counted out more bills. "This stack says you disappear, forever.

Anybody sees you pokin' 'round again, kid—" He sighed and repeated: "I'd hate to say what could happen." He thrust the money toward me. "One grand."

There was a long silence as my mind raced. To refuse the money would be dangerous. To accept was equally so. Still, Decker had to think he'd gotten rid of me—that I was gone for good. Bought off.

I opened my palm and extended it.

27

The Child Resource Center was a large one-story building at the center of a small complex of doctors' offices and insurance agencies. All were connected by a consciously "old-fashioned" wooden walkway painted white and shadowed by a pseudowestern overhang. The pillars that supported it were made of tin.

The offices inside resembled bureaucracy anywhere, or everywhere. There was a reception area, a divider with a gate, and behind it rows of modular cubicles buffeted by wall carpeting. Women of every nationality worked the cubicles, which were open-topped and open-ended. My first impression was of an ant farm; after standing there a moment, however, the room began to remind me of a smaller version of the IRS offices in New York. I'd been audited a year before; they'd gouged me for another thousand dollars—for a year in which I'd only earned twelve.

A tickle of reminiscent fear ran up my spine, and sweat. Bureaucracy can do that to a fellow.

A black woman greeted me at the reception desk. I asked her for the manager.

"Mr. Wise isn't here this afternoon," she replied, enunciating her words clearly. "Can anyone else help?"

"I don't know. I'm trying to trace a baby."

Her politeness faded ever so slightly.

"We don't give out that kind of information."

"Ah, well. I'm working with the police on this. Maybe I should come back with them."

A small man suddenly materialized next to me like a bureaucratic angel. The bureaucratic God had sent him on a mission of frightening delicacy.

"Oh my, sir. Is there a problem?"

"Maybe."

"I'm Mr. Olivera." He extended a limp white hand. It felt cold and lifeless, as if it wasn't connected to his body. I was reminded of the severed limbs of Chase and Goody, and withdrew my palm, then wiped it off on my jacket. Olivera's ass tightened around a stick.

"Come with me."

I followed him through the gate and down an aisle that cut an angular path through the cubicles. It led to a series of glassed-in offices; his was marked ASSISTANT MANAGER. It was hot back there. I took off my jacket, thankful that I'd unburdened my sore shoulders and locked my .45 in Stanley's trunk.

"Sit down," Olivera said curtly. "I've only three minutes."

"Then I'll be quick." I remained standing. "I'd appreciate any help you can give me in trying to trace a particular baby."

"Highly irregular. Why?"

"Because I believe that a stolen child may have been routed through your company."

"Then you believe wrong. No such thing could possibly happen here. I resent your—"

I cut him off. "Tell me why it couldn't."

He stared at me wearily. "Who are you?"

"I represent the mother. I'm not a cop but the cops know I'm here. Call it a private inquiry."

A voice boomed from behind me. A deep, powerful bass.

"Private is a word we respect around here, sir."

I turned to face a tall, thin man with a hawkish nose and

spectacles. Behind the glasses a pair of tired, lonely eyes tried to sum me up, not in the usual sense, but in a deeper, more thoughtful way. Quietly, he seemed to be probing the veracity of my soul as well as my story. A smile caught the corners of his lips and pulled up.

"You're young."

"Thirty-three."

"Young." He waved his hand. "This way. My office is air-conditioned." He turned to Olivera. "I'll take care of it, Al."

Olivera's eyes followed me down the hall until I reached an office labeled NATHAN WISE, MANAGER. The room was chilly; I put my jacket back on.

"I usually don't come back after a day of meetings," he said, "but there's so much to do." He spread his hands out over his desk as if blessing the mass of papers on it. "So. Here I am."

"I appreciate your time, Mr. Wise."

"And you are?"

I told him. We shook hands and sat down.

"Why do you believe the stolen baby was routed through here?"

"You were listening."

"I prefer to call it eavesdropping. I do it very well. My employees hate me for it."

"That's healthy." I was being facetious.

"Very," he said earnestly. "Now, answer my question."

"It's a complex question, and I'm not sure I can answer it."

"You've got to try, or I'll be no help to you."

Something sad was lurking under his relaxed manner. An awareness that was hard to peg.

"All right, I'll try." I had to make a quick character judgment—a dangerous one. Nathan Wise was going to hear my story. If he was connected to Decker or the baby smugglers, then it could be my last story. I pressed forward.

"A baby was stolen last April. A little girl. She's only part of a larger case, one that includes a lot of death."

"Death," Wise repeated.

"Yes. Eleven years ago a couple were butchered in their house on Mildred Avenue. A Mr. and Mrs. Farrer."

"There's not one person in Poughkeepsie who doesn't know

that story, backwards, forwards. Especially me. Ralph Denington—their next-door neighbor—was my partner here. He disappeared that same night."

"Yes, I know. Taking the Farrer girl."

"That—that's never been determined."

"Where else would she have gone?"

"I couldn't begin to guess. But Farrer's oldest friend, Pete Dillery, he and his wife and their young son—they disappeared that night, too. And haven't been heard from since. That's rather a strange coincidence, don't you think?"

Puzzled, I made a mental note of the name. Dillery.

"You're saying *they* might have taken the girl?"

"I haven't the foggiest. It's possible. I just know Ralph could never have killed anybody, let alone in that way. Nor could he have kidnapped a young girl. He's a good man."

But I wasn't listening to him. A thought had struck and shook me.

"The Dillerys' son—how old was he?"

"Four or five."

"Do you remember his name?"

"Of course I do. I held him on my lap many times. Billy Dillery."

I shuddered.

"I knew Billy," I whispered.

"Knew him?"

"He was shot to death before my eyes. I made off luckier." For some unknown reason I felt suddenly compelled to rip my shirt open and show Wise the bullet's scar.

He sat motionless.

I added: "It's his little sister who I'm looking for. Ralph's daughter."

Wise stood silently and peered down at his desk as if from a vertiginous height. He swayed.

"To hell with my work," he said. "C'mon. These walls have ears."

He left his papers as they were and led me out through the front door into a descending twilight. We walked around the far end of the parking lot to an ice-cream shack. He bought me a vanilla cone and ushered me to one of a few battered picnic tables sitting in a grove of dusty trees. The sun had not yet plunged below the distant Catskills. It still raged, bold orange against a pale blue sky.

"Tell me more," Wise said.

After a calming slurp of vanilla ice cream I continued. "Ralph and Julia Denington obviously saw something they shouldn't have. The murder, presumably. The murderers. They took the girl and ran. They've been running ever since."

Wise lowered his head into an awaiting web of fingers. "Julia," he whispered.

"I helped deliver her baby," I told him.

His eyes snapped up at me.

"Is she . . . ?"

"She's alive."

"Thank God." The silence that followed bothered me.

"Ralph was your partner, wasn't he?"

"Yes."

"And you're not concerned about him?"

He looked up at me and blinked. "Of course I am. It shattered me when he—I thought he was dead, too, lying somewhere. He was my best friend, above anything else."

"But you were in love with his wife? With Julia?"

He was slow to answer, his voice miserable. "I was. Who wouldn't have been? She was—is . . ." He paused, calmed himself, whispered: ". . . beautiful. And that voice . . ."

"Did you know the Farrers?"

His tone stiffened.

"I'd met them, of course. At Ralph and Julia's, several times. I didn't like them, though."

"Why?"

"I should say that I didn't like him. He was wild, a real social boor. He drank and cursed. Once he even smashed a mirror, an expensive one. He was drunk. It was the last time we—my wife and I—saw him. Ever. It was at Julia and Ralph's. A small dinner party. He just smashed one of her parents' mirrors, an heirloom. She was terribly upset. She cried."

"Why would he do that—break the mirror?"

"Farrer was like that. No respect for property, for possessions that were dear to people. When Julia told him casually that the mirror was an heirloom, he just up and smashed the glass with his fist. We all stood around, shocked, of course. He just got this strange look on his face, really strange, and said he was tempting fate, bad luck. Whatever. We all realized then, of course, that he was truly imbalanced. Even his little wife was stunned."

"Did Julia and Ralph ever see him after that?"

"I don't know. I would think they didn't. He was killed only two weeks later. And I know Julia was terribly hurt about the mirror and the way he ruined her party. I've often thought about what he said. Fate, bad luck, broken mirrors. Spooky."

"Was Julia upset enough to kill him?"

"The cops asked the same stupid question. But no one kills over a mirror, especially . . . especially in that way."

I licked some melting ice cream. It made me think of that little boy who'd knocked on my door one night last April.

"Was Billy Dillery adopted through your agency?"

Wise was visibly surprised. He looked as if I'd slapped him. "How'd you know?"

"Lucky guess."

"I worried for Billy. But Ralph insisted. Farrer's friends, the Dillerys, were desperate for a child, and Julia—even she put the pressure on. I relented, for her sake."

"Did Dillery work for IBM?"

Wise chuckled softly as he said: "No. But it's where Farrer and Ralph met. The very beginning. But—but then Farrer left the company and fell in with a wild crowd. Fast horses—even faster women. He ran around, to put it mildly, with a tough bunch."

"Did Julia have an affair with William Farrer?"

"The police asked the same question. The answer is no. But he did have affairs with every loose woman in town. In fact, so did his wife. With the same women."

"I thought you said you didn't know them very well."

"Well, I researched Farrer and his friends before sending Billy. They were all part of a context that I felt it was my responsibility to find out about. Ralph and I had quite an argument about my little research study. He told me to throw it away, to go to hell, you name it. It was the only real fight we ever had."

"Did Ralph Denington run around with Farrer?"

"With a wife like Julia?"

I understood what he meant. Julia had left her imprint on both of us.

"To answer your question," he continued, "no. He didn't run around, to my knowledge. And I knew him damn well."

"Why would the Deningtons have defended Farrer?"

He spoke archly, as if the truth were a formal affair.

"Not Farrer, but Farrer's friend, Pete Dillery—who Julia and Ralph had become chummy with. They were a decent enough couple, actually. In fact, they represented the best part of William Farrer—the only good side he had, as far as I could see. Pete had been a lifelong friend of Farrer's—their parents had been best friends. And it was only when Pete was around that Farrer seemed—well, normal."

"How could Billy Dillery possibly have ended up with Julia in New York City—not three months ago?"

"I've been running that in my brain since you told me. It's dumbfounding. I've no idea."

I let a buzzing silence surround us. Flies swooped and dove; rush hour traffic moaned from a distant avenue; a row of street lamps popped on just overhead. A motor chorus. Like those Greek choruses that long ago might have told you a character was lying.

"Did you sleep with Julia?"

"It's none of your business."

"No, you're right. It's not."

He leaned toward me. "No. I did not sleep with her. I would have left everything for Julia. But she was devoted to Ralph, I saw that. Everyone saw that. To have even confronted her would have been betraying Ralph—and her too, in a way, because to betray Ralph was to betray her." Wise spoke so quietly I could hardly hear him. His face had reddened. "I never even kissed her."

I hit him with a side punch: "Mr. Wise, aren't you aware that A. J. Farrer owns the Child Resource Center?"

He took a long time to answer.

"Yes." His voice was thin. "Farrer Enterprises owns it. You've done your homework."

"Since when have they owned it?"

"Since the beginning."

"Who bought it—Farrer or his father?"

"The son. But Farrer Enterprises reverted to his father after William died."

"Why did you lie to me?"

"Lie?"

"Of course you'd supply Farrer's friends with a son. He financed your dream—right?"

"Mine and Ralph's."

"With what money? He worked for IBM."

Wise was good at sitting very still, but I could tell he was on the verge of leaving me. He moved slightly, but the sound of a plane overhead caught his attention. Another motor. He focused his eyes on it and tilted his head as if listening to a signal from God. When he lowered his gaze his face had changed. He seemed older, prouder, and scared.

"It was illegal money, I'm sure. All cash. I never asked where it came from."

"Mob money?"

He nodded. But there was something more he had to say.

"That's not the only reason I lied to you. I—we, this whole operation, pays."

"Pays?"

"The Cubans. Each month."

"Cubans . . ." My voice trailed off.

"Half of Poughkeepsie is owned and run by them."

The plane left a white trail across the sky. The dying light reached up and singed the underbelly of the trail and made it bleed wisps of scarlet, like an ephemeral scar cut across the heavens.

I asked Wise: "Who runs the show: their don, whatever?"

"I don't know him. From what I hear, no one seems to. A different fellow stops by each month, collecting. I give him cash that amounts to a month's salary. In fact, that's how we handle it. There's one extra name on our payroll, a phony employee."

"Why are you telling me?"

Wise smiled and shook his head. "I don't know, exactly." He was lying.

"I think you do."

"Think away," he dared.

"You've found something out recently, haven't you? You suspect that someone's using your organization, tapping into the files and selling the names and addresses of the couples who're looking for children. You suspect the Cubans, probably, and are frightened, for good reason—but you have to tell me, Wise. Tell the Feds, or the police."

He laughed. "They own cops."

"They kill them, too." I told him about Chase and Goody. About the similarity between their deaths and the Farrers'. He was visibly shaken.

"My God." He inhaled, then exhaled. "Maniaco."

I wondered what he meant but didn't get a chance to ask before he slammed his fist against the picnic table. A couple of blue jays squawked angrily from a branch overhead. They flew to another tree and watched us with heads turned in profile, eyes glaring.

"I take my life in my hands by speaking to you, but to hell with it. Someone should know."

"Know what?"

He formulated his thoughts, then began. "You're not the first person to make this accusation. Let me tell you, if you had been, I'd have walked and told you to go to hell. My company—it's like my baby, my child. It's grown up well, through it all. At least I thought it had. We've provided a great service to a lot of honest couples, helped create families. I'm proud of it—even now, now that I know we've been corrupted worse than we had been. After being contacted I was in shock, because the man who came to me—he carried such weight that I had to believe him . . . enough to check his story, anyway, so I did. I went through our records. We hadn't been doing so well for the last few years. Business was slacking off more and more—even with the new yuppie boom. We thought more parents would want adopted children, but fewer were registering. When I checked the inquiries against the registries, I was shocked. There were so many more. . . . Then—well, it's too tedious to say how—then I discovered that someone was contacting those inquiries and selling them babies without a wait. No wait! Two months, maximum. People who had contacted us originally suddenly had babies that weren't delivered through our agency. No one would say where they'd gotten them. It turns out the yuppies are there after all. They have money. They just don't have time to wait for our agency to provide, legally. So they pay a premium. Upwards of fifty thousand a baby, I've been told. But they can afford it because we're talking lawyers and stockbrokers and ad executives in every urban center in the country."

"Where do all the babies come from?"

"I wish I knew. It's an incredible source of—of available children. Newborns. They've got to be coming from somewhere." He took a breath. "I'm sure it's an illegal source. Illegal importation of children."

"It's called smuggling."

"I know what it's called."

I remembered all those blood-soaked pictures scattered around Amanda's body. I had to fight away the image, and couldn't bring myself to speak of all the babies that were dying in transit.

"Who contacted you, Nathan?"

"I can't tell you."

"That's all right—I can guess. You see, he's contacted me, too, in a way." I rubbed the back of my head. There was still a bruise. "I've seen Ralph Denington."

Wise lowered his head. "Poor Ralph," he moaned. "He looked so horrible."

"What did he say to you?"

"Just what I've told you—to check my files, to verify his story."

"Which was?"

"That we'd been infiltrated by smugglers. And not just us—all of the Resource Centers, all around America. We—we're linked to over twenty of them in nine states. It's like a chain."

I remembered that Billy had lived in nine states.

"How are you linked?"

"Single ownership. Individual franchises. Like hotels."

"And you share the same computer system—like hotels?"

"Yes, of course."

"Where's the central terminal—the mainframe?"

"IBM. At IBM."

"Where? Here?"

"No, no. In a strange place. This little town in Michigan."

Bingo.

"And there's also a center in Los Angeles?"

"Yes."

"One of your larger ones? Or—is there anything special about it?"

"Not that I know of. Except, well, one thing."

"What?"

"I believe it's where Ralph was going."

"L.A.? He told you?"

"In so many words. I asked where he was off to again—I'd pleaded to see more of him, to talk, to help. He said he couldn't stay—he actually laughed, a horrible laugh—said that he was off to the fallen angels."

"That's all he said?"

"That's all."

The two words had a finality that seemed to wound him. Like the scar in the sky, Wise was visibly bleeding regret. He let his head fall back into his hands. I stood up and paced for a moment, my thoughts on Los Angeles. So many threads of the case led there. I remembered Julia's airline ticket, and the postmark on her letter, and Denington's tweed jacket; it had fit me well. Both Ridley and Bridge had traveled to L.A., probably following Julia's husband. And now he'd returned there, again. I felt a growing urge to know why.

"Mr. Wise," I asked gently, my voice hoarse, "can I see your computer files? See what information we could find about your centers in Michigan and California? Maybe I could take a copy of a disk?"

"It would be several floppies and that would be impossible. Illegal, even."

"We could meet later tonight—"

"Out of the question. Besides, you'd only find subterfuge."

"Is there anything you can show me?"

"No. I've said enough. Please don't ask me to risk my life." He sounded as if he was talking to someone else, or to himself. "Please don't ask."

"Do you have children?"

Nathan Wise stood, his lanky frame swaying with fear and fatigue. He was shaking, almost crying.

"Stay out of my life, Byman. Why did you even have to come here?"

"Answers."

"At my expense?"

"You seemed to be a man of conscience."

"Shut up." He took a few quick paces toward his offices but stopped and turned. He had something more to say and was torn between saying it and getting the hell away from me. I didn't blame him. I was beginning to feel like bad luck, even to myself. But his feet were frozen in place. They wouldn't let him leave.

"I can't do it—you understand?"

"I understand that you don't understand. People are being killed. Children are dying by the dozen, in transport. They're being stacked in piles."

Wise stared once more at the sky, as if an answer to his quandary might be lurking there. It wasn't. He turned without a word and walked back across the parking lot. I followed at a sauntering pace, easing toward Stanley's Chevy. Its putrid color glowed in the twilight. Wise put his hands on its luminescent roof and stopped. His back straightened. He turned to me and spoke from across a cement expanse.

"He—he said something else. I remember now, and it confuses me. But you should know." His bass voice had risen to a tenor whisper. I stepped quickly toward him, until we were only a few feet apart.

"What did he say, Nathan?"

"He said that it isn't only the Cubans."

"What?"

"I mean—I think they're still involved."

"What exactly did he say?"

"It didn't make sense, what he said. He said even the crazy Cubans were afraid, now—'cause it wasn't their operation anymore. I don't know what it meant, but he said they're scared as hell."

28

I gave Nathan Wise Helen Gladden's number and got out of there. But no sooner had my car turned out of the parking lot than I realized I was being followed, by a newish sedan, green. It looked like a Chevy. Maybe a Chrysler. I wasn't very smart about cars.
    Sometimes I wasn't very smart.
    I'd taken Decker's money and was beginning to regret it. Though I'd hidden it away in the trunk, along with the .45, I had a sudden and burning desire to get rid of it altogether. I drove as fast as I could and ran a couple of stoplights. The green sedan ran them, too. He kept an unnervingly consistent distance behind me. Every move I made, he shadowed precisely. If I hadn't been so scared I'd have been embarrassed.
    I swerved into the parking lot of a Grand Union, hoping for a back entrance. There was none. I turned into an alley behind the store. The sedan passed me, realized what he'd done, and, as I sped out of the alley, knocking crates left and right, he—rather calmly, I thought—did a one-eighty on a dime and tailed me out of the lot.
    To hell with it, I thought. Let him follow.

Finally I found Mildred Avenue and pulled the Chevy up alongside a fire truck. A few firemen were drinking beer and cavorting on its back end, as if the murders had been cause for celebration. I climbed up onto the truck and scanned the entire area. No green sedan.

"Hey!" one of the firemen yelled, "that's a fire truck!"

"Oh, shut up," I answered. He shrugged his shoulders and sat back down and cracked another Genessee.

A few minutes later I found Stanley hunched over a portable typewriter. He was pecking out his reports, one for the Feds and one for the police. I placed my wad of hundreds on the keys.

"Forgive me, father, for I have sinned."

He looked up at me, ragged and mean. "This a joke?"

"No joke. I've been bribed."

I told him the story of my afternoon. While I was talking Cussone had to silence me twice while federal agents wandered through. Helen's living room had been turned into a battle command, but none of the agents seemed sure of where the war was. Or whom it was against.

When I was finished Stanley said to me: "I'll tell Haley myself, what you've told me. And I'll take the heat for letting you go out there. But that's it, Byman. No more of this shit. Go home."

"No."

"Don't contradict me, damn it. Just sit and wait for me and I'll drive you in a few hours."

"Is that the gratitude I get?" I was angry. "I want you to do me—"

"You're not going out there again."

"I'll leave Poughkeepsie."

"Good. It's fucking dangerous for you here."

"Let me go where no one knows me."

"What are you talking about?"

"California."

"Jesus, Byman. You can't . . ."

It took me half an hour of badgering to convince him that it just might be a good idea for me to do a little legwork in Los Angeles.

"How do you expect to pay for your trip? Certainly you don't expect the police department—" He stopped when he saw my devious smile. I was staring at the thousand dollars Decker had placed in my palm.

"Oh no," he said.

"Oh yes. Think of it. They're paying for their own demise."

"Or yours."

"I'm going, no matter. I'll find the money."

"What about your screenplay?"

A consideration I hadn't taken into account.

"Three days," I answered. "Please, Stanley."

He winced, hating the sound of his first name. But he handed me the money all over again.

"You're on your own. I have no responsibility for you. I know nothing of this fucking bribe. And I don't give a shit about your ass. Understood? Any other way and it's *my* ass," he said, "in the holy grinder."

Outside, night had fallen. The radiant sliver of a new moon looked like a white-hot scythe cutting at the trees surrounding Helen's home. I stood out on the porch, waiting for Stanley. I waited a long time. Hours passed. Then Helen came out onto the porch. The case and its complexities had been swimming in my mind so long that when I said hello to her I spoke as if from under water.

"Hello," she said plainly, sober. "You don't look so good."

"Been a long day."

"Yes." She moved closer. "Thank you for being kind today. I mean it. You're a gentleman."

"Thanks." I worked up a smile. "Truth is, Helen, under all of it, I think you're a hell of a lady."

She grinned. We took each other's hands and held them awhile. Then her wistful smile faded in the moonlight. She took hold of my shirt and pulled me close and kissed me with more sadness than sensuality.

"Good-bye," she said.

The door opened and closed and she was gone.

29

I drove.

Headlights on the Taconic were sporadic. Driving seemed a constant process of being swallowed by the darkness.

I glided back onto Route 87, then wound along the murky contours of the Harlem River. We crossed over it, back into Manhattan, at Willis Avenue. Stanley had closed his eyes near Beacon; the cobblestone on upper Second Avenue bounced them back open.

"Shit," was his declaration.

I dropped him at his home, parked in a lot, then stuffed the parking ticket into his mailbox. It was one in the morning. I had two dollars. I didn't want to face the subway, so I walked to Lola's.

I hiked along an old Indian trail called Broadway, past an oversized mausoleum called Lincoln Center, across the narrow strip of grass they call a park, Needle Park, over to a place that used to be Columbus Avenue. Now it was a theme park for the New Consumers. Proprietors along its sidewalks packed their wares and closed their gates and seemed to be wondering why no one was buying today. Maybe the market was down.

Lola's block was full of shadows. A bum slept on her stoop. I tried not to wake him as I rang her buzzer.

She stood in her open door at the top of the stairs wearing a short white bathrobe pulled tight as a straitjacket around her slim black body. Her fists were clenched. She opened one and slapped my cheek, hard.

"Who the hell do you think you are?"

"A jerk."

"Goddammit! Do you realize how I've worried today?"

"I'm sorry." I walked through the door and closed it. I tried to hug her but she hit me again, on the arm.

"Christ! Never again—do you understand? A simple phone call—a simple phone call! That's all you needed to do, Luke, just call me!"

"No one can ever reach you at the hospital."

"Fuck that," she spat out. "Fuck you! You could have called me here this evening!" She slumped onto the sofa. After a few seconds she added: "Don't ever—ever—do this again, Luke. Or I'll throw your bags out the window."

I sat next to her on the sofa and tried to smile. "I get the message."

"Good." Her eyes curled in my direction. A trace of good humor flashed in them. "At least I know now. You can be a bastard." She leaned into me and feigned hitting my chest, a love tap. "Hope I didn't hurt you before."

"I'll live."

"Maybe I should take a look at your wounds." Her hand found its way inside my shirt.

"Sorry, Lola," I whispered above her head. "Really."

"At least you're all right."

Our lips met. Her tongue burned. I didn't have the heart—or guts—to tell her that I'd be leaving again. Tomorrow.

I put in a phone call to Weiss and informed him that a personal matter had come up. He barely said a word in response. When he did his voice was almost toneless.

"You know when the script is due."

"Yes."

"Just don't fuck me up."
He didn't say good-bye.

The coroner's office didn't know. Neither did the police. Then I was referred to Manhattan County's public morgue. They transferred me to three different offices before a woman on the wire was able to trace Billy's name and identification number, replete with an amount owed "to whom it may concern" for the expense of his burial. One hundred forty-seven fifty.

"He's buried?"

"Of course. Three months we keep them in the cooler. Then . . ." Her voice hushed. "Are you a relative?"

"No."

"Good, because I'm afraid he's over in seventeen."

"What's that?"

"Section seventeen, Forest Lawn. Likewise known as potter's field."

It was just a small plot amidst a city of gravestones, Queens. A single, blank slab of bluestone signified the end place for dozens of unknowns. It was stenciled "17." I tried to imagine Billy's name inscribed on it.

Sitting down, I crossed my legs and placed a bunch of wildflowers that I'd bought at the foot of the stone. I thought of Billy's short life, yet, strangely, not of the violence that had permeated it. Rather, it was the memory of his putting his small hand in mine that kept repeating like a visual mantra. The repetition of the image infused me with fear: fear for that delicate balance that binds what we were to what we'll become.

Gravestones all around me were reflecting a bright white light. I rose awkwardly and stretched my legs. They were trembling, like before the First Time. A nest of butterflies fluttered in my gut.

I hoisted my small suitcase and walked back along the trimmed alley of tiny evergreens—past sections sixteen, fifteen, fourteen—past all those men and women in the Potter family.

An hour later I was hovering over them, banking west in a 747 toward Los Angeles.

Part Two

LOS ANGELES

30

The plane descended over the San Gabriel Mountains, passed through that crown of smog L.A. wears most days, as if in penance, then touched down on its runway at LAX with cat's paws. By three P.M. I'd found a dingy little room in a shabby one-story called the Ivanhoe in West Hollywood. The "Hills" might have been a nicer choice if I'd had two-twenty-five a day. Anyway, I hated flowered pink wallpaper.

I rented American, at Rent-A-Wreck; a little Plymouth Reliant. Its horn didn't work, but at least it was cheap: twenty-nine dollars a day. No insurance. I wheeled its ugly frame down Fountain, avoiding Sunset, and turned left onto La Cienega. Its double lane stretched into infinity.

I stopped along the way at a little shack that—once again—resembled a caboose. This one was red, with tables that were shaded by umbrellas on an outside deck. With the thick smell of exhaust in my nostrils, I wolfed an avocado-and-sprouts sandwich.

In stop-and-go traffic I made my way to the address I'd looked up: 6750½ La Cienega, the Hall of Records. It was a smaller building than I'd expected, until I found out its main resource of records was a three-story library built underground. I was led down through several hallways to the appropriate desk, in Section C, Sales and Ownership, and with great efficiency was provided with a wooden chair and a microfilm machine. A tight-lipped young woman in a blue blazer and skirt handed me a microfilm cassette labeled "T, #4." Half an hour later I'd scanned through more documents of sale than I ever care to see again: all of the Ts in Los Angeles County. Finally, I found what I was looking for: the photographed documents of ownership for Trion Entertainment, Inc.

But I was not prepared for what became evident in the small print. One of the owners of Trion Entertainment was Farrer Enterprises, Poughkeepsie, New York, and A. J. Farrer had signed. With his one arm, I thought. Two co-owners were listed: Lithen, Howard, and Spear Entertainment, with a signature by William Howard; and a company known only as the Group. It was that signature that surprised me most. An actress of great repute had penned her name in tiny letters: Anna O'Reilly. I smiled a moment and thought of that freckled girl I'd grown older with: those incredible blue eyes, and that smile, and those breasts. Age and experience had seemed to nurture her beauty; or perhaps I simply had the healthy habit of being attracted to women who were my own age.

Then my smile faded. It dawned on me that the couple killed in Black River, Michigan, seven years ago, were named O'Reilly. Julia's maiden name. A surge of adrenaline jolted me. Anna and Julia . . .

I kept reading.

Apparently, the offices of Lithen, Howard, and Spear had merged with Farrer Enterprises and the Group. L.H.S. was a talent agency that had been bought for what was noted as "half its estimated net worth"—in cash—by the two other corporations, and the merger gave equal ownership to the three of them. The merger had taken place in May 1980, eight years ago. According to the records, no broker had been involved. These facts festered in my mind while I had the documents copied six times, at three dollars a page. It ran me fifty-four bucks.

In rush hour traffic I sputtered out along Wilshire Boulevard, through herds of leased Mercedes, to Century City. There, clumps of squat, shining cubes of glass and metal formed a series of connecting complexes joined by cement parks and elevated walkways. Trees sprouted like decoration. Parking lots roiled busily under every building; salesmen, stars, secretaries, and savvy executives left their status behind, collected a ticket, then rose from the depths on elevators to their appointed caste.

Sunglasses seemed to be in favor, and linen suits. I saw Don Johnson clones half a dozen times on my way through the lobby of 2122. I rode up with two of him to the fifteenth floor. They peered at my dark socks with a smile.

"New York," one of them muttered.

Trion Entertainment occupied a luxurious suite of offices. The walls were mauve, the huge plants a fertile green; the trim was pink, desks black; ashtrays chrome, like the smiles.

I asked one of the two receptionists for Mr. Howard. When she said he was "in conference" and that the next available time on his calendar was next week, I pulled the same stunt I had with Decker. I asked her to hand him a copy of the records I'd just copied. She complied.

It was a good tactic. Within moments he was standing over me in the reception area. He was youngish, thirty-eight or forty, and upwardly mobile with a vengeance. His pants and jacket were made of a shiny linen that absorbed the color of the walls.

"What's this supposed to mean?" he asked with a steel smile, waving the copies in front of my face.

"Your office," I replied.

It looked out over a river of automobiles that ran their slow course along Wilshire. Howard sat at his desk before speaking. He didn't suggest that I sit, too, but I did.

"So?" he asked.

"So I need information, is all."

"You think you can barge in here—"

"Yes."

I didn't like this guy, didn't mind being rude.

"I can," I added, "because I think you'd rather talk with me than with the cops."

"And who the hell are you?"

"It really doesn't matter. I'm working privately, but the cops—in New York and L.A.—know I'm here."

So I lied.

"I don't understand."

"Maybe not—maybe not at all." I pointed to the Xeroxed document I'd given him. "Can you describe the man who signed that document?"

"No."

"Why not?"

"I wasn't there when he signed it."

"Who was?"

"I don't know why I should—"

"Because he may be a killer and a smuggler. And much much more."

"Get out of here. I'm calling my lawyer." He put his hand on the phone. I stood and prevented him from lifting the receiver.

"Don't," I said. "All I want is information, no more. Call your lawyer and everything comes out of the closet."

"Like what?" he asked with a childish whine.

I avoided the question. "Were your lawyers present when this document was signed?"

He hedged. "I suppose so."

"Be truthful with me, Howard. I don't care about you, and though I do care about the smuggling you're involved with, I don't think I can do much about it. I'm just looking for one particular child. A little girl named Genna Denington."

He became still. His hand slid limply off the receiver. He rocked back in his soft leather chair.

"I don't think you know who you're talking to."

I tried to hit him from a lateral tack.

"Why did you merge with Farrer and the Group?"

"Money."

"Weren't you doing well?"

"All right."

"Why did they need you?"

"I don't know. Tax write-off, I presume."

"You represent actors here, right?"

"Right."

"Anna O'Reilly?"

He took a breath before answering. "Yes."

"Who are the Group?"

He thought for a moment. "An actors' group."

"I don't believe you."

"You can go to—"

"You represent actors all around the country?"

He stood up. "What is it you want from me?"

"Do you?" I pressed.

"Yes, of course. You can read the trades and find that out."

"I don't have time. Do you operate by computer?"

"Of course. I'm going to call the cops, I don't care what you say—"

"Oh shut up. Do you realize how many children die on those planes, Howard?"

He couldn't hide the sweat. He loosened his collar involuntarily.

"I don't know what you're talking about—" He didn't finish. Two young men in similar suits and ties were standing at his door.

"Any problem, Bill?" one of them asked.

Howard straightened himself. "Get this jerk out of my office. He thinks we have to represent him. He's dead wrong."

Each of the young men felt that it was necessary to hold my elbows as they walked me through the corridors to the elevator. They shoved me onto it and threw me the bird.

I waved good-bye.

31

I gave the parking attendant ten bucks. This bought me an hour parked near the entrance of his garage. As it turns out, it didn't take that long. William Howard ran out through the glass doors that opened into the lot and fidgeted while he waited for his Mercedes. It was scarlet red, easy to follow.

He was too hurried to notice my Reliant. I followed him out to Wilshire, then for half an hour we weaved together through miserable traffic. It took us an arduous hour to fight our way up Bundy, wind west on Sunset, then finally spill out onto Route 1. I found myself gliding with him along the coast toward Malibu. I had no idea where he was leading me. Perhaps he was just going home and heading straight for a tall gin and tonic. Or perhaps it was his lawyer who would be providing cocktails.

He pulled off into a little canyon drive. There was no sign, just a warning: MUD SLIDES. I waited briefly at the bottom of the road, allowing him to get a few turns ahead of me, then forced my shoddy Plymouth to chug its way upward.

The little car that couldn't.

It coughed, it stalled, it started and then coughed again. Steam began to spew from below the hood. A few minutes later I found myself standing at the side of the canyon kicking its doors and cursing its name.

A pickup truck pulled over. An old horse farmer and his wife very nicely offered me a lift to the nearest station, six miles up-canyon. I thanked them and hopped into the back of their pickup. I peered at every house along the way but didn't see Howard's Mercedes until I was almost at the station. He was coming back the other way!

I watched as he made a left onto a tiny dirt road, hidden from the other direction. He'd obviously missed it and had had to turn around. I banged on the glass behind the older couple. They pulled over.

"It's only 'nother quarter mile!" the farmer shouted over the roar of his engine.

"Thank you!" I yelled, and hopped out. "I'll stop by my friends' first."

They watched me as I headed for the dirt road. The woman got out of the cab.

"Those your friends, live up there?"

"Acquaintances," I answered dubiously.

The old man shut his engine off and got out.

"You tell 'em we sorry to call the cops—but we do it again, they make that kinda ruckus. Hell, scared the animals half to death. Half mile all 'round."

"What kind of ruckus?" I asked. My question made the old woman squint at me, hard and long. Her husband watched her.

"You ain't their friend," she said.

I was silent.

"You ain't even from around here."

"No."

"Don't even go on up there, is my advice, son. You don't wanna be their acquaintance."

"Why not?"

She paused awhile, trying to figure a way to say why.

"She's not the way she seems," was all she said.

"C'mon, Hilda." Her husband grabbed her arm and dragged her back to the truck. She got in, but he didn't. Instead, he turned to me and spoke again, quiet and angry: "Those weren't M-80s they were shootin' off up there, like the cops try 'n' tell us. They must think we fools. I know the sounds—I been infantry." That thought absorbed him for a few seconds. He looked at his feet, then up again. "You be careful."

"Thanks."

He started his engine and sped away.

I walked for what seemed like miles, uphill, dust seeping and chafing under my trousers. The road wound up and around a broad knoll that loomed out over the distant ocean. I climbed the knoll, carefully, and found myself hovering over the roof of a large cabin. Wicker rocking chairs swayed below me on a front porch that was made of slabs of rock and built into the ground. From there, an angry sun could be seen colliding with the Pacific. On the other side of the cabin was a closed garage and a small parking area, where Howard's car was parked. There was an elegant pool behind the garage. Though the pool area was mostly obscured, I could see a woman dressed in nurse's garb walking to and fro, picking up glasses, books, towels. The sun's warmth had faded, swimming gear no longer needed. I wondered if there were children. Beyond the pool was a large fenced-in field. In it, two sleek horses danced together, round and round in circles. Howard stood on a stave of the fence, his jacket off, watching a woman whose back was to me. She wore blue jeans and riding boots and carried a saddle she'd just taken off one of the horses. Though she was smaller than I'd expected, Anna O'Reilly easily hoisted the saddle up onto the fence. Her red hair floated behind her like part of the sunset.

They talked for a moment, way out of range. I tried to make my way down the other side of the knoll toward the garage, so that I could hear them, but their conversation broke and they started walking to the house. She motioned for Howard to walk around to the front porch while she went inside. Distracted, he headed in my direction.

I scurried up the slope in time to disappear behind it before he could see me. I listened as he scuffed along a stone path that bordered the house, then heard him slump into a wicker chair. It creaked under his nervous weight. He tapped his foot.

Fifteen tapped-out minutes later Anna O'Reilly opened a sliding glass door and walked out onto the porch. I peeked around a very prickly bush and saw that the "nurse" had followed with a tray of drinks. Anna handed one to Howard, took one herself, then held the door open for the older woman.

"Thanks, Ruby," she said in that so very familiar, slightly southern drawl. Everyone in America had seen at least one of her movies, or had seen her innocently accept an Academy Award. Now here I was, peeking at her from behind a bush.

At first the porch roof obscured my view so that I could see only her bare feet. When she sat down I saw that she'd showered and changed. She wore a gauzy white skirt and blouse. A blue turquoise necklace rattled around her neck. Her skin was tanned and freckled, her eyes green, her smile ingenuous. She used it on Howard.

"Why are you here, Bill?"

"Something's come up."

"Take it up with the others. You've kinda fucked up by coming here, if you know what I mean. Did anyone follow?"

"No one followed."

"Well," she sighed, "you're here. Big as life. Say what you have to say."

"Someone's looking for the baby."

She sat stringing her hair through her fingers. She said in that winsome southern whisper: "Yeah?"

"He's—he's a young guy. Thirty, maybe."

"I don't care how old he is, Bill."

"He came to my office."

"When?"

"This afternoon."

"Calmly, now. What did he say?"

"He handed me some copies of Trion's documents of sale—then he asked me about Farrer."

She sat up, slowly. "What'd he ask?"

"What he looked like, for some reason, and if I was present when Farrer signed the merger contracts."

She thought for a moment. She rattled the ice in her glass.

"He's a smart guy, Bill. What'd you say?"

"I said I didn't know, of course. I wasn't there. Not really. You both kept me in the other room, remember?"

"Hmmm." She breathed. Then, quietly: "With good reason."

"That's not our biggest problem, though. He—hell, Anna, he seems to know about the shipments."

She said in a strained whisper, "Jesus! Here you are, doing what I asked you never to do, Bill—coming to my house and risking someone following."

"I'm sorry. He seemed to know a lot—too much. Not enough to put it all together—not yet."

"Do me a favor, let us decide that."

Howard slurped part of his drink while Anna contemplated. "Anyway," he added. "Sorry. I thought you needed to know."

She sighed. "Who is this guy?"

"I don't know."

"You didn't even get his name?"

Howard said feebly: "No."

"What about the baby?"

"He called her Genna Denington."

Anna O'Reilly slumped back in the wicker chair and pulled her fine legs up to her chest. She rested her chin on her knees. Though the pose was gentle, her eyes were not. They looked like the barrels of two loaded rifles.

"Christ, another one," she whispered.

"Yeah," Howard reiterated.

"You're sure it wasn't—?"

"I'm sure. I know that Denington's in town, but it wasn't him. I have his picture."

Anna smiled, slightly. "Red called. We may have found him. Anyway, they've got his address."

Howard tried to share the smile, but Anna's gaze turned cold. He turned away from her, sipped from his glass.

A baby's whimper drifted out of the second-story window that was closest to me. Like the start of an engine, the tiny voice rose to a piercing cry and filled the house. Anna groaned, then went inside, leaving Howard alone on the porch. He finished his drink. Then he finished Anna's drink. When the door finally swung open Anna stood in the shadows cuddling a crying baby in her arms. She rocked it and sang a little song, then let Howard pinch its cheek. Wearing a strange smile that seemed glued to her face,

Anna carried the child out onto a patch of brown lawn that faced the canyon and the dying sun. The queer red hues of the sunset lent an eerie glow to the tiny face of Genna Denington.

Anna O'Reilly turned and unleashed that strange smile on Bill Howard.

"Get out of here," she whispered.

32

She watched Howard's car disappear down the canyon road. The trail of dust that he left in his wake surged up like smoke from a California brush fire and reflected the twilight. It changed colors with the swirling beauty of a chemical experiment. Deep orange, first tinged by a putrid yellow, was mixed with a grayish blue that swept in from the shadows. The result was an ethereal purple-green that darkened, then dissolved, then gave way to night. Wisps of purple dotted the dim sky like vagrant pieces of that wake that had tried to float to heaven. Curiously, I hoped that Anna had been savoring the sight with me. More than likely she'd just been watching for any signs that Howard had been followed. I gave her no signs. Quietly, she went inside.

I waited for another half hour before moving, nearly falling asleep on the knoll. Then with stiff knee joints I skidded on my heels down the dusty bank and hiked around on the road to the garage. I found myself crawling under Anna's kitchen window, trouncing a few rhododendrons. From there I could hear the network news mumbling from a back room. Dan Rather mentioned something about an arms scandal. Over that, and closer to the window, Anna suddenly spoke in a tense, controlled whisper. At first I thought she was speaking to me, but soon it was clear that she was on the telephone.

"No!" she lashed out. "Jesus, Dooby, when're you going to realize—I'm worth more than both the others put together."

Silence.

"Still not enough."

More silence.

"I am being reasonable. I don't need to do their picture. Not for what they're offerin'—don't you see?" She whined: "I got a baby now."

In the distance Dan Rather said: "Good night."

"Shit," Anna continued. "OK. I'll go as low as two, but no less. Fair?"

A short silence.

"Fair?"

She laughed, so sweetly that an indescribable sadness overwhelmed me.

"Yes, you're still my agent. Don't be stupid, Doobs. I love you. You just want every package that comes along."

I crawled to the open garage, making as little noise as possible, but within seconds Anna opened the back door and stared out into the night. I worked my way behind a dormant BMW, a couple of yards from her trash cans. It was a close call, but she didn't seem to see me. When she went back inside I peered out from the shadows again. Through a tall window that connected the first and second floors I could see Anna ascend a wooden staircase and enter a bedroom whose window overlooked the backyard. A light switched on in the room and she began to undress. A song suddenly wafted through the window, Patsy Cline's mellifluous "Crazy."

I emerged from the garage and quickly snuck around its corner. Out of view from Anna's window, I tiptoed close to the pool's fence, then, to the slow country rhythm, bounded softly across an expanse of horse shit toward the barns.

There was a dirt road that connected the driveway with a sliding door at the back of the largest of the three barns, the middle one. I unhitched the sliding door and rolled it back gently. It still made an awful noise. I froze and listened. Patsy sang to me: "Crazy, for tryin'. . ."

Yes indeed.

I entered the barn and lit a match. Bales of hay were stacked everywhere, on all sides. The match went out, so I lit another one. It was then that I realized the middle structure was connected by inner walkways to the other barns on either side. Both the left and right walls had doors built into them that had been covered up with bales of hay.

I lit another match and made sure there were no cracks in the walls or windows. Then I cleared a space on the dirt floor and piled some hay and started a small fire. It gave me light long enough to shift a stack of heavy bales away from one of the doors. There was a metal latch. I opened it.

Darkness. I had one match left.

I struck sulfur to flint and a small flame cast its dim light on a hundred wooden crates. The nearest to me was already open. Russian symbols had been stenciled on its side and on its lid. Inside, a half-dozen pistols had been packed in heavy wads of waxy paper. Some of the paper lay on the ground; a few of the pistols had been taken.

The match fizzled, but it didn't matter. Someone was breathing behind me. Long, steady breaths.

"I guess I'm not very good at this," I whispered.

"I guess you're not," breathed Anna O'Reilly.

She switched a flashlight on. It silhouetted the Kalashnikov that she was aiming at my head.

33

On our way out she shined her light on a small apparatus that resembled a gas lamp. It was riveted into the ground near the sliding door, obscured by its dark color. There was another one on the other side of the door.

"Little portable electric eyes," she chimed, as if giving me a casual tour. "Neat little gadgets."

"Really neat."

She motioned with her gun for me to step outside, then gave me a small poke with it. I felt like her horse. She rode my back up the dirt road to the driveway, then to the main house. The nurse stood in the back doorway, waiting, a phone in her hands.

"There's been no answer," she said in a thick Irish accent.

"Try again," Anna ordered.

The nurse dialed a long series of digits, then held a small black box to the mouthpiece and beeped it three times. When she hung up, we all went inside.

I turned left into the living room and was directed to sit on one of those Japanese futon-type couches. It was hard as nails. Anna sat in a designer chair across the room from me. She had a curiously wistful manner, a country girl with a lot on her mind. Her gun was what was on my mind. It kept staring at me.

The nurse dragged the phone in on a long extension wire and placed it on a table next to Anna.

"I'll see after the child," she said, then went upstairs.

Anna glanced at the phone with expectation, then worriedly shifted her eyes to the gun. They were big and green against her pale skin. She rolled them up and leveled her gaze at me and winced.

"Whoever it is isn't calling back," I said.

"He will." Her Texas accent stretched out each word.

"You may have to shoot me yourself."

"Oh, just shut up."

I was quiet for a moment. Far in the distance the Pacific crashed against Malibu. The muted blows against the shore faintly resembled a gravedigger's shovel strokes. The sounds made me remember all the graves that'd been dug in this case—remember how the waiflike woman sitting across from me had been so much a part of all that dying. I wasn't quite sure how. But I knew. A sudden rage swept into me, singed my guts, then passed, as quickly as it had come. It left behind a dull hatred.

"Have you renamed her?" I asked with such quiet anger that it engendered a whispered response.

"Dolly."

"Dolly," I repeated.

"It was my mother's name."

"In Black River."

She took in a deep breath. When she spilled it out she said: "Who are you?"

My anger snapped for a moment. I had to chuckle.

"A filmmaker, believe it or not."

She laughed a cruel, sardonic laugh. The gun kept pointing. I lost my grin.

"Why did you follow Bill Howard? Why are you here?"

"You know why."

She thought for a minute. "The baby's mine now."

"Why? I mean, with all the others you have access to—all those babies . . ."

Her eyes hardened and burrowed into me. "What others?"

"The ones you've been smuggling with a group euphemistically called Farrer Enterprises."

"I see."

"With all of them—why take Genna? Why keep her? Let me have the girl. Let me bring her back to her mother—"

"You know where her mother is?" she asked.

"No. But I can find her."

"No, I don't believe you can." She spoke with a weary finality: "Not anymore."

Terror filled my chest like a liquid. "Julia," was all I said.

"Did she get you, too?" Anna asked quietly.

"Get me?"

"Under her spell."

I didn't answer. The waves in the distance now crashed like remote heartbeats.

"None of us know where Julia is," Anna said.

I breathed a tremendous sigh. Cold beads of sweat ran down the center of my back, as if that brief fear of losing Julia had coalesced, then been wrung from my body with a single shudder. To lose another woman would've broken me.

I tried to relax, to focus.

"Who's us?"

She answered my question with a question. "Why so much interest in my girl?"

"She's not your girl. I should know, I delivered her." Anna inched closer on her seat. Her eyes widened. I continued: "Then I watched as her brother was killed—the first thing Genna ever saw. A big, tall man with red hair killed him. A friend of yours, no doubt. Killed an old woman, too. Then he stole the baby." I added: "I feel close to her, Anna."

Anna O'Reilly's mind worked backward and the process was revelatory. "You didn't die?" she whispered.

"No. I didn't die."

She dialed the phone, a local call. Someone came on and she asked for her husband. There was a pause, then someone else must have come on the other end. Anna listened for a brief moment. When she spoke her voice was all quiet nerves.

"I don't care if he's on the crane, Stan. Get him a mobile phone—now!"

She waited, not looking at me. Finally her husband was at the other end of the line.

"Jack . . ." She pleaded, then begged him to break the shoot and come home. When she hung up she fell back into her chair and smiled at me. "He's coming."

"Bully for Jack."

"He'll know what to do."

"I'm relieved."

"You're a wiseass, aren't you?"

"Not really, just scared. I don't much like the fact that you've been calling him to come over and pull the trigger."

"I'd pull the trigger if you forced me to."

"I don't doubt it."

"Anyway," she added, "we haven't just been calling Jack."

"Who else?"

But she didn't respond.

We stared at one another as if sharing a scene in one of her movies. Here I was, finally one-on-one with Anna O'Reilly. She was freckled and petite, with long, silky red hair that flowed over her shoulders and touched two soft globes that swayed under her blouse. She reminded me of Julia.

"Do I look like her?" she asked, reading my mind.

"Yes."

"So it's been said."

"Anna?"

"Yes?"

"Can I see her? Can I see Genna?"

"Dolly," she said coldly.

"Please. I don't know what's going to happen to me. Just let me see her before I leave."

She sat very still for a good long while. An answer finally came. "No tricks."

"No tricks."

She poked the gun in my side again as we walked upstairs. Genna was in a room to the left. She lay asleep in a large, expensive wooden cradle. Frilly sheets puffed out of it like sea froth. The nurse was rocking the cradle.

"It's OK," Anna said to the nurse. The matronly woman yielded her place with quiet disapproval.

I sat in a warm chair and looked down on Genna. Her eyes were closed, tongue partly out. It was a goofy expression, one that I'd carry with me as long as I could. Genna's tiny fists were clenched. I pried one open and stroked her soft hand. When the other fist opened, so did her baby blues. She smiled hazily at me; I thought I saw a question in those eyes, then she closed them again, and her fist closed around my finger. Anna allowed me to sit like that for a while, rocking the cradle. She still held the gun on me, but its barrel was down, averted from the baby. Then a wind blew up from the ocean and through the window and seemed to sweep away her tolerance.

"That's enough," she ordered. "Get up."

I got up. The wind swept in again, whirling some pages of blue stationery off a bureau and onto the floor. I picked them up and placed them back on the bureau before the realization hit me. This was the same stationery that Julia had used to write me from Los Angeles. I lifted the pages in my hands and smelled them. The fragrance was wildflowers.

"What are you doing?" Anna demanded.

"Nice smell," I said.

The top drawer was partly open. I opened it farther and saw that the box of stationery sat next to a plastic container of scented flowers meant to lend a fresh scent to the drawer's undergarments.

"Get out of there!" Anna demanded.

She went to the drawer and closed it. Just then we both looked down through the window to see headlights brightening the driveway. A black convertible Jeep screeched to a halt behind the BMW. Anna leaned toward the window—

"Jack!" she shouted.

Her gun lowered for a split second. It was time.

I grabbed her wrist with my left hand and jerked my right knee into her ribs. The gun went off, shattering the window. Through it, as I struggled with Anna, I saw her husband grab a pistol from his glove compartment. I shook Anna's gun to the floor and kicked it away, but she dove for it with a maniacal lunge. I jumped on top of her and we rolled together on the floor. For an instant I envisioned our tumble as kinky sex, but then her hands found the trigger again and she squeezed another shot off. The bullet whizzed under my head and ricocheted around the baby's room. Genna woke—crying. I managed to pry the gun out of Anna's small hand and get to my knees. But she was up in a flash. She kicked me in the groin, hard. I nearly buckled but managed to grab her leg and force her to fall to a kneeling position. Regret pulsed through me for a split second—but I had no choice. I swung the pistol into Anna's face. Her front teeth buckled and snapped. Blood spewed from her million-dollar mouth.

She sat down with a thump, shaking with her mouth closed. Then she screamed and spit out a spray of blood and ivory.

"My teeth!" she howled. "My teeth!!"

I grabbed her from behind, seconds before her husband bounded through the bedroom door with his gun extended. I stuck the barrel of my gun into Anna O'Reilly's ear.

"Oh my God," her husband said, trembling. "Oh my God."

Anna wept in my arms, limp and beaten. I'd hit her where it counts. Blood flowed from her mouth and over my arm.

"Don't shoot her," Jack whispered, and placed his gun on the floor.

"Kick it over here," I said shakily. He did as I asked.

A large shadow loomed behind him in the hall.

"Get her in here!" I demanded.

The nurse stepped out of the hall and into the room, carrying a shotgun with a defiant swagger. She seemed more frightening than the others somehow. It took her several moments to relinquish the rifle. When she did I ordered them all to sit on the floor and keep their hands up.

"Oh God, her mouth," Jack whimpered. He turned to the nurse and whined: "Where's Red?"

"He never answered."

"Shut up," I told them. "You're going to talk to me, now; tell me what the hell is going on here!"

"Never." The nurse was cold as stone.

Jack just stared at me.

I stood and grabbed those pieces of blue stationery.

"Julia wrote me on this same stationery! From this room! Goddammit! Why was she here?" I lowered the gun at Anna and faced Jack. "Why did Julia come back?"

Jack looked at me as if I was stupid.

"Family," was all he said.

I stared at Anna again. Blood trickled in a steady stream from the corners of her mouth. It soaked her white blouse, pressing it against her full breasts so that they shone in scarlet relief. I was reminded of one of the roles she had played where she'd been drenched in pig's blood. As they had in the movie, her sad eyes gazed up at me with a potent passion; she was not beaten, would never be, not till the day she died. I'd seen that look, though softer, in Julia's eyes, seconds after she'd given birth. And now it was easy to notice that Genna had inherited those same eyes. And a look—a melancholy look—that could launch a thousand ships; or just one, just me.

"Family," I repeated wearily.

But there was no more time for conversation.

Another car tore into the driveway and skidded to a stop. I hobbled to the window and saw four men burst from the doors of a Cadillac. One of them was huge—he towered over the car as he emerged from it. He was holding an automatic weapon in his hand, a thick-barreled, long-stemmed pistol. Streaming red hair poured over his enormous shoulders. But the top of his head was as bald as a monk's. He lifted a pair of devastating green eyes up at me and pointed his weapon toward the window. I should have jumped but instead I just stood there, transfixed.

"You're dead," he said to me, in bleak baritone.

There were steps on the stairs. Metal rubbed together like a premonition—a gun's bolt. I took one more split-second glance at Genna—then lunged for the door. The nurse tried to trip me but I jumped her leg and burst out of Genna's bedroom as one of the four men was ascending the stairs. He was pale and dark-haired and black-eyed. The clothes he wore were leather. He squeezed two shots off and they hit the molding that framed the door to the master bedroom. I smashed into the door but it stayed closed. The second that it took me to turn the knob allowed Jack to grab his gun off the floor and fire at me. He missed once, but his second shot scraped my arm as I collapsed into the room.

More feet on the staircase.

"*I want him!*" That dark, powerful bass register unleashed from the big man's lungs seemed to shake the house from its foundation. It shook me. It was difficult not to resign my fate to him.

But I couldn't. I got up just seconds before he reached the

doorway. Thunder blasted from his pistol. He was swinging it wildly. One of the scattering bullets caught me in my heel as I dove headfirst through the second-story window.

I screamed the whole way down.

The roof over the front porch broke my fall. I slid sideways over it and landed on the slab stone like a sack of wet laundry. There was movement behind the front door, so I got up on my sore legs and ran left under the roof until I was out of view. Then I sprinted right—into the darkness—and rolled down a gully. Gunfire fell like a hailstorm at my heels. But whoever was firing now was firing blindly. They couldn't see me, not yet. Not until their car crashed up and onto the back porch and aimed its beams into the brush. Then four silhouetted figures appeared at the rim of the canyon with their weapons poised. Someone switched off the car motor and a sudden silence squeezed around me, like a vise. The figures spread out along the rim. I was pinned—ten open yards from the tumbling shadows of the canyon.

I hefted a cold rock in my palm and threw it uphill. When it rolled and struck a sapling four machine guns aimed there and sprayed their fire. I seized the moment by hurtling myself downhill. I hit the ground with a thud and heard as I tumbled: "There he is!" Dirt exploded around me. A bullet must have hit a rock and sent chips flying, because I found myself pulling a piece of stone out of an indenture in my forehead. Blood trickled into the corners of my eyes and over my nose—but I made it to the woods, out of direct light.

They were coming, barreling downhill. A few shots were fired in my direction, but they couldn't see me. Then, suddenly, a flashlight beam waved around ahead of me like a lonesome spotlight looking for a soliloquy. It was coming from the upper window of Anna's house.

No Hamlet here; I turned and fired at the window. I probably missed the house. Bullets sliced the air around the spot where my gun had exploded—but already I was moving laterally along the cleft of the canyon, over an old streambed and into the woods. The flashlight retreated long enough for me to run beyond its reach. When its beam reappeared it only served to illuminate the four dark figures that pursued, imbuing the scrawny forest around them with a theatrical inertia. I crept quickly through a moonlit grove of brush pine that somehow reminded me of my youth, the days when Jim and Charlie and I would sprint the Catskill trails. There was a certain lonely enchantment under the low boughs, as there had been on those trails twenty years ago. A bond as strong as music: a bounding rhythm. I found it now, again. I found it and followed its traversing beat down the wall of a steep gully, splashing hard through low water, running up again against the roots of a dusty hill, in step with all the memories I'd lose if a bullet caught me now and took me down—in sync with my little white twelve-year-old ghost and his thin, resilient legs.

The noise behind me faded. I lost them.

It took me hours to wind through those high woods that paralleled the main road. I followed above its vague outline as it writhed and descended toward a black-and-blue ocean. Once, I stopped to ease the throbbing in my heel and heard two cars pass below. A searchlight shone up into the woods where I lingered, gracing them with a surreal blue light. It touched upon a bird's nest like an errant ray of bottled moonlight. When they'd passed I crawled to the edge of the embankment.

I'd reached a sharp curve that I recognized, where a squat dark shadow sat at the edge of the road like a sleeping Cerberus. But it didn't bark. It didn't start, either. Old Reliant was still just a vague lump of steel, its purpose a memory. I jumped off and into the woods just in time to avoid Jack's Jeep as it cruised back up the canyon. The powerful beam of its searchlight painted the contours of the forest with a fleeting hoarfrost. The Cadillac, never far behind, pulled to a stop. Both vehicles inspected my dead rent-a-car, then moved on.

So did I. When I finally made it through the tearing shrub brush to a knoll overlooking Route 1, the sky was just showing signs of brightening along the horizon. Three, maybe four A.M.

I had to hit the ground rapidly when the Jeep and Cadillac reappeared. They pulled a U-turn in a dusty turnaround below me, then slowly cruised back up the canyon road. That meant it was time to make a move. With my heel now numb with pain, my arm grazed and bleeding, my forehead feeling as if a dagger were jutting out from it, I slid down the sandy knoll on my ass. It seemed to be the only real estate I owned that didn't ache. When I reached the roadside I peered carefully around and up the canyon road entrance. No headlights. I took a deep breath, then sprinted out across the near-empty highway. A truck's horn whined from far off, perhaps worrying that I might throw myself in front of it.

When I reached the other side I didn't stop. I jumped a fence that bordered the beach and plodded along in the thick sand to a spot beyond the nearest dune. From there, I looked back out along the highway.

There they were.

They'd probably heard the truck's horn and come back. The Cadillac parked in the turnaround and the big man got out, carrying his weapon. In the headlights his hair looked like a bright red wig. Though I knew he couldn't see me, he looked in my direction—he knew just where I was. Then he and his black leather partner hopped onto the runners of the Jeep. Their guns swung out like fins. The Jeep skidded in the sand, then barreled out across the highway and crashed through the flimsy beach fence.

I ran deep into the winding dunes. They loomed like giants around me—huge shadows. A mist filled their cleaves and gaps. The sand was cold. Occasionally old wooden steps led up and through their soft fissures, but I had no idea where the paths were taking me. I just tripped and scuffed and ran like hell.

The Jeep drove along the beach, and its light shone through cracks and crevices and touched on me once. From behind there were voices, whispers that drifted through the dunes' winding tunnels. I was scared—there didn't seem to be anywhere to go. I felt like a rat in a maze, a maze with steps, steps and stones that were leading me gradually up and over the crest of the highest dune. From there, through the weeds, I could see the Jeep far below. A high tide had blocked its access to the other side of the dune's ridge.

It was quite a drop. A dark ocean roiled up against the shore. The light from the Jeep sprang in my direction and I lunged to avoid it—lunged the wrong way.

I hit cold, wet sand that gave in under me. I rode a wave of it innocently enough, thinking it would settle after a few yards. It didn't. A whole precarious ridge gave way, and I dropped through midair and landed several seconds later—a tremendous slop of sand coming down on me like wet cement. I tried to get up but my legs were trapped.

Voices, overhead. Sand scuffed and fell from where I'd just stood, many, many feet up. A flashlight beam poked around above me. Luckily I was guarded on one side by a small tuft of weeds that hung over me like headfeathers. When the flashlight pointed in another direction I took the opportunity to bury the rest of my dilapidated body in mounds of Malibu. I tried to imagine that I was actually enjoying the organic wonder of my immersion.

I must have tried pretty hard. I woke up hours later, in full daylight, frozen into the earth. The wonder was gone. What remained were buzzing flies and that strange and sticky taste of near death that had glued my lips shut.

34

Once I'd wrenched myself from the hungry sand I was confronted with another slight problem. I was teetering on the sandy ledge of a steep-sided old dune. It looked like it'd been blasted and soot-streaked like those elegant prewar buildings south of Twenty-third. Somehow, I wished I was hovering on one of those old ledges, looking down over Fifth Avenue, on all those girls in business suits and sneakers walking to work.

Anyway.

Up or down. Either way was a drag. I chose up, but when I sank deep into my first foothold, the hill chose down. All the way down. I slid, I tumbled, performed a one-and-a-half gainer. I finally landed in an ocean puddle just a few feet from sharp rock. I floated there awhile. A few sea gulls drifted over me like angelic vultures.

A young blond couple strolled by holding hands and laughing like a Pepsodent commercial. Their smiles faded when they saw me rise out of the puddle. The girl tugged hard on her boyfriend's hand—she wanted to get out of there. I looked like hell, I knew. But the blond boy's baby blues showed more feeling than I might have expected. He squinted at me.

"You all right?" he shouted over the surf.
"All right," I answered.
He waved good-bye.

I was already trudging down Route 1 when I realized that my wallet was gone, buried somewhere back under the shoreline. In it had been one hundred and forty dollars, my last credit card, and all my identification, including a driver's license replete with a silly picture that had been pressed in plastic on its right corner. It'd been the only photo taken of me in the last few years. Except for the one by that little man in Poughkeepsie.

I ripped my shirt open. Jack's bullet had only grazed the flesh in my upper right arm and left a cut that was healing poorly. It resembled a nightmare rainbow: a red tear in my skin surrounded by greenish white pus that was circled by blue and yellow bruises. Also, my heel had bled inside my right sole. Washed in salt water, blood had soaked through and tinted the whole sneaker. A never-ending flow of sand spilled out of the bottom of my chafing trousers like cells of my own disintegrating identity.

I walked—walked ten miles or more. Finally a sign declared that I'd arrived at Will Rogers State Beach. There, among a ridge of beach shacks that looked out over the ocean, I homed in on a group of young blond teens and managed to convince them to drive me in their daddy's convertible back to the Ivanhoe. I offered them ten dollars for my safe delivery. They talked me up to twenty.

I sat in the back seat between two breasty seventeen-year-olds and had the queer feeling that I'd died and been reincarnated inside a Beach Boys song. We sped along the shore, swayed east onto the Santa Monica Freeway, followed it to Route 110, cruised north a few minutes, then circled west onto the Hollywood Freeway: a huge U-turn. When we arrived at the Ivanhoe, just a few bleak blocks off of Santa Monica Boulevard, the kids waited as I picked up my backup key from an incredulous desk clerk. The balance of my money was in a sock in my suitcase. I got out twenty and handed it to the driver of the convertible.

"Lay off whatever you been drinkin'," he said to me, then sped away. Their cackles faded as they turned the corner.

A shower was foremost on my mind, but I forced myself to

rummage through the notebook I'd brought and dial the number Cussone had suggested I call in case of trouble.

555-2315.

A gruff voice chewed his name like cow cud.

"Sansino."

"Detective Sansino, my name's Luke Byman."

He didn't answer for a few seconds.

"Hello?" I asked.

"Yeah, I'm here." Some paper shuffled. "Got a note here that warns you might call. From—what is it?—Cussone, Homicide, Nyork?"

"Right." There was another pause.

"Well?" He was chewing tobacco. I heard him spit into a can. After I told him my story he waited a moment before responding.

"Very interesting. But you know what you just did?"

"What?"

"You just accused Pollyanna of arms running."

"Yeah, I guess—"

"It sounds like horseshit."

"There was a lot of that up there."

"Don't get cute."

"I assure you, Sansino, I don't look cute. I have a grazed arm and a hole in my heel and have half of Malibu in my shorts. Please, Detective, I need your help. Just come out there with me. Now."

A small squirting sound was his response—then the ring of his spit hitting in the can.

"Where are you?"

"West Hollywood. But I don't have a car."

He didn't seem to care.

"1600 Beaudry, downtown. Twenty minutes," he said, then hung up.

I was there in thirty. A cab dropped me in front of a squat little two-story slab of cement that was passing for a police station. He was waiting for me, a small Mexican-American with a flat upper lip and a mean little smile. He wore a checkered golfer's hat and a powder-blue polyester suit. It seemed to clash with his two-tone squad car and the harness around his shoulders.

"You look like hell," he said, then motioned to the squad car. "Get in."

I got in. He slid softly into the driver's seat next to me.

"I'm off duty now. Maybe I can get this over with in time for a few holes."

"I don't play golf."

"Wiseguy," he muttered.

I sniffed a little, then realized what I smelled. I'd never taken that shower.

"Shit! Man—you stink," Sansino whined as we sped back out onto the freeway.

It was four P.M. when we turned up into the canyon, nearly twenty tiring hours since my Reliant had overheated on the side of the road. It still sat in the same spot, a little shorter than it had been before. Its tires were gone.

I reached into my pocket and pulled out the crumpled Rent-A-Wreck contract and waved it in Sansino's face.

"See? That was my rental. It overheated."

"You walked the rest of the way?"

"An old couple—farmers—gave me a lift to the station, six miles up. I walked from there."

He drove without responding. Six miles later we missed the turn to Anna's. Annoyed, Sansino swung his squad car around, then turned onto the dirt road.

"Slowly," I cautioned. "We don't want to kick up a lot of dust."

Sansino didn't seem to care. He sped up and around the twisting curves until we reached the knoll. Slowly, then, he crept around it, onto Anna's blacktop driveway.

But there were no cars in it, or in the garage. All the doors and windows of the house were locked shut. There weren't even any horses in the barn.

"Look." I pointed. "The horse shit's fresh."

"A real Sherlock Holmes."

We knocked on the front and back doors. No answer. I walked the length of the stone porch to try to find some indications of the gunfire that had chased me down the gulley. But the only remnant of the night's violence was a set of tire tracks embedded in the brown lawn that looked out over the lip of the canyon—and the footprints smudged around them in the grass.

Passing the pool, we tiptoed across the field of shit to check the barn. Its sliding panels were all locked solid, but a fresh set of tracks plowed heavily out from the middle barn through the burnished soil and back up onto the driveway.

"Looks like a truck." I pointed again.

"Yeah," Sansino said, kneeling and running his finger along one of the treadprints. He didn't dare look at me. He might have betrayed that he was curious now. "Doesn't prove anything," he added perfunctorily.

"No."

"So." He stood up and cased the barn.

"So?"

"Stay here."

He followed the tracks and disappeared. I remained in place while he drove his car around, parked it, then opened the trunk. He rummaged through it and came back to me. He stood staring at the structure, a crowbar in his left hand. He handed it to me and spoke softly.

"So break it open. But if Anna O'Reilly should come back, I'll have to arrest you."

"Thanks."

He shrugged. "You must understand."

"They're not coming back," I told him, but was nevertheless discomfited.

Ten minutes later I'd snapped the rigid lock and broken a few redwood staves. The panel wouldn't slide open, so I broke a few more staves and climbed through the hole. Before Sansino crawled in, I used the crowbar to smash the electric eyes, just for the hell of it.

"What was all that noise?" he asked in the darkness.

"Flashlight," I said.

He went out to his car and grabbed a light and climbed back into the barn. I pointed to the now defunct electric eyes.

"These are what tripped me up before."

"Jesus," he whispered, "expensive."

I led him to the right side of the barn and heaved several bales of hay away from the hidden door. It, too, was locked, tighter than it had been before. I smashed the wood panels with the crowbar and worked up a good sweat breaking through. The flesh wound in my arm began to bleed again. But all of it was pain without gain.

The room was empty. Nothing had been left behind, not a book of matches, a gum wrapper, a bullet casing, a footprint.

Nothing comes of nothing.

"Here I was just getting excited," Sansino needled with his malicious smile.

"Shit," was my only response.

"That's all we've really found. Some tire tracks and a whole lotta horse shit." He gestured with his light. "Let's go."

We went. Sansino wouldn't let me break into the house, but it didn't matter. I knew that Anna and Jack had fled and had taken Genna with them. And William Howard had by now been called away on a sudden business trip. I would check, of course, as I would check Beverly Design, where Ralph Denington had bought that tweed jacket that he'd left in Julia's apartment. But I knew I didn't have much hope of finding much through either source.

I was nowhere, again. I had no idea what to do next, where to go, or why.

And I had no idea who'd started tailing us when we turned down the canyon road. For a moment I thought it might be Red and his boys. But it couldn't be.

The car was the same make of green sedan that had trailed me in Poughkeepsie, just two days ago.

"We got tailfeathers," Sansino whispered. He turned and sighed at me with disdain, then took out his .38 and placed it on the slippery seat between us.

"Trouble follows you, doesn't it?"

"Yup."

He pounded the pedal to the floor and we lurched forward with a sudden jolt. Within seconds the car was careening down the twisting canyon like a bullet. I clutched the dashboard.

"Jesus!" I yelled, but Sansino only smiled.

The green car followed with tremendous precision yet kept its distance. I tried to distinguish the face of the driver but it was in shadow, as was the passenger. There was also someone riding in the back seat: a large, dark silhouette.

I turned back to the road in time to witness the sight of a truck plowing up and around a steep curve. We swerved sharply to miss it. Our right tires rolled up onto the dirt embankment, and we were partially airborne for one vertiginous moment. We came down hard and hit rocks and swayed back onto the road and into the other lane—where a row of three cars suddenly appeared. They slammed brakes and hit one another with a triple crunch, as Sansino wedged his squad car between them and the trees on the left shoulder of the road. Dust kicked up with explosive swirls behind us. But that damned green car emerged from it like an apparition.

We flew. I closed my eyes as we spun around the last sharp curve at the bottom of the canyon. We took it sideways—but there was no point in righting our direction. Sansino and I shared a quick, split-second glance as the car screeched and slid and finally sputtered to a stop.

At the base of the canyon, another green car blocked our way. Its doors were open. Behind each open door a man was perched; they were dressed like Crockett and Tubbs—and they were armed. Every gun pointed at Sansino and me.

The car that had followed stopped just behind us, and two men got out with their weapons poised. A third emerged from the back seat, a big man who was dressed sharply. He strolled toward us with a strangely effeminate demeanor. He held a small handgun and waved it at Sansino.

"Throw me your piece," he said with a surprising, high-pitched voice.

Sansino complied.

The tall man smiled, then reached for his wallet. He walked closer and let it fall open in front of us. The silver badge inside was circled by black letters that read "Federal Bureau of Investigation."

"You two turds are in a kettle of shit," he said.

"Remind me not to like you," Sansino whispered to me as we were led to one of the cars and shoved into its back seat like hoodlums. We waited there a few minutes until the large man finally climbed daintily into the front seat and grinned. He reminded me of a fashion designer I'd known in New York. A real prick with a ten-dollar smile.

"Don't you realize what you've done, Byman?"

I didn't answer.

"You've fucked up months of hard work on our part."

"Sorry."

"Sorry, he says." He slapped his open palm against the dashboard. It took a moment for him to cool down. "There's only one thing to do now. Salvage what we can." He turned to Sansino. "Detective Sansino, first-class for only three months. Slight problem with white powder held you back from the promotions, though no one ever really spoke of it, or helped you. Your wife ditched with your son two years ago. Your parents died last year. Turned you around, somewhat, but now some whore you knocked up is suing. Seems she's pregnant."

Sansino lunged forward. "She's no whore!"

I held him back. Under that powder-blue suit his skin was quivering.

The big prick continued: "And, by the way, you should give up golf. You haven't hit under a hundred all year."

Sansino slumped back, a pathetic sight.

"You're an asshole," I said to the man.

"Yes, I am."

"What's the point of this?"

"The point is we've tied in heavily with LAPD on this score, and you, Byman, have fucked it up. Our men inside determined who could and should be trusted, and Sansino wasn't one of them. That's the point. Now," he spoke in Sansino's direction, "get the hell out of here and don't ever think about this day again for the rest of your life."

Sansino edged his way out, slowly. I rested my hand on his thick shoulder. "Sorry," I whispered.

His arm swung around with sudden force, and his fist caught me in the jaw. My lip split open like the skin on a plum and a thick dark blood began to trickle from my nostrils. Then, with feigned dignity, Sansino rose and walked to his squad car. He didn't look back.

35

The large man lent me his handkerchief. I dribbled blood over it as I held my smarting lip between my fingers, but it wouldn't have mattered if I'd bled over my disheveled clothes. They were so sandy and decrepit that by now it would be merciful to burn them.

"Who the hell are you?" I mumbled through the handkerchief.

"Call me Rose."

"You've got to be kidding."

"Mr. Rose."

"Well, Mr. Rose, you can't hold me. I haven't done anything wrong. I wanna get out of here."

"We're not detaining you, Mr. Byman. We're going to use you. Just sit back now, shut up, and listen."

He waved for another fellow to jump in beside him. The second man was young. He wore jeans and a T-shirt and a light linen jacket. A gun was tucked under it. He started the car, slipped it into gear, then led the other car down and out of the canyon. The second car drove off in another direction.

"Don't want to look like a funeral march," Rose said.

We headed east, southeast, east again, then north. All the while, I listened.

"We're going to use you," Rose said again, his monologue beginning.

My fate as bait. The idea was to hole me up back at the Ivanhoe. They would tap my lines and listen from a block away, just waiting for something to happen, on taxpayers' money.

"You blew our ever knowing where those arms were going," Rose continued. "We just got wind three days ago that they'd purchased again—through contacts we have in certain dealing circles. These folks have lots of cash. They've been buying and buying. Several years now. And this was the closest we've ever been to them."

"Who are they?"

He turned to me with an incredulous smile. "What an asshole you are." He faced the road again. "You don't even know."

"No."

He just wagged his head. "Why were you up there?"

"The baby. It's stolen. They make their money smuggling babies."

He pondered this a minute, bemused. "God damn. I've allowed you to fuck up our whole operation for a fucking baby."

This didn't sit so well. I considered punching him.

"Whaddya mean—allowed?"

"I mean I could have had you removed."

"When?"

"Yesterday, of course."

"Why didn't you?"

He didn't answer, just kept wagging his head. I imagined that he'd had some sort of vague moral crisis at the thought of shooting me and now regretted being part human.

The driver got off at an obscure exit and wound the car through the back streets of L.A.'s never-ending suburban flatlands. Tract houses by the thousands sped by like pastel matchboxes. Brown and black matchstick people watered weed-eaten lawns and yelled at their tiny matchstick children. Then their pastel poverty yielded to a world of brighter paint jobs. Barbecues were beginning to heat up, and the wavering reflections of swimming pools wafted up from backyard after backyard like ghostly mirages of luxury. But there were no people, no one walking on the sidewalks, no signs of life. The palms grew taller, statelier, if there's such a thing as a stately palm. Houses expanded but remained the same, somehow, in design and attitude, as if all the money had bought was more, not better. The Hills of Beverly seemed barren.

"We're taking a very long way around," Rose explained. "Enjoy the view."

To think, I thought, I might have missed all this.

Finally the crumbling sign for the Ivanhoe crept into sight like the ghostly landmark of a ruined future. The driver let me off a block from it. I stalked past the partially lit Vacancy sign, a ruin in my own right. Inside, I realized the room had been searched, probably by the Feds while I was being given the scenic tour of Los Angeles. Anyway, it didn't matter. Nothing mattered till I took a shower.

Sour L.A. water poured over me like a tawdry baptism. It cleansed me—I felt almost innocent again—even with the funky smell it left on my skin. My eyes were red from its chlorine.

I rolled on a pair of crisp jockey shorts, fresh socks, laundered khakis, some old sneakers. I didn't need a shirt; the room was too warm and the air-conditioning didn't function properly. It whined and clattered and was altogether too noisy to make phone calls over.

I dialed Cussone's number. Another detective answered and said Stanley'd have to call me back—he was in the can. I used the time to dial Lola at the hospital. The woman on duty had never heard of her. I flushed with worry and began to sweat again. I dialed her home number but there was no answer. As soon as I hung up, Cussone's call came through.

I told him that I had a hell of a lot to tell him but couldn't do it right now. My phone wasn't "secure"—a word Rose had used in warning me not to speak of what I knew to anyone. I would, of course, tell Stanley what had happened, but not yet. Rose himself was probably listening.

"Anything new on your end?" I asked.

"If your phone's not secure, dunghead, how'm I supposed to tell you?"

"You have a point."

I wished Stanley well and asked him to check up on Lola for me.

I continued by dialing Ros and Marty's number, but their machine answered. I tried to be witty but the humor fell so flat that my message ended up on a tone of despair. I folded with a toneless "Don't worry."

I called Beverly Design and asked for the manager, and when he finally arrived on the other end I asked if he'd ever served a customer named Ralph Denig or Denington.

"I don't answer those kinds of questions on the phone," he responded priggishly. "You have to come in. Even then, I don't know if I can help you. The name doesn't sound familiar."

Next I dialed Rent-A-Wreck.

"Ah. You're the one whose car was towed," said a friendly woman's voice. Her name was Mrs. Cortez. She spoke with a flavorful British drawl that was spiked by a twist of Mexican. "The Los Angeles Transit Authority got the report from the police and finally picked it up—towed it—just an hour ago. There were no registration papers in the glove compartment, but they recognized our sticker and called us. The report just came across my desk. Mr. Byman, there's no wheels on the car!"

"No!" I said, feigning surprise.

"I'm afraid they've been taken."

"Ah."

"I'm afraid you're responsible."

We haggled for a while as to who should pay for the wheels. She won. I owed Rent-A-Wreck two hundred and ten dollars. I told her to charge it to my credit card number, then she put me on hold; when she came back on the line her friendly voice was scarred by a trace of condescension.

"We've just checked your credit. I'm afraid you're way past the limit already. You'll have to pay in cash, Mr. Byman, or certified check. Two hundred and—"

"I know." I groaned with weary resignation. "I'll be in tomorrow." She hung up. Next time I would get insurance.

I tried Lola over and over but with no luck. In a fretful state I dialed Amanda. 212-555-7616. A dead number. I lay there and held the phone and felt as if it were ringing deep inside, where no one else had ever known me. No one answered.

When I let the receiver fall back on the phone I was shocked out of my stupor when it rang in my hand. Someone breathed painfully on the other end, then hung up. A pay-phone call.

Spooked, I sat upright like a jack-in-the-box and realized I was weaponless.

Panicky, I searched the socks in my suitcase and unraveled the argyle that had my money in it. It was all there; at least the Feds hadn't gotten greedy. I stuffed the wad in my pocket and went to the window as a car pulled in. A tremor ran through the muscles in my gut as its headlights brightened my dingy room. I backed against the wall and peered out my window. A middle-aged couple emerged from a rusty Buick. They argued over the room they'd chosen. They bickered as they carried their suitcases, bickered as they unlocked the door next to mine, bickered on the other side of the wall.

"Go to hell, will you!" the man shouted.

"You go to hell! All you ever do is—"

Their television switched on. The wife's voice droned under it for a moment but then stopped, in mute response to the words uttered over the tube. A woman's voice, rich, with a romantic timbre, vibrated through the wall and floor and sent a chill up through my shoes.

"I love you," she moaned to some unknown man. "Don't you see? Don't you know that I've always loved you?"

The couple quieted completely. I pictured them sitting down without a word, propping up the pillows on their separate beds, abandoning negotiations till tomorrow morning. Their movie mumbled on from behind the wall like a parallel world. A world so disembodied that it might as well be floating out among the satellites.

Mood music swelled. So did the sound of a siren. It cried out like the voice of a ghost, rising in pitch, coming closer. I paced the room, wishing for a weapon. The most I had was a nail clipper.

Then—one block away—an explosion roared. The siren died. I went to the window and saw flames shoot up high above a distant row of palms, and almost instantly they caught fire. Their huge long leaves swayed like begging, burning hands.

A small red car swerved around the corner, screeching. It tumbled over someone's yard and broke through a fence that bordered the Ivanhoe's parking lot. It slammed into a parked car, setting off a horn that wailed and wavered like a crying bird. A man got out of the red car seconds before it caught fire. He stumbled and fell, wide-eyed and blood-streaked. He got up again. Flames followed him toward me. I wanted to help him but I couldn't move. I was frozen to the rug under me, watching as Ralph Denington traversed the parking lot in a death dance.

A Cadillac scraped a fender against asphalt as it hurled around the street corner. It followed Denington's tracks across the lawn and through the fence, and I knew it was now that I had to move.

I saw myself from above—sprinting across the parking lot, sweeping Ralph Denington into my arms. I fell and hit my knees. His weight was dead weight—he was on his way out. His eyes had closed. I slapped him.

"No!" I screamed.

He cried out with closed eyes: "Julia."

The Cadillac sideswiped a car, tore against it, and hadn't even come to a stop before the big man was out of it and leveling his cannon at us. His eyes burned green above the gun barrel. I dropped Denington and dove behind my neighbor's Buick as he fired four times in succession. Cement shattered around me. One shot hit Denington in the gut. He screamed. But—strangely—the pain seemed to wake him. His eyes opened again. He spread his arm out for me on the pavement.

He held a bloody piece of paper in his fist.

Red was coming toward us—stalking like a hunter—loading his weapon with another clip. Two of his men followed, but stopped when Rose's two green cars sped into the lot and blocked the entrance. A megaphoned voice rang out from somewhere, but I didn't bother to look. Ralph Denington was, amazingly, standing up. He faced me and threw his arms out. I made the leap across open ground, grabbing his hand as Red fired again. Bullets slapped against Denington's body as I pulled him behind another car. One of the slugs tore at my leg. Looking down, I saw that I'd been grazed along the knee. I was bleeding.

I heard another clip snap into place.

And then, another shot—another gun. I got up on my good knee and looked out over the car long enough to see Rose firing his handgun. One, two shots. Misses. The big man turned his cannon on Rose and fired. Rose's head flew in two directions. His tall body crumpled onto the asphalt.

Flames from the red car sent black smoke drifting through the parking lot. I dragged Denington toward my open door, then collapsed with him in the doorway. Red aimed at us again, but his arm was ripped suddenly—his gun fell. The young agent who had been my driver had shot him. I watched from my doorway as the big man turned and ran. His red hair disappeared into the neon shadows cast by the Ivanhoe sign.

He was gone.

His man was trying to escape. The Cadillac had started moving but was hit by a barrage of bullets. The gas tank caught fire. The car was rolling toward us. The man dressed in leather staggered out and fell. I managed to kick my door closed before the car hit the motel. Glass blew in over my bed and suitcase. And flame. The Ivanhoe was burning. More sirens whined. The woman next door wailed. Voices and flame and smoke and the sirens surrounded my room like the muted whispers of a nuclear nightmare.

Ralph Denington stared up at me through the blood and smoke. I moved him so that his head rested in my lap. I held him. He tried to say something but couldn't. His lips moved, his eyes closed. He died in my arms.

I held his hand. The piece of paper in it was so smeared with blood that I could barely make out the word:

Sondra

There was nothing else. He hadn't finished what he'd tried to write.

I searched his pockets. A plane ticket was stuffed in his jacket. A bullet had nearly ripped it in half. I wiped the blood off and saw its destination.

Grand Rapids, Michigan.

On the back of the envelope he'd made notes: numbers, with initials next to them. "A" and "H" and "B"—finally, "RAW," with the number of Rent-A-Wreck next to it. He'd traced me through the car rental.

I didn't have much time—it was getting hot. Smoke was pouring in and I'd started to cough. I felt like I was sitting in my own cremation chamber. I got up but screamed aloud with pain and fell down again. My leg hurt like hell. I ripped Denington's shirt open and tied a piece of it around my wound.

I left him lying there.

A back window in the bathroom was open. I used it—I had to get away. Who cared if they knew if I was alive or dead? I squeezed through the opening, slid over an aluminum sewage tank, and hit cement. I dragged myself away through a nondescript grove of palms and brush that bordered the back of the motel.

I watched the poor Ivanhoe go up in flames from a backyard a block away. All of the possessions that I'd brought with me to Los Angeles were gone now. Consumed, together with Ralph Denington. It would take hours, maybe days, to determine that it wasn't my charred body in there.

I finally found a cab parked on Fairfax, and had to offer the driver a couple of twenties before he'd unlock his doors. He drove along the small ridge on Sunset that looks out over south Los Angeles. It lay spread to my left, a pulsing grid of colored light that seemed, somehow, to reek of both romance and decay. The cab swung left on La Cienega, and we descended through the colored light.

I was dead, for now.

At the airport I bought socks and a shirt and a shiny jacket with "Hollywood" spelled out on the back of it. Then I bought an electric shaver, toothpaste, a brush, soap, a towel, and a bag to put it all in. It was one in the morning. I washed and shaved in a desolate bathroom that was bigger than my apartment. Then I realized that I didn't have an apartment anymore. I wondered if I ever would again. With that thought, I carried what was left of me to Gate 29 and slept there till seven A.M. on a row of vinyl chairs. It was a fitful sleep. I dreamed that Lola had joined Amanda and that they were waiting for me in a heavenly version of my room at the Ivanhoe.

At 7:36 the plane to Grand Rapids left the runway. I sat in a window seat and smiled as we ascended through the brown ring. The thought of leaving Los Angeles lent a warmth to the pain that surged through me. I closed my eyes and felt the plane lift me away.

It was a full day before I opened them again.

Part Three

BLACK RIVER

36

"Where am I?" I asked, but no one answered. I was alone, under a white ceiling in a white room.

A calendar hung near a window, a solitary spot of color. It had been issued from Mapple's Hardware in Walker, Michigan. A month of small squares called July was decorated on top with the small dark rendering of two huge fins sounding in a swirling ocean.

I tried to get out of bed. It was then that I realized that my ankle had been handcuffed to the bedpost.

I closed my eyes again.

"Hello, young fella."

His name was Svenquist. His uniform was blue. The handle of his .38 was worn smooth. He unlocked my ankle bracelet, speaking with the slightest trace of a Nordic drawl.

"Sorry 'bout this. But I did have to go out to lunch, an' they said you might be comin' to. Couldn't let you run off."

I grunted.

"What's your name, son?"

"I'm not that much younger than you."

"Oh, I dunno." He smiled. "This good ole Swedish skin and blond hair can be deceiving." His smile faded. "Name?"

"Luke Byman."

"I didn't figure you were that same fella that got shot up and burned in Los Angeles."

"It's news already?"

"It was news a whole day ago. You know, kid, you been out twenty-four hours. Anyhow, it was big news on TV 'cause they say he was on the lam—for killings he committed in some town in New York years back. Real grisly murders, too. That's why I think it strange you have his ticket—know what I mean?"

I knew what he meant.

"He didn't do it," I said weakly.

"Lots of folks say he did."

I didn't have the energy to argue.

"I know you're tired," he said with a mixture of compassion and annoyance, "but give me a few minutes."

"OK."

"Why'd you have Denington's ticket?"

I took a deep breath. Wearily, I said to him: "I want you to know right now I'm not crazy. I have a story to tell you and I want you to listen. When I'm done, I don't want any patronizing comments or questions. I'm tired. I hurt. I just want you to get up and confirm at least part of my story with a detective named Cussone in New York City, ninth precinct. Then if you feel you have to you can call Detective Sansino of LAPD. He doesn't like me very much, and he's scared, but he's honest. I think."

Svenquist sat back in his chair. The mention of other cops seemed to have had an instant effect on him. He folded his arms, as if ready for deep meditation. I told him everything—poured it all out and hoped the middle-aged Swede would believe some of it.

He didn't, but he did as I had asked and called Cussone from the phone in my room. He charged it to his office. When Stanley got on the other end he talked quickly. I couldn't understand what it was he was saying, except that Svenquist kept looking at me strangely, as if a sudden ambivalence was creeping up his spine. Uh-oh, I could hear him think—trouble.

"Christ," Stanley said after Svenquist handed me the phone. "Jesus fucking Christ."

"I love you, too."

"You've made a mess out there in Los Angeles."

"I didn't like it out there anyway."

"And I have government officials crawling down my neck. They're looking for you."

"I've done nothing wrong."

"Says you. You ran from them, for Chrissake." He got serious. "You gotta come back, Luke. I've cleared you—I think—long as you get your ass back here."

I was getting dizzy. "Can you come out?"

"Of course I can't. It would do no good anyway."

"It would keep me company."

Silence. "You can't stay, Byman."

"Just a day or two. I have to." I didn't tell him about the piece of paper that had been in Denig's hand. His last message to anyone. Soon, not yet.

"I don't want you dead."

"Thanks for the sentiment."

"Your script!" he exclaimed, trying to exude hope.

"Shit." I'd certainly forgotten Weiss and his screenplay. My screenplay. Whosever.

"Come back and write it, Luke."

"Soon."

"It's your funeral," he finally said.

He hung up, severing the telephone connection just as he would any feelings he had for me. That way, my fate wouldn't linger in his gut, as it obviously had the last few days. If I died the pain wouldn't kick him so hard.

Svenquist stared at me. "You got nerve, you little shit," he said.

37

I spent a restless night at Walker Memorial, tossing, turning, dreaming. Hurting. A blue jay squawked at my window the next morning, as if it'd been his appointed mission to annoy me. I'd just fallen into deep sleep. I wished I had a gun.

July twenty-seventh. Thursday.

A nurse appeared magically. It was only later that I realized she'd been stationed outside my door, salaried by Svenquist and the greater Grand Rapids Police Department. She opened the closet and there hung a new set of clothes, along with the Hollywood jacket I'd bought at LAX. The only items that remained of my former wardrobe were my sneakers and socks. All else, I learned, had been sent to the Salvation Army. They'd probably rejected it.

The little kit I'd bought with razor and accessories sat on the floor. I used the razor, the soap, the towel; threw them back in the bag; then slipped on the pair of blue dungarees and denim shirt Svenquist had seen fit to buy.

"Has that sort of neo-jailmate appeal," I said to him in the parking lot.

"Shut up and get in the car."

I got in. A few blocks from the hospital an exit ramp led us onto 96, which carried us around Grand Rapids to Route 131. Svenquist was in a worse temper than I was. He set his square jaw north and didn't move it. It looked like a plaster mold of a Swedish statue.

"I don't know why I'm doing this," he finally said.

"Because it's important. Denington was headed for Black River, I'm sure of it. I don't know why, but we can try to find out."

"All it is is a town of IBM employees."

"Maybe so. But one or more of those employees is dirty. Hooked in somehow to the smuggling scheme. And, at the very least, Denington's wife's family used to live there. The O'Reillys. They were killed—murdered. But I don't know how it all connects."

Svenquist shook his head slowly. His doubt was at least a sign of life.

"It all sounds too fanciful to me."

"You have a point."

"If it weren't for that detective friend you have back there in New York . . ." He didn't finish.

I'd had to do some fancy talking to get Svenquist to take me seriously, to take a day and follow the strange case that had fallen in his lap but not into his jurisdiction. Another, private conversation with Cussone had convinced him that I was on the level. His curiosity was piqued; he smelled an important case. But he was angry with himself, as most cops are when they break routine.

"This could all be just a lark," he added.

"We may not find anything in Black River, but this isn't any lark, Svenquist."

I sketched in some bloody details of Amanda's death. I didn't want to—it hurt to speak of it—but Svenquist had to know. I added a bit about the babies stacked in piles and the two FBI men who'd been hacked apart. About the weapons in Los Angeles and those first murders in Poughkeepsie eleven years ago and in Black River seven years past. The Farrer family, the O'Reilly family. And this year those two Latin families butchered in New York. Then there was Ridley, and Bridge, who'd died a year apart, one of them in my apartment. And as I finished I once again reminded myself why I was following this chain of death in the first place: because a little boy had been shot before my eyes, and his little sister taken.

Svenquist didn't say much more the whole ride, just faced northeast, blue eyes strained by more than the sun. Me, I allowed the events I'd just recounted to tumble loosely in the creaky mill called my mind. Events and lives and families and death rolled against one another and sometimes connected briefly, like disparate molecules hoping to somehow form some clear-cut organism. But an overall connecting tissue never jelled. I didn't have a grip on the big picture. And every time I tried to see all the pieces of the puzzle organized and in focus, understand what had been happening to me, the image would loosen and the pieces would tumble about again like an endless laundry cycle.

I felt a hand grip my arm and shake it. It took a minute for me to open my eyes, realize that I'd been asleep.

"Boy, when you go out, you go hard," Svenquist said, parking the car in a small lot off 131.

I shook my head and tried to snap out of it.

"You need breakfast," he added.

I got out, still tugged by a nagging REM cycle. My dreams floated around in the parking lot.

"Where are we?"

"Hope you got an appetite," he said.

"Always."

I stood before the place and laughed aloud. It was another caboose, an old wooden job that needed repainting.

"What's so funny?" Svenquist asked.

"America," I answered, feeling particularly cryptic.

After a breakfast of poached eggs over toast with mashed potatoes lathered in cream sauce and gravy and garnished with bacon and orange slices and followed by a gallon of coffee, Svenquist allowed me to pay the bill.

"Cheapskate," I chided as we got back into his squad car.

"You bet."

An hour later we were approaching the outlines of a small city called Big Rapids, but we never drove through the town. Instead,

Svenquist bore left at an intersection and angled his jaw west, away from the sun. Forty-five minutes later we passed a good-sized lake, where children swam and boats zigzagged like skating bugs.

"White Lake," he muttered.

The road curved around the contours of the water, through miles of dark groves of white pine. A small dam at the far end of the lake spilled into a roiling basin where older boys dove from high ledges. The water disappeared for a while, then a break in the forest revealed it again as a small brown creek. A flock of white heron or some such bird landed in unison on the muddy surface.

"Black River."

We followed it into town.

The northern hub of Black River was a quaintified village of novelty stores. Burgeoning out from its main street were miles of row houses shaded by the boughs of elm and maple, small-town suburbs that gave way to the malls and shopping centers and supermarkets on which the town thrived.

"Stop," I told Svenquist in the middle of Main Street.

"What?"

"There." I pointed to an old hotel that must have dated back to a time when the innards of the town had thrived, before the malls and Holiday Inns.

A painted sign hung over a row of chipping columns and labeled it THE BLACK RIVER HOTEL.

"I don't know why, but that strikes me as a place Julia would stay if she were here."

"Denington's wife?"

"Uh-huh. Her family's house burned down."

I got out and crossed Main Street, leaving Svenquist with his motor running. A cheap glass door opened into an even cheaper lobby, which had been grafted into the hotel, along with a bar and a cigarette machine and a jukebox. Grafted, indeed. An Italian bartender stroked his bar, which was in full view of the front desk. A lonely-looking man tended the desk like a sparrow being watched over by a hawk. He offered up a little smile. I returned it.

The more I saw of the place, the less I thought Julia would be here, but I went ahead and asked anyway. Five dollars later I learned there was no one by the name of Denig or Denington in the place. I offered a twenty to see the register, but the proprietor's frightened gaze drifted toward the bar. I turned and saw the bartender shaking his head slowly, but not so subtly. I walked to him. Halfway across the room I began to speak:

"You seem to know everyone—"

One of his hands raised. The other fumbled curiously below the bar.

"Get outa here," he said.

I got.

"Swell place," I said as I climbed back into the squad car and told Svenquist what had happened.

"Hope you realize why I can't go throwing my weight around here," he said.

"Jurisdiction."

"More than that, damn all. I'm not a cop from these parts. I have to save my uniform like a trump card."

"Well, as a trump card, have any bright ideas what hand to play next?"

"You're the boss." He produced his first smile of the day. He enjoyed watching me squirm.

"The other hotels and motels in town."

"Helluva plan."

But we followed it for nearly three hours, scouring every joint we'd found listed in the Black River Yellow Pages. With no luck. We had lunch at three o'clock on the vinyl seat between us. Roast beef sandwiches and apple juice. Svenquist bought. He spoke with his cheeks full.

"She could have registered under any name. If she's even in Black River."

I knew she was. It was hard to say why, but I knew. Perhaps it was something in the way Denington had uttered "Julia" before he died, his last word. He'd been on his way to her. I heard it, then, in his thoughts. Now I felt it in my gut.

Yet our day was rapidly waning and we'd produced nothing.

"We have to try a different tack," Svenquist added.

He hadn't wanted to go to the local authorities; he hadn't wanted to embarrass himself. But I could tell by his featureless gaze that he was resigned to it now. I looked at him directly and said: "Police station."

We were there in minutes. Washington Street, where four brown slabs of sandstone had been hoisted up, buttressed, then cemented together. They'd even lowered a roof on them. More than a few had urinated on the back wall in the parking lot. Bright weeds and flowers had grown up there.

There were no precincts in Black River. This was the only station, and its interior was as drab as the overgrown block on which it sat. Svenquist inquired as to who the officer had been seven years ago, at the time of the O'Reilly deaths—who'd actually found them. We were given a cold reception by the officer on duty, but finally extracted the information. Minutes later we found ourselves in a tree-lined cul-de-sac knocking on the door of a retired detective, Roger Blum.

He was enormous. And sharp-eyed, like a hawk.

"Svenquist?"

"Right."

"Station called. C'mon in."

"Thanks."

A ridge of gray hair ran around the sides of his skull. His hair on top was black as coal, and sticky. His hand was big and limp and dry when I shook it, as if it were stuffed with hay. A huge old leather chair begged for forgiveness when he sat down in it. The room around us was filled with worn furniture, but none too worn to be presentable, just. A bay window looked out on the cul-de-sac. The wall was blank next to it, but for a hook, from which a holster hung. The .38 was polished like an objet d'art. Its bullets gleamed. Blum noticed me noticing it and smiled.

"Love that damn ole thing. Never used it, though." His smile faded and he looked at his shoes. "Luckily."

"We need your help, Mr. Blum," I said, sitting down.

"And who the hell are you?" he asked quietly.

Svenquist recited my name.

"Oh."

Blum turned his gaze on the Swede and bore down on him with an ageless doubt.

"I—need your help," Svenquist said.

The whole drive up I hadn't known—the entire afternoon had been a question mark. Now I knew; I saw. Svenquist was going to stand in the batter's box and swing. He was hooked.

"What is it I can do for you?" Blum asked.
"Tell us about the O'Reilly fire seven years ago."
"Arson," was all he said.
"Can we see the place?" I wanted to know.
"Burned to the ground. Another house there now. But . . . well. We could go for a ride."

We went for a ride. Twenty-seven stop signs later we turned onto Elm Street. Number 44 was midway down on the left, a brand new split-level ranch house. Its white siding was gleaming so brightly amidst the neighboring wooden houses that it reminded me of a nonbiodegradable piece of garbage, one whose brightness would never relent.

We parked under an elm and strolled partway up a pitch-black tar driveway. It had been shoddily laid over an older gravel drive. Blum climbed the steps awkwardly and rang the doorbell. No one answered. No cars were in the garage.

"Guess it's OK if we wander."

He led us around back. Behind the garage and back patio we found a quiet, mysterious piece of land, strange and swamplike for a suburb. Birds spoke to one another in the trees. The last of the afternoon's rich sunlight descended like an ethereal remnant of the fire that had consumed the O'Reilly home.

Blum spoke quietly: "It was here we found 'em."

"Who?"

"The O'Reilly couple. The house was still burnin', the smoke something terrible. Wasn't till later we realized it was 'cause there was so much fiberglass in the attic. Some of us still got throat problems."

"Were they dead?"

Blum stared at the ground beneath him. "They were dead. Layin' right here. Arms entwined."

Svenquist spoke up. "How'd they get here?"

"That's the trick question. You see, there's more. It was night when the house burned. We—police and fire departments—we had our hands full evacuating all the other houses and sealing off the street, watering down everything, everywhere. It was a hell of a fire. It wasn't until the following morning we found the blood."

"Blood?"

"Where these two had been laying, or nearby. I lifted them

away myself. I know the position they was in and where they were. When morning came we were able to determine a few things. One, they'd been dragged from the house, one of them already dead, prob'ly, or both on the verge."

"Why do you say that?"

"Well, heel marks were dug real deep into this soft earth—quite nearly a swamp here—left by someone who'd dragged the old folks out. Then, their arms were entwined. That led us to believe that they knew they was dyin' . . ." His voice lowered. "So, in their last moments . . ." He lifted his hefty arms, as if to wrap them around the memory of an unrequited lover.

"We get the picture," Svenquist whispered.

"You know, it gets me every time I think of them," Blum said, then added: "I don't have someone like that." His words floated out over the dry land swamp and were absorbed there, with all the other lonely sounds.

"Anyway," Blum continued, "there was blood on the ground—but it wasn't their blood. They weren't even wounded. Not shot nor stabbed, or nothing. It was someone else's blood and there was quite a bit of it." Blum scraped his big toe along the soft dry earth. "All in here."

"The person who dragged them out was bleeding?"

"Apparently."

"Do you know who it was?"

"We know who we think it was. The daughter—the good one, I mean."

"Julia O'Reilly," I said, a sudden chill running through me at the thought of her true name.

"Hell no."

"No?"

"No. Anna. Little Anna O'Reilly. The good one." His eyes misted over. "She's famous now." And then he spit out the word: "Julia!" His ears reddened, his eyes burrowed deep inside his cheeks. "She's the one set the fire. She and that husband of hers. The one who just died in Tinseltown, I read. And I say good riddance. They was on the run, we found out, when they came here. An' if only—if only we'da known we'da blasted them in jail faster than—oh, Julia was always the bad one. Everyone always knew. Anna, she never did nothin' wrong her whole life. She deserves to be where she is. She was a fine girl and she's a fine woman. Comes here often, back home. Keeps the old friends." His voice growled again: "Julia. She deserved the husband she got."

He was panting. Svenquist and I stayed silent awhile. There was no use in antagonizing him with facts.

"Was there—did Julia have a boy with her?"

This startled Blum. He raised his fat cheeks.

"How'd you know?"

"I knew Billy and Julia. Was there any sign of him after the fire?"

Blum eyed me suspiciously now. "No sign."

"What led you to believe the fire was arson?"

"An open tank of gasoline in the house. It didn't burn."

"Were there any other remains?"

"No bodies, if that's what you mean. There was some pipes and furniture and kitchenware that somehow made it through the fire. Didn't shed no light to anything, though. 'Cept—"

"What?"

"Those footprints weren't the only ones."

"There were others?"

"Yep. Looked to me as if they were all in the house when the fire was heavy under way, then bolted. Anna was the one who dragged her parents out. What I always figured was that Julia actually shot Anna—that Anna was gonna turn her and her husband in—so they tried to kill her, along with the parents."

"Whaddya mean—you figured?" Svenquist asked. "Didn't you question Anna O'Reilly?"

"Well, yes."

"Was she shot?"

"Yes. She had a bandage on her arm."

"Did she go to a local hospital?"

"I don't know where she went. We'd all have to admit she was kinda mysterious. She disappeared after the fire, then reappeared at the funeral. Julia didn't come, of course. She and her husband, they ran." He was trying to deflect the issue.

"And you questioned her then? Anna, I mean."

"Well, we did, but I'll tell you flat out she didn't say nothing. Clammed up. She told us it was tragic what had happened to her folks and was all upset, but she said to us that as long as she lived she'd never incriminate a loved one." He added: "We couldn't blame her—I tell you—enough bad had already happened. We were left to figure out what happened ourselves."

"So you don't really know that it was Anna who dragged her parents out of here that night? Who saved them?"

Blum scuffed the ground with his feet. "No, but—"

"You didn't check to see if she was really shot up?"

No answer.

"You didn't take molds of the footprints and try to match them to a pair of shoes?"

No answer.

"You just let her go?"

"You can't blame me. The whole town was on her side. The papers. The whole force. I—I still am." But he didn't sound so sure. "After all," he whined, "she was—" He cut himself short. His tiny eyes stared at us like a pair of pathetic marbles.

I finished the sentence: "She was Anna O'Reilly."

"Hell, she'd just won the Academy Award."

"Jesus!" Svenquist turned his back on us and pondered the events that had tainted the tiny patch of woodland swamp. It looked, now, like a mire. I caught a whiff of someone's barbecue. It reeked of burning flesh.

Blum's head was lowered. I tried to hoist him from the shame Svenquist had made him feel. We still needed him.

"The past is past," I said. "Can you help us now?"

He slapped at his empty sides. "I'm no cop anymore. My weight . . . my heart. Early retirement." He whined again. "What can I do?"

Ten minutes later we pulled up in front of the Black River Hotel. It was where we'd started, hours ago, and once again I felt the vague sensation that we were close to Julia. The same desk clerk was still behind the counter, still the same pert and formal wimp. His eyes grew a little larger at the sight of us.

"Oh, no—you again," he said to me.

"With company."

"This wasn't necessary, sir."

"Yeah, it was. Now, Mr. . . ."

"Bask."

Blum cut in. "How about showing us the register, Henry."

"Officer Blum? You're working again?"

"A little."

"Good to hear it," Bask strained to add. He tilted a large red portfolio our way and held it up for us.

Svenquist and I pored over the names scratched into the registry. She hadn't logged in on Tuesday or Monday. Finally Svenquist struck his middle finger on the Sunday page, like a small arrow hitting a bull's-eye.

"Got it!"

It was her handwriting all right, distinctive enough for me to remember from the letter I'd received months ago. But that wasn't what first caught my eye—or Svenquist's. It was the name she'd logged in under:

Lucy Byman.

"As if she's expecting you," Svenquist whispered.

"Mmmm."

I felt a breathing behind my back, hot, alcoholic. When I turned the Italian bartender stood there, his big chin up against me. His fists were clenched.

"Thought I told you to get lost."

"Too bad," I said. I'd had enough of the jerk. I also had a cop on either side of me.

"Do you have a warrant, officers?" he asked them.

"No," Svenquist answered. "We're just here to see a guest."

"I have to let them," Bask said. "They're police."

"No, no you don't. This one here"—he pointed to Svenquist—"he's from downstate, out of his territory and harmless. This one," he chided, poking Blum in the gut, "was too fat and too drunk to run fast. Couldn't save his own partner. So now he's pensioned off like an elephant to his graveyard." His big mouth opened in an obnoxious laugh.

I'm not sure what came over me. My hand accidentally swung up and smashed his teeth. He gulped his laugh down his throat, then rolled back on his heels. I'd never used my fist on anyone before, and for a first time it was a doozy. I nearly broke my hand. There were teeth marks on my knuckles. They started to bleed. But the bartender lay on the ground cold as a cucumber. Svenquist knelt beside him.

"Out cold," he said with a smile.

"That wasn't so wise," Blum whispered. "These guys run more than you think around here."

"It certainly wasn't wise at all," Bask said. His hand crept for the receiver. "Chief Trell will want to—"

"No you don't," said Svenquist. "Just give us a few minutes upstairs and we'll be out of your hotel in no time." He held out his palm. "Room two-twelve. Lucy Byman."

Reluctantly, Bask handed the key over.

"What if he wakes up?" Bask asked about his friend. He leaned over the counter and a trace of satisfaction creased his thin lips. The Italian was slobbering on himself.

"Blum, here, will hold him." Svenquist spoke to the worried ex-cop. "Tell him he's under arrest if he interferes any further. If he wants to he can call the cops here. We'll explain."

"That won't go over so well," Blum said worriedly.

Svenquist smiled and handed Blum his gun. Blum was grateful for it. He took the dulled steel into both palms and shivered slightly.

I was already headed upstairs. My hand was throbbing; the knuckles had expanded, but it didn't matter. Julia was in Room 212—I hoped.

We knocked on her door but didn't get an answer. When we opened it the room looked empty. Would that we had been so lucky.

I stepped into the room, near to the bed. A new nest of butterflies came alive inside of me when I smelled that faint trace of perfume, a scent I recognized.

I didn't see the blood, but I stepped in it. It was thick and rich—and scarlet, as Amanda's had been—and I felt that same sad dizziness coming on, the same forever rhythm banging my head inside again. It hurt. My eyes blurred.

"Julia," I said aloud, then fell to my knees. In that dim red mirror spreading on the rug, I saw my reflection rush toward me. Later, Svenquist would inform me that I'd fainted and fallen smack into a tidepool of Type O.

I woke peering sideways along a soggy carpet, straight into the dead eyes of a bald man. He seemed to be smiling at me.

38

They carried him out on a stretcher. His feet didn't even reach the end of it. Police found his glasses shattered under the bed, but his wallet was intact. We searched its contents on the round Formica table that was the room's only semblance of respectability. A tacky replica of a Tiffany lamp shade hung from an adjustable wire. Svenquist pulled it down over the open wallet, then dumped its contents.

His name was Benjamin Kelly. The cowhide contained all of the respected credit cards and his Social Security card and a driver's license. Also, a few identification cards, one for the IBM in Black River, a typical ID with picture; another for classified areas in that same plant; then another for those classified areas in the IBM headquarters in Poughkeepsie, New York.

Kelly was also a member of some local organizations. The Lions Club, the Veterans Association. Tucked away with his money was a season's pass to the local track, along with two tickets to tomorrow's race. He'd had twenty-seven dollars on him when he died, and some change. And a few phone numbers.

Two of them were on business cards; professional associates, it seemed. Svenquist muttered that we'd have to call each one. The third number had a 213 area code. I lifted the tattered little piece of paper in my palm and walked to the phone.

"Not now," Svenquist said.

But I had to.

I lifted the beige receiver and a sputtering came over the wire. Then the hotel operator picked up as if I'd woken her.

"Hallo," she whispered lethargically.

I gave her the number.

Six rings went by. I almost hung up, but before I did the rings stopped. There was a strange clicking sound. Then a mechanical woman spoke to me.

"Enter the code," she breathed hypnotically, "now."

It was then that the local chief of police made a showing, with his coterie of grim uniforms. They stood in the open doorway, toting heavily. And aiming. The bartender smiled behind them.

I suddenly had a very funny feeling.

The big, red-faced cop stepped forward and announced himself with a gust of sanctimony.

"I'm Chief Trell. Chief of Police. Don't move." He had his men frisk us.

"I'm a cop," Svenquist said as he leaned against the wall. "We reported the murder."

"I don't care who the hell you are," Trell barked.

Another cop pushed Blum into the room. He fell to the floor with a tremendous thud, then stayed there, sitting like a gigantic boy in an oversized playpen.

"What were you doing here?" Trell asked harshly of all three of us.

I answered: "Looking for someone."

"Who?"

"Lucy Byman," Svenquist said.

"My wife," I added.

"You're lying." Trell came close to me with his gun still extended. It hung close to my belly. "Why the blood all over you?"

Svenquist spoke for me: "He thought it was his wife under the bed. He fainted in the blood."

Trell grabbed my hair and pulled. I tried resisting, but his .38 tapped my chin so I went along. He dragged me across the room to the bartender and shoved my face close to him.

"This the one that assaulted you, Tony?"

"He's the one."

Trell spoke to me with a macabre theatricality.

"You've assaulted one of our more respected citizens."

Blum made a sneering sound.

"You have something to say, Roger?"

"No."

"Good," Trell said, " 'cause you're a pig's hair away from thirty days."

"Give him thirty days," Tony said.

Trell walked back over to me.

"No," he said. "Then we'll have these assholes in our hair for another month. No," he repeated. Then he grabbed me by the hair again and shoved me toward Tony. "Say you're sorry."

"I'm sorry."

"Whaddya say, Tony?"

Tony didn't say anything. He let a punch fly—into my abdomen. I buckled, but before I fell he swung another, an uppercut into my jaw that straightened me again. A third punch hit my neck and sent me to the floor.

I learned then that it's the third punch that always hurts the worst.

Svenquist rushed to me. He helped me sit up, then sprang to his feet, ready to do battle with Trell.

"You asshole," he said with a surprisingly Swedish intonation. His fist rose, but one of Trell's lackeys caught him from behind and held back his punch. Trell took the opportunity to throw one of his own, into Svenquist's gut. The big Swede fell to one knee. Trell pushed him to the floor with the sole of his shoe.

"If either one of you two are in my town in ten minutes, I'll find a way to hang this murder on you. Consider yourselves lucky I don't just do it right now."

He shoved his gun back into its holster.

"As it stands," he said, "we know who to hang it on." He heard what he'd said and revised it. "Who did it."

"Who?" I asked through my bleeding lip.

Trell smiled, and I saw that his teeth were rotten.

"Your 'wife,' " he said, then spoke to one of his men: "Put out an all-points on Julia O'Reilly. Again." He looked down on Svenquist and me, and spoke condescendingly. "You see, we know she was in town. We know she had this room. And we know she met with Kelly here and had an argument."

"You seem to now everything."

"That's right. I have trustworthy informants."

"Oh."

"Now get out of here!" And he added: "Blum—go home and stay there, you big jackass."

Tony the bartender snickered as he faded back into the darkness of the hallway. Trell followed.

"My gun!" Svenquist shouted after him. "I want my gun!"

"Forget it," Blum whispered hoarsely. "Get out of here, like he said."

Trell's men lifted us to our feet, then shoved us by the shoulders till we were out the door. From the hallway I caught a glimpse of one of them as he slipped Benjamin Kelly's twenty-seven dollars into the breast pocket of his uniform. Our eyes met briefly, and I thought I caught a trace of the way he'd look on judgment day.

The door slammed shut.

39

I was shaking as I left the hotel. Trell and his men had carried themselves with such cocky assurance that I felt close to shooting them.

"This town went bad," Blum said sadly as we drove him home. "They think they can do anything here." He crawled through traffic jammed along a main thoroughfare where lounges and pizza parlors and an OTB had replaced Cromwell Hardware and the Village Deli and Bank's Bookshop. The old establishments had not yet had their painted advertisements sandblasted off the exposed brick at the sides of each building. Their faded letters seemed to speak of another era, just as the faint marks below them spoke of earlier enterprises that had thrived before the turn of the century. A movie marquee at the end of the block guaranteed triple-X satisfaction, yet, as if clinging to that dying other world, its wall posters spoke mutely of an old-fashioned Disney matinee. Next to the theater was an old alleyway. In it, slovenly, curvacious forms melded with the shadows, black on black. Blum hung both arms over the window's edge, like paws, his sad eyes gazing wearily at the confusion that seemed as rampant and frenzied as a border town. Just down the street a church bell rang without hope. "Maybe they can," he added.

Svenquist rounded the corner of a tree-lined avenue and pulled to the curb. He slammed his steering wheel, then threw the door open with a quiet, searing anger that was frightening. I could feel the heat he left behind him in the car. He paced across the street. After a few cars went by he paced back. He stood at the side of the car for a long minute, his holster empty, then reluctantly lowered himself back inside. He sat quietly, but his knuckles were white against the wheel. I saw the years he'd spent on the force etched into the corners of his eyes, like those circles inside tree trunks. The man had just witnessed the dark side of his profession, and perhaps for the first time that dark side had not been remotely worried. Frustration pulsed within him like a loosed animal. And defiance.

"You must help us," he said to Blum.

"Don't involve me—I don't wanna be involved. This is where I live."

"IBM?" I asked.

Svenquist nodded. Not another word was spoken till we'd dropped Blum in his cul-de-sac. He waddled toward his home, confused, turning often to look back at us as we made the U-turn and sped out of there. I glanced back for a last look and saw him leaning against his front door. He might have been crying.

Svenquist reached into the folds of his uniform and produced Kelly's two IBM security cards.

"We may need these," he said.

I smiled and opened my fist. My knuckles were bruised and sore; it hurt to open them. But I hadn't let go of that tiny slip of paper with the 213 phone number on it. I told Svenquist what I'd heard on the other end of the line.

"Hmmm," was his only response.

"We're looking for that code," I said. "I think."

We found our way to the central plant, just on the outskirts of town. Its elongated form was hidden among a flat forest of shopping centers. Once there, however, it seemed that all the shopping centers spread out from it, as if the plant were their mother bee. It was a huge pentagonal building, divided in sections. Each section had a parking lot labeled A through E. We parked in B and walked over to A, but were directed to C by a security guard.

A bell rang as we opened the door, and we thought for a moment that we were violating some obscure bureaucratic rule. We stared at one another, confused, until, seconds later, a thunderous sound emanated from the interior hallways. Then droves of IBMers stampeded toward us, their day over. Svenquist dodged to the left, I to the right. They charged by with a velocity that matched a crowd at rush hour in Grand Central. A minute later it was all over.

We stalked the hallway and found an empty receptionist's desk. I sat down in the warm chair and browsed through a catalog of names and numbers, all the employees and their extensions. Kelly's was 1612.

"Excuse me—what are you doing?"

A young black woman stood over me, a symphony of fresh ruby makeup. She smelled of hair spray.

"Get up!" she said with more surprise than anger.

I got up and held out my hand.

"Hi, I'm with this officer here, and we're looking for Benjamin Kelly. There was no one here, so I . . ." I gestured to the extensions catalog. "Sorry," I concluded.

"Well," she said, "you caught us changin' shift. Who was it you wanted again?"

"Benjamin Kelly."

It took her more time than it had taken me.

"Sixteen-twelve!" she said, excited. "I'll buzz him."

"Don't bother," Svenquist said in a commanding tone. He was wearing his uniform, but redundantly, and with some effect, he flashed his wallet badge. "We'd like to . . . surprise him."

"He might not even be here!" She was excitable.

"That's all right, we'll try it anyhow. Where's sixteen-twelve?"

She pointed down one of the three hallways that converged at her desk. "Right at the end of the hall, umm . . . then your first left—maybe it's your second. Down that hall."

"We'll find it," I said, and thanked her. She smiled worriedly. People were always worried, nowadays, when they looked at me.

It was a long, wide, low-hung hallway that was paneled overhead. I could have touched the ceilings. We followed it, made the right and then our first left, but found only a series of janitorial chambers.

We backtracked, then made the second left. Half a mile down another corridor we came across number 1612. It was locked.

"Here." Svenquist handed me one of the security cards. "I'm not allowed to do this."

"Chickenshit," I muttered, and slipped the card into a metal slot—a fancier version of those new hotel key-locks. The door popped open.

"Presto."

"Quiet."

We stepped into a dark room. Motors hummed, wavering like mechanical tuning forks. Svenquist switched on a light. The room that was revealed was small and tidy, devoid of personality. Six computers blinked at their various terminals, left running to remain up to speed. Svenquist opened a drawer.

"Figure out which desk was Kelly's," he whispered.

"Right."

We rifled and searched before realizing that there was a door in the room. It opened into another, smaller cubicle, with only two terminals. The computers were of a higher quality. A framed photo of Kelly, sailing on a lake with his wife and two children, stood near one of the terminals, below a phony window that had been painted on the wall, replete with curtains and potted plant.

I searched in his only drawer but found nothing but pencils and paper clips. Near his computer sat mounds of printouts, their numbers and characters indicating nothing but the fact that Kelly had apparently designed software, not programmed it. Sifting through them nearly put me to sleep.

"The problem is I wouldn't know a code from a phone number," I told Svenquist.

"Depends on where it's kept," he said obliquely.

He made a cursory search of the other desk but found nothing. He had just rolled the drawer closed when the room's door popped open and we were accosted by a broad man in a cheap suit.

"What the hell do you think you're doing?" he bellowed.

Svenquist stepped forward, flashed his badge, introduced himself.

"I don't really care who you are," the man said warily. "This isn't right, you being in here."

"Under normal circumstances, you might be right," said Svenquist. He lifted Kelly's picture. "Do you know this man?"

"Of course I fucking know him. Now get out, please. We'll talk about this elsewhere."

"He's dead," I said bluntly.

"Dead?"

"Dead."

He staggered back against a flimsy Formica desk that was built against one wall. It sagged under his bricklike trunk. His upper legs spread flabbily on it; his face reddened. A stubby hand reached with the deftness of a pickpocket into his trousers and removed a pack of butts. He lit one.

"Jesus." The word breathed smoke. His eyes rolled back.

Svenquist helped him to a rolling chair. Its wheels ground along the floor and came to rest in little grooves that had been worn into the carpet by years of bearing his weight.

It took him a full moment to overcome his dizziness.

"We work together," he said hoarsely, "here." His hands gestured slowly and expansively, as if the room were large. Then he turned and with a forlorn grimace waved the cigarette before his computer screen. "This is my desk." We watched silently as he peered toward Kelly's old computer. "That—was—Kelly's."

"So we gathered."

"Car accident?" he asked Svenquist, his voice meek.

"What?"

"How'd he die?"

"No accident," I said.

His eyes widened with a muted fear, but no surprise.

"He was a terrible driver," he said in monotone.

"What's your name?" Svenquist got around to asking him.

"Augustine." His body went limp at the sound of his surname.

"What were you working on?" I asked.

"What?"

"Together, you and he?"

"Oh. Well. Nothing that important. We were just redesigning the company's program for word processing."

"That's it?"

"Yeah—Easywriter. You can check. But . . . why?"

I showed him the 213 number scrawled on that tiny slip of paper I'd found in Kelly's wallet. He stared hard and long at it, as if it were a clue to his own malaise.

"Ever see this number? Ever dial it?"

"No." He looked up at me. "Are you interrogating me, or what?"

Svenquist soothed him. "Of course not. We need to ask these questions. We need answers fast. Bear with us."

He sat, recalcitrant as a fat bird. Emotions seemed to pass through him like clouds, enhancing then obscuring his outward character. From somewhere deep inside his belly came the words:

"All right."

"All right," Svenquist echoed. "Dial this." He plucked the number from my fingers and handed it to Augustine. His square frame swiveled in the chair and punched a touch-tone with effortless speed. He ran his stubby fingers through his hair as he listened.

"It's just ringing," he said.

"Keep holding."

"Wait—" he said, cutting himself off. His look was intent for a few seconds. Then he hung up.

"Well, it's another modem, most likely." He spread out his thick arms. "To what I can't tell."

I asked him: "Can you figure where he might have kept the code?"

"His head. Anyway, how do you know it's his?"

"We found it on his body," Svenquist answered.

Augustine tilted his head back, stretching his double chin into a single slope of flesh.

"Isn't that illegal?"

Svenquist said nothing.

"Who the hell are you guys?" Augustine asked impatiently. He pointed a stubby finger at Svenquist. "You're not even local." He eyed me with the intelligence of a wild boar. "And you're just a kid."

I suppose I looked younger than my age, but his comment was so far afield that I lost patience.

"C'mon—" I growled, but Svenquist cut me off with the wave of a hand.

"Mr. Augustine. The local cops will be along, I'm sure. I could hasten that eventuality by asking you to take a ride down to their station. I don't want to do that. I want you to help us find that code."

"Why?"

We weren't sure why. I wasn't sure of anything.

"Sondra" was all Denington had written. It might be that something was about to happen at Sondra's Marina in Poughkeepsie. Yet here I was in a tiny cubicle at the center of a gargantuan computer plant—on the outskirts of a corrupt small town in Michigan—facing a sudden crisis in understanding why. I gazed at my bruised right hand. It was curled like a question mark.

Svenquist sat down in another roller and leveled his eyes at Augustine's oblique gaze.

"Lives may depend on it."

I crouched down to face the broad man, and to take some weight off my bad leg. For some unexplained reason Augustine simpered with defiance.

"Hook your modem up," I whispered, "and dial the number again."

"You're saying Benjie was bad."

"It's possible."

"Well, I can't do anything against him. Sure, everyone knows Benjie had a slight problem with the horses. But, hell . . ." He pointed with his cigarette across the room. "Look at that picture," he said. We looked. The woman Kelly stood near had a dark complexion and dark curly hair. She was small and broad and looked like she could have lifted Kelly with one arm.

"He's married to my cousin," said Augustine with a shallow gust of self-pity, as if this was his predicament. He repeated: "I can't do anything against him."

"Was married," I said.

His hands spread over his knees.

"You can't make me."

A voice spoke from behind us, low and ornery and full of itself.

"Sons of bitches," Trell said. "You are dumb." The barrel of his revolver was level with my eyes. His middle finger stroked the trigger. "Now get down," he ordered.

My crouch turned to a kneel.

Svenquist remained solid as a spur of granite.

"No."

Trell's voice squeezed with anxiety: "Down!" Then his walkie-talkie buzzed. He answered: "I got 'em."

A voice blared: "What next?"

Trell said: "Stand by."

"Right." The static died.

Trell waved his gun and smiled at us. "Did you think Blum wouldn't tip us?"

"You're scum," Svenquist spit out.

"Get down on the floor."

Augustine backed toward the doorway, behind Trell.

Trell said to him: "I'll need your statement later, Bobby, how these men have been harassing you." Augustine nodded to the cop's back. Trell added with a smirk: "Your brother'll be proud'a you."

"I don't care," Augustine said before making for the hills.

There was an eerie pause. I knew anything could happen now.

Svenquist stood up. I grabbed his leg—

"No!"

Trell fired. It seemed as if the bullet entered the Swede's right shoulder and popped out his back in slow motion. It hit the wall and spattered a few drops of blood. They dripped down as if the wall were wounded and bleeding.

Svenquist collapsed nearly on top of me, moaning. His head slumped under the desk, out of sight. All I could see were his thrashing legs.

"He's hit!" I screamed up at Trell.

"I know." He actually smiled. "I shot him."

"Call a dcotor!"

"No doctors. Get him on his feet."

Svenquist writhed and twisted, and in that painful moment it struck me that Trell was mad. Down, up. He was unsure of what he wanted. His gun waved.

"Stand him up!"

For a moment I thought he was going to shoot. His gun shook, and his middle finger squeezed on the trigger. My whole body convulsed and I closed my eyes. But no shot. Instead Trell pulled at Svenquist's left leg, dragging him out from under the desk. The

Swede's face was drained. He shook. But there was a gleam in his eye, and he grabbed my arm, pulling me toward him. I didn't know why. I leaned closer—until I felt the barrel of Trell's revolver poking in my ear. The cold steel found its way inside the chamber. I heard the ocean.

"Stand him up."

I pulled Svenquist's good shoulder up and over mine and hoisted him halfway. But he was two hundred pounds of sodden weight. I nearly fell. Trell's words cut through his delirium.

"Use your legs, flathead"—he kept his revolver up against my head—"or I'll kill the kid."

Svenquist tried. His feet scraped along the carpet, hoping to help push him up. We made it together as far as the edge of the desk, using it as a rail to lean on.

"Quickly!" Trell shouted.

Again his walkie-talkie snapped to life and he barked into it: "Stand by!"

Svenquist rose shakily to his feet. I supported his left shoulder. We wobbled like two drunk sailors.

Trell smiled. He thrust his gun out an extra inch toward us, as if it had a bayonet.

"Can't have bullets embedded in the floor. Wouldn't look too good." I'd never seen anything with as much clarity as I saw his stubby finger curl around the trigger. A last image to remember all those years in purgatory.

"Good-bye," he said.

In my death flash I conjured up my long-gone parents and the big old house they'd raised me in. Huge run-down rooms with comfortable sofas. Now here I was about to die in a sterilized cubicle with a Styrofoam ceiling. It didn't seem right, I thought. Briefly.

I closed my eyes and the shot fired. My heart stopped a beat. I jumped—so did Svenquist. But neither of us fell. Neither of us was hit.

My eyes opened.

Trell stood strangely before us, his gun hand down but his fingers still clinging to the revolver. His eyes had changed from black to dull gray; his shirt from gray to blackened red. Blood soaked the left sleeve and ran down his arm. A cup of it collected in his palm. His mouth opened and all at once the blood from his head seemed to drain from it. He toppled. Blum stood behind him, fat, beaten, bruised, his eyes puffed red and black, his cheeks swollen with welts. That silver .38 he'd had hanging on his wall was in his hand, still smoking.

A tear wound its way through his welts and fell to the floor. He slumped down on a desk against the wall, grimly contemplating what he'd just done.

"They'll never believe me," he whispered.

I had no time to answer.

Svenquist fell to the floor and dragged me with him. Then the Swede pulled me toward him. Again, his face stretched into a grimaced smile. I smiled with him.

"We're alive," I said, confused by his painful grin.

He waved that off with his eyes and then used them to indicate that something was behind him, over him. Under the desk. I crawled under. His left hand slapped the wood above him and pointed. I followed his finger.

There, taped under Augustine's computer, was a dog tag. I untaped it and held the small piece of shiny metal in my hand. It was worn smooth on one side, as if it had rubbed against an anxious palm since World War II.

On the other side six numbers were printed: 447212.

Trell's radio buzzed again.

"Chief?"

I got to my knees and fumbled for a switch on Kelly's modem. Finally I found it. A red light faded on.

"Chief?" the talkie whispered.

I didn't even try to answer—no time.

I opened the drive guards and found Easywriter on one side but nothing in the other. Rifling through his catalog of disks I found only one that was unmarked. I hoped it was the right one.

"Chief, respond!"

I pressed Enter. Nothing.

"Coming in," the talkie said.

I shared a glance with Svenquist and saw his mute concern. He tapped my leg and pointed to Trell's body. I nodded, then crawled over and grabbed the .457.

"Blum!" I yelled. "Cops coming! Cover the door."

But he just sat there, chin against his chest. His gun drooped.

I turned back to the computer and pressed Clear and Enter at the same time and the screen blanked. Then the computer greeted me:

"Hello."

I called up the only file on the disk. Then I dialed the 213 number on the modem. My few turns with a word processor had done me good; the modem channeled the number so that it read out on the screen—as did the words of the mechanical woman who answered. "Enter the code," she said again, "now."

I punched the keys: 4-4-7-2-1-2.

A word flashed in bold letters: LINKING. . . .

I heard the static of a walkie-talkie outside, and footsteps. I ran to Blum, shook him.

"Help me!"

He wagged his greasy head.

"I'm sunk."

A voice in the hall said: "Chief?"

The eye of his gun peered around the door.

I kicked the door, pinning the cop's arm. His gun fell and went off, and the shot breezed by my foot. I yanked the door open and quickly slammed my gun in the direction of his face. I missed. His foot came up and hit me in the chin and I flew backward, knocking a computer to the floor. Its back end shattered. Electrical sparks sprayed the air like a shower of miniature fireworks. I looked up at the cop I was fighting and saw that he was young, younger than I was, and flying down on me like Chuck Norris. I braced myself—but he never landed on me. His young body broke sideways with the force of the bullet that fired over my head. He crumpled on the carpet to my left, a hole in his side. Blum sat in his chair like a slumping Buddha, the barrel of his revolver swaying with the rhythm of a tree branch. He was drooling. His eyes were glassy. An aftershock shook his rotund body and his eyes closed. Tears squeezed out of them. But I felt no pity for the man, only disgust. He had saved my life by killing Trell. But now his trigger was hot. Out of control. He'd just murdered a boy.

"Look what you've done!" I cried.

We stared together at the young cop. He had fallen in the fetal position, and his hands were cupped together as if in prayer.

My chest pounded with grief and guilt and a crashing wave of self-disgust.

"Oh God," Blum whispered.

I pulled myself into the other room, breathing heavily, and faced the computer. A date flashed on the monitor: May 5, 1989.

The cursor pulsed as fast as my heart. I pressed the Page Down key and up from the bottom came a list of names. They were gathered like ghosts on a spread sheet. Mary Gordon. Constance Gravitz. Beth Lumley. Others, many others—with addresses.

There was a date column, and across the screen, in another column, a number that corresponded to each name. Under a column headed "Referenced From" were corresponding sets of initials.

My finger lingered on the scrolling key. A flood of names continued to roll past, with their corresponding columns of initials and numbers. I remembered the numbers marked on those Polaroids that had been spread in Amanda's blood. I could only guess that each of these numbers now scrolling by identified a baby, and every address listed was a family due to receive that child.

The initials didn't take long to figure. "IBM" was the key. "EG" most likely stood for the Entertainment Group in Los Angeles, where all the information that I'd called up was most surely stored. "AA" could mean an adoption agency, and the specific one would be indicated by the number that followed. These initials seemed to clarify only which of the many sources had produced a needy couple. Perhaps a legitimate agency that had been tapped; or IBM's family files; or one of the many actors and actresses, producers, directors, or writers referenced through the Entertainment Group.

Every now and then the steady flow of the list was broken by other dates; "Delivery Dates." Under each of these were varying numbers of names. The last delivery date read: "Delivery due July 28."

Thirty or more names and addresses were listed under that date. Thirty or more numbers, babies. Most of the receivers had been referenced from anonymous adoption agencies. Some from IBM; some from the Entertainment Group. Only one had no reference at all: "7."

I had no time to think. Svenquist was grabbing at my leg.

"Doctor," he groaned, barely conscious.

I nodded silently, but remained focused on the screen for a moment, staring at the file's final words. They glowed like uranium ore.

> Schedule =
> Panther Field drop 2100.
> Sondra's Marina pickup 2400.
> Arrival Clinic 0600.
> Exchange and expediting as per MOTHER.

There was nothing else.

After I pocketed the disk and dog tag I pulled Svenquist by his legs until he was out from under the desk. Then with one surge of effort I hoisted him to his feet and we staggered out together, into the front room. I opened the door and edged out into the hallway carrying Svenquist's dull weight. Before going any farther I turned to Blum, who still sat inside.

"Let's go," I said.

"Nah," he whispered. He didn't look up. "I'll face them. I'll tell 'em. They'll believe me." His voice seemed queer and ethereal.

"C'mon, Blum—get out of here!"

"You go on."

I went on, dragging a tall Swede.

A crowd had gathered at a remote corner of the hallway. Muted sirens were making their way closer. A security guard stood in the center of the hallway, a thin scarecrow of a man. I threw Trell's gun down, still dragging Svenquist along the tiles. His shiny shoes squeaked a high-pitched rhythm. The crowd dispersed, away from us. I yelled that it was all right, that we were cops. I wasn't quite sure what I was saying. The security guard stood like a frozen stick as we glided past him. I made a left at the end of the corridor instead of a right, away from the route we'd taken in. A few suited men cowered in an office. I shouted:

"Hospital! Where's a hospital?"

They saw his uniform, my eyes.

One of them pointed. "East on Route Twenty."

"Thanks."

We exited through two glass doors at the end of another corridor that opened out onto the back parking lots. From behind some bushes I watched as two police cars sped across lots D and C and screeched to a halt.

I had very little time. I left Svenquist in the bushes and ran, hard, fast, nearly screaming from the pain in my leg. I fell once, but finally made it to the car and started it and pulled out in time to miss being seen. But only seconds after I'd reached Svenquist I heard their sirens again. I got out and literally carried the Swede into the back seat. Before his door was closed I was gunning the gas and squealing around another corner of the pentagonal building.

Svenquist yelled from the back seat: "They'll come from both directions!"

He was right. I could hear stereo sirens behind me.

I hit a cement curve and the car flew up and then down again into the parking lot of an adjacent shopping center. Svenquist cried out—he'd fallen to the floor, onto his arm. But it didn't matter. All that mattered was losing two cop cars that were boring up my ass fast. Ready to pin me for one, two, three murders.

"Christ," I said aloud.

I pressed the gas pedal all the way down and wove at a maniacal pace through the busy parking lot. People were everywhere, hurling themselves out of the way. The two cop cars matched my every move, barreling down the lanes that ran on either side of me. One of them used an outside speaker and commanded me to stop; his voice sounded like a tin God in a bad movie. I didn't do as he asked.

But I did slam on the brakes. The sound was deafening, a screech that was matched, twice, by the police units. But I'd surprised them—they were well ahead of me when they stopped. I twisted the car to the right, through an empty parking space, then roared the engine again, bearing down toward a green light at the entrance to the shopping center. Beyond it. Route 20.

The light turned yellow. My speedometer rose past 70.

Red.

I jumped a median strip that divided the road from the shopping center and at full speed careened across the intersection, squeezing between two facing rows of cars. I hit a guardrail as I tried to veer up a cloverleaf ramp that led to 20. My rear wheels waved in graceful fishtails. I tried to keep control of the wheel—

but then a car came speeding down the ramp. I was going the wrong way.

I veered in time; so did the other fellow. I caught a split-second glance of his wide eyes behind a pair of glasses. Then I heard the crash.

Behind me in the mirror I could see how he'd rammed into the first police car broadside. I slowed slightly. The driver got out—so did the cop. They ran, but neither car exploded. When the other cop arrived on the scene he couldn't get through.

I sped up over the lip of the ramp and started to my left, the wrong way down Route 20—west. I wasn't daunted. I simply drove across the grass median that divided the two highways. It dipped and formed a ditch that I very nearly remained in. My wheels spun and ground and then finally took. They kicked back a spray of soil as the car lurched forward up onto 20 east. But I didn't stay there long. A tidal wave of cars was heading toward me. Their horns sang. I was off the road a second later, on the right shoulder, swerving to avoid a nosedive into a small and slimy stream of stagnant water. It was coated with green swirls of oil. A little sign-marker there on the highway read BLACK RIVER. I ran it over as I merged left.

Ten minutes later I dropped Svenquist and his car at the County Hospital. He was unconscious. A doctor in the emergency room said he'd lost a lot of blood but would be all right. I watched as they wheeled him away on a stretcher. His hand fell off it and his fingers fluttered, as if he was waving good-bye.

I never saw him again.

40

Focus.

I had to pull my mind's eye into focus—beam it in on one goal, then get there, increment by increment.

Car.

I had no ID, no credit card. That meant no rental. And I had no idea how to start a car without a key; I couldn't steal one.

My nerves were frayed, my hands shaking. A siren sang in the distance. The distance grew shorter.

Airport.

I inched out from the emergency ramp along the hospital's red-brick wall. I stepped through some bushes in time to see a taxi—straight from heaven—pull up at the front entrance. A nun got out. I ran to her and she stopped, frozen in her tracks, as if she thought I might have some earthly intent. A stern, round, featureless moon with brown eyes peered out of her black habit.

"Bless you, sister," I said. "I needed this cab."

My ragged voice grated against the hospital hush. She just stared at me.

So I blessed myself and got in the cab.

"Thank God you're here," I said.

"I'm waiting for someone," a female driver barked harshly.

I handed her a fifty.

"No, you're not." I was too tired to say any more.

There was a brief silence, then: "No, I guess I'm not." She drove off.

When I turned to see if I'd been followed, the nun was still staring after me, even as the cab turned out of view.

"Airport," I said.

"Which one?"

"Grand Rapids."

"Shit! That'll cost ya another fifty—in advance."

That would leave me three hundred.

"All right."

"OK."

We had a deal. I handed her another fifty.

I fell asleep somewhere along the interstate. I dreamed of Lola, that she was pressing her naked breasts against my chest. I heard her laugh in my ear, softly. She was speaking, whispering to me, when the whisper turned fierce, loud like thunder.

I woke to see a plane cross just inches overhead. It rattled the taxi windows as we drove under it. Its roar filled the cab, like a magnified version of the ocean in a shell. When I finally stepped out of that shell it was onto the beach of a neon airport. Its lights washed green against a bluish twilight. Sounds seemed magnified. I stood there in a daze, feeling like I'd just been borne into the fray.

I had no bags. My clothes had been stained by both Kelly's and Svenquist's blood. People stared as I limped my way to a United Airlines counter. My right arm was still so sore and my right hand so swollen that when I tried to count out cash with it I failed. Finally, I laid my wad on the counter and removed bills one by one with my left hand. I counted out two hundred and fifty-eight dollars—a one-way to LaGuardia. That left me forty-two. The plane was set to leave in twenty minutes.

"No bags?"

"No bags."

The clerk spoke with a tone of apprehension tinged with sincerity.

"Have a nice flight."

I carried myself through the X-ray scanner, then made for Gate 23. Before boarding I realized how hungry I was and bought myself a miniature hot dog at a food stand. It cost five-fifty. I ladled it with mustard and sauerkraut and wolfed it down in two bites.

Two and a half hours later, touching down in New York, I still hadn't digested it. It roiled up and down and sideways in my stomach. Churned there, as if I'd swallowed a gulp of the Black River.

After I arrived I left that part of me behind in a bathroom at LaGuardia. When I hoisted myself off my knees my head was spinning. I hung on to a wall and tried to focus on my cheap watch. It was 12:03.

I wandered through the airport like some past image of myself, someone I once knew. Electric doors opened for me as if they were glad to let me outside. A cool breeze blew across my face like holy water. I let my eyes close, and when I opened them only moments later the spinning was gone. A black man with a red cap was leaning his sad eyes toward me.

"You o-right?"

"Better."

"Das good." He went back to performing some obscure duty.

I stepped out into the darkness of the roadway and faced the night. Somewhere beyond the streetlamps were stars, the origin of the calendar that we humans had constructed to delineate our days. They were circling now. A new day had spun into place. July 28th.

Focus.

Part Four

NEW YORK AGAIN

41

"Manhattan," I said. "Upper West Side."

I slid onto the crisp back seat of a new cab. Inside, the taxi felt as windless and compressed as a space capsule. The silent driver quickly maneuvered his capsule out along the Grand Central Parkway and aimed it toward Manhattan. To my right, planes rose and fell like giant ghost-birds in an ephemeral aviary.

I asked the driver for a pen and paper. He handed me a red ballpoint and a pad, and I scratched on it, from memory:

> *Panther Field drop 2100.*
> *Sondra's Marina 2400.*
> *Clinic 0600.*

And then that enigmatic phrase:

> *Exchange and expediting as per MOTHER.*

I racked my brain. Perhaps someone I'd come in contact with during the course of the case might fit the description

"MOTHER"—someone other than Julia. I tried to think: a literal or figurative mother, an expediter. But I came up empty. Empty but for the nagging sensation that the answer was within my grasp.

Then, curiously, Billy's rabbit's foot and its sad inscription came to mind: "She is not my mother."

Perhaps the expediter had sent him to Julia.

Without thinking, I scribbled the number 7. It'd been the only number on that computer that had had no identifiable source. I had a trembling suspicion that it might be Genna—that Anna O'Reilly might finally have considered Genna a liability and put her up for sale. If I was right, the baby would be dropped along with a lot of others at Sondra's Marina, tonight, at midnight—2400—alive or dead.

A row of lights rushed by along the parkway and flashed against the pad of paper, causing it to blink eerily in my hands like some staccato pocket-cinema. I thought I saw Genna's face flicker there, briefly, flicker with the weary radiance of a fading Polaroid.

The cab let me off at the corner of Central Park and Eighty-second Street. The echoes my footsteps made bounced along the brownstone canyon. They lent a punctuation to the silent wisps of light that raced down Broadway. I smiled at the juxtaposition.

It was good to be back.

I climbed Lola's steps and rang her buzzer. I rang it three times before she answered. The speaker had broken since I'd been gone. Her voice was gruff and mechanical.

"Who's there?"

"Luke."

Silence.

The door buzzed like an alarm clock that could wake the whole building. I pushed the door open, apprehensive. Something was wrong—I could tell by the length of the buzz.

I ran up the first flight quietly, trying to get there before anticipated. I paused before the door and listened. There was a muffled whisper inside.

"Luke?" she said weakly. Scared.

"Yeah."

The door opened and her eyes told the story. Go away, they said.

I should have listened. But how could I? She looked so sensual: halter top and jeans and unkempt hair swinging down around her sleek shoulders, a black Cleopatra. I was drawn in, a moth to light.

I took the bold step and grabbed hold of her two bare arms, squeezed them as I pressed my lips against hers. My tongue stroked along her tongue. I felt that wonderful surge of warmth in my groin.

Then the bolt hit—against the back of my skull. I fell to my knees. The warmth between my legs disappeared and reemerged at the base of my neck. It spread from there, across my shoulders. I felt blood trickle down my spine. The original wound had reopened. I swooned there for a moment, aware that Lola was frozen—eyes wide. I stared up at her. Her hands rose, palms forward.

"No!" she screamed.

But the gun slammed me again, this time in the side of the head. I fell to the floor and lay there on my back. My eyes were blurred but I still saw the tall, thin figure that hovered over me. He held a .38 at his side. Our eyes met.

Nathan Wise spoke to Lola as he stared down at me.

"He—he's recognized me, Lola."

His gun arm straightened. The barrel pointed at my head. His hand was shaking.

Lola's voice was a terrified whisper.

"What are you going to do, Daddy?"

His eyes stared down past me, as if his gun were aimed toward hell.

I blacked out.

42

I woke up. That was the best thing I could say about the morning.
A cop was sticking the point of his shoe in my side.
"Ouch."
"Get up," he said, with blasé disapproval.
I tried, but nothing worked. My head felt like someone was behind me—a malicious guardian angel—twisting a vise around my ears. A high-pitched tone kept ringing, a discord of the spheres. The cop yanked me to my feet. My leg hurt so badly I fell again. I tried to brace myself, but my bad shoulder had frozen up, so I just collapsed like a sack of potatoes.
I moaned pathetically; no sympathy came from above. The cop grabbed my collar and pulled me across a tiled floor. It was an old, dilapidated lobby, huge. A chandelier hung over my head. Its bulbs had been stolen. Our tinny echoes bounced against the walls and like boomerangs came back to slap my ears. What was worse was the light when we got outside, lots of brittle rays that made my head feel like exploding.
"Get a hold of yourself," the cop told me.
He left me sprawled across the front steps and went to roust

a bum in the adjacent alley. Another bum. They had a similarly enlightening conversation.

I tried to sit up. It was then that I smelled the liquor that had been poured all over me. Perhaps it'd been poured down my throat, too; my lips were parched enough. I licked them with a sandpaper tongue, trying to determine where I'd been dropped.

It looked like Harlem. A welfare hotel on 121st or 122nd, maybe 123rd. The steeple of Saint John the Divine was peeking out of some trees to my left. I got up on two of the wobbliest legs ever and started walking toward it. It was a goal, at least.

"Hey, hey, hey!" The crop grabbed me. "Where do you think you're going?"

"Home," I said, but realized I had none.

He escorted me to the back seat of his squad car. Another cop escorted the bum from the alley and rudely shoved him in next to me.

"Careful," my cop said to the other. "They're fragile."

"Yeah."

They got in the front seat and both turned to look at us.

"Good morning, gentlemen," the first one said.

"Jesus," said the second cop, staring at me. "They're getting younger every day."

They drove us down Riverside, to a church on Ninety-ninth that had no steeple. They pushed us out of the back seat with the words: "This is our good deed for the day. Stay sober, goddammit."

A young man wearing a sweater that was too small for him grabbed us each by an arm and led us briskly through an arch adjacent to the church façade.

"We can't have soup lines out here," he said with a cartoonish voice. "The neighborhood will be up in arms."

Inside was a courtyard where a few dozen vagrants sat idly at temporary tables, most hung over and weary from a night on the sidewalks, waiting for food that they'd been told they must eat. A few actually looked hungry. Most, like me, wanted to get out of there. I tried, but an overzealous young Christian caught me sneaking out and, seeing that I was young, paid special attention to me. He actually patted my head.

So I ate.

It wasn't so bad, either. Even though it was morning, they

served us stew. Beef, potatoes, carrots, bread. I ate ravenously, as did all but the hard cases. They sat with their eyes fixed on a faraway drink.

My watch was gone, so I asked my Christian friend the time.

"Nine-thirty."

"I've got to go, now. But—thanks."

"Go and be with God," he whispered, putting a Bible in my palm. There was a dollar bill in it.

Since I had no more money in my pockets, I used his dollar to hop the West Side IRT. I rode it all the way downtown, to Christopher Street. From there I limped east, seven long crosstown blocks, to the ninth precinct.

Cussone was exactly where I'd have pictured him being, sitting with his legs up and his eyes fixed on that opaque window. He had a cup of coffee in his left hand and a Danish in his right, both poised evenly, untouched. He resembled that sculpture of the scales of justice.

"Hello, Stanley."

It took a moment for focusing. It must have been a bad night for him, too. He delicately set down his coffee and his Danish, as if not to be too loud about it. His eyes were riveted on me.

"Jesus . . ." he whispered, standing.

I looked down at myself and tried to smile.

"That bad, huh?"

"That bad."

He handed me his coffee and his Danish with a bit too much emphasis. Too much worry. I'd seen that look before. That Goodbye Look people give you when they want to throw one last show of decency in your direction. Before you go all the way down.

"Stop staring, Stanley." I drank the coffee. It scalded my insides.

"You're in a lot of trouble, kid. And look at you; your life's fallen to shit." He spoke softly: "What's happened?"

I didn't want to talk, not just yet. I was still trying to figure out what had happened to me the night before. To comprehend how Lola was a part of this case, how she had been all along. I said sadly:

"Let's not talk, Stanley. Not yet. Just dial this number—use one of your computer modems." I recited the 213 number.

A breath of luck had been with me over the course of the night. The only thing not taken from me was Benjamin Kelly's old dog tag, which I'd hung around my neck. I handed it to Stanley.

"Listen for the voice," I told him. "Then punch this number in."

"I don't understand."

"You may soon."

He sat and blinked at me a couple of times, slow basset hound blinks.

"I'd have to run this next door."

"Then run it next door."

He stood up again, aggravated.

"You come in here, like—" His voice halted. "Like some—" He swung his arm down in open air. "I mean, Jesus!"

"I'm happy to see you, too."

He strode the length of the second floor. At the other end was an arched door that led to a set of stairs. They spiraled down into the basement of the next building, the "dungeon," a room filled with computers and phone tappers. Cussone stopped just short of the arch and yelled back to me:

"You know where the locker room is. Take a shower." He paused for emphasis. "Please."

The tiles were cold, the water lukewarm. The soap was Ivory. It seemed ridiculous to lather myself in it, rinse, dry, then put those same clothes back on. But that's what I did. They were sticky with sweat and bourbon and blood. I gritted my teeth and smiled, trying to make them feel like home.

Cussone was waiting for me at his desk. He seemed dissatisfied.

"Those same clothes again?"

I threw my hands out gently and let them fall at my sides.

"Oh well," he added.

"Did you see the lists?"

"What lists?"

I sat down. "Oh no."

"There's nothing on the other end of this number. Just a woman's voice saying 'Disconnected.' Over and over. I asked the guys to take the trouble and trace it. The wire. But the main trunk lines seem to be out of operation. We can't come close to pinpointing an address." He breathed one long breath, putting his fingertips together. "What lists?"

I told him. The whole story. The circuitous gauntlet that had passed me through Los Angeles and Black River. The three partners in Trion. Anna O'Reilly and her barn full of Kalashnikovs. The huge man with red hair—Red, Billy's killer. A man who'd also killed a Fed named Rose. I told Cussone how Denig had died at the Ivanhoe, and of his bloody note. Stanley already knew that I'd used Denig's air ticket to Black River.

I spoke kindly of Svenquist, with respect. I told Cussone how we'd found Kelly in Julia's hotel room. And of Kelly's passkeys for IBMs in both Black River and Poughkeepsie. Then there was the number in his wallet—and the lists I'd seen on that computer. I added that there were two more murders to consider, deaths that were surely connected to this case, but had been covered up by a corrupt sheriff in Black River.

"I think Anna O'Reilly might have killed her parents," I told Stanley. "But the whole town's blamed Julia for the last seven years."

"Why would they blame Julia?"

"Because she and Anna are sisters."

He stared at me, then turned away toward his window.

"O'Reilly," was all he said.

I leaned forward and put my arms on the desk.

"Stanley."

"I'm trying to sort this out in my head."

"It's difficult. Impossible. We don't have all the pieces."

He thought for a moment.

"If I had a blackboard—"

"Not now. We don't have time."

"What? Why?"

"It's tonight."

I wrote them on his office pad—those same four phrases that had been etched into my memory. I slid the pad across the desk.

"What is this?"

He read the phrases silently, then ripped the page from the pad and stared at them some more.

"Those were the last words on that computer in Black River."

His eyes rolled up at me. "Exactly?"

"Exactly."

He looked down at it again. A breath squeezed out of his lungs. "This fits in with Denig's note."

"Yup."

"And—we don't know who all the players are yet—but if this is correct it begins to clarify their operation."

"It's correct."

"And tells us where to be at midnight, I suppose. You're sure it's tonight?"

"July 28th."

He laid the paper on his desk and flattened it with both hands.

"You know, I can't expect much help on this. Two, three men, tops. The case has gotten nowhere, from our department's angle—after months . . ." He smiled at me with all the charm of a double-edged razor. "And you're not exactly a reliable source, as far as the Feds are concerned." His smile faded. "My name could be shit if we come up empty on this."

I watched and waited. It took a while, but the tumblers between his ears finally clicked into place. He said sternly:

"I'll make some calls."

43

"Meet me here in six hours." Cussone's basset-eyes were blank, his voice a monotone. "I'll have all the forces I can muster here by that time. Six o'clock. Until then you go get something to eat, to wear, and get some rest. You'll need it."

He pulled a twenty out of his wallet as if it were a thousand-dollar bill and handed it to me with as much reluctance.

"Thanks."

"Now get out of here."

I stopped at a deli and got some change, then used a phone booth on the corner of Fourth. My first call was to Richard Weiss. His machine answered, affording me the opportunity to leave a rather inscrutable message about the screenplay's ephemeral progress. It was Sunday; I hoped I'd be able to start writing again by Monday. I hoped. Then I called New York Hospital and got the answer I'd expected: Lola wasn't there.

I decided to make a personal visit. I needed to know how phony she really was. It seemed important for me to verify that I'd been used—though for what I was too tired to guess.

I used a dollar out of my twenty and took the Third Avenue bus up to Thirty-second Street. From there I walked east to New York Hospital, catching a glimpse of the East River shimmering behind it. Its smokestacks billowed with white smoke, lending the impression that the whole ugly structure might break anchor and steam away on its own power.

Inside the main lobby a receptionist pointed me toward a room labeled SWITCHBOARD OPERATIONS. Beyond the door three operators fielded all the calls made to the hospital. Each wore headphones, and each worked a computer, searching for patient and employee extension numbers. When none could be found, they made a general paging call. One of the operators was a young black man. His voice was familiar. So was the name on his nametag: Ronald. I put my hand on his shoulder and yanked his headphone off.

"What . . . ?" he said in shock.

I had to be quick. I lifted him gently but with force up out of his seat and flattened him against the back wall. The two women who operated the other switchboards stared with their mouths open as the switchboard buzzers sang in chorus.

"I just want the truth," I said, my voice calm, "and I won't take you to the cops."

"I haven't done anything wrong!"

"How much did she pay you?"

"Who?"

"The fake nurse, Lola. She doesn't work here, does she?"

His eyes swayed nervously from me to the other operators. They were all ears.

"I don't know who you mean," he said weakly.

"I know her as Lola Wilson." I turned to the two others. "I'm working with the police. Find out—is Lola Wilson on your computer? She's supposed to be a nurse."

They eyed me but didn't move. Finally the bigger of the two spoke up, laconically, I thought, given the situation.

"I don't have to look 'er up. She ain't on there. All calls to her we was to forward through him." She pointed to Ronald. Ronald smiled at me. "She gone now," the woman added.

Before he knew what I was doing, I managed to reach down

and slip Ronald's wallet out of his back pocket. I stood between him and the door, trying to appear broad-shouldered, and opened the wallet.

His name was Ronald Spears. He had over a hundred dollars in his wallet, a bank card, a driver's license with a bad picture. And a few phone numbers. One of them was Lola's.

"Just tell me the truth, Ronald, and you'll get your wallet."

"Outside," he said, his eyes cold and sad and ever so weary.

We sat in the lounge, on a faded orange sofa. In adjacent seats around us a family waited, six kids and their mother, all perched on the edges of their seats with hands in their laps. They'd all been crying, but their big eyes were calm now. Over the shock. Prepared.

I whispered to Ronald: "Tell me."

"What?"

"How much?"

"Twenty—a day, for however long it lasted."

"How long's it been?"

"I dunno—since this one guy came in the hospital. Few months ago."

"That was me."

"Aw, shit," he said with a frightened whisper. The mother of the family eyed me sternly.

"Quietly, now," I said. "How could she—and you—get away with this? She's not a nurse."

"But she is—from another hospital. A degree, the whole thing. She had the certificates, so they allowed her temp status. Anyway, that's what the other nurses . . ." His voice drifted off.

"Did she say what hospital she came from?"

"No."

A sudden flush came over me. The center of my palms beaded with some instant sweat.

"Did she mention that it might have been a clinic?"

"No—she didn't tell me anything. Honest. Except . . . except."

"What?"

"Well, except what she'd told you. The excuse, I mean."

"Excuse?"

"After you left the hospital the first time she thought the job was over. Me, too. But you tried to reach her here, after she'd already gone. I don't think she figured that. She told me that she told you that—that I was a jilted lover. Jealous . . . That I wasn't putting your calls through."

"I remember."

We were quiet for a moment.

"An' then," he continued, "you kept calling. I had to let the other operators in on it. I told them that I'd take all her calls. I played it like I really was her lover. A protective one. That there was this other guy—"

"I get the picture."

He paused, hands folded in his lap.

"Who were the other nurses?"

"I won't tell. They're awful nice to me. I know they wouldn't have done it, you know, but for the fact that she was another nurse. Registered, the whole thing. They're the ones who saw the certificates. She gave them money."

I got out a pad and pen I'd lifted from Cussone. I tried to sound mean.

"Their names, Ronald."

"I can't tell you. Please don't make me."

"I have to."

He brooded for a moment, then muttered their names: Brunetta Mack and Mary Bonfiglio. I put the pad and pen back into my pocket.

"Am I gonna go to jail?" Ronald queried.

"I don't know. Tell me, did she ever receive any calls from anybody else?"

He didn't answer at first. Finally he nodded.

"An older man," he said. "A few times."

Nathan Wise.

"Anyone else?"

He shook his head.

"Answer me one more question."

"All right."

"Why was she doing all this? What did she have to gain?"

"Man," he said breathily, "I can't begin to know. I asked her, you see. But she never said a word about it, really. I never knew."

He stared down at his hands, twiddled his fingers for a while, then looked back up at me. "She's a good person, I think. I wouldn'ta done all this otherwise."

Just then a doctor approached the family next to us. His face was grim. The mother stood and took a few awkward paces toward him. Her hands gripped his arms. He looked her in the eye and smiled wearily. I didn't hear what he said but it didn't matter. Everyone in that lobby got the message. She leaned her head against his chest, crying and smiling. "Thank you," she cried. "Oh God, thank you."

She turned and knelt and her children threw their little arms around her. They wept happily together, their whimpers the only sound in the enormous lobby.

I stumbled away from Ronald, exiting the building through glass doors that spilled out into a concrete garden. A fountain sprayed small arcs of water at its center, and I sat on its edge, exhausted. I wished I could cry. Not with relief for the woman and her children, but for myself. Lola had used me all along. I didn't know why, but it didn't matter. I felt bruised inside, cut to the bone. The marrow was infected. A poison was thickening my blood. Bitterness. Maybe I'd never cry again. Maybe nothing would ever be the same. This case had swung down on me like a butcher's cleaver and severed the umbilical that had connected me to the first half of my life.

A large hand rested on my shoulder.

"You all right, buddy?" asked a man with dirty jeans and a hefty paunch. I didn't look him in the eye. I spoke to his lunch pail.

"Yeah. Thanks. Just tired."

"Feel better," he said as he backed away.

I tried to take his advice. I got to my feet and let the dizziness subside before I started drifting in a daze along Thirty-third Street, east, to a cement footbridge I knew that crossed the FDR. I climbed down to the shining river and gently stretched my bruised body over a concrete bench along the running path.

The sun had warmed it.

44

As if my timetables were reversed, I woke promptly at the crack of dusk. Headlights on the FDR washed over me. From where I sat they seemed to meld together like a string of glowing pearls clasped around the silhouetted skyline.

I stood up and tried to straighten my hair. Just above me, on the highway, traffic had stalled. A young, well-dressed woman in the passenger seat of a BMW stared down at me through a wire grating. Her hard eyes softened with a distant pity, as if I were a photograph of an Ethiopian child.

Shit, I thought, I'm tired of this. I need new clothes.

I crossed the footbridge, hiked to a deli on Thirty-fourth and Second, and bought myself a triple-decker sandwich and a Coca-Cola. I scarfed them in the cab that took me downtown.

"You're late," Cussone said harshly. Too harshly.

"What's wrong?"

"Nothing."

He led me angrily to his Chevy and pointed.

"Get in and wait."

It was seven-forty. By eight we were under way. All three of us.

"This is Detective Denoy," Cussone said wearily.

I shook hands with a black man in his late thirties, a comer with black leather jacket and striped tie. He chewed gum.

"Hello."

"Dan. How ya doin'?"

"Denoy is with us," Stanley said, "as a favor to me. We're lucky to have him."

"No one else?"

Denoy said with some amusement: "Chief threw him out on his hands. You shoulda seen your face, Stan!"

"All right, all right," Cussone said.

"Not all right!" I tried not to sound too worried. "What are we going to do?"

"Here," was all Cussone said. I looked down on the seat between us. With his right hand he pushed a gun across the vinyl. It was in a holster.

"Don't say I never did anything for you."

"It's a beauty," said Denoy, leaning over the front seat. "Nine-millimeter automatic. Fifteen shots. Fourteen in the clip, one in the chamber. And you can leave it cocked and locked."

I lifted the weapon in my hands.

"It usually takes some getting used to. Too bad you don't have the time."

I gulped. "What about the FBI?"

"I've informed them as to where we'll be and what we think is going down. They were curious as to who my source was. When I told them, they laughed. The last thing they said was 'Good luck.'"

The ride to Poughkeepsie consisted largely of my learning from Denoy the proper manner in which to reload a Beretta 92F with a fresh clip. It took some doing. I had it down so that I could snap a clip, remove another from my belt, and pop it in in a matter of ten seconds.

"Too slow," said Denoy. "Under pressure the time it takes doubles, at least. That ain't too healthy."

"Thanks."

"No problem."

Our tires rumbled under us, a metallic thunder.

"Mid-Hudson Bridge," Cussone reported. "We're here."

Denoy handed me two full clips. I slipped one of them into the handle chamber and then switched the safety lever. I tucked the other into my belt, at the back and to the right. I strung the holster around my shoulders, pulling on the little strap below my arm to tighten it. When it was snug, I sank the heavy nine-millimeter deep into its stiff leather pouch. It was not comfy.

Poughkeepsie loomed like a dark dream. Its tarnished city lights spread out in various directions but seemed not to connect. Black structures—whole neighborhoods—brooded in shadow. Rolling off the bridge, we entered an area lit with tall streetlamps that seemed themselves to deny any human activity. They umbrellaed an entire avenue with the sterility of a city under martial law.

"Nice place," Denoy said.

We wound our way around some back streets in a few forgotten neighborhoods before finding the road to the river. Far from the hill that led down to Sondra's Marina, Cussone stopped the car. He left the engine running.

"What now?" I asked him.

"Coffee."

He pulled a U-turn and we drove up the road approximately half a mile, to an all-night grocery. There we bought three coffees and a few wrapped sandwiches and some granola bars. Cussone also picked up three quarts of milk.

"Do we need that much milk?" I asked.

Denoy smiled. Cussone slapped his money down and we got out of there. Outside, we pulled up along the road again.

"If you wanna take a leak like a normal human being, do it now."

The three of us wandered like vagrants into some roadside bushes and wandered out again a minute later. Across the street, some tiny black faces peered down at us from a second-story window.

"Shameless and proud of it," Denoy said as we got back in the Chevy. "Let's go, Joe."

We went, without lights. Cussone curved our car down the

driveway toward Sondra's. We passed the road to old man Farrer's trailer on our left. The trailer was perched on the hillcrest like a silent, silhouetted tomb. We inched under it, down the gravel driveway, blinded by a sudden, total darkness. Finally the surrounding trees opened out onto level ground, where Sondra's barn and office sat in shadow. Two dark winches rose up into the night, cables and hooks swaying like pendulums. Stanley backed his car along the perimeter of the open ground, away from the barn. He found an ample opening, then revved the engine a little, wedging the back end of his car up into the forest. We scraped along a tree to our right, but managed to submerge the entire vehicle in a tangle of underbrush and low trees. He turned the engine off.

We were pitched at a steep angle, facing downhill. I almost slid off the seat, spilling my coffee on myself.

"Shit."

"Shhh."

"Fine night for a stakeout," Denoy whispered, stretching his legs out on the back seat.

We were silent. The night woods crawled around us. After a few minutes Cussone spoke.

"Doesn't seem like anyone's around yet. Let's cover for possible reflections."

We all got out and covered the right side of our vehicle with brush and loose branches. Cussone climbed in from the passenger side. I followed. Denoy spoke softly, still outside.

"My turn?" he asked Cussone.

"As good a choice as any. Keep to the upper right."

"Two o'clock high," Denoy said cheerfully.

"Roughly. But not too near the road."

"Right."

Denoy removed a camera from a bag in the back seat. It was wrapped in a green fatigue warmer. Only the telephoto lens and remote trigger were exposed. He snapped a practice picture. I barely heard the automatic wind.

"Two hours," Cussone whispered.

Denoy waved. He was already heading uphill.

"Where's he going?" I asked.

"We might be seen. We don't want all of us in one place."

"Oh."

"Get your gun out."

"What?"

"You heard me."

The gun slid out with a whisper, an unmistakable sound.

"That's what I wanted to avoid at a touchy moment. That sound's tipped more people than you know. And, speaking of sounds . . ." Stanley reached up and unscrewed the glass dome that covered the car's ceiling light. He removed the tiny bulb. "Now, open your door, quietly." We both opened our doors and left them only slightly ajar. "That takes care of that," he said. "Now . . ." He removed the food from its paper bag, then rolled his window open. Quietly, with a steady hand, he poured out two of the three containers of milk.

"What're you doing?"

He threw the containers on the floor and smiled.

"Those are our porto-johns."

"Christ."

"Beats holding it." He placed the gun on the dashboard. "Now be quiet. And keep an eye just above the riverline. If you look slightly away from something in the dark, you see it better."

"What am I looking for?"

"Whatever floats upriver. If anything. Now quiet."

We didn't speak for over an hour. The wind rose and fell in strength and pitch, sometimes carrying sounds from the city. When it lulled I heard the river lapping gently against the two wooden pylons on which the old dock had been built.

I began to think clearly about Lola, how she'd called Nathan Wise "Daddy." It was odd to think of him as her father. It made me realize, for the first time, really, how many families were involved in this case. The Denigs, Ralph and Julia and Genna; and Julia's family, Anna and their parents, who'd died in that fire seven years ago. Then there was the mysterious William Farrer, who'd been hacked apart with his wife eleven years ago; and his father, a poor, destitute drunk who owned half of Poughkeepsie. And there were Farrer's old friends, Pete Dillery and his wife, who had disappeared. Maybe they'd murdered Farrer and then run, or maybe they'd been killed, too. In either case, young Billy Dillery had somehow ended up with Julia. And had knocked softly on my door four months ago.

A damp gust of wind swayed the two tall winches. They creaked under its force. Some loose tarps fluttered; the barn shook; my bones rattled.

"Stop shaking," Cussone said, his first words in sixty minutes.

"I don't have a jacket."

"Whose fault is that?"

"My fault," I whispered, though I'd already heard the car coming.

"Jesus." Cussone spoke to me, barely audible. "Gun."

I took hold of the nine-millimeter. It felt as heavy as a sledgehammer. My wrist and hand shook.

Cussone brought a finger to his lips. "Just watch."

I watched.

The car was an old Lincoln Town Car, its lights off. It seemed big and bulbous in the darkness. Two men got out and stood near their open doors. Gradually their eyes adjusted and they spread apart, away from the car, each carrying a large pistol. They were policing the area.

Cussone and I were crouched down. I saw the whites of his big dog-eyes turned on me.

"Shit," he whispered.

One of the men from the car walked in our direction. His pistol was aimed toward the woods where we sat.

Cussone brought his lips close to my ear.

"Get ready to slide out on the ground."

I nodded.

The man seemed to be walking right toward us. I heard his footsteps crunching over leaves at the perimeter of the forest.

A sound. We all heard it. It sounded like a rock hitting rock.

From far off I heard a voice—a grating whisper:

"Elwin!"

Our man ran back to his partner. Cussone and I peeked over the dashboard in time to see both figures taking to the woods above the marina barn.

"Denoy," Stanley smiled. "Threw a decoy."

"Saved our ass."

"Maybe. Let's get out of the car."

We slid out onto damp ground, both from the passenger door. We lay still. The next ten minutes were spent listening to various footsteps clamber in the woods a good distance away. When the wind kicked up we'd lose all sounds in its flurry. It rustled through the fallen leaves and gave me the impression that the ground was breathing.

Finally—confusingly—the two men got back in their Lincoln and drove off. I watched them from under the right wheel of Stanley's Chevy.

"Denoy may have spooked them," Cussone whispered. "They may not bring their principals down."

Five minutes passed.

"Shit," I finally said. "We'll never know when they'll be here again."

But Cussone was listening to something I couldn't hear. "There's just one thing worse than not getting what you want," he said, his voice low, his eyes locked on the road. "Getting it."

A faraway rumble approached. It rose in volume. The ground shook under us. Faint cold rays of artificial light streaked through the woods on both sides of the hill, then grew brighter, as if an angel were descending. Or a machine God. An engine thundered. A flood of light aimed down the gravel driveway, then scoured the woods to the left of the road.

"They're looking for Denoy. Let's get out of here."

I followed Stanley. We dragged ourselves on our stomachs, uphill, deeper into the woods. We heard voices. I turned and saw two men prowling the road, eerie silhouettes that carried rifles.

The light shone in our direction. Luckily our car was covered well—but we weren't. We'd been caught on an awkward ridge, naked of trees. We both lay behind a small bush. We didn't move. The light seemed to freeze us with the harsh blue of a slow-motion flashbulb. But no one saw. The light passed over us. We squirmed along the ground faster than I'd thought humanly possible and hid behind a clump of trees.

Stanley was sweating. He wiped his face with his sleeve and then reached into his inner jacket. He fiddled with something in his hands for a moment, then brought a pair of tiny binoculars to his eyes.

"Christ," he whispered, "that thing is service issue. Army convoy. Big."

"Soldiers?" I whispered.

He looked down at me. "Not our army."

He handed me the binoculars. They were light and waterproofed. I held them to my eyes.

The two armed men had taken positions at the entrance to the marina. They stood just inside the woods on either side of the road. One was wearing a red baseball cap. It caught the wash of brakelights and glowed like an ember in the shadows. I couldn't see his face accurately, but I could see that his skin was white. He wasn't Cuban.

I watched as the convoy truck circled around on the flat, engine roaring. It backed its tail end over the dock. The driver got out, brandishing a rifle like a palefaced Sandinista.

The doors to the back of the barn were being opened. It was hard to see what they were taking out. Something metal. Long. It rattled. Two other men carried it. Cussone took the glasses from me.

"Let's see."

He watched for a while without speaking.

"I'll be damned," he said.

"What is it?"

"A conveyor belt."

We stared at one another for a moment. Stanley shook his head with a weary resignation. I knew why: we'd both seen that conveyor in the boat shed.

He raised the binoculars again, but lowered them immediately. He didn't need to see. The engine of the truck had shut down with a growl and a sputter, then left a sudden silence in its wake. Slowly, a strange, haunting sound filled the night. It ran through me like a sonic knife. I got up on my knees and clung to a tree, listening to the voices crying from inside the truck.

The searchlight swept in our direction. We both fell to the ground, pressing ourselves into the soil. I caught a glimpse of Stanley in the severe light. His cheek lay against the leaves. His eyes were unfocused.

"Bastards," he whispered when the light had passed.

Then we heard another sound coming from the river—a deep, rhythmic, frightening motor that seemed to swell and subside like the breaths of some huge beast. Its shadow drifted up and down near the shore, splashing waves against the pilings. No one turned a light on it. No one spoke a word from shore. It approached through the darkness. The engine cut and there was a lapping silence.

A dim figure knelt on the boat's bow. When he stood, I knew him immediately. His enormous silhouette seemed to dominate the horizon. His long hair drifted behind him. A rifle crossed his chest. I had the silly thought that he was an enormous Christian hood ornament. Then his huge arm swung up and he lofted a line toward shore. Someone on the dock caught it and held it as the boat rotated on a tight axis. Its hull scraped against the pilings as it backed in along the wooden dock. The startling squeak of wood against fiberglass pierced the quiet of the operation with a noise as unsettling as a coyote's howl.

The boat was secured and Red jumped from its bow to the dock, a nimble move for a man his size. His voice was hushed as he spoke to the men onshore. At his command the back gate of the truck was opened, intensifying the sounds that emanated from it. The babies' cries seemed to drift out along the river surface, slap against the other side, then bounce back to Cussone and me. A delayed, anguished echo, not easy to sit still through. My fist involuntarily squeezed the butt of my revolver. I wanted to shoot somebody.

The conveyor belt was hoisted up over the lip of the truck's tailgate. It stretched down to the dock. Someone on the far side of the truck started a small putt-putt generator, no more than a few amps, and the conveyor started to roll. The truck's red taillights were switched on, and in their glow I saw the bleached white canvas revolve around on its rollers. A man inside the truck sent the first baby down the conveyor. It screamed the whole way, sending a terrible shudder through my gun arm. A young man, who had piloted the boat, waited at the other end. Under glasses and a wool knit cap, his face was ashen. Red watched him closely as he lifted the baby and relayed it to another man waiting in the hull of the boat. I saw only his hands. He took hold of the child carelessly and pulled the baby into the bowels of the hull.

The system worked, so they began in earnest. Babies were sent down rapidly on the conveyor belt. Cussone and I watched as over thirty of them rolled into awaiting hands.

"There's more than was on the list," I told Cussone. "They've moved up another shipment."

"Thank yourself for that," he said, then passed me the binoculars. He tried to sound objective.

"I count eight men."

"Three of us."

He sighed. I raised the binoculars in time to see the conveyor slip from the back of the truck and a half dozen of the infants fall to the ground. One went into the water near the dock. It sank. The boy with the blue knit cap jumped in after the child but came up empty-handed. He pulled himself to the dock, soggy and flustered. No one helped him. No one acknowledged his effort. The man inside the truck kicked a man standing near the tailgate, and I heard something about "fifty fucking thousand," but the generator coughed like a mechanical child and I didn't hear the rest. Within seconds the fallen babies were carried to the boat and passed inside. The conveyor was rerigged. Someone tied it down this time.

The operation continued.

"We could get them all right now," Cussone said in a strained whisper. "Murder one. If Denoy got the pictures."

A voice spoke from behind us and my heart stopped.

"Would be nice," a man whispered with a seedy elegance. He sounded like Ricardo Montalban.

We turned to see him standing in shadow, above us by two yards. The hammer of his gun clicked back.

"Do not move," he said. "Do not speak."

Along the forest ridge, all the way past the marina, a dozen figures stood waiting in shadow.

"The weapons," he said to us politely.

We gave our guns to him.

"Up."

We got up.

From his general vicinity we heard a small beep—no more than the sound of a watch alarm. It signaled once. Responding, the Cuban produced a compact machine gun from under his leather jacket. A silencer extended from its barrel.

"Time," he said. He had a rather nonchalant attitude.

The other figures along the hill began marching down in unison. The Cuban pushed us forward. We walked ahead of him by one pace.

"Who are you?" Cussone asked.

"It's not who I am." He poked me in the ribs. "It's who you are." The Cuban spoke with delight. "You are my barricade."

I glanced at Cussone; he glanced at me. Mute terror clouded his eyes.

"Damn you," he said to me.

The gunfire began.

45

We stumbled ahead of him, not comprehending the scene that spread out before us. Cubans had come out of the woods firing on the truck. Two men had already died. The kid with the hat and glasses fell onto the dock, screaming, then rolled into the water, following that drowned child for good. A cacophony of pathetic screams came from the hull of the boat. They echoed. The sound was ghastly.

One of the guards on the road fired at us. Instinctively, Cussone and I hit the ground. A spray of bullets that were silenced fired just over our heads with the suction sound of rapid-fire spitballs. The man along the rim fell with a scream.

Our Cuban shook his arm and seemed only annoyed at the blood that was running out of his sleeve.

"Damned potato-eaters." It was a surreal epithet. "Get off your ass!" he yelled at us.

"What the hell is all this?" Stanley shouted, a shudder of desperation in his voice. The Cuban grabbed him by the scruff of the collar, dragged him up, and kicked him forward. He poked the barrel of his gun in my back and I was up in a flash.

Spits of rifle fire whispered near us. Red stood on the bow of the boat and fired several rounds until his rifle failed. I was pushed forward, with Cussone, as our Cuban fired in Red's direction. A wash of icy floodlight spilled over us. It was then that Red saw me. He lowered his gun a split second, confused. A bullet caught him in the leg.

He fell to one knee. I turned in time to see the Cuban aiming his Uzi at Red. His shots went off and nearly took my ear with them. But he missed. The Cuban was about to fire again when I grabbed his gun and kicked his groin. His gun quickly slapped my chin. His knee rammed up into my chest. I buckled—and the barrel of the Uzi lowered in my direction. But before he could fire, Cussone threw a left into his stomach, then a right into the side of his head. Two muffled shots punched holes in the ground. The man fell. Stanley grabbed our pistols out of his belt and shot him, twice. Once in each arm.

He gave a gun to me. The barrel was hot.

"Let's go."

But I couldn't run. I knelt there and watched as the last of Red's men jumped on the boat. The engine rumbled. Its stern fumed with fire. It sputtered away from the dock.

"We have to get out of here!" Cussone yelled.

I watched the boatload of babies disappear across the river. Red was at the wheel, navigating with a pistol in one hand. His bright hair caught a glint of the fire that grew astern, then he was swallowed by shadows. All we could see was the flame that burned its way south, down the Hudson.

A sudden quiet spilled around us. Someone had switched off the generator. A car's searchlight popped on with a hum and shone in our direction. It caught us, mid-field, poised like two amateur thespians waiting for a cue.

"Drop the pistols!" a Latin voice shouted from behind the light.

Our cue.

"God damn you," Stanley cursed.

Our guns hit the ground with two dull thuds.

A strange haze filled the air, dust and gunsmoke and burning motor oil. Through it, the searchlight reflected and refracted and bounced in a thousand directions. A handful of Cubans approached through the drifting swirls, weapons extended.

"God damn you," Stanley whispered again.

There was a finality in his tone this time.

They remained in a wide circle around us, a group of silhouettes that might as well have been spirits. They were walking us across the field, a walk where the smallest sounds seemed magnified to me: our crunching footsteps; the lapping of water aginst the dock; all the dozens of pulsing breaths and erratic cries that drifted from the back of the truck like mingling echoes from a well. They swelled in pitch like a dissonant concerto, rising to a dreamlike crescendo. Then all at once I realized I was on my knees. There were voices and they weren't American. They were shouting. I felt Cussone's hands under my arms, hoisting me to my feet again. My legs were shaky. A thousand needles pricked around my body. Someone yelled close to my ear—but I didn't see him. My head was still spinning. His rifle slammed me between the shoulder blades. Again, I landed on my kneecaps.

"Get up," Stanley said. He was frightened. "Off your knees!"

I tried and made it. My head felt clearer now—pain can do that—but my legs were still wobbly. We all took a few more steps forward, to the truck. Some of the men dispersed, breaking the circle open. A few guns raised. One motioned for us to step forward. Slowly, we took the steps. I thought it was all over, then, that they were going to shoot us. So did Stanley. I saw eternity floating behind his eyes.

Someone turned my shoulders and faced me toward the road. Up on the hill I saw a pair of headlights flash on and off. Once.

"Shit," one of the Cubans spit out.

Then his arm raised and lowered and his gun cracked down against Cussone's skull. Stanley fell to his knees. It took another hit to lay him flat.

"Oh, no," I said aloud.

There it was again, that old familiar feeling. Cold metal slapping the back of my neck. I felt myself fall—felt my knees hit ground—but it wasn't ground. It was water. Deep, black river water. I sank in it. Down and down. Past the other children. Their blankets had drifted off and they were naked, suspended in water. They were crying out to me.

I hit bottom.

46

I woke up with my hands tied. I was being dragged by my shoulders over what I thought to be a riverbed. It was the road. My eyes opened and closed involuntarily; I was not fully conscious. I caught brief glimpses of the muscular shadows that pulled me along. Through the corner of my eye I saw the sparkle of a white limousine that was parked at the top of the hill. Then I was hauled off the road and dropped like useless luggage. My head landed against a tin can filled with small metal objects that made a rattle like maracas. They spilled over the ground. I ended up with some of them in my mouth. Nuts and bolts. They tasted of oil. It didn't take long to figure where I was.

Old man Farrer's trailer.

I heard a car door open, close. Light footsteps strode across the gravel. A pair of five-hundred-dollar shoes looked me in the eye. His voice spoke over me. A smooth voice. American.

"Bring him to me. Both of them. Inside."

He stepped over me and kept walking. The trailer door opened. I was lifted again and dragged over some sharp objects that were strewn over the ground. Metal tire rims and other junk.

Someone, somewhere close by, was trying to start a small engine. I thought of the generator—but that wasn't it. Generators don't roar like lions, putter out, roar, putter.

"What's that?" I mumbled aloud. I was frightened. Maybe I already knew what it was. As they dragged me through the open door of Farrer's trailer the engine finally started. I knew the sound.

I was dropped again on the floor of the trailer. My lips tasted a dirty yellow shag. When I rolled over, a dim bulb waved overhead, making the trailer seem to be rocking side to side. The elegantly dressed man stood under it, his back to me. He took his coat off. I tried to focus my eyes, my thoughts. My memory. Then he turned and stared down at me with a malicious grin.

I recognized him from the picture I'd seen of him as a boy, standing arm-in-arm with his best friend on the dock below. Back when it'd been Farrer's dock, before it was changed to Sondra's. I remembered the sign: LIVE BAIT. Me.

"William Farrer," I said.

He smiled.

One of his men walked in with a tiny little chain saw. Its motor purred.

Farrer motioned with his left hand. A hefty Cuban grabbed me by the shoulders again and pulled me into a chair. I was bound to it, my chest wrapped in rope to the back of the chair. But they cut my arms free. Blood surged into my fingertips.

Moments later Stanley was dragged in. He was still out cold. They sat him in a chair next to me and bound him in the same way. The rope seemed to wake him. Groggily, he pitched his big eyes my way. He said nothing.

Farrer put on a pair of gloves. They were long and sleek and shiny. They matched his thousand-dollar suit. He took the chain saw with deft fingers and swung it as if it were a six-shooter.

His smile corroded my nerves.

"I'm getting pretty good at this," he said.

I'd never been one to sweat profusely, but that changed. Beads of the stuff rolled from the base of my scalp over the crest of my forehead. They splashed on my nose and cheeks and pants. My breathing began to accelerate—I was heaving, short, terrible breaths. Tears squeezed from my eyes. I jerked a glance at Stanley and felt even worse.

He was shaking. His eyes were wide and he was crying. He knew what was coming and all he could do was whisper his wife's name, over and over.

"Annie . . . Annie . . ."

Farrer came closer with the chain saw.

"You've been a terrible nuisance to us, Mr. Byman. I've been keeping track."

I had to pull myself together. I had to know.

"You're supposed to be dead," I said.

He waved his right hand, gripping the saw in his left.

"Alas."

"It was your best friend that you killed that night."

"What night would that be?"

"The night you were supposed to have been murdered."

"Ah. That night."

"I saw a picture once, you and a small boy arm-in-arm down there on the dock. It was him, wasn't it?"

Farrer's frivolous air seemed to evaporate.

"Peter was a good friend," he said. "I regretted carving him to pieces. I really did." Then he smiled again. "But I've developed a taste for it."

To put it mildly, the man was insane.

"Now it's your turn—or would you rather it be your cop-friend's first?"

"Mine." My voice sounded squeezed and high-pitched. "But give me a last request."

Farrer paused. He didn't say yes; he didn't say no. He waved with an infinitesimal motion.

"Answer me a few questions," I said.

"But you're going to die."

"Then I'll go to heaven with my curiosity satisfied."

"Or hell."

"That's your domain."

"Maybe." He didn't switch the engine off. "Ask."

"Eleven years ago—what happened that night?"

"Simple, my friend. I killed Peter Dillery and his wife and set it up so that it appeared as my death." He said more slowly: "And my wife's."

"What about Billy?"

"I didn't even know he was in the car. Little shit saw the whole thing. Did his mother first, too. Cut her head clean off."

I almost fainted. My head swirled with the image of a small boy watching as his mother's head rolled to the floor. I nearly spit a curse at Farrer. But I needed more.

"He ran . . ." My voice was a groan. "He ran to Julia."

Farrer's eyes looked past me for a moment, into the shadowy world of his past life.

"Julia," he said. Then his eyes met mine with a harsh humor. "Great fuck, isn't she?"

"I wouldn't know."

"Oh. I thought you two had . . ." He waved his hand in the air again. I was getting tired of that waving hand.

"No. You did?"

"Yeah," he said with gusto, stretching out the word. "What a voice that woman had."

"Has. She's still alive."

"Unfortunate. Luckily that asshole husband of hers is gone." He stared down at me. "You seem to have taken his place."

Farrer crisscrossed the chain saw in front of my eyes.

"How 'bout your nose?"

"I like my nose. I like to smell."

"Ah," he said to his men, "he wants to smell the death. Very well." He smiled. His eyes glazed over.

I was scared as hell.

The trailer door opened. Old man Farrer stood just inside, a captain's cap tilted over his forehead. He wore a thick blue captain's jacket. One sleeve didn't have an arm in it. He seemed to be waiting there—perhaps to take me across the river of death.

His voice swelled like a preacher's.

"I suppose you're going to kill him, too."

William Farrer spoke softly to his men: "Get him out of here."

"He's just the age Peter was," the old man said.

Farrer swung around and yelled: "Get him out of here!"

They got him out, but the old man was still cursing his son to hell. We could all hear him outside.

Farrer stepped close to me. He raised the saw.

"Hold out your hand."

My peripheral vision turned a murky shade of gray. I was on the verge of fainting.

"Don't do it!" Cussone yelled. He'd been in a stupor but his eyes were clear now. His cheeks drooled sweat.

"Hold out your hand!" Farrer bellowed.

"No," I whispered.

Someone did it for me. I didn't even see his face. My eyes were closed. The sound of the saw revved to a high pitch and came nearer to my ear.

The back window broke. The side window smashed open. Windows behind me shattered. Gunshots. No silencers. My eyes opened. Before the Cubans could fire they were dropping. I looked up to see a bullet hit the back of Farrer's head. It came out through his eye. Farrer fell, onto the running chain saw. It groaned loud and long under him before hitting bone and stopping.

A few seconds went by in bleeding silence. When I turned to Cussone he was already smiling at me.

I heard old man Farrer outside, asking: "Did I do all right? Did I do all right?"

"You did fine," a familiar voice said.

Detective Dan Denoy stepped in.

"Hi, guys."

Officers Stephano and Williams were not far behind.

Cussone said: "I never thought I'd be so happy to see your ugly puss." Denoy laughed. But Stanley began to shake again.

"Jesus, thank you," he cried.

"Untie him," Denoy said.

Our ropes were cut. Cussone was breathing hard, but he was OK. Denoy knelt next to him and wrapped his arms around him.

"I'm glad to see you, too, Stan."

I could have stood up, gotten out of there, but I didn't. I stayed in that chair for a moment. A chair I might have died in. It was an ordinary hardwood chair. For an ordinary guy. Tears flowed freely but I was smiling.

Old Man Farrer stepped in and turned the body of his son over. The chain saw was embedded in William Farrer's chest. His dead arms swung wide. His thousand-dollar suit was soaked with blood.

"All these years," the old man said. "All these years I've wanted to bring him down. I didn't have the guts. I tried to stand up to him once. Right off—in the beginning. I tole him flat out I wouldn't lie about whose body that was all cut up on Mildred Avenue. It was poor Pete an' his wife—an' he wanted me to identify it as him and his terrible woman. I wouldn't, I tole him. I hated them both. Then he killed my woman—his own mother." He groaned: "I loved her." His voice lowered. "Took all the steam outa me when she died."

He squeezed his empty sleeve.

"Then he cut this arm off, to keep me quiet forever. I—I kin still feel it, sometimes."

He bent over and spit yellow slime on his son's bloody face, then wandered out of the trailer.

I rose out of my ordinary chair and for the first time saw things clearly. The walls were light blue, the rug yellow, the light a grungy iridescent. Four Cubans lay dead on the floor in a circle around the two chairs. Their blood had begun to canal its way through various fissures in the shag. Two cops gave them their final photo opportunity, then began to drag their bodies out.

I looked through one of the smashed windows and saw that Denoy had apprehended a few Cubans outside. They held their hands on their heads. They weren't saying much. Their compatriots had disappeared long ago with the half truckload of babies.

I tried, momentarily, to assess all that had happened. I remembered what Julia had said in her letter: that she and her husband, Ralph, had been caught "between two dark clouds converging." Cussone had thought the line poetic. I'm sure he felt differently tonight. Yet it was hard to figure out what we'd seen, what had actually happened and why. I still didn't know who Red was working for—who the Group was. It was hard to concentrate. My hands were shaking. My mind kept deviating to thoughts of my gangly limbs being taken from me, one by one. The imagination was working overtime.

Instinctively, I tried to calm a set of rattled nerves by rummaging around the place—although there wasn't too much hope of finding anything. I stumbled across the room to a nest of plastic drawers in the far corner. Other cops had begun to appear, to work their way inside for a look at the carnage. I wound my way through them. Flashbulbs popped like strobe lights at a high school dance. Only there weren't any pretty girls in pink dresses.

I slumped down near the drawers and opened the first one. Some old tools. The second: cartons of nails and some sandpaper. The third: extension cords, a box of Band-Aids, string. The fourth held nothing but bullets, different calibers.

"What are you doing?"

It was Cussone. He stood over me like a reincarnation of himself.

"Searching."

"I figured that. Don't."

For some reason communication had broken down to simpler forms. I pointed at the open drawer.

"Bullets."

He looked down at the odd assortment. "Bully."

"What are you so mad about?"

"Ahh—" He waved his hand impatiently. "Just don't smear your fingerprints over everything." He turned to leave me but then swung back again. He pointed to the door. "Why don't you wait outside? It's a nice night."

"It's cold as hell, for July."

He didn't respond. He turned and knelt down near Farrer and, with the help of another cop, removed the chain saw from Farrer's midsection. Then they searched his body. They retrieved a gun, a wallet, a couple of cigars, a key chain. I didn't see what else. Cussone had spotted me watching and once again waved his hand toward the door.

"A nice night."

"After all I've done for you," I said, but he pretended not to hear.

I stood up. I felt the way people do after a car accident—every bone shook inside my skin. My head pounded. The hairs on the back of my neck still stood at attention. Goddamned Cussone. You'd think he'd've been grateful. It was my life, too. You'd think maybe there was a medal in it for me. Or some honorary mention, for Chrissake.

"Chrissake," I said to him as I walked to the door. My eyes scanned the trailer a last time. The place where I came close to buying the big one. I took in its decor: a dirty little kitchenette, an unmade bed, some cases and shoe boxes piled near a closet that was so stuffed its door had popped off. It hung on one hinge. Glass from the broken windows had shattered over everything. Shards of it reflected light from the hanging bulb like broken pieces of a dream.

I almost walked out. I hovered in the open door, over the cement steps that led down to the old man's junkyard. But curiosity held me, like a drug.

I was drawn by that open closet.

My mother had once saved all our family letters and heirlooms in shoe boxes. Maybe old man Farrer had, too—once upon a time, before the drinking. Or perhaps his wife had.

His silhouette ranted loudly some yards down the hill. He was crying out curses to a shadowy river. Sometimes he just cried out noises. Questions put to him now would be useless. And there were a lot of questions.

I went back inside.

"What are you doing back in here?" Cussone asked.

"Keeping warm."

The place was small. I took about three steps and stood before the closet. The shoe boxes were mostly in bad shape, so I was careful with them. They were stuffed to the limit and were nearly bursting. I lowered two of them onto the bed and opened the first one.

There were letters, mostly from old man Farrer to his wife. They'd been sent from a ship in the Pacific, circa 1944 and 1945. All of them began with "My Dearest Margaret." It struck me that the old man had not always been what he was today. A passionate love had once brewed in the letters I held, a love that was finally consummated—then cut short by the fruit of their consummation.

I opened the second box.

Pictures, more pictures. Near the top was the same old photograph I'd seen in Helen Gladden's bedroom. Billy Farrer and his best friend, Pete Dillery, stood on the dock arm-in-arm. Only now did I find Pete's distant resemblance to Billy. It wasn't striking, but it was there.

I found some other pictures of Pete and his wife. Marriage photos. Probably copies from an old portfolio. In the mother, Pete's wife, I saw Billy's features distinctly. His Buster Keaton eyes and nose and deadpan melancholy. She'd been a striking woman, almost as small as he was. I found it hard to imagine Farrer slicing her to pieces.

There were some other pictures of Farrer as a boy: fishing, running, standing proudly with his father, wielding a slingshot. And there were the usual nameless faces caught in time by the camera. Suspended there, for no reason.

That was it. I closed the box. I faced the closet again.

A third box sat in the shelf shadows. It was a crumbling pink cardboard hatbox that fell apart in my hands. Its edges shed clumps of cardboard that reminded me of asbestos. I brushed them away and opened the circular lid. The box sides split open. A pile of black-and-white photos spilled across the bed, mingling with the shards of glass.

"What the hell are you doing?"

Cussone stood over me again, but I didn't answer him. I don't think I'd have answered the Pope. My breath had disappeared. It'd been knocked out of me, knocked clear out the door and was probably gusting downriver.

"I asked you a question."

I stared up at him, oblivious to his anger. My jaw literally hung open. I didn't seem to be able to close it.

"What?" he barked.

I stared down at the picture at the top of the pile.

Cussone knelt. His voice squeezed out:

"What?"

I could only point. To the picture. A marriage photo, the standard kind. An ordinary album portrait. William Farrer wore a white suit and dubious smile. His wife was on his arm. She was short and sweet and had a blond pixie hairdo. Even through the layers of wedding frill her ample breasts were evident. Yet, even then, there'd been something lurking behind her blue eyes. Something I'd seen often. That strange theatricality. As if nothing she did or said was real. As if she were secretly mocking everyone around her.

William Farrer had married a young girl named Gina Wilkie.

My next-door neighbor.

47

A pale light bled life into the river. Rose hues undulated on its surface, spreading like ephemeral capillaries through the surrounding shadows. Then for a fleeting moment the Hudson burned a fierce red. It had the deep, unsettling glow of an open aorta.

I remembered the river's original name—Shatemuc, Mother of Rivers—and daydreamed that it was a bloody umbilical winding from its mountainous womb toward the city to the south. Then the morning sun climbed over the edge of the world, and the river turned a shade of lacquered blue, and everything again seemed almost normal.

Cussone spoke to me from across the junkyard.

"I'm finished."

I turned and faced him but said nothing.

"Here, anyway. The FBI's on their way. I don't even want to be here. I'm too tired."

"Right."

He jiggled his keys in his hands. "Can you drive?"

I drove. Somehow I missed the turn for the Taconic and ended up on River Road, a driving exercise that wound through the woods along the river. Faint blotches of color sparked the predominant green. The river shimmered through the trees.

"We wired in about the boat," he said.

"Anything?"

"Nothing."

"What about helicopters?"

"There were two. They must have missed it."

I drove some more.

"We should talk, Stanley."

"I know."

A few more minutes went by.

"Talk now."

"Later. We need to sleep for a few hours."

I breathed. "All right."

"But I'm interested in that picture," he said.

Interested.

I was still too stunned to talk about it. The thought of Gina and Farrer—together—pressed on me like a nightmare. Yet, like a nightmare, there was a strange logic in it. I felt that somewhere deep inside of me something had clicked, something solid, like the sound of a deadbolt unlocking. But I needed sleep so badly that I put my spinning thoughts on hold, gripped the wheel, and drove like one of George Romero's zombies.

Instead of hooking up with the Taconic, I opted for Route 9, a road that twisted us through a series of linking towns: Peekskill, Croton, Ossining, East Nyack. Just past Tarrytown I spun the Chevy up a ramp and merged with morning traffic on 87. It was seven A.M. By eight we'd inched over the Willis Avenue Bridge. Traffic was terrible. Once again, I avoided the FDR and braved the cobblestones on upper Second Avenue. It was another forty minutes before I landed on Cussone's couch. I put a pillow over my head and closed my eyes.

The phone rang.

An hour later we were standing on the banks of the Hudson again—this time on an old pier under the Tappan Zee Bridge, forty driving minutes north of New York. The low bridge curved over the water with a feminine elegance. Near shore, on one of its enormous pilings, someone had painted "The Dead," meaning the Grateful ones.

In the water under it an expensive fishing boat floated aimlessly. A plume of smoke rose from its engine. I only heard a few babies crying from inside its hull.

A police boat snagged it with two grappling hooks and dragged the craft to safe harbor near the old pier. Instantly, a team of officers, including myself and Cussone, were employed to relay the infants from the hull. A line of us stretched uphill to a piece of flat ground. Blankets had been spread out over red clay. The babies were set there in a line. We left their tags on.

I waited near the water after the last baby had been wrenched from the burning boat. Paramedics took over on the hill. They had their hands full trying to breathe life into several of the babies. The police helped—but I couldn't. I knew that some of the children had died. It was hard to say how many. Finding out was a job I couldn't handle.

Instead, I watched two cops on the police craft use thick hoses to water down the smoldering fire. But water didn't seem to work. They boarded the boat and smothered it with fire extinguishers.

All the while Cussone had been deep in conversation with a local precinct chief. When he was through he joined me, crouching on the bank. I noticed that he had no socks on.

"Can we get on the boat?" I asked.

" 'We' can," he said, meaning only the police.

I nodded.

"Something else," he said. "There's a dead man about a half mile north of here. Night guard for that factory over there." Cussone pointed upriver. Two black smokestacks poked up over a row of dusty trees. "He was shot. His car's gone—an old Nova. We have the plates."

"Time of death?"

"Few hours."

I sighed. "He's gone."

"Probably. We have an APB out, though. If he's still driving, we'll get him."

"Hmmm."

"I wish I knew who the hell he was. Interpol came up dry, I should tell you. No one by the name of Red in their computers." Cussone added: "Christ, he sure as hell was big."

The local chief called down from the hill.

Stanley stood up. "C'mon," he said.

I followed him. Up on the flat the babies were lined up, like an ungodly caricature of a maternity ward. Police stood around them like a crowd of desolate fathers. I scanned the few dozen faces closely. I had to. Genna might be among them, though I was almost sure she wouldn't be. Strangely, some of the infants smiled; some drooled over their pudgy jowls. Others cried. Some hadn't opened their eyes.

"Six dead," the young chief told Cussone. He swung around. "God fucking damn it!" he yelled, then pounded his foot into the clay. He wore a name tag over his badge: "Wall." He was thin-framed and pockmarked, and at closer inspection I realized that he was probably older than he looked. He stepped away from us and leaned against an old wire fence.

A few ambulances arrived. They were empty. Paramedics gently cradled and cuddled and tickled each baby as it was carried into one of the three vehicles. Some responded. Others remained in a daze. I prayed for them, that their daze wouldn't be permanent.

White smoke billowed uphill. It came from the boat. Someone growled about the wind changing. I left Stanley and walked downhill.

The two cops had jumped back onto their craft and were putting on their gas masks. I used the smoke as a thin shield and leaped from the pier onto the boat's deck.

It was slippery. I almost slid into the open hull. Smoke bellowed out of it, and I caught the glimmer of fire down below.

"Get off the boat!" someone yelled. "The tanks may blow!"

I decided to give myself sixty seconds. I started counting aloud but heard Stanley's voice shouting at me and lost my count. I started over: one-thousand-one, one-thousand-two . . . and lowered myself into the hull. There was too much smoke; I couldn't see. I climbed back out again. Quickly, I opened the door that led down into the boat's cabin and slid down the metal stairway. I bumped my head and my ass and landed on the floor of a small kitchenette. There wasn't any food in the refrigerator, just beer. New Amsterdam. No pots or pans or utensils in the cabinets and drawers. Nothing. I opened some overhead storage compartments and found supplies: rope, slickers, a knit cap, some pulleys, a fire extinguisher, two rubber boots. They were the same boots that

Red had worn the first time I saw him—in Julia's apartment. There was mud on them. And drops of blood. He'd probably changed out of them before jumping ship.

"Get out of there!" Cussone was shouting from outside.

Twenty seconds to go.

I walked to the far end of the cabin, where a handful of life jackets were stacked. I looked under them. Nothing. There was a low drawer under the aft bunk. I opened it. Smoke began to fill the compartment. I couldn't see my own hands. I felt inside the drawer. Whatever was inside had been shrink-wrapped in plastic. It was long and hoselike, and I decided, To hell with it, I'll take it.

I felt for the ladder. It wasn't where it was supposed to be. Or I was turned around. I stumbled to the other side of the cabin and found it. But I was dizzy. I couldn't inhale. I felt as though my lungs had collapsed—that they were stuck like a wet balloon. I fell to my knees.

"My hand!" I heard through the smoke.

I saw nothing.

"My hand!"

I reached up into the nothingness and felt a strong hand groping there. It grabbed me. For some reason I clung to the shrink-wrapped hose, even though it blocked my exit for an excruciating moment. Finally my body went limp, but I wasn't unconscious. I felt every contour of that boat ladder and deck and felt the hands that grabbed hold of me and threw me over for a crash-landing on the pier. A pair of feet jumped next to me and then that same someone took my arms and dragged me over the slats. Splinters jabbed into my ass. I moaned on the cool ground.

"Are you happy now?" Cussone was asking me. Wisps of smoke drifted around us. "Now that you have your toy?"

He was right; it looked like a toy. It was long and white and had a hose and handle and a little crank that was painted red. A portable water pump.

"Aw, shit," I wheezed.

"You're an asshole sometimes."

"Yeah." I was trying hard to regain my breath.

"Don't you know about smoke?"

"Do now."

He left me there. I closed my eyes. Within minutes a paramedic bent over me.

"I'm all right," I said.

"Yeah, well we'll see."

He took my blood pressure and asked me to breathe a few times and gave me a glass of water.

"You're all right."

"Tend to the children," I said.

"What's left of them."

I lay down again to digest his bleak comment. And to avoid anyone else staring at me as he had—as if I were a fool.

I held my new "toy" over me. There was lettering on the wrapper. It told me that the pump had been made in Sweden and distributed in the USA. It gave the company names. There was a serial number on the end of the package. And that was it.

"C'mon," Cussone said. "We better go."

I stood up.

"Hey, Stanley."

"What?"

"Thanks."

"What is it with you anyway?" he said, and tried to smile. I tried back.

"Stanley?"

"C'mon."

"All right, but—let me ask you something."

"What?"

"This pump."

"What about it?"

"There's a company name on it. A distributor." He was silent now, staring at me. "And a serial number."

Wall had overheard me. He stepped closer. Stanley took the pump into his hands.

"I have to admit, you've got a point," he said.

"Listen, Detective . . ." It was Wall. He sidled up to us reluctantly, as if wanting to remain at a safe distance. "What if I— well, you're on your way to New York . . ."

"Yeah?"

"I mean I've got to *do* something!" He pointed uphill, toward the babies still being carried to the ambulances. "This is my jurisdiction. I get the sense that all this is bigger than what we see here. Hell, one look at the both of you tells me that. But you can't shut us out up here in Westchester. This is our backyard. I wanna help."

"All right," Stanley said, and handed him the pump. "Trace it. Maybe the distributor knows where this particular batch went. Maybe we'll get lucky."

Wall grabbed the pump solemnly, his Excalibur.

"Thanks."

"But first thing—get this damn boat hauled up and put the fire out—quickly. Let's salvage what evidence we can."

"Right."

"And walk the trail from here to the factory—where you found the stiff. Maybe he dropped something."

"Right."

"And—that's it."

They shook hands.

"Ninth precinct," Cussone said to him. "A few hours."

Wall nodded and turned without another word. I tossed Stanley the car keys.

The road shook under me like a river. I dreamed that I was being carried in the hull of a boat and that there was a porthole down there where I could see the Statue of Liberty disappearing. When it was gone the sea became still, and I was floating, alone and adrift in a black ocean.

Not quite alone. I woke up and saw Stanley sleeping behind the wheel. We were parked at an angle on Fourth Street east of Second Avenue. A few doors down the precinct buzzed with activity.

"Thought I'd catch a few winks," he said with his eyes closed. "Before we go inside."

He opened his eyes. They were red and bleary and it stung just to look at them. I peered into the side mirror and saw that mine were the same color.

"Smoke," he said huskily.

"Christ."

"It'll go away. Sooner or later."

I looked at him again. He sat in a haze of cruel morning light that streaked in through the car window like spaghetti through a strainer. I'd never seen Stanley so down-and-out ragged as he was now. His clothes were crumpled and damp with stains, and his hair, what there was of it, was sticking up every which way. There were streaks of gray along his jowls from the smoke, and dried blood on his fingertips, which were the same color as his eyes.

He seemed to be sizing me up in the same manner. The only difference between us was that my week-old clothes were now beyond description. And the smoke had singed my entire face. I looked like Al Jolson in *The Jazz Singer*. My head had a lump on it the size of a tangerine, and a fine patina of dried blood ran from it down the base of my neck all the way to the crook of my butt. It'd dried and was flaking off.

"Put this hat on," Cussone said, smiling as if he'd tasted bitter medicine. "Your head looks funny."

It was an old hat but a good one. Olive drab. The inside label spelled "Cromwell's." The ribbon was black.

I put it on.

"Let's go." Stanley opened his door. "We have a hell of a day ahead of us."

48

He sat down in his chair and it moaned under him, this time, it seemed, with the fondness of familiarity. He closed his eyes and grabbed hold of its wooden arms and squeezed them as if a mystical strength were flowing from the mahogany into his limbs. Then he leaned forward and his eyes blinked open like bright lights in an old house and he said:

"Tell me about the picture."

It took me a moment to begin. I hadn't tried to think about Gina's connection to the case; events and weariness had not allowed for thinking. Nevertheless, the connections had boiled underneath for a while, trying to find themselves.

"I think I've got a handle on it," I said. "But I don't know about long-winded explanations." I looked at a clock. It was almost two P.M. "She works at a clinic for addicted children. If I remember right, it's not too far from here."

"There's one in this precinct. They took over an old warehouse on Centre Street—" He stood up. "Shit—I see what you're getting at."

"Right."

"We should move."

It was tough to stand up again.

"This time," I said, "it wouldn't hurt to have some backup."

He organized two other squad cars, six men total. Denoy had phoned in a report about our night in Poughkeepsie, and the whole station now seemed to be treating Stanley with some deference. The squad cars were readied in minutes. One of the cops even fitted his shoulder holster. I stood and watched from a discreet distance as they defined a plan. When they'd finished a brief conversation the other cops moved past me as if I were invisible. They headed downstairs.

"Let's go." Cussone waved to me impatiently.

"Am I invited?"

"Don't get sensitive." He was in his "boss" mode again.

This time there wasn't any mention of a gun for me.

The clinic was a four-story brick warehouse. Like most other buildings in the area it had been built around the turn of the century and sandblasted recently. Its finely detailed window arches were newly refurbished and stood out in bright relief. Old streaks of black dirt still hung down below them like painted stalactites.

There was a small sign over its entrance: CHILD REHABILITATION INSTITUTE FOR STABILIZATION AND THERAPY. To its left was an overgrown alley with a signpost labeling it a street: Mulberry Place. It was wide enough for one car, or a truck. There were loading docks in the back. A silver semi was parked in one of them. Its rig was pointed toward the other end of the alley, which connected to Crosby Street.

Dozens of employees filed into the building next door, their lunch a memory. No one was walking in or out of the clinic. The place looked deserted.

We got out of our cars. A few officers ran up the front steps; one ran to the right, around the block, checking the possibility of another back entrance. I followed Stanley and two other cops as they stalked into the alley toward the three loading docks. Two were empty. The one truck that was there was a refrigerated rig that had nothing stenciled on its cab or box. Its doors were unlocked. I checked the glove compartment for a registration, but there was none. Stanley and the others had already jumped inside. I followed them.

The fresh smell of oil and exhaust lingered on the shipping floor, as if more trucks had been recently parked here and had gunned their engines and fled. I wondered if there'd been any cargo. Perhaps those babies coming downriver were not the only shipment expected.

Three workers in overalls seemed more than surprised to see us. Less than glad. One of them ran back into a dispatcher's office that had been built of glass. It looked like an oversized phone booth. A short, wide gentleman stood up in the booth, threw a clipboard into his desk drawer, locked it, took his glasses off, then emerged.

"Yes?" he said from across the stockroom. His voice was calm and serious.

Cussone raised his badge, an unnecessary gesture since two uniforms stood on either side of him.

"Police," he said.

"I gathered." The wide man didn't move. Under the dusty glow of the overhanging lights I could see his tiny eyes bearing down on us from the center of his face. He carried considerable authority, even from a distance. He'd been around.

"We have reasonable cause to believe," Stanley told him loudly across the echoing room, "that illegal merchandise has been traveling in and out of this warehouse."

"It's a clinic."

"Nevertheless."

"What reasonable cause?"

Stanley stood there. I realized what he realized: We had none.

"Do you have a warrant?" the man asked, taking one step closer. It was a tactical step. It seemed to underscore his willingness and ability to play hardball.

"A John Doe, yes." Stanley removed it from his inside pocket.

"I know my rights—and the rights of the clinic," the man said, quivering with calm. "John Doe warrants require reasonable cause. I ask you again—where is it?"

It'd been a long night. Cussone was weakening. He was stuck.

Hell, I thought. I'm not a cop.

I turned and took a few strides and stood at the tailgate of the unopened truck. Its back end was snug against the rubber guard along the loading dock.

"Get away from there!" the man's voice boomed behind me. "You have no warrant."

I spoke to him softly. "I'm no cop."

His voice rose a few intervals: "I'll have you arrested!"

"Then arrest me."

I grabbed the metal latch, flipped the bolt, folded it over, and lifted. The door slid upward with a metal roar. To my dismay, a pile of boxes stared me in the face.

I lifted one. It was heavy. I opened it and found inside one large plastic bag stuffed with individually wrapped cloth masks and one similar bag filled with rubber gloves.

His voice was calmly hysterical behind me: "Arrest this guy!"

A hand came down on my sore shoulder and pulled me out of there. My elbow jerked back—it hit the wide man squarely in the gut. He took a step back.

"Sorry," I said, and jumped over the boxes in the truck.

"Jesus Christ, Byman!" The cops were scrambling inside as the man kept screaming:

"Arrest him! Arrest that fucker!"

One of the cops climbed after me, over the façade of boxes. He grabbed me hard but quickly let go. We stood there quietly for a moment, behind the cardboard wall, staring at the back end of the semi.

Each wall was lined with a double-decker row of cribs; I counted twenty-four in all. They were actually built like shelves into the walls. The walls themselves were ribbed with what looked like a ventilation system of metal tubes and hoses. These were connected to the refrigeration unit built against the front end.

I heard a scuffle outside. The cop and I knocked the boxes down in time to see Stanley's gun extending toward one of the overalled employees. He'd tried to run.

The four of them were gathered, cuffed, their rights read to them. The wide man's name was Cole. He kept mumbling how his lawyer would declare this bust as unconstitutional.

"No," Stanley told him. "You asked us to arrest this man." He pointed at me. "We all heard it." He spoke to one of his men. "Arrest him."

"Stanley?" I whispered.

The cop lassoed a pair of cuffs around my wrists. Their snapping bolt switched on an inner fear in Cole that made his eyes bulge.

"Get the key," I said to Stanley.

"Key?"

"In his pocket. The one to the desk in there." I nodded toward the oversized phone booth. "The bills of lading." Stanley stared at me so sternly I thought I was a criminal. "Just helping you out, Officer," I added with a smile.

"Ahhh," he growled, then searched Cole's inner pockets. He came up with a set of keys.

With my hands behind my back I followed Cussone to the glass office and waited while he tried each one. The last key finally worked.

"Wouldn't you figure," he mumbled, pulling the drawer open. He leafed through the clipboard with a few officious gestures, then snapped the pages back. His head jerked up with a precise movement and his bellowslike cheeks exhaled. Bad breath blew across my face.

"Book these fuckers. Charges forthcoming."

Three of his men shoved Cole and his partners across the shipping floor. Cussone yelled to their backs:

"Donetti!"

The oldest of the cops turned to him. Gray-black hair sprang out from under his hat. His uniform was rumpled. His eyes were intent.

"Yeah, Stan?"

"Your collar."

The other men smiled. Donetti's lips curled up for a split second, then flattened out again. He nodded. Then with one quick straight-arm he shoved Cole out the open loading dock as if he were a bloated bag of garbage. I heard the fat man's body hit pavement. The sound resembled someone stepping on an eggplant.

"Sorry, fella," Donetti sang down to him.

I stared down at the clipboard on the desk. It brought back recent memories that seemed already dim and dying: of Black River and Svenquist and of a computer whose program spewed names, addresses, numbers, more names. They were printed out this time, probably by the computer that rumbled next to me like a cement mixer. It rattled the windows. All the names were there: Mary Gordon, Constance Gravitz, Beth Lumley, tugging at me with the potency of familiar faces. Somehow I felt for them, the expectant couples who'd more than likely laid half their money down. There'd be no fifty-thousand-dollar baby coming their way now. No reimbursement. No consolation. I almost hated to disappoint them.

Someone grabbed my wrists—Stanley. He unlocked the cuffs and swung me around by the shoulders and smiled.

"Released on your own recognizance."

"Thanks."

"Don't mention it."

Together we found the sliding door that led to a huge freight elevator. Stanley pressed the button and we waited. The door slid open quietly. We stepped into what looked like a padded cell and rose in it to the second floor. Stanley drew his gun, but when the door opened one of his other men awaited.

"Nothing much unusual up here, Detective."

Stanley sighed: "Let's see."

The floorboards sang under us as we marched around a corner stacked with maintenance equipment. We came upon a well-lit hallway, a dozen rooms branching off of it, six on either side. There were half a dozen beds per room, most of them empty. A few small children were in some of the rooms toward the far end of the hall, nearer to a pair of swinging doors that led to a lobby. I ducked into each of the rooms on the off-chance that Genna might be among the children in the ward, but again was out of luck. All the kids in the place were either black or Spanish, no more than ten years old. They stared at us fearfully, some sucking their thumbs. Morning light streamed through yellow curtains and seemed to cloak the dark children in a haze of optimism. They were well cared for; their hospital pullovers were clean, eyes bright, sheets and blankets orderly. Quite a contrast to the babies we'd found in the hull of a boat only hours ago.

"Look," Stanley's man said to both of us. He held up one of the children and spread out its tiny hand. Between the child's fingers were faint black dots and scars. Old needle marks. "Most of these kids were once addicted. Prob'ly born that way. Their withdrawal hurts so bad that some-a these ignorant mothers stop their kids from crying by keeping them high." The child started to moan. The officer patted its dark hair. "There, there," he whispered.

"There's no one up here?" Cussone asked.

"Jimmy's got the nurses in the waiting room."

"Where the hell is Slattery?"

"Basement."

"Oh. Good."

We left the officer to calm the crying child and exited the hallway through swinging doors. A small, sterile anteroom lay beyond, tidily decorated with paintings and plants. A pair of nurses sat rigidly on a puffy vinyl sofa, hands in their laps.

"They're tight-lipped, Stan," the cop named Jimmy said with his husky Irish accent. He sat perched on the edge of a chair, hands on his knees, staring at the nurses.

Stanley knelt in front of the women, practicing his gentle approach.

"I'm Detective Cussone," he said smoothly.

But he was interrupted.

Slattery cried from the other end of the hallway—from the freight elevator. His voice sliced open my nerve ends.

"Detective!"

Cussone was on his feet and through the doors. I followed quickly down the hall and around the corner to the elevator. Slattery stood frozen in a grimace of indescribable melancholy. The wind seemed kicked out of him.

"What?" Stanley was scared.

"See for yourself."

And so we did. The elevator took us down to B level. We stepped out of it into a cement hallway painted hospital blue with tawdry white trim. Dying fluorescent bulbs blinked overhead. They'd have made our skin turn green, but that had already happened. We had to pause—stunned by the smell of feces and vomit. Slattery handed us handkerchiefs and I tried breathing through the cloth, but it made no difference. Tremors started shaking through my legs. I prayed I wouldn't find what I was imagining. But the utter silence of the place seemed to scream at me.

Slattery whispered: "Not one nurse."

We turned a corner and faced another long hall. A dozen rooms led off from it on either side, a vertical mirroring of the configuration upstairs. But these were smaller, narrow rooms, and windowless. They were all the same. A few cribs filled each one. They were made of shiny new plastic but the sheets and mattresses were stained with days of use. The babies, again mostly black and Puerto Rican, were naked. Some had been left untended, unclean, rolling in their own mess. Some stared with eyes as blank as a blindman's. And as always, a rare few smiled.

"Thank God they're alive," Stanley whispered. We were all whispering. "But—there's no crying, nothing. Not a sound."

Slattery turned to me, his eyes carrying a world of weight.

"It's what I was thinking, too." He gasped. "Christ, I got babies of my own. They make a hell of a noise."

"What's your point?" Cussone's throat seemed pinched with disgust.

"Look."

Slattery led us into one of the far rooms at the end of the hall. A tensor lamp sat on a stool. It was the only light in the room. It shone through the slats of the cribs and cast ribbed shadows over three quiet children. From the first bed a little Spanish girl with unkempt curls reached up for me with tiny extended fingers. But she didn't make a sound. Or smile. Her eyes looked up at me from another world.

I'd witnessed that look before—recently. That queer faraway gaze that had veiled a pair of beautiful dark eyes.

Gina's lover.

Sondra.

I took a step back, gasping for air. I didn't need to see what Slattery was showing us. But my eyes were riveted. He held up the baby's tiny hand—as the other cop had—and spread her fingers. Small red blotch marks were encrusted between them.

"Some of these marks are fresh, Detective," he was saying. My mind reeled. I stepped outside the narrow door, but heard his voice drone on:

"And it ain't methadone—look at her!" He extended the baby at arm's length and groaned: "She—she's high." After a few deep breaths he put her down, gently, his eyes remaining on the child. "Hooked."

I slumped down in the hallway, against the wall's sandpaper stucco. It chafed me but I hardly noticed.

I'd finally begun to see the whole case clearly.

"You all right?" Cussone asked from the baby's room.

"Sondra," was all I said.

"What?"

"It's Gina's daughter. Her name is Sondra."

Cussone lingered in the door frame, a silhouette. He whispered: "As in the marina."

"Yes."

"But . . . so?"

"I don't know. Gina can't be working for her husband."

"Her husband?"

"Farrer—Farrer! She took their kid. Don't you see?"

"No."

"She must be working for the others—the Group."

"How do you know?"

I didn't.

"I'm sure of it."

"Why?"

"Gina!" I stood up.

"Damn it. You sound crazy."

"She's got to be 'Mother.'"

Cussone leveled his eyes at mine and let a quiet moment pass. A furnace rumbled somewhere close by, its pipes clanging.

"Who in hell is this Group?" he asked.

I couldn't answer him.

"It's time to go back to my old building," was my response. But we were already distracted.

"Those pipes."

Slattery came out: "They weren't banging like that before."

The clanging was rhythmic. A faint tap that was broadcast through the water pipes overhead.

Cussone ordered: "Follow it." Their holsters unsnapped in unison. Slattery led the way.

We forged ahead cautiously, around a second corner in the hall. There weren't any lights. Just shadows, and a deeper dark ahead, around a third corner. Stanley nudged me.

"Check the walls for switches."

I rubbed my hands against the stucco. Paint chipped. I found a couple of cockroaches but no light switch. Then I waved my arms overhead and hit a dangling string. I pulled it. The bulb must have been a full ten watts. But it was better than no light at all.

"Listen!" Slattery raised his hands and we stood still at the verge of total darkness. The clanging had stopped. We waited a few seconds. One faint tap. A few more seconds . . . another.

"We're close," I said.

"Around the corner."

We stepped into the darkness. Slattery felt the left wall, I rubbed my arms along the right. My palm hit a loose doorknob. It was locked.

"Help," a man's' voice whimpered from inside. I vaguely recognized it.

I shook the door.

"Step behind me." Stanley's voice was firm.

I stepped. He fired.

A shower of splinters hit me in the face, and the door still didn't open. Slattery investigated.

"There's a second bolt."

Cussone fired again and the door rattled on its hinges. Slattery yanked it open. He and Stanley went in at a crouch position, just in case.

They were silent for a few seconds, groping the walls. I went in after them but couldn't see.

"Where are you?" I heard Stanley say. His voice was close by. It was a small room.

"Here."

I knew the voice.

"Got him!" Slattery hoisted the man in his arms and walked him out the door. Once in the hallway, the angular contours of his jaw and cheekbones made Nathan Wise look like the skeleton he would one day be.

"My daughter!" His voice was a cloudy whisper.

I went in after her, into the pitch-black. I felt like I was floating in there—as if I'd submerged myself in one of those lonely isolation tanks. Groping for a woman. Always groping for a woman.

I found her lying in a far corner, damp with sweat. She seemed so small and frail and cold. She was barely breathing. I carried her out of the room and around both dark corners of the hall, back under the blinking fluorescent lights. I laid her shaking body down in the cement hallway and held her. The tips of her fingers touched my chest. It was pounding.

"Lola," I whispered.

"Luuuke."

The timbre of her voice scared the hell out of me. I recoiled and saw the sleeves of her shirt rolled high. Blood had trickled from a careless puncture in her upper arm. Her eyes opened blearily. She stared at me as if she were lying at the bottom of an inferno.

"Again," was all she said.

49

Slattery took charge of the "evacuation." He barked orders like a traffic cop. A milling crowd stood by and whispered as Lola and Nathan Wise were carried away by ambulance to New York Hospital. Children and adults alike moaned at the sight of each new baby carried out in the arms of blushing cops or paramedics. Large white Red Cross vehicles were used, the babies placed lengthwise on canvas stretchers that hung horizontally from the inside walls, like bunks.

An ABC News crew arrived. Their video camera and small sun-gun lamps flashed over Cussone and me but didn't linger. We stood cemented to the sidewalk, watching Lola's ambulance disappear. Its red light pulsed like a heartbeat that was flying away forever.

"Gonna rain," Stanley said.

"Yeah."

He breathed a long, deep sigh.

"I take it you knew she was—adopted."

"Christ—I don't know anything anymore."

I spit the words out bitterly. Before I could soften my attitude a little, Slattery came bounding down the clinic's steps and touched Cussone's arm. He whispered:

"Detective—something you oughta know."

We turned to the building. Slattery seemed to be pointing at it.

"That hall downstairs. The basement."

"How could I forget?" Cussone said.

"It goes on, the corridor does, all the way to another entrance. We got the flashlights and're checking every door and all, but you should know that there's a staircase at the other end that leads into the basement and then the lobby of 419 Broadway. A big building. Lots of businesses. Near Crosby."

"A back door," Stanley said.

"Yeah."

"Thanks, Slattery. I'll take a look."

Slattery leapt up the stairs and disappeared.

"We've got to get to Gina," I said. "Quickly."

The commotion was escalating. We pushed through the melee of crowd and cameras and went back up to the second floor.

The waiting room's bright decor seemed an insulting counterpoint to the squalor below. The two nurses were crying now. One of them was howling like a dying coyote.

Stanley grilled them quickly, harshly.

"Read them their rights?" he asked Jimmy, who still sat at the receptionist's desk like a guard in his sentry box.

"Yep."

Cussone crouched and faced them.

"I'll put it to you bluntly, ladies, because I don't have time to fuck around. Talk to me now or forever hold your peace, in prison."

The coyote-woman howled for forgiveness: "I'm sorry, I'm sorry!"

"I'm not interested in sorry. Who runs this place?"

They both began to mumble in Spanish.

I took out Farrer's wedding picture and handed it to Cussone, and he showed it to the women.

"Is it her—is she in charge here?"

The crying woman took one look at the picture—gasped—then began to howl louder than before.

"Maniaco!" she screamed. "Maniaco!"

Stanley slapped her. It brought the woman to an abrupt and simpering silence.

"Maniaco," she repeated weakly.

I knelt beside her.

"He's dead."

"No," she responded, wagging her head.

Cussone added: "Yes. The man with the chain saw. We killed him."

She stared at us with huge red eyes.

"Butcher . . ." She spat onto the floor.

"Who has he killed?" Stanley asked.

But she sat quietly now, sullen, rocking her body as if silently mourning a loved one.

I asked: "His wife. Is she in charge here?"

She took the picture in her hands. Her fists held it so tightly they began to crack it. I yanked it away from her.

"We did not know they were married." She was breathless at the thought. Her hands opened and closed in midair, looking for something to crush.

"How do you know him?"

She continued her rocking.

"Do you call her 'Mother'?"

A bitter smile cut across her face like a festering wound.

"Never. She is no longer the nun."

"Nun?"

Her smile disappeared. "Sí."

Stanley said: "You've been injecting the babies downstairs with heroin."

She looked him in the eye and repeated the word with a despairing monotony. "Sí."

"And 'Mother,' she sells them that way?"

She said nothing. Her eyes glazed over. There seemed to be nothing left inside of her except a show of repentance. Her lips quivered in silent prayer. She produced a rosary and kneaded it through her jittery fingers. For some reason, I remembered the warm feeling their clatter used to evoke in me when my own mother would knead her rosary on Sunday mornings. Now they looked to me like a string of poison pills.

Cussone stood up.

I, too, got to my feet. Fatigue tugged at my backside like a pair of invisible hands. They were trying to drag me into a horizontal position, and I wanted to let them. I almost asked the nurses to shove aside so that I could lie down. But the stench below that had singed my nostrils still seemed to cling to me. I needed air.

Cussone barked to his men: "Book them, for Chrissake." Then he said to me: "I'm gonna take a look at that tunnel. C'mon."

I didn't have the stomach to go down there again, and told him so.

"Then wait outside," he ordered. "Ten minutes."

I nodded, guiltily. There wasn't much left in me, but I knew what I had to do. This wasn't the time to stand around on a sidewalk waiting for Stanley. Damn his methodical procedure. Gina was packing her bags right now, if she hadn't fled already.

I stepped outside again and worked my way through the crowd to his Chevy. Like all cops do, he'd left his keys hanging from the ignition. I started the motor, wishing I had a shiny new set of armor that would brace me against all that was to come.

Instead, I put my new hat on.

50

I drove north, past the point where Centre Street segues into Lafayette, rushing through yellow lights at Broome, Spring, Prince, until a red light caught me at the corner of Houston Street. I sat there and watched in silence as a commercial was being filmed on the sidewalk outside the grand Puck Building. Three men dressed as chefs danced in unison like seals in a water show. There were cameras and lights and reflectors and a crowd of crew and production staff that stood in an enormous circle watching them. The dancers all wore big mustaches and sang a song. They all carried boxes of frozen pizza.

The light turned green. I stepped on the gas and their song rushed out of memory as quickly as it had come. I rolled slowly now, as if the car were contemplative, past Bleecker and Great Jones and the methadone hotel on Bond Street. I parked below Tower Records, emerging from the car to a less-than-musical chorus of "Got a quarter?"—sung by one of the ever-changing trios of bums that were always pissing and parading and generally loitering on the corner of Fourth and Lafayette. Seeing them reminded me that I had a whole ten dollars in my pocket.

Two women with matching streaks of bluish green in their hair were carrying a piece of Hamlet's castle across Lafayette toward the Public Theatre. A yellow cab came speeding up the street, honked its horn, nearly hit them, swerved, then screeched to a stop across from number 419. Its ass end jutted out into the avenue, rudely blocking a lane. Several cars used their horns but to no avail; the taxi remained inert. An implacable Oriental sat behind the wheel, stone-faced as a boat master on the River Styx.

I figured I knew who the cab was waiting for.

I rang Gina's buzzer and prayed that she was there. No answer. I rang again and waited. The speaker popped with an electronic buzz. Her voice sounded small and tinny, like a long-distance connection.

"Yes?"

"Gina. It's Luke. I don't have my key."

My old hallway seemed so much the same as it had in those days when I'd first moved in that I stopped for a moment, took pause outside the elevator, let its muted sounds and sour smells work me over like old ghosts slamming on a living punching bag. Their special cadences brought to mind that confident fellow that I once knew so well. Luke Byman, filmmaker. Lover. Success.

I found myself tugging at my fraying jacket, trying to straighten it, but there wasn't any use. I wasn't him anymore.

To my right, around the corner and all the way down the hall, was my old apartment. Gina's was next to mine. Closer, at the hall's corner juncture, just down from the elevator, was Julia's old place. It had already been rented to another tenant. The police bolt had been removed. I smelled garlic frying.

When I turned the corner, Gina was standing there—quiet—waiting. She startled me. I jumped back.

"What were you doing there?" she asked sharply.

"Remembering."

She was backing down the hall, stepping cautiously in high heels. Her appearance was a surprise; with the heels she wore a black skirt and gray silk blouse and—makeup. It was strange to see her transformed. First Ivory Snow, then Manhattan sophisticate. She said:

"Not all good memories, are they?"

"No."

"In fact"—she laughed, strangely—"you've had a hell of a time here."

"Yeah, you could say." I stopped midway to her apartment. Hearing her heels tap against the tiles brought back a very particular memory. One I didn't cherish. Something started to burn inside of me, as if I'd swallowed a red-hot coal.

Hatred.

"I suppose those were the heels you were wearing that night you killed Bridge. In my apartment, of all places."

She was silent.

"The night you slapped me on the skull." I rubbed two fingers against my temple. "I still have the bump."

She whispered:

"I didn't want to kill him. But he barged in with a trick key—surprised me."

She opened her door.

"You know," she said disconcertingly, "I don't think I can find your key, Luke. It doesn't matter though; your apartment's been rented." She smiled. "Come in."

As always she positioned herself so that I'd have to brush against her. This time it had no effect. I stepped inside.

"Sit down." She closed the door.

I stood.

"Then—" I said. "Then Bridge put it all together. Along with everything else, he realized you'd killed his partner."

She spoke with her back to me. I watched her reflection in a mirror that hung on the wall near her old diplomas. She was reaching into her pocketbook as she said:

"Yes. Those creeps—Bridge and Ridley—they'd come to much the same point that you find yourself in now."

She turned and faced me, this time with a third eye. A little Luger that looked strangely at home in her palm.

"I liked you, Luke—really. I didn't want to hit you on the head that night. What'd you have to come here for?"

I just stared at the barrel.

"I mean," she said flightily, "this is so terrible."

"Stop it. I hate it when grown women talk like little girls."

"It is, though," she said, her voice cool and distant. "Terrible."

295

"What's so terrible? All I want is to know what's been happening to me."

"You want more than that."

"Just information."

"No. No, Luke. You want more. We—it's all wound up like a little helix, all your little strands of information. Any one of them will explode in your face." She creased her lips into a smile that could have soured milk. "I think you want them to."

As she spoke she wound a metal cylinder onto the barrel of her Luger. It squeaked like violin accompaniment.

"I think you've been flirting with death."

I sat down on the couch, trying to appear relaxed, and failing.

"I don't want anything exploding with me around. I came just to talk—to ask you questions. I don't even have a gun."

"Talk?"

"Talk."

"Raise your arms onto the top of the sofa."

I did as she ordered. She frisked me, as much for a wire as for a weapon, then said:

"Take your right shoe off—using your other foot."

I slid off my corroded sneaker and revealed a ratty blue sock. I smiled at the holes over my toes. I barely heard the gun fire.

The bullet slapped into my upper leg. It tore an instant gape in my trousers, burrowed through my flesh, then hit bone. The vibration on impact rattled my insides—I think the bone fractured, or the bullet lodged in it. Whichever, I screamed. And screamed some more. My hands came down and groped for the wound. I fell off the sofa and rolled onto the floor.

"Get up!" she yelled, waving the gun judiciously. "And please shut up."

I tried, but couldn't stop moaning. My head felt like it was about to explode; a feverish sweat spilled off it. I was nauseous, out of breath, as if I'd also been shot in the gut.

Gina said quietly: "Two or three minutes and I'm gone. I've got a cab waiting and—well, I'm anxious to leave. Compose yourself, Luke Byman. You can ask a question if you want."

I pulled myself onto the sofa, half prone there, ready for the flashing blacks at the perimeter of my vision to take over completely. Unconsciousness was close. Maybe worse.

"Well?"

I breathed hard a few times. It seemed to punch some life into me. A few minutes worth.

"Where's your daughter?" I said, struggling with the words. She stared at me with a queer, blank hatred.

"She's safe." Her mood changed, and she said with some surprise: "Already you know more than I thought you knew." She raised the barrel of her gun and touched her smiling lips with it. "You've spoken with him?"

"Your husband?"

She sighed. "I thought so." She aimed the gun at me again. "I didn't think you could be bought."

"I can't. The scumbag is dead."

Her eyes changed from playful to hateful like rolling license plates.

"Dead." She said it as a statement, her voice starched.

"This morning." I groaned.

She sat motionless. Her eyes underwent another transformation.

"You look—sad," I whispered to her. "I thought—I mean, I had the idea you ran from him, took the child."

"I did." A strange smile appeared. "But I suppose I am a little sad. We loved each other, once." She squeezed herself with her upper arms. "He was a great lover."

"Not anymore."

"Not for years. He went crazy. Really crazy."

"He's not the only one. What happened to you, Gina—eleven years ago?"

"He killed his best friend, you know, and his best friend's wife. Chopped them apart and set it up as his own death. And mine."

"But why?"

She thought a moment.

"He had to go 'under.' Someone . . . someone in the organization was informing on him. He was about to be busted, go to the can for a solid ten." She remained silent for a moment. "He had his father identify the bodies as his and mine. Without even asking, he killed me—my identity. Do you know how that felt? How he tossed me out like a piece of old junk?"

Her whole body quivered, and as the hate shook out of her

she fired another bullet into the sofa. It split a blackened hole in the fabric. The hole puffed smoke.

"And he took Sondra."

"Yes."

"What—" But my voice broke off as if disembodied from my mind. I was near to the darkness. I pictured it a swimming pool filled with ink. I was mid-gainer and descending.

"What did I do then?" she mimicked in singsong. "You mean, 'What did a pretty girl like me . . .'" She didn't finish.

I nodded bleakly.

"When Bill discarded me like that I actually didn't even know who I was. If I liked men or women. Anything. It was as if he really had killed me, inside. I felt so low—I don't know if you've ever felt that down, Luke. Down enough to change your whole life. Well. It's what I did. I went to a Catholic school. Studied social medicine. Courses, degrees, the whole Good Samaritan thing. And it wasn't show, either. I meant it all, mostly."

"Then how could you become—how could you be . . . 'Mother'?"

The word seemed to slap her. Her head rolled back, as if on a spring. She spoke tremulously.

"It's an involved question, Luke." She grimaced. "My husband was the one who dubbed me 'Mother'—because I used to take care of all his operations at the adoption agencies with my father. And my sister. They were just one of Billy's schemes back then. It's where we found Sondra." She spread her hands. The gun pointed toward a far wall. "Believe it or not—it's when I ended up in the convent that I met the others. Men and women already involved with the same kind of operation that William had created—it was just on a smaller scale. They needed what I knew."

"Your contacts."

"Yes. Rosters, agencies—the computers. The whole network, such as it was five years ago."

"You muscled in on your husband's operation."

"More than that. We took it over, outright. Billy was forced to buy back his share in our foundation."

"And you created Trion."

"Yes." She blinked. "Very impressive, Luke. But you've dug your own grave by finding all this out."

"You're going to shoot me again, Gina?"

She brought the gun to her lips again. "What's a girl to do?"

"Who—" A surge of pain shook me. I rolled with it, then continued. "Who was it that you met . . ."

She breathed quietly for a few seconds.

"I have to go now, Luke."

"I wanna know."

"I'm not going to tell you."

"And you sell babies for him?"

"Them."

"And buy arms?"

"That's not my business, really."

"Why sell addicted babies?"

"They are addicted when they come to us, first of all. We just keep them that way. Just for a while."

"I don't understand."

"It's really very simple—but we won't go into it."

"Your husband—he killed those Latin families?"

"Ah. Billy loved sending messages. Threats. Those men were my dealers. He wanted to cut our operation, scare the rest off—and it almost worked. No one in town would deal to us anymore. We had to go directly to Miami—but all this doesn't really matter."

Everything was quiet for a moment. I heard distant traffic on Lafayette. A faraway horn blaring. The taxi.

"My cab's waiting."

"I think I see, Gina. It must have been you—you were going to turn on your husband in the beginning."

She sat quietly, the pistol's barrel askew as she folded her hands. My grandmother used to sit the same way.

"Very perceptive."

"He 'killed' both of you by faking your deaths, then held Sondra to keep your mouth shut."

Her silence answered an affirmative.

"Why lie to me now?"

She smiled a motherly smile and with a sweet voice said: "You just don't understand." Her gaze hardened and she was tough again. "You really don't."

"I understand a little. You're a liar. But one thing I don't understand is why in hell Julia was living down the hall."

She smiled, said inexplicably: "Money, of course."

"I don't understand."

"I didn't make the arrangement. I abided . . ." She raised her gun toward me. "But it doesn't matter anymore."

The taxi's horn squealed again. I was getting nervous, looking up that little black barrel.

"Who is the Group, Gina?"

"You'll never know, Luke."

"Where's your daughter?"

"Safe and sound. Her little pussy waiting for me."

She aimed at me. My heart was pounding, trying to figure out a plan—where to move, if I could move. I managed to spit out:

"Humor me, damn it. One more question."

She stood and faced me. Though I was burning with pain her eyes alone made me shudder with a freezing tremor. Her skin had fallen slack. Everything pretty about her vanished. Her gaze was grim. Her voice sounded like a man's:

"Ask."

It was the only question I could think to ask.

"How is it that scum like you sleeps at night?"

I was lucky—her hand jerked before she pulled the trigger. I threw myself to her left, landing on my bleeding leg. She fired once. A bullet ripped through my other pants leg, missing my flesh, and stuck in the floor. The gun swiveled on her wrist. She aimed again and I screamed for my life—

But then three explosions rocked the front door.

Her door lock shattered into pieces. Stanley kicked it open. Gina's gun swung for him, but Stanley was crouching and firing—and I guessed he'd heard it all, everything, because he emptied his weapon into her. She took his first two shots standing. Blood spurted from her stomach, her shoulder. She staggered back, hit a wall, then fell to her knees. Gina turned a startled gaze on me before Cussone fired again. Then her head snapped back. Her neck cracked. Blood hit the wall. Then Gina's tiny frame collapsed backward, her knees buckled under her. Two dainty arms sprawled out from her body like broken wings. Cussone walked closer, stood over her, and fired another two shots. Her body bobbed as the bullets hit.

"Stanley!" I screamed. Painfully. "Stop!"

Cussone stood hunched over, breathing heavily, shaking. Oddly, though, when he looked up at me he produced a weary look of hope. Hope was on his breath when he said:

"You all right?"

"I hurt like hell."

"Ambulance," he muttered.

But before he dialed, Stanley raised his gun over Gina again and pulled the trigger one last time. The hammer snapped, click. My motor sputtered.

Late, late that night, I woke up in New York Hospital again. I half expected a gold plaque labeling my room "The Byman Suite."

My leg was in an awkward sling. Light spilled over it for an instant. I turned my blurry eyes to the left, to the door.

Someone had just come in and was standing in the shadows. A shiny piece of steel caught a ray of moonlight and gleamed in her hand.

51

A squeaking sound.

Suddenly, I noticed that there were two shadows. One was tall and thin and metallic, the other human. They approached in silhouette, and I had a vision of them as a mad scientist, hair in wild disarray, with an accompanying robot. Its wheels needed oil.

Lola's face emerged in a patch of moonlight. She looked like an ancient fresco of herself, pale and washed-out and hollow-eyed. She wheeled a metal stand along with her. From one of its arms hung a bag of plasmatic nutrient, fauceted into her arm by means of a plastic tube. It was multicolored in the moonlight. It swirled into her veins like gasoline.

She carried a small picture frame in her good hand.

I managed to say: "Hello."

She said nothing, but pulled a plastic chair near to me, sat in it, slid off of it, knelt on the floor, then hung her head on the side of the bed. She was shaking, and crying, and breathing hard. It took her a while to speak.

"Luke."

The voice tore at me. I took hold of her hair and stroked it. Her ears were red-hot. Her soft cheeks were ice-cold.

"It's all happening again," she said, "all the same. It's so strange, you know, but I remember."

"The heroin."

She nodded, her cheek on the sheets near my pillow. I tried to roll and face her. Sharp pains erupted in my leg.

She said in monotone:

"I was barely three when Nathan weaned me off of it. But I can still remember the feeling. The floating. Then, this horrible need." She repeated: "A horrible need. And so many other memories coming back with it now. Strange faces."

She flinched, as if those faces had hands that were grabbing for her through the steel cage of memory.

"Whose faces?"

"My real parents, I suppose. Both addicts. I don't know who they are. Never have. Nathan always said I didn't want to know."

"He adopted you?"

"Yes. Knowing we were addicted. They were so good to both of us, he and Joan."

"Us?"

"My—" She stopped again, took a few breaths. "I have a sister. We were adopted together."

"Blood sister?"

"No. No, another orphan. A white girl."

Her eyes tore into me.

"We'd both ended up abandoned, in the same clinic, in beds next to one another. Fate. Nathan and Joan had wanted to adopt. They came to the clinic to see my sister. You know, the official meeting between parents and prospective child. She was white. That's what they wanted. I was the afterthought. It was Nathan who took pity." She smiled weakly. "He used to say that the moment he saw me he fell in love." The smile vanished. "And it was true. Nathan treated me wonderfully. And he's always said that adopting us prompted the idea of his starting his own agency. He'd been a pediatrician for the local hospitals, and, well . . . suffice it to say that he's been a very loving father, Luke, to both of us. But there's always been something different about my sister—something that didn't take to the rest of the family. As we grew up, she separated herself from them—from all of us, early on. I hung in with Nathan. Helped him." She added, as if with some secret meaning: "I guess I feel I've had to do some things I didn't want to."

"Like what?"

But she said nothing—or there was nothing to say. Her silence made me think. It became obvious that by helping her father she had been forced to use me—though for what reasons I still didn't know. But the certainty of it shook through me like a bitter wind and blew away all traces of a morphine shot I'd been given earlier. Suddenly my eyes were clear, my legs ached again, and the plaster cracks that webbed the ceiling seemed revealed in greater detail. They were tangled like branches of overlapping family trees.

"Where is this sister?" My voice was harsh.

"New York." Her voice hushed. "She's bad, Luke. A monster. It's why I came here, to this hospital. Posing as their nurse." She said with a sad spark of pride: "I"ve been a nurse almost all my life, you know. Upstate first—at the same clinic where I was adopted. Then when Denington and my father merged I worked at their adoption agency. I loved it, but I hated Poughkeepsie. Lately, these last few years, I've been at a local adoption clinic here in town." She produced a forlorn smile. "It's where I always was when you could never reach me."

I didn't see anything worth smiling about. I turned away but she continued:

"At first I was using you, I admit. We thought you were involved with her. Or had been."

"With your sister?"

She let a long moment slide by.

"Then I fell in love with you, Luke."

"Give me a break."

"Please—"

"Who is she?"

Another pause, for breath. She was short of it. She spoke haltingly.

"It took us years to find her, you know, to try and stop what she's been doing to us—to all the agencies. She's working with others, tapping into our inquiries file, finding the families, and then making the illegal pitch. Their babies are a lot more money but there isn't any wait. Or papers, or questions. Anyone can adopt, for the fee. There's—there's been a lot of loose money around. She's been very successful. They. It's an organization now. My sister has become a conduit for them. She was extremely able because she knew the business, the whole system. She'd learned it well enough, from her father."

"Nathan."

"Yes. A long time ago she even married Nathan's and Ralph's financial backer. A hateful man, but he had money. Sometimes I think it was all part of her plan. I know her very, very well. She used my father to get to her husband. To money. Then she used her husband to get where she is now."

I whispered: "Farrer?"

She nodded quietly in the moonlight, lifting the silver frame and resting it on my chest. It was one of those that had been missing from her bedroom wall. I raised it and saw two tiny girls dressed in frilly First Communion dresses. The dresses were an identical blue, but one of the girls was black, the other white. It didn't take a genius to recognize them. Lola and Gina. Sisters.

I turned my eyes up, again, and stared at those cracks in the ceiling. It seemed as if they formed a spider's web, a web that was descending on me. "Christ," I said aloud, hurting, not from any bullet wound, but with a dull pain in the left side of my chest. I felt as if the wind had been kicked out of me, or the blood squeezed out of my heart.

Two pairs of sisters, four very different women. And at least three of them had either betrayed me or tried to kill me. Or both. "Christ," I said again, then blurted out: "She's dead."

Lola leaned her young body closer to me. When she tried to speak the word struggled out of her, like an old woman's gasp.

"Gina?"

"Gone."

The room hummed. Mute sounds of a hospital hallway pressed around us. Lola said so quietly:

"You killed her?"

"Cussone. He shot her."

With desperation she asked: "Definitely?"

"Definitely."

With the sudden force of a dam splitting open, she burst into dry heaves. She hung on to the side of the bed with one hand, and a quiet moaning emanated from deep inside of her—as much from relief as from sorrow. Finally, her breathing steadied.

"Don't think I'm sad." She reached up and tried to touch my cheek. She missed. "I'm just so sorry, Luke—for everything."

I didn't feel forgiving.

"I still don't understand," I spat out icily, "why you came to me."

She pulled herself up, away from my anger, and wheeled the metal stand into the corner, near a basin. She ran water and splashed it on her face and then slumped below the sink, resting her head against the porcelain.

"It was the private investigator my father hired. Over a year ago now."

A cog snapped into place. I sat up—in pain.

"Ridley?"

"Yes."

"Tell me."

"It's a long story, really. He and his partner, they found Denington—years after he'd run from the police. They followed him to your apartment building." She took a breath, then exhaled: "You see, we had nowhere else to look. Gina had disappeared. She'd been gone so long, after the retreat."

"Say again?"

"The convent. She spent a lot of time there after Farrer—he . . ."

"He phonied her death."

"You know?"

"I know."

"He's a horrible man. A murderer."

I let the present tense pass.

"Go on."

"Well . . ."

"The retreat."

"Yes. She disappeared there but after a couple of years we got a note. Nathan and I. She'd joined an order—a convent, really—and was just a year away from taking vows. Imagine." She imagined for a few seconds. "Anyway, she was letting us know that she was fine—a weak moment, I suppose. She never really kept in touch, or was close at all. As a kid—"

I broke her off. "I'm losing strength, Lola. What happened at the convent?"

"I don't really know. She met someone. I don't know who it was. She left the convent with her."

"Her?"

"From what I understand. Ridley visited the place a year ago. They told him what they could, but she'd left a full year before that." She stared out the window and said dreamily: "We just lost track of her."

"How'd you know to follow Gina? That she was undercutting your business?"

"Farrer. He told Nathan. I don't know how he found out, but he threatened Nathan and me, to try and make her stop. Luckily, we had her letter from the convent. So we hired Ridley to try and trace her from there. It didn't work."

"Where is this retreat?"

"Oh. I don't remember. On a mountain someplace. The Catskills."

"What happened after Ridley lost track of Gina's trail?"

"He found Denington."

"How?"

"Ridley was casing all the clinics in town, trying to find the one Gina might have been operating through. He spotted Denington at one of them. We know now that Ralph was doing the same as Ridley—tracking Gina. But Ridley didn't know that. He thought it was some prearranged rendezvous." She sighed, then went on. "He saw Ralph let himself into your building, moments after Gina had gone in, so he suspected that Ralph and Gina were working together. He didn't even know your Julia was down the hall. Her mailbox had some other name on it."

Your Julia.

She added: "Imagine Ralph's shock when he found out Gina Farrer was living just down the hall from his wife."

But it couldn't have been a shock: Denington must have known. Julia did, or so Gina had said. The thought had been plaguing me ever since I found out that Gina had been Farrer's wife. Why would Julia knowingly live down the hall from Gina Farrer?

Gina had told me before she died that money had been Julia's reason—yet she'd lied to me so often that I couldn't believe her. What profit would there have been in staying down the hall from that killer? Maybe Julia had been held captive by the Group, or perhaps held under a threat to someone she loved. I wouldn't know, not for sure—not until I found Julia and asked her myself. If I ever found her.

Then another, even stranger thought crossed past me like an experience from a previous life: before being born into the case I'd already been involved. A brief and painful laugh forced its way out of my gut. Lola seemed to know the cause of my astonishment.

"Yes, Luke, I know what you're thinking. I first heard your name through Ridley. After a day or two of surveillance, he realized that Ralph was actually staying somewhere in the building. At first he thought Denington was living with Gina, but we discounted that later. He broke into her place and didn't find any trace of Ralph. Then, well—he began to think that you were Ralph—I mean, that Luke Byman was Ralph Denington's alias." She hesitated. "But . . . he never got the chance to search your place or he'd have realized his mistake. Soon after he tracked Denington to your building, Gina and Ralph were off to Los Angeles."

"Together?"

"Separately, but on the same plane. Ridley assumed they were together."

My mind was racing. I muttered:

"Trion. She went to sign the papers."

"What?"

"Nothing. Ralph was following her."

"I wouldn't know why. And I don't know what happened out there," she said. "We never knew. Ridley was killed and dumped on a beach out near Malibu." She sighed. "Then Dad went a bit crazy. He actually suspected Ralph had done it."

"So did Bridge. Why?"

"Because Ridley had sent Bridge a key. To that safety-deposit box."

I knew the one.

Lola continued quietly.

"When Bridge traced the key he found that the box was under

the name Denig. It was obviously Ralph's. There were those pictures in it. . . . Nathan was horrified. He didn't realize it was Ralph's evidence—ways to destroy Gina and Farrer." She sighed. "It's only when Ralph resurfaced that my father realized he was truly innocent. He came to Nathan for help—to get the box and pictures back." Her eyes scanned me. "He was a shell of himself."

"But Nathan didn't give it to him."

"No. But he told him where the key was."

"In Bridge's office."

"Yes. Where—where Ralph hit you on the head."

"Why didn't Nathan come forward with the pictures?"

"Farrer has had Daddy in the palm of his hand for years. You don't know him. What he's capable of doing."

I did, though. For a split second I relived the near loss of my left arm to his chain saw. The thought made my fingers go numb.

I said after a moment: "I know that he's dead, Lola."

"Dead?"

"Very."

She clutched my arm and bowed her head and released a shiver. We sat for a few moments, shivering together.

When Lola finally lifted her eyes, I saw that they were webbed with veins, like the ceiling.

"It's over," she said, her voice cool and hollow.

"No, Lola. Not over. Not yet."

A few seconds stretched by.

"Luke?" The way she said it, my own name pierced me with a chill.

I raised my hand in the air to stop her from talking further. There were more questions. Recriminations. A long, drawn-out talk about how it could never work, not now. Not ever.

I didn't have the strength.

"Please, just go," I said.

It didn't take her long. She pushed herself up and wheeled the metal stand to the door. When she opened it the hall light shone through her hospital dress and revealed a lithe body frozen underneath. It was my final, fleeting X ray of Lola.

52

My eyes opened.
    Rose hues washed the cracked ceiling with a life all its own. Its colors deepened to blood red, undulating like an upside-down ocean. Then a clear white light took over. I had to squint. A flock of bird shadows passed along one wall.
    I didn't move. My breathing stopped, and a strangely mellow sensation filled my limbs. Not pain, nor the absence of it. It was a warm sensation, sad and sure, nearly exultant.
    I waited for nothing in particular.
    Then all at once I made the move—I swung my leg out of its sling and to the left, off the bed, and sat up. For one blank second I felt nothing. Then a gush of pain clobbered me and forced me down again.
    I waited some more.
    It took six tries. Each time I got a little farther. Each time I ended up on the bed again. Finally my body agreed to make it as far as the closet. The sight of my dirty clothes inside almost seemed comforting.
    It was a painful process, slipping the pants on over my wounds.

The hole in my leg burned. It bled slightly. My bones ached like little freeways of pain inside of me. It was rush hour. I didn't cry at the hurt, but tears squeezed out of the corners of my eyes. I kept telling myself that pain didn't matter. I'd come this far, goddammit. I'd take the plunge.

"Good-bye," I muttered, but had no idea if I was going anywhere. I sat on the edge of the bed, rolled open a metal tray and found my ten dollars and my cheap watch. It was seven-thirty.

"Christ!" I said aloud, recalling a vague obligation I'd already fucked up beyond repair. Perhaps it was an odd time to think of it, but hell, I'd had a life once.

I tried to remember his number. Digits spun around in my head like a slot machine as I sang "Da-da, da-da" out loud like an idiot. Seven numbers clicked into place. I dialed Richard Weiss at home. I caught him as he was going out the door.

"What?" He was trying to remain calm. I was giving him bad news, but it was his first call of the morning.

I said it again: "I won't be able to write your screenplay."

"I heard you the first time," he said. "But I'm not listening. You have a commitment, Byman. You gotta write it."

"I find myself unable to."

He tried to speak with casual assurance.

"Don't do this. I could come after you, you know. We got a contract."

"For how much?"

"Nothing now, you know that. You trying to squeeze me?"

"No."

"Then what?"

"I just can't do it, is all. I'm sorry."

"Sorry? You better fucking give me a goddamned good reason."

I said quietly: "Well, your idea stinks. The script will stink. As a matter of fact, your whole deal stinks, too."

I hung up on him, feeling vaguely satisfied.

"Heartening way to start the morning," I said brightly to no one.

I stood up again, and took stock. A bandage was wrapped around my left thigh where Gina had shot me. A spot of red shone through, like a Japanese flag; the wound hadn't healed yet. My right heel was still swollen to the size of an orange. An oval Band-Aid hung on it. I had an image of my body whistling in a strong wind.

The phone rang.

I perched my damaged inventory on the edge of the bed and picked up the receiver. They seemed to be making phones heavier lately.

I answered without irony: "Good morning."

"I got something."

Cussone. His voice was bright.

"Me, too."

"You up?"

"In a manner of speaking."

"I'll be over. Half hour."

"Pick me up outside."

"What? You can't—"

"You heard me. The fountain."

The shirt, my jacket, belt, even the socks—no problem. The sneakers were the hard part. I had to bend my aching legs to get them on. I cried out once. No one heard.

There was a walker in the hallway, so I used it. The elevator rolled open. My nurse popped out of it, smiled, and only as the doors rolled closed did she turn and realize who I was. She was saying:

"Wait!"

So I took the elevator to basement level. I stepped out into a bright, tiled hallway that slanted up and became a ramp to a freight entrance. Through its doors were a set of stairs I had to stumble down to get out of the garage. This took me past a garbage truck that seemed, from the smell of it, to be loading all of last night's bed-mess.

I emerged at the back entrance of the hospital and had to shuffle the full length of the block, using my walker, then around another half block to the front entrance. My nurse stood with a hospital guard near the fountain, scouring the area for me. The guard wore a stern expression. His hand rested on the butt of his holstered pistol, as though a lunatic had escaped.

Perhaps he was right.

I waved to them as I walked to Stanley's car. I opened his door. He had half a bagel in his mouth.

"Get the hell out of here," I said to him, falling backward onto the front seat. Like Lloyd Bridges off the boat.

His "What?" came out a grunt.

I yanked his automatic transmission into Drive.

"Go!" I said.

The nurse and guard ran toward us. They were yelling to us. Stanley finally saw them.

He said: "Oh," then hit the gas. Horns blared on First Avenue. Brakes screeched. His hot coffee slid off the dashboard and poured into his lap.

He screamed "Shit!" and patted a napkin on himself, panting heavily.

I was happy to stay prone on the seat awhile, bumping up First, staring at the vinyl ceiling. Cussone cooled off. When the pain of scalding his genitals had subsided, he broke our silence.

"Soggy crotch," he said, resigned to that fate.

"I had to get out of there," was my answer.

We stopped at a red light.

"Hungry?"

"You bet."

"I have to get to a men's room."

A few moments later the car slid to a stop. I sat up and blinked at the sight of a pretty woman bending over and picking up her dog's poop with a toy shovel. We eyed each other warily as she dumped her prize into a corner trash can. Above her, the sign for Seventy-sixth Street was bent at a right angle.

"There's a good coffee shop across the avenue," Stanley said. "Come on. Maybe you can help make something of what Chief Wall had to say."

"He called?"

"That's what I said, isn't it? Let's eat."

He strolled easily across the avenue. Without my walker I hobbled like Walter Brennan.

We had coffee, French toast with eggs over easy broken over the slices, bacon, syrup, orange juice. More coffee. I thought of nothing else but eating. Only afterward did Stanley remove a folded piece of notebook paper from his breast pocket and read its scribblings aloud.

"Wall traced the little hose you grabbed in that boat yesterday."

"It's a bilge pump."

"Whatever."

"So?"

"I'll go through it. The manufacturer's and distributor's names were on the package, so he called, and was diverted to yet another number, a sales office. After some haggling the guy there lays it out for him. There are nine digits in the serial number. The first three indicate the model, the second three are its batch number, and the third three are sort of stamped on. They identify the distributor it was sent to. After some more haggling Wall gets the guy to look up 339—the last three numbers—and he gets the distributor. A dump all the way in Schenectady. The guy there was too busy to trace the thing—so, get this, Wall hops in his car yesterday and goes up there. A three-hour drive. He appears and scares the shit out of this rude distributor. The guy crawls on his knees to his books and here's what he came up with. Their company, it keeps track of what they send out by using the batch number—the middle digits. The first number of the three labels the county. The next two digits identify the store or local distributor."

Cussone stopped to slurp some coffee through his smug grin.

"So?" I said again.

"Greene."

"Greene?"

"County."

"Greene County?"

"Uh-huh."

"Don't play games. What town?"

"Catskill."

I said: "Hmmm," and thought for a moment. I knew the place. Not so many miles from where I was born. "It's on the river," I said.

"Thirty miles north of Poughkeepsie. Not too bad in a speedboat."

"No, or by truck."

"How do you figure?"

"I may be wrong. But I think we're looking for the airfield."

"Panther Field."

"Yes. The babies arrive there. Then they're loaded into the truck we saw."

"Taken to Sondra's Marina."

"And from there to New York. The clinic."

"And dispatched in those fucking tractor trailers. And—" Cussone winced. "It occurs to me that since the kids are high, they make no noise. It's possible they may be routed through legitimate businesses in the towns where they're dropped."

"Gina said the reason was simple."

"Reason?"

"For keeping them high."

"Oh." He paused. "Yeah, simple."

"Yeah."

I waved my spoon around in my coffee cup, thinking of Genna. Cussone went on:

"And those legitimate businesses might be hospitals, you know. Or other adoption clinics."

"Or medical supply companies. That's what the truck was filled with."

"Right." He inhaled some more coffee, whispering again: "Right."

"And there's something else."

"You have something, you said."

"Lola. What she told me."

"Last night?"

"It's confusing as hell. Gina was her sister."

Stanley sat like Buddha and pondered the connection.

"Jesus."

"I'll tell you more in the car."

"My God . . ." he said to himself, then snapped out of it. "Are we going somewhere?"

"We have to, Stanley. Again. If I'm right, we don't have much time. We may be too late already. They may be gone. Or maybe I'm not right at all."

"What are you talking about?"

"We have to get a map of New York State."

Cussone leaned back in the booth. He fixed his implacable gaze on me, the way he would on his office window.

I said quietly: "Red was headed for the city in that boat, but I don't think it's where he went in the car he stole."

"Then where?"

I, too, sat back, prompted by another surge through my limbs. That same mellow sensation, adrenaline from another world.

"We have to find a convent," I said.

Part Five

PANTHER MOUNTAIN

53

Stanley held the left side, I grabbed the right. We unfolded its squares across the front seat. We'd had to drive down to Rand McNally to find it. Now, reflections of Fifty-third Street traffic glanced across the colors of the map like bright shadows.

Stanley took a pen from his pocket and traced it along the routes that extended out from the Catskill basin, north and west to the mountains. Dark splotches of green indicated forest preserve, and a lot of printing was lost in them. Bending down to see, we bumped each other's heads.

Cussone held his bald spot.

"Christ! You have a hard head."

We continued scanning the map, looking for an airfield, but none were shown anywhere in the highlands. The nearest was the Kingston airport, where 32 north meets 209.

"We could try it," Stanley said. "Look around."

I was disappointed. It wasn't the airport. It couldn't have been. Too high-profile.

"We could call Kingston. I know a uniform up there. Maybe there's a convent on a mountain nearby."

"Yeah, I guess."

Stanley opened the car door. "I'll call."

"Right."

So I waited for him, still staring at the map. I lifted it into my lap for a closer look. The printing in the dark green came alive a little with some light under it.

I held the map up to the window. Shadows of the passersby shone through it like pedestrian spirits. From the other side they likewise might have seen my form, shadowed as it was, smiling.

There in the middle of one of the green blotches were two small words in fine print: "Panther Mountain."

When Cussone came back I didn't even let him say word one. He didn't get the chance. I was poking my finger against the map, against the green blotch, in Greene County.

"Found it," I said flatly.

He grabbed the sides of the map and wrinkled it up close to his eyes.

"Panther Mountain," he said aloud.

"There's a town, right there."

"Maplecrest."

"Call them."

I watched him. I could only see his feet and the bottoms of his bent elbows as he talked in the half-booth on the corner. He made very little movement at first. Then his hands got restless. His feet began to shuffle. They walked back and forth in the two-foot booth, turning, scraping, tapping. He hung up. Dialed again. Another call. This time the right hand was animated. It swung around, accentuating his words, then clutched the side of the steel booth. His foot stamped the sidewalk as he slammed the receiver down. A pause. A thought. Then another call. His body pretended to be calm. His hand waved in a gentle explication. He was coercing someone to do something. When he hung up he stepped back from the phone and gave it a dirty look. Then Detective Stanley Cussone lumbered toward me with his peculiar walk.

He sat at the wheel a few seconds before speaking.

"Well," he declared, "no airstrip." It was all he said for a moment, before adding quietly: "But there's a convent."

The thought of Julia surged through me with that same foreboding tincture. My fingers numbed. The numbness traveled up my arms and into my shoulders. From there it invaded the back of my neck and enveloped my head with a tingling that narrowed the focus of my eyes. For a split second all I could see were Julia's eyes, again lancing me all the way to the marrow. As if that one look had been the root of the infection.

"Julia," I said, inadvertently, aloud.

Cussone eyed me. "What?"

I took a deep breath. Changed the subject.

"What were the other calls?"

"Oh. The station. No one's fuckin' gonna drop what they're doing—" He caught his bitter tone in check, then continued more calmly. "Everyone's busy there. Same as before."

"FBI?"

"I didn't call."

I waited.

He looked me square in the eyes.

"You want me to? They'd take us off this for sure, handle it themselves. It's prob'ly the better way."

"Probably." It didn't take long to consider, though. "Don't call."

"All right, I won't."

"Then I guess it's you and me."

"Well, I did make one other call. To our good Chief up in Westchester."

"Wall?"

"We need all the help we can get, brother. He'll be in Maplecrest before us if we don't get our ass going."

Stanley edged his way into traffic. He inched along Fifty-third, across Sixth, then Seventh, then turned right onto Eighth Avenue. We followed it up past Columbus Circle, onto Broadway, and at Ninety-first he stopped again. We parked along the east side of the avenue and peered across the rush of traffic to the old gun store on the opposite corner.

"I don't know," I said hesitantly.

"I've only got my thirty-eight. You need a piece."

He left me in the car. It took six minutes. He came out with a paper bag full of bullet clips and another .45 automatic. It was dark black and worn smooth and heavy to hold. There were two silver clips.

"It wasn't much," he said. "There's a special on forty-fives, a whole crate of them he's got. Korean issue."

I hefted the steel in my palm. I held it for a full hour, all the way out of town. My fingers relented their clutch on it somewhere past Nyack, when sleep took over.

A while later I woke up to the words:

"Your life is shit, kid." Stanley paused, waiting for my eyes to open. He turned his glance down on me. "Ya know that?"

I had no relevant answer.

"I mean," he continued, "look at you. Your friends, where are they? I mean, maybe they're around, I dunno. Anybody call you lately?"

"I don't have a phone anymore."

"That's what I mean."

"What's what you mean?"

"Your life is just a pile of shit. Look at you. I've never seen someone go down so fast. I've never seen it. Your friends, whoever they are, are prob'ly way past the worrying stage. More in the pissed-off stage by now."

"Like you?"

"Well . . ." He said it bluntly. "I'm not your friend. I'm a cop, for Chrissake. Who am I to you? You're a film guy. You write big movies or something."

"Say what you mean or lay off."

"After today, I dunno. If nothing comes of this up here, well, I think it's time you go on to other things. Get out of my hair. Out of this whole business. It's not for you—look at you. I mean, you don't want it to be your business. Don't keep on this. It's worthless, thankless. What are you in this car for? You have woman friends, right? Guys. A profession?"

"Not much of one after this morning." I told him of my conversation with Weiss. My ex-script.

He shook his head. "What are you fucking doing, Byman? What are you doing with your life?"

A small Thruway bridge rattled under us like metal thunder. Its echo lingered in the car for a moment.

"I suppose I don't know," I said to him quietly.

The highway rose steadily for an uphill mile. When it dipped down again, faint forms of the Catskills appeared on the horizon like stark, shadowy whales surfacing on smooth water.

"Not after today, anyway."

The air cooled. We had to roll our windows shut, which only accentuated our rolling silence. Overhead, big white clouds made the bright sun blink at a slow-motion pace. Whenever the light was gone the mood inside our car grew somber, as it did also on the road, in hotel parking lots, Thruway road stops, mountain passes. All around us the world blackened, until, just a moment later, the sun would splash down again and create a sparkling landscape, a gorgeous day, worth the price of any admission. Or exit toll. I could feel each flashing change in my viscera, as if the earth itself was schizophrenic.

Stanley pulled the Chevy through the toll booth at Exit 21, Catskill. We drove west on Route 23, through large sections of road mainly populated by old resort hotels. They had once been at the height of fashion. Now they withered with age. Large women in sleeveless shifts and curlers mowed their lawns. Some of the husbands sat on their porches and stared out at the two-lane stretch before them as if it were Fifth Avenue.

We started to climb, past the old hotels, up large portions of bumpy road. We wove around the potholes, guided by a series of detour signs, themselves deteriorating. Farther up, slate rock had fallen in glossy piles by the roadside. One pile had half buried a small green sign for Maplecrest, on our left. A white arrow was painted on it, angled upward.

Route 296 went straight up the side of a mountain. Its curves were vicious horseshoes. They bordered steep slopes of loose shale that, to the left, went up, and to the right—all the way down. Groves of birch shone iridescent in the gullies down below. Amongst them, the husks of several crashed cars glittered like ancient relics. Stanley slowed down often, blinded on a bad curve as the noon sun flashed out of the clouds.

The road leveled off into a plateau, and we traveled on it for a while before Maplecrest came into view. The small white spire of a wooden church was our first sighting. Then a fly-fishing supply store, its siding lined with fishing rods. A huge brick liquor store was next. It seemed a seedy cornerstone of sorts for a row of shops that bordered the north side of town. Two bars, a junk shop, and a few run-down joints that defied definition. On the other side of the main street a different tack had been taken, as if Maplecrest had two owners. A row of precious renovation was heralded by an ornate gift mart, replete with phony gold leaf on all its trim. The other stores that followed were similarly self-conscious. An ice-cream parlor, clothing boutique, and a "General Store" that looked as old-fashioned as a Hallmark card. Some outsider's notion of quaint.

The one-room police station was at the far end of town. Four brick walls and a parking lot. It was tucked away to the right, behind the seedy side of town.

Inside, the walls were brick and plastic wood. Two desk areas had been compartmentalized by a wooden rail with a swing door in it. Cussone and I stood with our fingertips on the rail, waiting. An overweight cop in his mid-forties was on the phone. When he finally hung up, he stood and faced us, revealing a distended gut and an infectious smile.

"My mother," he said, holding out his hand for Cussone to shake. "She always calls at lunch."

"Knaust?" Stanley asked.

"That's me. Cussone, right?"

"Right."

"I can always tell the New York cops."

Stanley smiled. He waved a hand in my direction.

"Byman," I said.

"Howdy."

Stanley asked: "A lot of New York cops up this way?"

"One 'r two. Ski resorts bring the city shitheads. Present company excluded." Knaust grinned mischievously. He motioned for us to sit down in a waiting area near the door. Paintings of trout-flies hung at jagged angles over the chairs. "Fact is, there's a lot of petty crime up here during winters. 'Cause that's when this place comes alive with all sorts of folks. But summers, hell. They're dead."

Stanley leaned his elbows on his knees and clasped his hands.

"What do you know about the convent near here, Deputy?"

Knaust's face changed, like a mood of the sun. His expression went behind a cloud.

"Not much."

"And you're sure there's no airstrip around here?"

"Hell, no."

"Mind if we go up and take a look at the place?"

"Snoop?"

"Discreetly. Ask some questions."

Knaust sighed. "Sister Theresa's a tough bitch. And she runs the place. We'll have to call her, you know. We just can't go—prowling around."

"Don't call," I said. "Please."

"Well. Shit—What is it you want me to do, for Chrissake? I gotta know what you think we're gonna find."

Stanley weighed his response before speaking.

"We may be dead wrong about this, Knaust. If so, Byman and I will have had a pleasant trip to the country, nothing more. You can send us packing. But—if we've hit the right place, well . . ." Instinctively, Cussone fixed his implacable expression on a rack of rifles in the far corner.

Knaust's eyes turned reluctantly to the rack of rifles, then back to Cussone.

"That bad?" he asked.

"Could be."

Another police car pulled to a stop outside. The shadow of a uniform passed by the window blinds and opened the station door. Chief Wall stood there. A piece of white paper fluttered in his hand.

Cussone introduced them dryly. The two shook hands without a word.

Knaust squirmed before he asked Wall: "You in on this?"

"Doing what I can."

"What about? I mean, what the hell is all this?"

Wall flipped a short glance at Cussone. Stanley shrugged.

"Haven't told him much."

Wall seemed more formal than before. He took a military step forward and dropped the piece of paper in Knaust's fat hands. "It's about a lot, I suppose. Mainly this."

Knaust read. It didn't take him long. For some reason he turned his gaze on me, and held it there.

"It's my report," Wall said to all of us. "Yesterday's."

Knaust turned back to the page in his hands. Wall said to him: "Seven babies dead. It's lucky we found that boat when we did. It could have been a lot worse."

"And . . ." Knaust slapped the report with the back of his hand. "You think you've connected some of these goings-on with—with nuns up at the convent?"

"Maybe," Stanley said.

I stood up. "We should go."

Cussone remained seated. His eyes lingered on Knaust.

"You coming?"

Knaust just gazed at his feet, as if worried they might get up and take him out the door with us. He was trying to will them not to. He stroked his hand through what little hair he had and said to his feet:

"I don't have to, do I?"

"No."

"But—I can't just lend you the rifles without going."

"Then we'll have to do without them."

Cussone stood up. A tense moment passed. I took the opportunity to wink at a small sparrow that had alighted on the outside sill behind me. It seemed to be smiling.

Knaust attempted his own smile, but what broadened below his small eyes was a dubious grimace. He looked again at me, as if I'd brought him the trouble, then back to Cussone.

"Aw, hell," he said, and stood up.

He walked over to the rifle rack and unlocked it.

54

We went in two cars. Stanley and I in his Chevy; Wall and Knaust in the deputy's rig. It was the usual police unit—flat, ugly, dark green—except the back end had been jacked up like some country Camaro.

It led us through a network of connecting roads that all pointed up, none with guardrails. Looming hills of dark pine surrounded us. Among them, small groves of angel birch brightened like phosphor, then disappeared again, as the fickle sun continued changing moods.

I slapped a clip into the .45; made sure the safety was fixed, its white dot showing; then laid the gun back on the seat beside me. Inadvertently, I stared at it too long.

"Don't worry," Stanley said, catching me. "More than likely, you'll never use one of those. Not your whole life."

I considered this for a moment.

"Anyway," I said, "there's only one man I could think to shoot."

"I know."

Brake lights winked ahead of us. Knaust put his blinker on,

the right one. He made a wide turn up a steep road that was bordered at its entrance by stone columns. A gold plaque was embedded in one of them. It spelled out in script: CONVENT OF THE SACRED HEART.

Across from its entrance, the road gave way to a steep chasm. I couldn't see what was just below the edge, but it appeared to go straight down. Way down. No rail, no fence. Across the rift a waterfall spouted from the woods like a faucet, fell a long way, then crashed over clumps of glacial moraine.

"Treacherous up here," I monotoned as Cussone swung wide and made the right turn.

We followed close behind Knaust. The two rifles he'd dispensed to us started clattering together on the floor of the back seat. A blanket that had covered them had shaken loose. I reached back and hid them again.

"I'm feeling sort of silly, carrying those things to a convent," Stanley said.

"But not really."

"No. Not really."

A couple of sharp turns brought us up against a steel fence that crossed the road. It disappeared into the woods on either side.

"Shit," Knaust said as he got out of his unit. "Didn't know they had a fence installed. I thought I heard about everything up here."

We all got out. There was an intercom at the gate, and Knaust used it.

"Yes?" a woman's voice responded over it.

"Hello, ma'am. Sister. Deputy Knaust from the village police here."

"Yes?"

"Like it if you could buzz us in."

"To whom do you refer?"

"Have a couple gentlemen here with me. We'd all like to chat with Sister Theresa."

"Hold on."

We held, hands in pockets, mine sweating. We were close, I knew it. This wasn't the way most convents greeted the world. We were close.

The voice buzzed again.

"I'm sorry, Deputy, the sister is busy presently. She says you should have called. Call her tomorrow, she says."

"Sister . . ." Knaust clutched his fingers in the fence grid.

"Yes, Deputy?"

"It is most important that you let me in. Now, Sister. None of this appointment crap. Am I gettin' through to you?"

A pause, then: "Hold on."

Another few moments of wind in the pine boughs. None of us said a word.

"Shit," Knaust finally drawled. His foot slammed the fence and the intercom snapped to electronic life.

"Deputy?"

He smiled at us. "Everything works if ya kick it." He talked to the small box. "Yeah, Sister?"

"You can come up alone, for now, if you like. Or come with your friends tomorrow."

"What the hell . . . ?" he said to us. Then, to the receiver, "All right. Fair deal."

The fence buzzed open. Knaust turned to us, his concern apparent. He said with no humor:

"Fuck her. Let's go."

We jumped into our seats. I closed my door, slipped the .45 down into the back of my belt, then put my jacket on. Stanley drove inches from Knaust's car, through the gate and up a steep hill. Around a snaking curve, the convent came into view, high above a sloping lawn that was dotted with plaster religious sculptures.

It wasn't what I expected. The old mortar mansion was brightly painted burnt umber, with a white stone trim that was too ornate for its own good. Its front section was a tall four stories, a towering façade. Its back section was wide and more modern, a squat two stories. The old and new sections had been grafted together by a connecting archway. I was struck by the juxtaposition of windows. Arched stone in the original house; square, routine storm windows in the back section. The new building looked like offices, or dormitories, a place where the business of the convent was centered. A satellite dish sat on its flat roof.

A paved road led off from the back of it to a small stone stable or gatehouse. A black Jeep was parked there. A light was on in the upper window.

As we swung around the circular drive, a chapel came into view to the left. It was small, and built long ago with rough blocks of mountain stone. It wore a bluish green roof that looked like an unpolished copper cap. Its bell was tolling, slowly, like a dirge. A dozen nuns were filing into the chapel, walking in pairs, their heads bowed, hands clasped in prayer. They kept their eyes on their feet; none of them even glanced at us as we pulled up in front of the convent.

"You are disturbing us, Deputy," were the first words we heard. I hadn't even gotten out of the car.

"I'm sorry, Sister." Knaust took his hat off.

"Sister Theresa."

"Sister Theresa—we had to. Let me introduce you to—"

"I don't care who they are. You should go, Deputy, before I lose my temper. We are mourning today, and it is not appropriate for you to be here."

"Mourning?"

"One of our beloved older sisters passed away yesterday evening. It was expected. Nevertheless . . ."

"Sorry, Sister Theresa, but we have to—"

"Is there something momentous you feel forced to ask me?"

"Well . . ." She was rattling Knaust's nerves. Stanley jumped in. He flashed his badge but not his smile.

"We need to look around, Sister. Please."

"Whatever for?"

The bell stopped tolling. The five of us stood silent in its wake.

"An airstrip," I said bluntly.

She turned a gaze on me that nearly shrank my manhood. She turned it back on Knaust. I think it did shrink his.

She spoke harshly to him. "Explain this to me, Deputy."

"I can't, really. Detective—"

But her eyes were burning with vituperous glee.

"You can't explain—?" Stanley cut her off.

"If I could only—" She cut Stanley off.

"No. Do you have a warrant, Deputy?"

"Of course not, I didn't think—"

"No, you don't, do you? I could, right now, arrest these other gentlemen for trespassing, couldn't I?"

"Well, I suppose . . ."

"Never mind, I won't. But I'm angry enough to. You barge up here without invitation and disturb one of our most sacred services, a very private one, with—with—cops." She composed herself with a visible show of discipline. "Leave now. Come back with a warrant, if you like, if you ever figure out what it is you're looking for."

A smart cookie. A deft allusion to reasonable cause.

Too bad for her that I'd already noticed them—that pair of dirt lines etched across the lawn behind the chapel. They wound their way back into the forest.

I raised my eyes to the heavens and made a quick apology to Tom and Ben and all the other framers of the Constitution.

But to hell with a warrant.

I got in Stanley's Chevy. Closed the door. Started it.

"What . . ." The sister came toward me. Her eyes burned.

The window was down, so I said to her out of it:

"Go to hell."

I flipped the shift into gear, pulled a one-eighty on the grass near the rectory, scattered some sod, then sped across her lawn, past the chapel and into the forest.

I heard some yelling behind me. Knaust's red light snapped on in my rearview mirror. It rolled around at a lopsided angle as he sped across the lawn after me. I hoped Cussone had gotten in with him.

The Chevy clattered and rocked over tree roots and tire ruts. I was taking them too fast. The side of the car scraped along a tree trunk. Branches broke against the windshield. It was too dark under the pines, tough to see. I swerved back and forth through a slalom of tree trunks. I grazed another one, swung off the road, down a steep little gulch, then humped over a dry streambed. Something shook loose from the chassis. A muffler. The engine groaned. Dust flew and shafts of light seeped through it like rays from the other world. I sputtered at an angle along the stream bank, then crept out of the forest into an open field. It spread out before me like a green pond.

I shut off the engine and staggered out of the car.

The open area seemed as haunted as a battlefield. It emanated an unearthly silence, reminding me of an enchanted place that I was drawn to as a kid. We called it Magic Meadow. I used to sit there for hours, always sensing that I was surrounded by spirits. Now I felt the same way. I strode into the field, trying to understand the oppressive sensation. As if I'd been here before.

Knaust's rig skidded down the gully and bounced along the streambed. Its engine growled as it conquered the stream bank, then its motor cut off. The silence was complete. Cussone ran toward me, ahead of Wall and Knaust.

"Christ almighty, Byman."

He approached me, panting. I said to him:

"I recognize this place."

He stopped near me, leveling a mean gaze in my direction. He spit out: "Get back to the fucking car."

"No."

"It's too small to be an airstrip!"

I turned from him and plodded deeper into the field.

"Byman!" Knaust was running toward me. "Byman, you bastard!"

They followed me to the middle of the field. We didn't say much there, not for a few moments. We all saw it: the circle of sod cut from the middle of the meadow. The floodlamps at its perimeter. The footprints.

Cussone bent over some tracks, but it was obvious what they were.

"I never considered helicopters," I said to him.

"No."

I walked away from them, still haunted by a tinge of déjà vu. I saw nothing at the far end of the field. No road, no other signs of mechanical life. I hiked back along the edge of the forest, where pine trees rose up from the dry streambed and shaded part of the field. Pine needles had fallen like silk over the forest floor. Laced among the shadows were several mounds of old dirt that had sunken slightly. They were clustered haphazardly, like graves.

I sat down in the damp weeds. All at once I knew where I'd seen this place—the pastoral groves, the gentle floor of pine needles, the stacks of dead children.

In those Polaroids soaked with Amanda's blood.

Stanley approached, behind me. I could feel by his breathing silence that he recognized the spot.

"Christ," he said.

"It's the place in the pictures."

"I can see." He grabbed me under the arms and pulled me up. "Come on. Let's get the hell out of this cul-de-sac and call for backup."

But it was too late.

A shot fired, crunching into metal. Then another. Inexplicably, music from a radio warbled across the field. Another shot quelled it.

"Jesus! The radios!"

Stanley pulled his .38. I was too scared to think about my .45. It stayed back in my belt as we ran to the cars, joining Wall and Knaust midway. We all kept along the perimeter.

Then I saw. Two nuns were at our cars, ripping apart the radios inside. A rifle emerged from Stanley's window.

Wall sang at a high pitch:

"Hit the ground!"

A few shots rang out as my chin slapped against some dandelions. Their dry floating seeds made me sneeze. I tried reaching back for my gun but I didn't have time—Cussone was up and running for the woods. I followed. Wall and Knaust ran with us. More shots fired. Some branches snapped near me.

"There's only two of them," Stanley panted.

"What'll we do?" My voice sounded like Mickey Mouse.

Cussone said two words: "Split up."

I ran with him, keeping low, away from the road. We sprinted deep into the woods, crunching over beds of needles, under low boughs. There was a silence in there as thick as sap. It seemed to slow us—or maybe it was my bleeding leg. It hurt like hell. But I wasn't about to pause and give it a rest. More shots had begun. Rounds of them, spitting like hail against the tree bark. Chips of it flew like shrapnel. A puff of dust exploded on the ground in front of me.

"Kalashnikovs," Cussone yelled.

I heard other guns, too. I turned to see Chief Wall and Deputy

Knaust crouching with their .38s extended. Their guns sounded like cannons in the quiet forest. None of us had had an opportunity to gather the rifles. None of us had much ammunition.

An old stone fence, one that had crumbled two centuries ago, crossed our path and wound its way through trees in the direction of the convent. We jumped it and ran along its other side, south. I hobbled as best as I could.

Stanley hit the ground. My legs were in such pain that I couldn't crouch. I simply let my body fall next to him.

I asked him again: "What're we gonna do?"

"I have to make it back to the car somehow. There's a second radio stashed in the trunk. And there's another set of keys taped to the wheel well."

"They'll be guarding it!"

"Probably. But I don't see more than three guns. I'll have to run around the perimeter of the field, circle all the way round. It'll take a while. Anyway, I have to try. Unless you have a better suggestion."

"No."

"Take your gun out."

"I can run better without it."

"Don't be afraid to use it, damn it!"

"Won't I be with—?"

"No."

We both saw them, far behind us, but coming. Two nuns, black shrouds with black weapons. We stared for an unbelieving moment. The sight was surreal.

"They're men," Stanley whispered.

"Christ."

"Look," he said. "Go." He pointed in the direction of the chapel. I could hear its bell tolling again.

"They'll be all over the place!"

"Hide. Just be near the road. If I come barreling out I don't wanna stop for very fucking long. I'll swing around the driveway. Listen for me, my horn, my siren. Anything."

"Jesus, Stanley . . ."

"Go," he said, and left me.

Shots were fired in our direction. I crawled beneath the fence for a few yards on my stomach—before struggling to my feet. I bent my legs to keep low. Pain started working its way up my body. I fell, got up, fell again.

There was light behind a veil of trees. The bell was tolling a frenetic rhythm. I crawled on my hands and knees toward it, to the edge of the forest. I leaned against rough pine bark and tried to concentrate, to shake away the fear. A group of nuns was running from the chapel, quickly, their awkward shapes hobbling over the lawn in their thick heels. They were heading for the main building.

There wasn't anyone at the back of the chapel. A wooden door was open, but I couldn't see if anyone was inside. Whoever had been tolling the bell had stopped. I was going to have to take a chance.

I got up, saw no one in the woods behind me. No one on the grounds who could see me if I made the run. If I was lucky I could hide in there.

I pulled out my gun. It felt as heavy as a bowling ball. I lugged its weight out of the woods, froze for a moment, then dashed for the chapel.

Its back door was thick old oak with black iron latches. It creaked when I touched it. There wasn't anyone immediately inside; no one seemed to hear me.

So I stepped into the dark.

I felt my way through the unlit foyer. My palm slid against unsanded wood paneling till it found another door. It was almost latched shut. Not quite. The bolt clicked when I pulled it partly open. I peered into the chapel, but it was half obscured. Candles must have been burning up at the altar. Their light made shadows jump up and down along the walls.

I stepped in, under an arched alcove.

"Come all the way in," a woman whispered.

I flipped my safety off. A red dot appeared. I closed my eyes and still saw that red dot. Beating. My heart pounded in my throat. I took another step.

Sister Theresa sat in the first row of pews, staring—not at me, but at the altar. She shriveled her lips into a queer smile and said to her icon:

"So fragile."

I took a few more steps toward her, cautiously. Her hands

were folded in her lap. She was holding something underneath them. Something small and silver. I kept my eyes on those hands and tried to answer her.

"Children are fragile."

She looked at me with an imploring bitterness.

"All of us, all of it." She breathed slowly in and out. Her voice was a high-pitched whisper. "You have no idea the damage you've done." Her pale visage creased into a knot of torment. She stared back at Christ on his crucifix and said: "It's over."

Her hand rose. There was a gun in it, a silver derringer. I thought it was swinging at me—so I jumped to my left, hit a pew. It rocked her. She stopped a moment, frozen.

"Over," she said coolly, raising the gun to her temple. "Forgive me."

"No!"

I lunged and slapped her arm with my .45. Her hand jerked back. The gun fired. The bullet seared the back of her habit and shattered a stained-glass window.

"Damn you!" she cried, and fell to the floor, just a puddle of black robes, like the melting Witch of the West.

Her sobs quieted when we heard the sound. It was far away but unmistakable.

A baby was wailing.

Suddenly I realized I'd been holding my breath. I let it out with a burst, gasping for air. Little Genna was close, I knew it now. I knelt down near Sister Theresa.

"Where is she?"

No answer.

I grabbed her arm and twisted her body so that I could see her shriveled face.

"Where's the baby?" I yelled again.

The sister stared up but didn't see me. She was gazing far beyond me, through a stained-glass skylight overhead, as if her past shone through it.

"It started off—so pure."

"Sister . . ."

"We weren't sinners. Not then. We were doing what was right."

"Sister!"

"Do you believe me?"

"Yes. But tell me—"

"You have to believe me!" she cried, clutching my arms.

I don't know why, but I lifted her close to me. Her fragile body felt like it had broken in half.

"No one would miss them," she whispered with a tiny voice. "We were trying to do them good."

"I do believe you, Sister."

She closed her eyes. Old tears fell from them.

"Above the garage," she said.

I used the woods as cover, running just inside the edge of the forest, around and past the chapel to a small grove of birch behind the stable. A light was still on upstairs. But the baby wasn't crying anymore. And the black Jeep was gone.

I was a good twenty yards from the back door—a long sprint. If I was seen by the wrong person they'd have several shots at me.

The front stairs were worse. Anyone from the convent could see me enter from there.

There wasn't much choice.

I ran—staggered is a better word—across the expanse. I carried the gun at my side. It slapped against my leg in an awkward rhythm, but it was a rhythm that I followed, like a fibrillating heartbeat. I used it to keep pace as my legs screamed for me to slow down.

I got to the back door, but it was locked. A window opened upstairs. Trails of auburn hair dangled out of it. A pair of haunting green eyes peered over the sill.

"Front door," Julia whispered.

I circled around front, underneath the side stairs, my back sliding along the wall. I held my gun the way they do in cop movies. Up. Toward you-know-who.

It was a long, rectangular building. In front, garage doors had been built in at ground level, where the horse stalls had once been. A staircase ran at a slant along the front wall, then pulled a right angle and continued up the side wall, above me. They led to an old hayloft door that hovered overhead, now an entrance to the upstairs apartment.

In plain view of the whole damn convent I leapt along the front wall and jumped the wooden steps. They sounded as hollow and noisy as African drums.

But no one saw me.

The door cracked open and I froze there, on the side landing. Julia stood just three steps up, her eyes bearing down on me, sad and penetrating. Her hair fell down around her shoulders like waves of the Red Sea. A simple white dress hung around her loosely. It was tied at her waist with a red belt.

"Come in, Luke," she said to me quietly.

I moved up the steps but froze again when I heard the shots—from far off, in the woods. Muffled automatics.

Stanley . . .

Julia pulled me inside and shut the door. She stood, a few feet from me, in semidarkness.

"You don't have much time here. You may have been seen."

"Julia," I said aloud, frozen by the look in her eyes. They seemed to implore me to go—to go away forever. Instead, she took a step toward me. Our hands touched first. Her breasts grazed against me. Our lips came together softly. We seemed suspended in time, dangled in a simple kiss. My hands slowly traced the contour of her body, up her thighs to her slender waist. I stroked along her back, then pulled her closer to me, so close that we were molded for a few seconds. Nothing was said, not till I opened my eyes. Over her shoulder I saw Genna's crib across the room.

"Genna . . ." I whispered.

"She's all right."

Julia and I parted, slowly. I hobbled across the small apartment and sat on a chair near the baby. Genna slept, her fingers wriggling.

"She's grown," I said.

"Yes."

Julia sat down across from me, on the other side of the caged crib. She grabbed the bars with her hands, leaned her head down on the rail.

"Luke," she said. "Go. Please. He'll kill you."

It didn't take a genius to know whom she meant.

"Where is he?"

She raised her eyes and tilted them toward the window.

"Out there."

I shuddered, thinking of Stanley. There was nothing I could do for him now but pray.

"I need to know, Julia. All of it," I said.

She leaned her head aginst the rail.

"All of it," she repeated, "is half a life."

"Come with me then, now. We can walk back to town if we have to. Talk later."

"No. No, Luke. I can't run any longer. Ralph is dead. . . ." Her voice trailed off.

"I was with him."

She said gently, "I know."

"Where's your sister now? Where's Anna?"

"In South America. They say you hit her pretty bad, Luke." There was a trace of anger in her voice. "She's having her teeth rebuilt."

"I did what I had to do."

She sighed, resigned. "Yes, I believe you did. Anna is—she can be capable of—anything."

"Like killing her parents?"

She didn't answer.

"Tell me, Julia." She said nothing. "Start—start at the beginning. Poughkeepsie. I know Farrer killed his best friend to fake his own death. Billy Dillery saw it, didn't he?"

"We both saw." She shuddered. "I'll never ever see anything so horrible." She had to breathe once before continuing. "Farrer must have asked Pete Dillery and his wife to come to his house. Pete and Sharon came, all right, but they brought Billy. He was waiting in the car but must have heard something—" Her hands took hold of one another. "God, Luke! He came to me—just four years old—to my front door. He was crying."

I remembered Billy crying at my front door.

"He dragged me by the hand and led me to the Farrers' back window. I saw, I saw inside, God, I saw him carrying Sharon's head." Her voice choked. "Another man was clipping fingers into a bowl—with garden shears! I screamed—I couldn't help myself. The man looked up and saw me. . . ."

She got up and stood at her window. She was breathing hard. The horror she'd witnessed lingered palpably after eleven years. I waited a moment for her breaths to subside.

"So you ran," I said quietly.

"With Ralph. We didn't stop to pack, nothing. We went to our bank, got money, then disappeared."

"To where?"

"It doesn't matter. Everywhere. Ralph had money."

"Hadn't Farrer recently funded his and Nathan Wise's clinic?"

"Yes," she said, surprised that I knew.

"Did he take Nathan's cash, too? The company account?"

"Half of it. Fifty thousand. It seemed a lot then, eleven years ago. But it was his rightful half."

"Then . . . then you went to Black River?"

"After five years of running. We'd been hunted by the police for those murders. They blamed Ralph, you know. So we had to stay way off the beaten path. Move around. So many different cities."

"Why didn't you go to the cops?"

"We tried, by phone. They replied by telling us that we'd be given a fair trial if we came back. But Pete and Sharon's bodies had already been cremated. There was no chance to exhume them, to prove they weren't Farrer and his wife. Anyway, Ralph suspected William owned half the cops and courts in Poughkeepsie."

"So you ended up in your hometown."

"We just wanted to visit. My parents were getting very old. It turned out that Anna was there. Meeting with this terrified little man from IBM. Benjamin Kelly. She . . ." Julia sat down again and clutched the bars of the crib. "We'd never been close, but she knew that Ralph and I had been on the run. That we were desperate. So she offered Ralph a deal, a deal to go in with her . . ."

"He knew the baby business."

"Yes."

"And they needed to tap into Wise's computer, with Kelly's help."

"Yes. They offered him a lot of money. Ralph knew the codes, what to do, how to do it. At first, I didn't know what he was doing those weeks in Black River. I didn't know what the project was. It seems foolish now, but I thought it was something to help Anna gamble—she loved putting lots of money on the horses. And she was tied in with a lot of the people who take money for that sort of thing. Gamblers, loan sharks. I thought she was hiring Ralph to help her beat the odds. He was great with computers. But that wasn't it. The day before—" She stopped abruptly. Quietly, she started again. "The day before the fire, I found out. I was horrified to see what she was doing, what she'd gotten my husband into. Poor Ralph, everything he did was for me and for Billy. We'd adopted him, you know. We needed money for us to leave the country, leave everything behind. But I was disgusted with Ralph, with my sister, with her awful friends. I spilled out everything to her, my hate, everything—in front of my poor mother and father. They heard it all. And they knew—they knew I was right, that I was telling the truth. Anna could see it in their eyes. They'd always been so proud of her, the grand actress, the nicest little girl. But they knew—always, deep inside—that she was bad." She hissed: "They knew. And she saw it in their eyes." She pressed her forehead with her scarlet nails. "That night Ralph and I were sleeping there, and the house caught fire. I'll never know who set the fire, if it was Anna herself or one of her paid friends. But I blame myself for involving Mom and Dad. I don't sleep a lot at night, thinking of them lying there . . ."

"You dragged them outside?"

"Ralph and I. But the smoke had already killed my father. My mother, she just hugged him." She wiped a tear that was floating down her cheek. "I was crying there with them when the shot fired. It hit me—"

She opened two buttons of her white dress and revealed the old wound I'd seen once before, on her couch, moments after Genna was born. She touched it again with the tips of her fingers.

"Yeah," I said. "I remember."

We were silent for a long moment. It seemed an eternity ago that Genna had been born; almost as long since I'd been in Black River. I remembered that little bald man I'd found lying in his own blood. I asked her quietly: "How did Kelly fit in?"

"The poor man. He owed some people a lot of money. Gambling, horses, I don't know which. Anna used her influence. She bought away his debt and then used that debt like blackmail. He became the foundation's link to the IBM mainframe. Ralph had found out what was happening to Kelly, and knew that he would break someday. A frail soul, that's how he put it. He wanted to get him to testify, to blow open the whole Black River connection. But—" She sighed.

"But they killed him."

She nodded. "We were to arrange a meeting with Kelly when Ralph came back from California. But then Ralph didn't show and didn't show. I was frantic. I knew, Luke, I knew that he was gone. I felt—I had to do what he would have done. So I called Kelly myself and arranged the meeting. I reserved a hotel room by phone, then went to meet him there. But he was already dead. Someone had found out about our meeting and gotten to him before we could."

I thought to myself that it might have been Trell that had killed him, or one of his slimy friends, perhaps on Anna's payroll. It didn't seem to matter much anymore. If Kelly had been such a weak link, his phone had probably been tapped. More than likely that's how they'd been tipped about his meeting with Julia. Anyway, there wasn't time to find out. Not now. I heard shots again, close by.

"What happened after your parents died? Where did you go?"

"Again we had to disappear."

"Is that the point when Ralph became . . . obsessed?"

"You could say that."

"And he took their money. That pile I saw on your bed."

Her expression turned blank.

"They never gave him a dime. But Ralph's hate wasn't about money. You know—he didn't realize at first how horrible their treatment of the children was. That babies were dying. When he finally found out—he'd stolen some pictures, you see, pictures I never saw, but he used to have nightmares about—when he saw those pictures he became obsessed with destroying their whole, foul plan. And with killing one particular woman. Not Anna. A woman we knew from Poughkeepsie. She'd begun to run the operation. To play hardball at the children's expense. Ralph loathed her."

"Gina Farrer."

She sighed: "You know."

"I know she's dead."

She stared at me. Her voice hushed. "You killed her?"
"My cop friend."
Another sigh heaved out of her.
"Luke—my God. You—you've done what Ralph . . ."
She was breathless and couldn't finish.
"Never mind that," I said. We had to hurry. "How—how does the whole thing operate? This place—it supplies the children?"
"Yes," she said, flustered.
"How?"
She shook her wonderful brown hair. "Orphans. Catholic orphanages. From all over South America."
"They're shipped in with helicopters?"
"Yes."
"By who?"
"Luke—"
"Why?"
"Guns!"
"For who, Julia?"
"I don't know, I don't—"
"Julia!"
"It doesn't matter who they are! It's political, is all. They train men, ship weapons. This is some sort of military camp. Important people invest in it."
I sat there like a stone.
"Then why—why are you here, Julia?"
"I wanted my baby!"
I didn't know what to say to that. I moved on.
"Is this where they met? Anna and Gina?"
She nodded.
"Anna used to come here between movies, you know. It was like rehab for her. We'd been raised Catholic, and it was her way to find a contrast to her life-style in Hollywood. It had become quite . . . sordid. Anyway, five years ago she invested in a 'recovery operation' for orphaned babies set up by some sort of charity foundation in Ireland. The nuns had convinced her to put money in it. They meant well, then, I suppose, but it turned political quickly. And Anna didn't back away—she got involved. She began to return more often. And, I think . . ." Julia bowed her head.
"What?"

"I think she was also coming back to see Gina. She and Gina got to be—close."

"Lovers?"

She nodded again. "And partners. With this source for children, and with Anna's money and clout, Gina convinced my sister that together they could eclipse her husband's business—within just a couple of years—and do it all for a cause they'd both come to believe in. Apparently, Gina was right. William Farrer was forced by good business sense to go in with her."

"Trion," I said.

"Yes—Anna met with Gina and with representatives of the foundation, in California, to sign the papers with Farrer—who was supposed to be dead. He signed his father's name."

"And Gina got her daughter back in the bargain?"

Julia blinked.

"I think that getting Sondra back from her husband was the reason for so much of what Gina did. So much of the hate between her and William. So much of what's happened."

It wasn't just Sondra, I thought. There was Billy, too, and Genna. Three children who had each in their own way originated a strand of this twisting case.

"Your husband followed Gina to your sister's ranch, didn't he?"

"Yes. To the house. It was a horrible night—another one. I saw Gina that night for the first time since Mildred Avenue. It was a shock to see her—and to see that she and Anna had become . . . friendly. And—that horrible night, I met Red. I don't have to tell you he's a dangerous man. He's full of terrible passions, Luke. He'd once been a priest in Dublin, then was excommunicated for bombing a British garrison. The foundation sent him over to co-run the recovery operation with Gina. He made it his first priority to get rid of Ralph. I pleaded with all of them to relent, to leave my husband and me alone forever. I begged, and I succeeded. Ralph wasn't Red's first priority anymore. I was. He made a violent pass at me. Anna and Gina just watched. . . ."

"Then Ralph showed up."

"With his gun. He actually shot at Anna. One of Red's men shot back at him. He managed to run into the woods and escape."

"I know those woods," I said.

"What?"

"Never mind. Did he take money?"

"No. No, I took it. Weeks later. After—"

She pinched her forehead with her fingers.

"After what?"

But she didn't continue. It didn't matter, though. That same old, plaguing question had come back to haunt me again.

"Julia—why did you move in down the hall from Gina's apartment? Why choose to live there?"

"I didn't choose."

"I don't understand."

She caught me in the cool clutch of an honest gaze.

"I was raped that night in California."

I leaned on the crib.

"You mean—Genna . . . ?"

She nodded, then spoke slowly. As she did I saw a discomfiting sight through the window behind her. The black Jeep emerged from the woods, on that same dirt road. It parked near the chapel. She continued as my eyes lingered on the Jeep.

"I suffered trauma. It took weeks to recover, and by the time I was able to leave California they knew I was pregnant. He knew. They made a deal with me. They told me it was the only way I could save Ralph."

"I don't understand."

"They wanted . . ." The words didn't come.

The Jeep started up again and sped across the lawn toward us. The big man sat in the open passenger seat, his red hair flowing out behind him like a scarlet cloak. He held his gun up close to his ear, barrel skyward.

I stood and picked up my .45.

"We've got to get out of here."

"He'd just find us."

"Move!"

I grabbed her wrist and pulled her up. I lifted Genna into my arms.

"I couldn't sell her."

I backed toward the door as the Jeep slammed to a stop downstairs.

"I took the money," she whispered to me, "but at the last minute, I just couldn't do it."

The man called Red was on the stairs. His weight shook the house. He kicked the door open.

I stepped back near Julia, holding the baby. It started to cry—the only sound in the room. Red stood there, his huge frame shaking with anger.

"Give her to the woman," he whispered, his bass voice frighteningly hoarse.

He aimed his gun at my legs. Two of his fingers curled around the long, thin rifle trigger.

"I'm taking her with me," I said.

He took a step toward me. His head nearly scraped the ceiling. He screamed like a devil:

"Give her to me!"

I jumped back. The baby started to wail.

Julia took a step. "Give . . ." she said.

I backed away. Red circled in front of the window. I could have shot him then, but I didn't. I couldn't. The gun shook in my hand. I stepped toward the door.

He said: "I'll kill you both before letting her go."

"No!" Julia grabbed his arm. "Let them go! Let them—"

He shoved her away, hard. She fell against the table and crib, smashing them.

"Julia!" I screamed, stepping closer—

—but Red's gun rose. He aimed at my head. His trigger finger squeezed.

I ducked—lunging for the door—shielding Genna.

"Luke!"

His gun fired. A bullet tugged at my side. I fell. Blood was dampening my back, but I didn't feel pain, only dizziness. I started crawling for the door, but as soon as I touched it I collapsed. Genna lay near me. Her white blanket was stained with a bright red blotch. My blood. For the briefest of moments I smiled. It suddenly seemed so fitting that I should die with her in my arms.

I was still lucid; my vision wasn't blackening. I saw clearly that Red was bending down over me, taking Genna away. He held her with one arm and aimed his gun with the other. It pointed down at me.

"Over, now," he whispered.

Then he screamed! Fell to his knees! One arm clutched Genna to his chest, almost crushing her. Julia kicked the rifle out of his other hand. It landed behind the door. The baby was crying. Red grabbed at his shoulder with his free hand. Blood coated his fingertips.

I rolled to my left and saw Julia holding the knife over him. She stabbed him again, between the shoulder blades. He screamed, but—amazingly—got to his feet. He wouldn't relent his grasp of Genna. Julia tugged at him, but he pushed her aside. Drops of his blood trickled down on me as he took a huge step over my body and out the door.

Julia screamed. "My baby!"

She fell next to me, hitting at me with her fists.

"Oh God, oh God! Again!"

She stopped hitting and started pulling. I didn't know if I could get up. She spoke to my thoughts.

"You can do it—you can do it!"

I staggered to my feet, crying with the pain—but still conscious. I felt my wound. The bullet had ripped through my side and exited, a flesh wound. I pulled my hand away. It was covered with a fluorescent red liquid that had once been inside of me. I wanted to faint. I stepped back, hitting the door, and fell to my knees.

"Get up!" she screamed—and I did it again. I got up. I obeyed.

"Keep telling me," I said weakly.

"Go!"

She put the gun in my hand and pushed me out the door. Red had already made it to the Jeep. His engine started.

Somehow the sound revived me.

"Shit," I uttered.

"The garage!" Julia cried out as she stormed past me. Something jiggled in her hands. Keys. She ran down the steps.

I followed—slowly. Blood flowed down my leg and over my right shoe, but a sudden clarity was taking hold. I saw the Jeep pull out and caught a glimpse of another weapon rising in Red's bloody right hand. I heard Genna's cries fading as they sped away.

Then another engine turned over, didn't start, turned over again—then started. It sounded like a tractor.

The far doors of the garage slapped back with a snapping sound. One of them broke off as Julia's car jerked out into the open. An old, round, Pontiac convertible. She backed up near me as I made it to the bottom of the stairs.

"Hurry!"

For a fleeting moment I wondered about Cussone—Stanley! I looked in the direction of the woods but saw nothing.

"Luke." The way she said my name. "Luke, get in."

I opened the door and fell into the seat. Before I could close the door she was barreling down around the circular drive—fast—past the convent and chapel, past the strange small figure of Sister Theresa looming in its door frame. We snaked around two curves—screeching—then Julia pressed on the pedal and raced for the fence. It sputtered with sparks as we hit it, pieces of metal flying over us, cracking our windshield. I closed my eyes, then opened them, and saw that Julia's eyes were still closed. We were lurching off the left shoulder. I grabbed the wheel—screaming with the pain in my side—and turned us right, back onto the road. We were flying. A sharp curve was ahead. I reached my leg over and pumped the brakes, slowing us, but not enough. I steered wildly around the curve, twisting the wheel back and forth, our right tires thundering over a row of rocks. They prevented us from skidding sideways into a ditch and somersaulting. Then—suddenly—we were careening toward the entrance. Julia threw her hands forward. She screamed: "Luke!"

Red was trying to turn his Jeep through the stone pillars onto the mountain road. He didn't make it. The car spun sideways, skidded across the road, and hit a tree on the far side. Its back right wheel went off the ledge. It teetered there.

"Genna!" Julia grabbed me. I tried to swing our wheel right, around the turn, but couldn't. The Pontiac slammed against the left pillar. Metal screeched. The wheel spun like a steamboat's. It made a snapping sound and something broke underneath the car. The wheel was jelly. All in a second we were skidding forward across the road, toward the edge. We hit Red's Jeep hard, and it stopped us from going over—but we pushed its other back wheel over the ledge. It was lurching toward doom. Julia was screaming. I pressed on our brake but nothing happened. We started rolling toward the cliff. Two of our wheels slid forward, over the ledge. Red's back wheels and our front wheels now spun free over the crevice—but then each car butted against the other and stopped the other from falling. They teetered on the cusp of the ledge like two seesaws. Red got out of his Jeep—slowly, so as not to rock it. It could easily slide into the gully. Julia jumped out of our car, and I followed, through the driver's door. There was nothing but air on my side.

I tried to hold my gun firmly. I walked to the middle of the road, where Red stood, facing me. Tears wet his face. And blood. He held little Genna up with one hand and squeezed her neck. The baby's face started turning blue. She was struggling desperately to breathe. She spit out mucus and small, choking coughs. He smiled at me—the strangest gleam in his eye—and whispered with the voice of a ghost.

"She's mine. My own daughter."

The baby dropped out of his hands. Genna hit the ground on her back. The thud she made seemed to echo across the valley and back to me. Julia cried out. Red's eyes rolled over. He lifted his gun at me.

I raised my .45 and squeezed the trigger.

I hit him in the gut.

He fired back and I took a bullet in my groin but somehow only fell to my knees.

Then he fired again—wildly. I felt a shot punch my arm and one whiz by me, but I stayed half up, shooting. The gun jerked in my hands like a wild animal. Red took my first two shots in his neck and leg, then I missed one. But my fourth caught him in the face. Blood spurted. He collapsed, screaming. I fell forward. I started to crawl to him. His huge body flailed near Genna, trying to get up. But he couldn't. So he raised his gun a couple of inches and aimed it along the road—toward me. I rolled. It fired. A bullet skittered into the woods. I crawled closer. For a split second I caught a glimpse of my own blood trickling down the asphalt. But I didn't stop. I kept crawling. His finger pulled the trigger again but the clip was empty. The bolt just snapped with a metallic twang.

I hoisted my body up and knelt over him. A third of his face was missing. One eye hung loosely from its socket, dangling from a few fleshy threads. His other eye rolled up at me, terrified. A tear fell from it.

We stared at one another for a moment.

"Forgive him, Father," he whispered, his voice so far away and deep that it sounded as if he were already speaking from the depths of hell.

I put the .45 to his temple and fired my last shot.

There was blood all over the road. It separated into little capillaries that webbed and flowed around Genna. Julia ran to her, fell over the small body, sobbing: "My baby, my baby . . ."

I was only barely alive. There wasn't much time.

I dragged myself to them and pushed Julia gently, gently away. I was afraid to do what I had to. I pulled Genna's bloodstained frills away and ripped her tiny sweater off. Then I dragged my shot-up legs closer and pressed my ear against the baby's chest.

A warm surge ran me through. A few of my last tears streaked over her soft skin.

"It's beating," I whispered to Julia.

We held one another, huddled over the child. Julia cried quietly, "Oh God, oh God . . ." but a small sound hushed her. Genna was whispering. Her tiny feet kicked.

I tried to laugh aloud, but the surge stabbed me—different from anything I'd felt before. The kind of pain that tells you that nothing will ever work inside of you again, not anymore. My mind reeled a moment. I nearly went out, all the way. But Julia held my head and spoke to me.

"My Luke," she said.

And I was alive again, for the briefest of moments, I knew. Everything seemed so clear. A road bathed in blood, winding its way down a mountainside to a town somewhere, I'd forgotten which one. Birds singing questions above us in the trees, and there were answers for them, from across the ravine. I felt the rumbling waterfall through the asphalt. The wind waved branches around. The sound of an engine approached through it, from behind us, perhaps a Chevy without its muffler. I turned my head as far as I was able and saw Stanley standing outside his battered car, begging quietly into a two-way. I clutched Julia. I scarcely had a voice anymore, but I cried to her:

"He's alive."

Julia took hold of me. She rested my head on her lap. Then she lifted her little girl and clutched us both in the same hug, staring down on me with translucent, farewell eyes.

A shower of little helicopter seeds fell over us, twisting in a gust of wind. I lifted one of them and felt its green seed between my fingers. I put it in Genna's tiny hand, just the way my father had once handed me a helicopter seed. I'd considered it a king's treasure.

The child opened her blue eyes and tilted them toward me. A curious smile curled her lips.

And it was over.

EPILOGUE

I never expected life.

But there it was, in all its fluorescence. Another hospital, yet another sanitary blank. I felt born all over again, into that same old empty panorama, void of any color, void but for those strange hues that were faces whirring by. Those fleshy blurs swam like first strokes on a brand-new canvas. They had voices that sounded like foreign music on late-night radio.

Two primal opposites were rearoused in me during those peculiar days in white-wall heaven. One, that the world was clean. Two, that I was alone in that clean world. It took a week to comprehend that I was wrong on both counts.

They'd put me in the Benedictine, in Kingston. Upstate. Up near the old town. After a few days the strange blurs that sang the foreign music rolled me a few feet, nearer to a window. A framed world of static blur. Lots of green and gray. Every day the same green, more speckled dots of gray. It was a long time before I found myself able to focus out that window—on the reassuring vista of a wooded cemetery next door.

Two incidents during that time should be remarked upon. One, the less important of the two, was when my nurse felt me—for several wonderful minutes—right where it counts. I think she thought I was in a coma. So, to her, whoever she was, I tilt my hat. My revival sped along quickly after that brief but life-assuring episode.

The second lasted longer but was less defined. It remains so. It seemed to last for days, and maybe it did. I've never asked. But it was Julia, I do know that. Julia, who sat there near me for so long, waiting, patiently, for me to go whichever damned way I was going—back into life, or back from whence I came thirty-three years ago.

On that first day when I was semiconscious, and more aware of the cemetery, and of her—her clothes, black; lipstick, bright red; cheeks, streaked with purplish mascara; and that auburn hair, so bright against the white wall—that was the day she left her letter.

It's on the top of the stack now. The first letter in my first file. Here in my first office, if I choose to call it that. It's more accurate, right now, to call it home.

I hold the letter in my hands before slipping it into the folder. It's on a light gray stationery, from a good press. The weave is in relief, as if someone had woven the paper on a loom. She'd written the note with an old ink pen, the kind I used as a kid, with a little ink tube inserted into the chamber. They had spreading metal tips that made blue spots in my trouser pockets on my way home from school.

I think about the pen in her hand as I read over the words for the thousandth time. The pen in her hand wrote:

Dearest Luke,

You will live. The doctor assures me, and I thank God. Truly, you have given me back my life. My little girl. The two are entwined for me, more than I ever knew. We will survive, and find happiness. You, too, will survive. I am so thankful for that.

I hope it comforts you to know that Genna will learn that she still has a father. I say this figuratively, of course. But I mean it, Luke. From my heart. I see no reason to tell her of her real father, or even of Ralph, bless his poor troubled soul. I will tell her of you. As much as I know. I will tell her how you saved us.

I know that I must go far away. I'll let you know where we are when we arrive. Whenever and wherever that will be.

I pray for you, Luke, and think of you, and wish . . . that it had all been different.

I will send pictures of Genna as she grows up.

Good-bye.

And that was her letter. Reading it again didn't help. I would read it a thousand times more and still churn out the same paradox. That feeling of nausea in my gut at the thought of Julia selling her own baby, no matter who the father was. And that feeling of emptiness in my soul, knowing I'd never see her again. I felt as tiny and useless as a common moth, fluttering around in the darkness, denied his one, his only, perfect flame.

A second letter came directly here. Stanley had been good enough to reroute my mail to this office when I was in the hospital, and this had been my first envelope. No postmark. No signature. Just a blank page and two words scribbled on it.

We remember.

I slipped it into the folder.

Under it were the various clippings Cussone had copied for me. The *Times, News, Post*, local reports from Poughkeepsie—where, after nearly a dozen years, Ralph and Julia Denington were finally exonerated in bold relief—and all the local rags from Los Angeles, Black River, even an article in the *Maplecrest Star*. The reporter there, a woman named Marjorie Cole, had written a remarkably astute summation of the events. Perhaps I felt this way because it was the only article—of all of them that had been written, anywhere—that mentioned my name.

It read:

A volcano erupted in Maplecrest yesterday. A volcano in the form of an explosively violent police bust of a baby-smuggling ring that had been operating out of our own backyard.

It was a shootout that, tragically, took the life of a beloved member of our community, Deputy Sheriff Ernest "Ernie" Knaust.

The fatal events were said to have transpired yesterday afternoon, on the grounds of the Convent of the Sacred Heart, a residence and retreat for Catholic nuns. Authorities verify that the mountain convent was indeed the "pit stop" used by mobsters and terrorists for their horrifying contraband: babies.

The nuns are said to have been involved.

This is the final and successful effort by the New York City Police and Federal Bureau of Investigation to root out the smugglers' operation and destroy it. The operation has extended around our country, and, indeed, around the world. Other busts, which came today, have closed businesses in Poughkeepsie, New York City, and elsewhere, most of them corrupted adoption agencies. Even a theatrical agency in Los Angeles, California, had its doors shut by federal agents, due to financial and other connections with the smugglers (see box).

Poughkeepsie's notorious Cuban mob is said to have begun the operation years ago, and to have allowed the participation of reactionary political groups. "Babies were often sold for huge prices," said one source close to the investigation. "Those profits were then turned into arms for groups like the IRA and others."

Three known members of the IRA were killed in yesterday's shootout, one apprehended. No one knows as yet whether the prisoner has revealed anything to the authorities, nor do they know if any other members of the group have escaped.

Two officers died in the line of duty. The second, Chief Michael Wall, of Westchester County's police department, was fatally wounded when the routine search of the convent turned into a bloody gunfight.

At 3 P.M. yesterday, Stanley Cussone—head of the investigation for the New York City Police Department, with a private investigator, Luke Byman, and Officers Wall and Knaust, together approached the convent, suspicious but not convinced the nuns or any members of the sect were involved. "We were greeted rudely," said Detective Cussone, "and told to get out by the head nun," Sister Mary Theresa (who is now in critical condition at the Benedictine Hospital in Kingston after suffering a self-inflicted gun wound to her temple).

"On our way out," Cussone continued, "we saw what she was trying to protect us from seeing—an airstrip for helicopters. It was then we knew that we had the right place—and that's when they started shooting at us."

At least three men appeared, with weapons, firing upon the officers and the civilian detective. After a harrowing chase within the woods on convent grounds, Cussone managed to reach his car, and from there radioed for help. Officers Knaust and Wall were not so lucky. "They were courageous men," Cussone added. State Police appeared on the scene several minutes later, and within the hour the situation was under control.

It has been relayed to the press by authorities that the smuggling operation began in South America and poor ghettos in America, where babies were sold to mobsters cheaply by Catholic homes and shelters and even hospitals. These babies were shipped by plane and then by helicopter to the convent, where it is said they may have stayed for periods up to three weeks before being shipped by boat to New York City, where they were "distributed" nationally by mob-run trucking firms. Babies were sold to wealthy impatient couples seeking children but not willing to wait what can sometimes be up to three years for a legitimate adoption. Indeed, the New York *Post* summed up the situation last night with its evening headline: "Baby Boomers Buy Smuggled Tots."

The profits are said to have been in the millions. Detective Cussone summed it up by saying: "That's a lot of guns."

The investigation continues amidst our shell-shocked community. Two local helicopter pilots have been arrested, names withheld, and the convent shut down permanently. "This has been devastating," said Father Steward, local priest of the Maplecrest and Tannersville parish. "No one has come through our doors since this has happened. It has sullied every honest, hardworking, God-fearing church leader, nationwide and especially locally. I urge our parishioners not to have a crisis with their faith."

Detective Cussone amazingly suffered only a flesh wound. Mr. Byman is in critical condition at the Benedictine Hospital. Deputy Wall is survived by his wife, Judy, and three children.

Our own Deputy Knaust is survived by his mother, Edith; his wife, Beverly; and their two children. Funeral services will be Friday at the Tannersville Funeral Home.

There were more articles, by Marjorie Cole and all the others, and then follow-ups, and follow-ups of the follow-ups. Some names never made it to the papers. Some were mentioned only fleetingly.

Nathan Wise was only connected to the case in the Poughkeepsie papers, where his ownership of the adoption agency was questioned by various public officials. Lola's name never appeared in print, and I was thankful for that. I didn't want her harmed. I even missed her, somehow, a vague hurt. But I wasn't going to do anything about it. I knew the way it had to be.

Chief Svenquist sent me a couple of clippings from Michigan. The first informed me that Roger Blum had been arrested for the murder of two police officers, one of them Chief Trell, and that a trial date had been set. The second relayed the grim news of Blum's final decision. He'd sat down in his living room chair, stuck that shiny .38 in his mouth, and ended his life.

Svenquist had added a cheerful little note. It said simply that he hoped he wouldn't ever lay eyes on me again.

Not once was Anna O'Reilly mentioned in any connection with the smuggling or the political groups or the death of her parents. A small article in *Variety* indicated that she had cancelled her next roles in two upcoming film productions, but that was all.

Nor was Julia ever mentioned in the national press. Cussone had done that for me, kept her out of it. He'd gotten her and Genna out of there that last day before police and reporters could descend on them. Now she'd disappeared again, for good.

Perhaps, one day, more would have to come out, when the FBI pressed deeper into the case. If they ever did. They didn't seem to want to talk much now—not to me, anyway—and that was fine. It was over. I had my life back.

* * *

There was a last letter. The mailman brought it up to me this morning with a smile—he knew I was sleeping in the office. He said with his cheerful white teeth shining:

"Make yourself official, will you? Get a mailbox."

I said, "OK."

The letter was from a completely unexpected source. Perfume scented the white envelope. Its lining was pink, and so was the paper. The postmark was from St. John's.

Luke Byman;

Meeting you may be the best thing that's ever happened to me. You turned me around. I haven't touched liquor since that day. Not a drop of it. And no more eye makeup! I left my husband. Just packed my bags and got out. I've filed for divorce, and, believe it or not, he agreed. Everything is going to be OK. After I left I decided to use the little money I had for travel, and ended up down here in St. John's, where I met a man—a wonderful man. I work for him now, helping to manage his yacht tours. I don't dare say what I hope may happen after my divorce is final. But I love him, and I think he loves me. That's enough for now. I've never really even had that before.

I write because I needed to tell you what a difference you made to my life. And to thank you, Mr. Byman.

Thank you.

Helen Gladden

I held her letter against my bandages. Under them, my heart was beating, in sync with the city lights that were brightening the dusk.

The scraping noise that had droned for so long behind me finally stopped. I turned, and the little man who'd been scraping the painted letters off the door smiled at me wearily. He wiped his brow with a soiled rag.

"Day's almost over," he said.

"Yeah."

He smiled gleefully. "Night's beginning, though."

I smiled with him.

"Quittin' time," he said. And he was gone. I suppose I couldn't expect much for twenty bucks.

He'd left the door glass only half scraped. The names Bridge and Ridley had been removed, but the other two words remained stenciled on the door.

Anyway, now the office was mine, my only reward from a less-than-grateful police department. It was all I'd asked them for. A place to live. Cussone had even issued me a cheap cot.

Now, looking out over the city, I wondered what I would do with myself when the wounds healed. I pondered whether the film industry would ever want me again. Or if I wanted it. Time would tell.

Shrugging off those thoughts, I slipped Helen Gladden's letter into the folder, closed it, then placed it carefully into one of the empty filing cabinets. I uncorked a bottle of great red wine that I'd bought to celebrate with, poured a glass, and took a few sips. Then a few more.

I pushed the door shut—and had to laugh out loud—my first laugh in a long time. The letters that remained on the frosted glass had been painted for the public, not for me. They faced me backward, looking like Egyptian hieroglyphs.

SNOITAGITSEVNI ETAVIRP

I poured another glass of wine.

I used my new cane to hobble over to the cheap cot in the corner and sat down. The cot squeaked under me like a plaintive Chihuahua. Ah well. This was home, for now. I swallowed a big gulp, smiled as the wine warmed my insides, and stared at those two words while night descended.